FOUL
APPETITE

Genevieve Lyons

LITTLE, BROWN AND COMPANY

A *Little, Brown* Book

First published in Great Britain in 1994
by Little, Brown and Company

A CIP catalogue record for this book
is available from the British Library.

ISBN 0 316 90704 9

Typeset by M Rules
Printed and bound in Great Britain by
Mackays of Chatham PLC, Chatham, Kent

Little, Brown and Company (UK)
Brettenham House
Lancaster Place
London WC2E 7EN

This book is for Lyn with love . . .
                    and Michele.

'. . . through the dark night he stealeth,
A captive victor that hath lost in gain;
Bearing away the wound that nothing healeth,
The scar that will, despite of care, remain.
Leaving this spoil perplexed in greater pain.
    She bears the load of lust he left behind,
    And he the burden of a guilty mind.

To the rough beast that knows no gentle right,
Nor aught obeys but his foul appetite.'

The Rape of Lucrece by William Shakespeare

PART ONE

CHAPTER ONE

Lonny Clebber was given a six-month suspended sentence for rape in Dublin in 1956. The judge, with solemn portentousness, told the jury that he was a first-time offender, never been in trouble before, an upright young man, a devoted son, his mother's sole support. Here he nodded towards the body of the crowded court and the jury stared at the vast tub of a woman in an astrakhan coat that smelled of moth-balls; Lonny Clebber's mother. She pressed a large handkerchief to her eyes and sighed audibly every so often as if she carried the weight of the world on her shoulders and wanted everyone to know it.

The court-room was packed. It smelled of polish and human sweat, and was charged with excitement. Such cases at that time were rare, and provided juicy copy and titillating listening. Women did not bring charges against men; they knew what the outcome would be and were loth to face the future of embarrassment their accusations would bring – the inevitable innuendos, the allegations of lying, the eventual isolation and ridicule.

The judge, continuing his summation, told the jury to note that Lonny Clebber was a diligent and sober worker. As if that had any-thing to do with it, one plump lady remarked, and drew frowning stares from not a few bright-eyed male members of the crowd near her. Lonny Clebber's employer had testified to the fact that he was an exemplary employee. He was assistant to Joseph O'Laughlin & Son, Undertakers, Capel Street, Dublin. He had given Lonny Clebber a glowing reference.

Lonny Clebber stood in the dock and followed every word with intense concentration. You would think to look at him that there was some question of his innocence. Detective Inspector O'Malley could not believe his ears. It was almost as if there were some excuse for the little runt. No one had denied that he had been guilty of the rape of Arlene Shaughnessy, but the judge seemed to be saying that under the circumstances, because of her clothes and because he was a diligent worker, Lonny Clebber was somehow excused from punishment. O'Malley ground his teeth together in impotent fury. This was a regular attitude in the courts and he deplored it. An all-male hierarchy had no conception of the outrage, the lasting damage this violence did to victims.

Lonny Clebber was a weedy-looking young man, pasty-faced with bad skin, but he was quite good-looking in a spiv-like way; black hair slicked down, eyes that ran away from anyone who tried to catch his glance. He was obviously deeply embarrassed as the counsel for the prosecution brought to light some of the less pleasant aspects of his actions. When Arlene Shaughnessy described her ordeal in a halting whisper, her head hanging down, hair curtaining her flaming cheeks, Lonny Clebber looked at least as embarrassed as she. Some of the women in the court stared at him with something like sympathy in their eyes and DI O'Malley marvelled again at human nature.

The judge, in his summation, told the jury that Arlene Shaughnessy had obviously been asking for trouble. After all, she was dressed in a tight sweater and bobby-socks – all the rage at the time no doubt, he remarked drily, but any girl in Ireland who was trying to look like Miss Lana Turner should remember what the consequences could be if she paraded about in such a fashion. If you looked like a strumpet, the judge insisted, you must expect to be treated like one. Arlene's mother glared at His Honour. Lana Turner was one of her favourite film stars and she resented the slur he cast on her 'Sweater Girl' image. Mrs Shaughnessy read *Picturegoer* and *Film Fan* and knew the state of the morals of every film star in Hollywood. Louella Parsons and Hedda Hopper reported regularly about all the most intimate goings-on in the lives of the glittering few and if they dared get out of line they were reprimanded vitriolically in print and their careers took an immediate downward turn. Miss Lana Turner was happily married, according to the latest gossip, to band leader Artie Shaw, and led a blameless life. Could she be criticized therefore for the ideas her image put in men's minds? Mrs Shaughnessy shook her head sadly.

Arlene, the judge continued, was the kind of girl who brought this sort of trouble upon herself. He stared at the jury with reproving eyes, shaking his head as sadly as the victim's mother but for different reasons. He appealed to them. Any reasonable person *must* agree with him! He methodically stripped the girl of her character and morals in his benign Father-Confessor concern for Lonny Clebber's good name and reputation. He guided them to the verdict he thought appropriate. He finished by stating bluntly that if Arlene Shaughnessy chose to wear her jersey (he called the garment the old-fashioned name instead of sweater which, Mrs Shaughnessy said afterwards, revealed how behind the times he was an' no mistake), if she chose to wear her jersey a size too small and thus reveal the outline of her breasts (gasp in court) in an obscene and provocative manner then she should not come crying to the law. She had, after all, got what she asked for.

O'Malley glared around the court. He could feel his blood pressure rise dangerously. He was the one who saw the end result of such cases and Arlene Shaughnessy had been a sad and sorry sight when she had reported to the Gardai the night she had been raped. He scanned the court-room. The faces were mostly reproving, staring at Arlene as if she had committed the crime. Even the women looked at her as if she had somehow let down her own sex.

Sex education in Dublin was non-existent. Children relied on their parents informing them of the mechanics of the 'facts of life', and a lousy job most of them did. O'Malley himself knew how difficult it was and had cravenly left that duty to Mary, his wife, when his daughter Colleen had reached the age when such knowledge became essential. A lot of kids had a very curious idea of what actually happened, whilst many more had no knowledge at all and were left to fend for themselves in an onslaught of intense and muddled feelings. Lust and romance and a terrible yearning confused them and aroused them and flung them into an abyss of guilt. O'Malley wished more than anything else that the church would keep itself out of that whole area and concentrate instead on spreading its message of love thy neighbour rather than trying to orchestrate the sexual lives of the whole of Ireland.

The all-male jury agreed righteously with the judge and Lonny Clebber toddled out of the court-room a free man with his suspended sentence a formality.

CHAPTER TWO

Detective O'Malley stood on the steps of the court-house, black rage washing over him. He was a big man, a gentle man, but now an angry man. Stupid old fart! Jasus, when would judges begin to understand the human race? Most of them came from a rarefied background, academic, prosperous. Protected from life's harshness, they didn't know their arse from their elbow. 'That kind of thing doesn't happen in nice circles,' one of them had confided to the detective and O'Malley couldn't resist replying, 'Not that you *know* of, Your Honour.'

For that little bastard Lonny Clebber to get off scot-free, for that was what the suspended sentence amounted to, was, in O'Malley's book, a severe miscarriage of justice. Didn't the judge realize that he was going to do it again? As sure as God made little apples that bastard was going to force some other poor girl and poison her life forever. He shuddered. He thought of Colleen, his lovely girl, and he shivered fearfully. This kind of case with its attendant high profile and publicity, gave men permission to think of women as mere objects for their gratification. It was a dangerous verdict. It sent the wrong message to Dublin thugs.

O'Malley glanced across the street to where Arlene Shaughnessy and her mother and father were getting into a taxi and his penetrating stare caught the young girl's eye. Her face was destroyed with weeping and she looked at him with startled accusation. He had told her it would be all right. She turned from him and ducked her head as she got into the car.

Her mother had said she was a joyous girl. Well, she had had all the joy knocked out of her. By Lonny Clebber. O'Malley doubted if she'd ever be happy and carefree again. No, Lonny Clebber had seen to that. O'Malley lit a cigarette. He saw the rapist emerge into the light. Clebber blinked rapidly. He looked smug. His shifty little eyes darted around and caught O'Malley's gaze, then darted away again, like silverfish. Then he looked back at the detective and O'Malley thought he saw the glimmer of a smile in the rapist's eyes. A tiny spark of triumph. He strutted down the street, swaggering, like he'd won a victory. Which, O'Malley reflected, he had.

O'Malley dropped his cigarette on the steps and ground it under his heel. 'I'll be waiting, Lonny Clebber,' he muttered. 'However long it takes, I'll get you, you little squirt. I'll be waiting.' Then with a heavy heart he went on his way.

CHAPTER THREE

Arlene Shaughnessy, nervous and subdued, went home with her parents. She was bewildered at what had happened in the court. She felt guilty and ashamed, as if she had been the one on trial. She lost her sparkle. She became middle-aged overnight, turned morose and reclusive. Her mother was irritated with her daughter. She too felt humiliated. As if she hadn't brought the girl up properly.

Arlene gave up her job at Guinness's, where she had been popular, a well-liked member of the staff. Now she found the sidelong glances of the girls and the covert, lecherous looks of the men unbearable. She never went out except for cigarettes and then it was only the short journey to the store at the bottom of the road where she lived. She used to love dancing but now she gave up going to the hops and avoided all social occasions. Her mother was at her wits' end. So she asked Father Connolly at St Alphonsus to have a word.

'Ye must make a pretence of living, Arlene, until the desire returns,' he urged her, but to no avail. She was like a zombie and she stayed that way, to her mother's despair and her father's shame.

His daughter, he told the boys in the local pub, was ruined. Shamed. 'That bastard got off scot-free,' he told them, not noticing their sniggering and nudging, 'and now she's shop-soiled goods. Sure no man'ud marry her now, would they? Wouldn't touch her with a barge-pole and she interfered with an' everyone knowin' it. Sure she's not a virgin any more, is she . . .'

'Ye can guarantee she's not that, John-Joe,' his mate replied, hardly able to stop himself from laughing out loud.

'. . . an' her name all over the papers for the world an' his wife to see an' no chance to keep it quiet,' Shaughnessy continued, taking a deep swig at his pint of porter. His audience smirked but they listened to him with fascinated attention. 'Twasn't every day you talked with a man whose daughter had been raped and whose name had hit the headlines in the papers. 'Twasn't every day you heard the words aloud, in public. Words like 'rape', 'breasts' (the judge had used that) and others they had had to look up in the dictionary. Words they still didn't understand like 'sodomize', words that were technical and therefore riveting.

'I'll never forgive her for goin' to the polis,' Shaughnessy continued. 'Never. What she want to do that for? I ask ye. What'll she do now? The nuns won't take damaged goods either. They won't have her. The missus went up to Larkhill an' the Reverend Mother said she had every sympathy, those were her very words, "every sympathy for the poor girl in her distress", but they won't have her. Ha! What'd ye think of that?' Den Shaughnessy licked the porter-foam off his lips and stared regretfully at his empty tankard until one of the men, feeling he had earned it, poor man an' his daughter ruined, offered to refill it.

All the neighbours stared at Arlene. They gave her funny furtive glances as she passed so she stayed home more and more. Only once the milkman's son asked her to the pictures and her mother persuaded her to go.

'Ah sure, what harm can it do, Arlene? He's a nice wee fella, so he is, an' it'll get ye back into the swing of things.'

She came home in tears for the milkman's son had taken her to the sand-dunes at Dollymount and tried to have his way with her. When she protested, then screamed and ran away from him as if from the plague, he called after her that he thought she'd like it now, after that first time women were supposed not to mind so much.

So she stopped going out altogether and became as reclusive as a nun.

CHAPTER FOUR

On superficial inspection Lonny Clebber looked a bit flash but quite presentable. However there was something furtive and unhealthy about him that put the girls off. He was certainly a snappy dresser. Mr O'Laughlin, the undertaker, had to ask him to tone down the ties he wore as they tended towards the Hawaiian rather than the requisite black, navy-blue or brown which was regulation in his business and showed respect for the dead. Lonny liked two-tone shoes but was not allowed to wear them, so he kept a pair in the back to change into when he left the premises of an evening. Though who he met to show them off to Mr O'Laughlin could not imagine.

His appearance, Mr O'Laughlin felt, was eminently suitable for the job. His black hair drenched in Brylcreem was parted and slicked flatly on to his bumpy skull. His wrists stuck out from his black gabardine jacket. He was tall and gangling, his slippery eyes veiled by heavy lids helping him to blend in beside the hearse. He appeared a natural part of the scene, shouldering the coffin. Mr O'Laughlin's son, Stephen, had a rosy, cheerful face split constantly in an irrepressible grin and looked right out of context anywhere near a coffin, so he had to be left in the office as he completely upset the sombre balance.

Mr O'Laughlin, a large egg-shaped man whose bleak countenance hid a cheerful disposition, saw no reason to dismiss his assistant after the court case. 'Silly piece of fluff,' he remarked to Stephen, referring to Arlene Shaughnessy. 'Anyone could see she was up to no good. Do anything to be noticed, these floozies will. You be careful of women like that, Stephen, y'hear?'

Stephen grinned. He had no need to use force to get what he

wanted and was the only one at the undertakers who had sympathy for Arlene.

'Lonny's not that sort of fella,' Mr O'Laughlin continued stubbornly. 'He's a nice, quiet serious class of a lad, a gem of a pall-bearer.' He shook his head. 'The idea!'

'But, Da, there was no question that Lonny was guilty,' Stephen replied. 'It was just that the judge didn't think the offence was serious enough to send Lonny to jail.'

'Well, as far as I'm concerned the fact that he's not in jail means that he's innocent. Ever hear of a guilty man outa jail? Ever hear of a guilty man get off scot-free? No, in my mind the boy had a raw deal from that floozie.'

Stephen held his peace. There was no point in arguing with his father when he had his mind made up.

Lonny loved working for the undertaker's. Mr O'Laughlin gave full, comprehensive service. He was a qualified embalmer, pumping preservatives into the veins of the corpses when necessary; doing it with a certain detachment, but with respect; allowing Lonny to assist him. That was another thing his son Stephen was best left out of as he had a propensity to faint.

'Ye have te treat the bodies with respect, Lonny,' O'Laughlin told his young assistant. But Lonny didn't need to be told. He loved the dead. He talked to them, massaged their cold hands. Mr O'Laughlin allowed him to rub them down. Formaldehyde was what they used and Lonny liked the smell. Mr O'Laughlin told him to treat the bodies as if they were his ma and da.

It was peaceful when he helped Mr O'Laughlin with the dead. The undertaker talked quietly to both him and the corpse. In a soft, kindly voice that reminded Lonny of his da. It was a reassuring voice as if he was telling the corpse that everything was going to be all right, that he or she would be laid to rest tenderly. Powder for colour and to dry the corpse out. Wash the hair. Put a bit of rouge on the cheeks, take the blue look away. So that the person looks asleep. Nothing to shock the mourners. Nothing to upset.

He let Lonny chauffeur the cars. The hearse or one of the limousines that the relatives rode in. He let him pall-bear. Everyone stops and stands respectfully as a hearse passes. Men raise their hats, women bless themselves. Lonny felt important when they did that. Like he was a king or something.

All in all the undertaker allowed Lonny to help more than anyone else. But never with actual communication with the bereaved family. He insisted on doing that himself. He prided himself on his reassuring and tactful manner and his instinct about their feelings. Sometimes they were devastated, drowning in grief, sometimes they were indifferent, sometimes they were relieved.

Upon their attitude depended the price of the funeral arrangements. Mr O'Laughlin would sense the relatives' requirements as he asked them about whether they wanted the casket open so that folks could see the face of the dead one or whether they wanted it discreetly closed. Some wanted it viewed, others not. The shock might be too great. It was a dilemma he helped them to solve whilst taking the measure of their grief. He talked to them about the purchase of the coffin – the casket, as he preferred to call it. He talked to them about the dead one's taste in music and flowers. At last, and governed by the information he had received, he talked to them about price. He was very fair about that. Most people were quite satisfied. Therefore he was popular.

He'd tell Lonny, 'Ring St Pat's. The coroner will give you clearance. He'll tell you when to collect the corpse. The bereaved want it to lay in the Chapel of Rest in St Ignatius' overnight. That'll be tomorrow so we'll have our work cut out to have poor Mrs Delahunty ready by then, looking nice and relaxed and peaceful. Now you mind, Lonny, drive that cadaver back *carefully*, as if she were alive. No risks. No recklessness. I want Mrs Delahunty to be resting in death. It makes my job easier. Bounce them over the place with careless driving and they look tight and tense and it takes hours to smooth them out. Now you remember.'

He'd help Mr O'Laughlin strap the corpse on to the trolley and screw the coffin-lid down. And with the dressing as well as the embalming. And in the purchase of drinks for the boys at the end of it all. Then he felt he'd done a good job.

Oh yes, Lonny loved his work. And he worked hard. Mr O'Laughlin testified to that in court. Sure he was peculiar but in Dublin a lot of people were peculiar. And Mr O'Laughlin knew that he could not easily replace Lonny. Stephen refused to have anything to do with the corpses while Lonny showed no such distaste. Mr O'Laughlin found it difficult to get staff because of the stiffs and he did not want to lose Lonny. So Mr O'Laughlin was relieved that the court found his employee guilty only of behaving the way any red-blooded male would under extreme provocation. Rape was not like burglary, stealing or destroying property. Women enjoyed rape once they got into the rhythm of it. God's sakes, Mr O'Laughlin muttered, it wasn't something to make a fuss over. So Lonny went back to work at the undertaker's the following Monday as if nothing had happened and everything returned to normal except that the other pall-bearers and Dessy, the cleaner, nudged Lonny and winked at him meaningfully every so often to let him see what a fine fellow they thought him, a man with a hidden talent. A man to be admired because he wouldn't take no from a slut of a girl like Arlene Shaughnessy. Showed the whoor who was boss. Gave it to her, that's for sure, gave it to her good.

And Arlene Shaughnessy smoked endlessly in the prison of her bedroom and could not sleep.

CHAPTER FIVE

Meriel Masters threw gloves out of the drawer in the bedroom she shared with her sister Phyllis, Fliss for short. None of them was clean and she needed a pair for the *thé dansant* in the Gresham Hotel that afternoon at five.

Her mother would be indifferent to her plight. So would Fliss. They would look at her coolly and tell her it was her own fault, which was true, but that didn't help at all.

She was eighteen, a chubby girl, but losing her puppy-fat, slimming down and promising beauty. Fliss was twenty-one and the right shape: thirty-six, twenty-two, thirty-six. The boys, the magazines, the newspapers said those precise measurements were humdinger perfect. Fliss would toss her cloud of hair and tell everyone that those precise measurements took no account of height, weight, bones or alignment and therefore people were foolish to judge by such criteria. But Meriel and her friends held on to that standard as gospel. Meriel wore a waspie to clinch her waist and her friend Sheeve padded her bra with cotton wool.

Fliss was perfect, Meriel decided furiously as she examined her last pair of kid gloves and found a split in the thumb. Those kind of things never happened to her sister. She bit her lip. No gloves. No tea dance. One simply *had* to wear gloves. It was *de rigueur*, and it was better for a Masters to stay at home than to appear in public inappropriately dressed. Someone would be sure to tell Mother and that would bring down a heap of trouble on her head. There were things a lady did not do and her mother was unyielding when those rules were broken. It simply wasn't worth it.

Meriel desperately wanted to go to the tea dance. She had a new dress, Bobby Mitchell had asked her and he was a swell guy, the best-looking boy in their crowd, *and* Geraldo was playing. She must, absolutely *must* go.

She stood still a moment then crossed the room to her sister's side and opened the small top drawer where Fliss kept her gloves. There they were, at least ten pristine pairs, perfectly laundered, perfectly arranged, the fingers smoothed lovingly outward like starfish. Meriel selected a pair of white nylon and silk mix, a small pair that frilled out at the wrist and had a pearl and a loop to fasten them neatly. She told herself that Fliss wouldn't notice, but even as she said it to herself she knew she was lying. Fliss *would* notice. Fliss in her precise and meticulous way would spot their absence the instant she opened her drawer. Well, let's hope she won't open it for a while, Meriel prayed fervently, and, hiding the gloves under her uplift bras in her own chest of drawers, she went downstairs to lunch.

Her mother was with her father in the drawing-room. It was Saturday so there was an air of relaxed celebration. Friends dropped in for pre-lunch drinks at the weekends or were invited to lunch. The house was full of activity, laughter and sunlight.

It was a large, gracious house set back from the road with lawns divided by a tree-lined gravel driveway. Rogan Masters, Meriel's father, was a heavy-set man, a little pompous but gracious. He stood now with his back to the fireplace. There was a Japanese screen shutting it off and in front of the screen a Chinese vase full of beech leaves her mother had preserved in oils last autumn. The room was high-ceilinged, a light, airy room. There was a long-playing record of the music from *South Pacific* on the turntable and the sweet melody of Bali Hi filled the room. Trixie, the maid, was moving about among the guests and family. She was in full uniform today as there were visitors, and was serving canapés and drinks. The short black dress, white frilly apron and cap did not suit Trixie's square figure and she stooped, carrying her responsibilities and her anxiety on round shoulders so that the maid's cap tilted forward drunkenly on her forehead and her skirts rode up at the back. Tessa Masters, Meriel' mother, could see the snag in Trixie's black stockings. She sighed, for she was weary of trying to make Trixie presentable, acquire a little charm, even a pleasant manner. Still, the girl did her job reasonably well, was hard-working and honest, and certainly self-effacing, unlike her predecessor Bette

McAlister, who had flirted constantly with anything at all in pants, from their old grandfather of eighty down to little seven-year-old Robbie, her son. It was all quite harmless on Bette's part and the girl was popular – in fact a sunny, happy-go-lucky creature who livened up the house. But then something had happened to Bette McAlister (who was named after Bette Davis, the film star, a deplorable habit in Tessa Masters' opinion, but all the rage these days when cinema was God and children named after screen stars instead of the saints as was right and proper). Bette McAlister had become impossible overnight and Mrs Masters could not fathom why. From a cheerful and bright-spirited, willing worker with the one flaw of batting her eyelashes and wriggling her bottom at any male person who came into her orbit, she had changed into a pale-faced, nervous, hysteria-prone liability.

Tessa had of course tried to find out what ailed Bette but had no success. Suddenly one morning she had simply refused to come out of her room and remained locked in there all day. The next day she emerged, grey-faced and shattered and would tell no one what was wrong. Tessa was certain that something terrible had happened to the maid but the girl would not confide in her. She became incoherent when questioned and deeply distressed when pressed. Tessa Masters put up with her behaviour for a couple of months, then had no choice but to dismiss her. That had been last winter; January actually, and now it was spring. Trixie had come to them when Bette left and now on this glorious Saturday in May Tessa noted with satisfaction that despite Trixie's rather ramshackle appearance she *had* succeeded in remembering that Valentine Bushell's tipple was a gin and it. Trixie might make it yet.

Tessa Masters was a cool, elegant woman, competent and efficient. She liked things to run smoothly, hated fuss and upheaval, loved her daughters and adored her son. A woman of taste and culture, she was also in complete charge of her emotions and never allowed her heart to rule her head.

Her family had been terribly well-bred but genteelly poverty-stricken. During her whole childhood they had been on the brink of disaster and had had to scrimp and scrape to keep up appearances. From her earliest years Tessa had loathed the deprivations the lack of money subjected them to, the terrible fear that insecurity produced, and had determined to marry a man who would provide for her and provide well.

She chose Rogan Masters, whose family owned the largest creamery in Dublin and who had enough money and prestige to give her the kind of protection she so desperately needed. She had married him, convincing him she adored him. It was a woman's role, after all. She was determined to be a good bargain and prove herself well worth the trust he put in her. She gave him all she promised and more and he never had the slightest cause to regret marrying her. She was an excellent wife and mother, a perfect hostess. She kept to herself the fact that she did not desire him and that their coupling (now happily over – since Robbie's rather difficult birth they slept in separate rooms) had always been distasteful to her. Rogan, an old-fashioned man, expected this – after all, no real lady *enjoyed* sex. Only cheap floozies like this Arlene Shaughnessy whose name had been smeared across all the papers last year actually *enjoyed* it.

Rogan was grateful to Tessa, worshipped her, saw her as the perfect woman, and counted himself damned lucky. He remained totally ignorant of her feelings, her character, her thoughts. It never occurred to him to be curious about her, to ask himself how she felt about this or that or why she behaved in one way or another. Any deviation from the normal he put down to her 'time of the month', about which he knew nothing and desired to know even less. One simply didn't discuss embarrassing subjects such as that.

His father had told him that women were strange and mysterious beings and the less a man tried to fathom them the happier he would be. Rogan took his father's advice and would have sworn on the Bible that their marriage was quite perfect.

It only pained him that he could not be open about his mistress. The moral climate of the times prevented him from being honest about that most civilized of arrangements. Carmel Kavanagh was a woman of doubtful past (which was all to the good for she was a demon in bed) and he had set her up in a nice little two-roomed flat in Molesworth Street. Her great talent was sex. She revelled in her body, his body, ways to prolong satisfaction, ways that drove him mad with lust. She used words that turned him into a raging bull, words that Tessa would not recognize and had probably never heard. Words that if she *had* uttered them would have had the exact opposite effect upon him than when whispered to him by Carmel Kavanagh, arousing him to near frenzy in the large warm bed where she played her erotic games with him. Rogan could not imagine his wife involved in any of the activities he got up to with Carmel, and if she had attempted anything remotely approaching the boldness of his mistress, he would have frozen in horror and been incapable of performance.

However, he was very happy with the situation as it was. There was no chance of Tessa finding out about Carmel. They lived in different worlds, connected nowhere.

Tessa too felt she had made a very good bargain. If she had missed the passion she saw depicted in films and plays and read about in books, the financial stability Rogan provided her with more than made up for it. Her burning ambition had been to live in style and comfort and she had succeeded. Her only regret was that her mother and father had not lived to benefit from her good fortune. It would have made them so happy. They would have appreciated the chance to sit back and enjoy life a little and not worry about bills. Particularly her mother. A great lady, a woman of grace and culture who surely was created to appreciate the finer things of life; a woman who yearned to smile, to laugh, a woman eager for abundance but who was doomed to scrimp and scrabble, always preoccupied with cutting costs. How she would have bloomed surrounded by comfort and plenty. But it was not to be. Tessa often wondered at the seeming cruelty of God's plan when a week after she and Rogan had returned from their honeymoon her parents were both struck down with pneumonia and died horribly quickly. They had been undernourished, the doctor said, and had no resistance to fight the influenza, which had rapidly turned to pneumonia and carried them off within a matter of days. It soured things for Tessa, who had so wanted to spoil them a little, but she never by word or intimation let her husband know what she felt.

She looked up now, a small sigh on her lips, as her daughter Meriel came into the room. Tessa beckoned her over. The girl was too plump in Tessa's opinion and she wondered briefly what to do about it. It was ironic. Meriel rode and played tennis and she ate sparingly. She did not stuff herself like Fliss tended to do sometimes when she was miserable. But Fliss never gained an ounce and Meriel did. Again Tessa thought of how unfair God could be. Picking on poor Meriel like that when she had done nothing to deserve it. It was simply her metabolism.

The sun streamed into the room and the long lace curtains billowed in the soft breeze from the front lawns. The cherry tree was a mass of pink blossom, the fresh-cut grass beneath it strewn with petals. Rogan was talking to Valentine Bushell and Clemmie, his wife, was sitting in an armchair across the room gazing out the windows. She was stylishly dressed, a stiletto-heeled shoe dangling from the tip of one toe, her net petticoats visible beneath her grey grosgrain full-skirted frock.

'Merry, talk to Clemmie, there's a dear,' Tessa instructed her daughter quietly. Meriel grimaced. None of them liked Clemmie Bushell. She had a sharp tongue and they were certain she used it against them with the same barbed accuracy she used it to them in condemnation of others.

'Mother, must I?' Meriel complained. 'Why can't Fliss?'

Fliss stood, her back to them, looking out of the window to where the drive swept up to the house. She was waiting for the Devlins: Bigger Devlin, Rogan's golf partner, his wife Agnes and son Derry, who was doing a line with Fliss.

'Fliss is waiting for Derry,' her mother said softly, looking at her eldest with affectionate eyes. She found the relationship between Fliss and Derry Devlin very touching. It moved her to tears just to think about them and she didn't know why. They were so in love, so vulnerable, like travellers wandering hand-in-hand, tentatively exploring the unfamiliar terrain, yet blindly confident. They were moving towards the altar and marriage, Tessa was sure.

Tessa and Rogan approved of the match, Bigger and Agnes were one hundred per cent in favour and the young couple, blessed and smiled upon by their parents, blossomed beneath the general approval. Nevertheless they seemed oddly defenceless, though why they should need defences, Tessa, for the life of her, could not think.

'She saw him yesterday!' Meriel said acidly, glaring at her sister's back. 'He hasn't been to Siberia!'

'Now, Merry, don't be like that. Over now, talk to Clemmie. We must do our social duty.'

Meriel put her hands on her hips and faced her mother squarely. 'I put twenty curlers in Fliss's hair last night,' she informed her mother. 'Twenty! Who's going to do that for her when she marries Derry, I'd like to know.'

'Oh, I don't think he'd mind what she did,' Tessa replied and they both looked at Fliss's slim straight back in her short tennis skirt and polo top. The white was dazzling against her tanned arms and legs.

Her hair had lost whatever curl the twenty rollers had put in and lay flat and gleaming on her neck, blonde and straight like leaves of gold in the sun.

Tessa smiled and shook her head gently. Her daughter wanted her hair to look like Gloria De Haven's – a mass of golden curls and waves, dips and frolics festooned around her head – and she dedicated time and effort and put up with a great deal of discomfort to achieve this. But Nature had decreed otherwise, and however hard Fliss tried, whatever curls and waves tumbled about her face and shoulders when she removed the rollers after a long night tossing and turning with them digging into her scalp, the glorious riot sank and sagged, deflating after a very short time so that, usually within the hour, it was flat against her head as God intended. And God was right, Tessa acknowledged, God had better taste than Fliss.

'Fliss's hair suits her straight,' Tessa remarked now to Meriel.

'But, Mother, it's *not* the *fashion*!' Meriel protested.

'Silly fashion then,' Tessa said serenely and patted her daughter's bottom. 'Off you go while I see about lunch.'

'Is it sit-down?' Meriel asked and Tessa shook her head.

'It's such a lovely day I thought buffet. I told Trixie to open the French windows in the dining-room and Nora has cooked a ham and there is salad and a cold salmon in aspic. I thought we'd put tables and chairs in the garden and let people help themselves and mingle.' She frowned. 'May is early for it but it *is* gorgeous out today.'

'I'll help with the chairs, Mother,' Meriel offered eagerly.

'Colm'll do that. Now, Merry, you are just trying to wriggle out of your job! Over to Clemmie, there's a dear girl.' She smiled at her daughter. 'It won't be for long. Lunch should be soon. Oh, there's the Devlins! I better get on. Fliss can greet them.'

The sound of the car in the drive sent Tessa scuttling to the back of the house to see that Nora, the cook, was, as she put it, 'on top of the food' and to tell Colm, the handyman, to put out the tables and chairs.

'Under the trees,' she ordered. 'Trixie, put these linen cloths on the tables. No, leave the napkins on the big table with the food in the dining-room. They can serve themselves in there and come out here into the sun if they wish.'

She hurried back into the drawing-room. Now that Trixie was helping with the food there was no one serving drinks. But she need not have worried. Rogan was pouring a Paddy for Derry and his father and Meriel was bringing a gin and it to Agnes Devlin. Tessa realized that she had used Agnes's need as an excuse to put off her social duty to Clemmie and she shook her head over her daughter's stubbornness.

Agnes was saying to Rogan; 'We're planning a visit to Rome. Isn't it grand to be able to do that? Go abroad again.' She had a sweet face that looked soft and crumpled, the skin crushed like fallen rose petals.

'And see the Pope!' Bigger Devlin nodded, agreeing with his wife. 'An audience with His Holiness. Just thinka that!'

'The Pope! God, he's a shocking spoil-sport!' Clemmie cried. 'Pious. Stopping us having any fun.'

Bigger Devlin tut-tutted. 'Now now, Clemmie. That's tantamount to blasphemy.' He looked around. 'Is Bren Greene not here? Was sure I'd see him here. He owes me a fiver and I want it off him. Man never pays his debts.'

'I don't know where he is,' Rogan said.

'He's in hospital,' Valentine Bushell volunteered. 'God love him. Walked into the glass door at the golf-club. Didn't see it. It was closed, see. He was drunk as a coot. Glass everywhere. Face cut and knocked himself out cold. Had to have twelve stitches. They kept him in overnight.'

Hoots of laughter all round greeted this statement.

'Where is he?' Rogan asked, a frown of disapproval on his face.

'They had to take him to St Luke's Presbyterian Hospital.'

'I hate that they call it that,' Rogan muttered.

'What?' Bigger asked.

'St Luke's Presbyterian Hospital. St Luke was *not* a Presbyterian!'

'No,' Bigger agreed. 'He was a Catholic.'

The two men nodded in agreement.

'Sorry, folks, but he was a Jew!' Clemmie said loudly.

Tessa looked over at her daughter. Meriel was leaning over Agnes's chair ignoring Clemmie. She still had not done her duty and that lady remained alone, swinging her foot to and fro in the toe of her shoe, her eyes challenging, asking for an argument. Tessa gave up on Meriel's help and went over to her troublesome guest.

'Are you all right, Clemmie?' she asked. The woman turned her cold and lovely face to her hostess and Tessa realized she had not noticed how discontented Clemmie looked.

'Fine thank you, Tessa. Men! They do talk such terrible twaddle. They have to reassure themselves that they are the chosen ones, that their way is the right way. God, what fools they are!' She glanced around the room. 'I see Derry and Fliss are all over each other.'

Tessa nodded. 'They are doing a very strong line,' she said.

'I know.' Clemmie's bright blue eyes narrowed. 'So I thought it odd to see him and Coralie Thompson sitting bold as brass in Fuller's in Grafton Street on Wednesday last drinking coffee and gossiping ten to the dozen, heads close together and all. If I were you, Tessa, I'd tell Fliss to keep an eye on our young Romeo.'

Tessa looked at her friend. She was always so eager to spoil things for others. Perhaps because she was unhappy herself. There was a desperate light in her eyes, a gleam of wild despair, and Tessa knew that Valentine had been up to his old tricks again.

Valentine Bushell was too handsome for his own good and had given Clemmie a hard time since their marriage. Tessa realized that Clemmie's whole outlook had been poisoned by her husband's infidelities so she forgave her friend her bitter comments and bit back the obvious retort of 'Don't judge every man by your husband, Clemmie!' After all, who knew how she would behave in Clemmie's position? She knew Rogan was faithful. He would never behave like Valentine Bushell. He had too much respect for the family. Even if he was tempted, which Tessa didn't believe for a moment he would ever be (he was not a romantic, she reassured herself, and he *certainly* was not sensual), he was too moral to give in.

No, he was not a sensuous man, you could see that by his mouth. A thin, straight line, not like Valentine Bushell's large bee-stung lips. Besides, Rogan came up to Communion with her each Sunday morning and that he could not do if he was committing adultery. Good Catholic middle-aged fathers did not behave like Valentine Bushell and poor Clemmie had suffered the indignity of it over the years.

Tessa said now, gently, 'Oh, I don't think we need worry about Derry and Fliss. One has only to look at them to see how they feel about each other. Besides, Coralie is Fliss's best friend and Derry was probably asking her advice about his present for Fliss's birthday next month.' She felt that she had disposed of that satisfactorily and took a deep breath and said, 'So! How's your drink, Clemmie?'

Clemmie tossed back the remains of the gin and it and held out her empty glass. Tessa thought that she drank too much. It crossed her mind that perhaps she would too if Rogan was playing the field the way Valentine was and then she decided that no, she would never let herself down like that. She handed the glass to Rogan as he passed and tried to shrug away the unpleasant train of thought Clemmie always triggered in her. It was such a glorious day and she would not allow anything to spoil it. The garden was at its best, the cherry and magnolia trees were in bloom and the lilac scented the whole garden with a heavenly perfume.

'We're going to play tennis, Mother. Have we time before lunch?' Fliss asked, her cheeks flushed, her hand in Derry's. The tennis club was a stone's throw away but Tessa shook her head.

'No, dears,' she replied firmly. 'Lunch is just about ready and I'll not have you come back here hungry as hunters when we're finished and disturb Nora's well-deserved rest. You can play this afternoon.'

Fliss and Derry had their arms around each other and, as Tessa watched, Fliss brought their clasped hands to her mouth and kissed the back of his. It seemed to her infinitely sweet, that gesture, ineffably loving, and for a moment her heart was gripped with a sharp pain, like loss. They always seemed to be touching each other as if they could not bear to be separate and Tessa wondered what it must be like to feel like that about a man. Then she put the thought firmly aside.

Rogan and Bigger were talking about the game of golf they had played that morning and commiserating with each other that Portmarnock, the club, was so far from where they lived.

'That drive in the morning across town is such a drag,' Bigger moaned.

'I don't mind *going* there: the journey *out* is okay – sun coming up, game ahead. No, it's the return journey that's such a bind,' Rogan stated.

'But you both have cars!' Tessa reminded them, thinking of the luxury of driving everywhere and the misery she was once familiar with of waiting in queues in the teeming rain, cold winds blowing her umbrella inside-out, for a bus or tram that never came.

'I know that, my dear, but after a game we're bushed and if we had a decent golf-course nearer it would save us no end of a drive.'

She shook her head. They had no idea. Both of them came from well-to-do families, neither had known any kind of deprivation.

'The roads are getting busier and busier,' Bigger said. 'Every Tom Dick and Harry is getting wheels these days.'

Valentine snorted. 'You should see London!' he remarked and shuddered. 'Can't *move* there.'

Valentine went to London a lot, a fact that made Clemmie nervous. She knew his women in Ireland. It was how she spent most of her time: spying on him, spying on them, driving herself mad but unable to stop. It included her somehow in that part of his life. When she tracked down the other woman, waited in the car outside her home, or a hotel, or simply watched the car they were in together, she felt part of them; contained in their activities. But when Valentine was in London and she had no such tenuous hold, she felt a loneliness that was almost unbearable.

'Let's go into the dining-room,' Tessa suggested, seeing Clemmie's pain. 'We're eating outside, if you care to.'

Colm opened the connecting doors and the group moved into the next room, chatting as they moved to where the food was laid out and a stack of plates, cutlery and napkins waited for their use. Nora had done a grand job, Tessa noted with satisfaction, and the ham – crusted with honey and brown sugar and stuck with cloves – gleamed invitingly. The salmon lay pink and tempting, glazed and garnished with cucumber, lemon and parsley.

'That salmon is so perfect it seems a shame to tackle it,' Bigger Devlin laughed and Rogan replied, 'That'll not stop you though, Bigger, will it?' Then, looking around at them all: 'Tuck in, don't hang back,' and he handed Bigger a fish-slice and soon everyone was helping themselves and each other, laughing and talking, delighting in the good things to eat and the warmth of the company. Plates were soon filled and everyone drifted through the open French windows, drawn by the sunlit garden.

'The lilac is gorgeous,' Agnes remarked. 'Listen,' she said and cocked her head to one side. 'That's a lark. What's he doing singing at this time of day?'

The birds sang, the fountain splashed and the record Meriel had put on floated into the garden:

> 'Imagine me with my head on your shoulder,
> And you with your lips getting bolder,
> Just you and me and a sweet melody,
> I'll buy that dream.'

Fliss and Derry sat together on the wide swing under the lilac trees. They both ate heartily, smiling at each other every so often. It was as if they were having a conversation without speaking. Valentine and Bigger were deep in conversation with Rogan. 'Men's talk dear,' Rogan told Tessa when she asked them to mingle. Agnes was telling Meriel about the new Christian Dior fashions in Brown Thomas. 'Smaller waists,' she said and Meriel groaned. 'Fuller skirts, petticoats galore.'

'Oh Janey,' Meriel sighed. 'It won't suit me *and* makes half my wardrobe redundant!'

Clemmie was alone again and Tessa, catching sight of her, sighed.

'Isn't it a great excuse to go shopping?' Agnes was saying to Meriel, who bit into cucumber and salmon.

'Help me to tackle Mummy,' she whispered to Agnes. 'She has this frugal streak. Comes from being skint when she was young.'

'Yes, your poor mam had a tough time,' Agnes concurred. 'Not that she has to worry about that now, pet – she could buy and sell us all – but you never forget the hard times.'

Tessa decided there was nothing for it but to sit with Clemmie herself and try not to be affected by her black conversation. It was daunting the way she sat there under the chestnut tree on the wooden bench that circled it, sending out her 'don't touch me' message loud and clear.

She did not eat much; she had no real interest in food, but she gulped great draughts of wine greedily as if it were water, and she pulled on her endless cigarettes as if an intake of smoke would save her life.

'Men!' she said when Tessa joined her. 'Men are such beasts. They none of them have an ounce of honour. Liars and cheats, all of them.'

'Oh now, Clemmie, that's a trifle strong, don't you think?' Tessa protested. The lilac scented the air and the heavy white and mauve blossom looked edible.

'I wish I could tell Fliss, explain what's in store for her, the poor girl, before it's too late,' Clemmie continued, staring at the young couple.

'If you try to disillusion my daughter, Clemmie, I'll never forgive you.' Tessa's voice was cold.

Clemmie shrugged and continued moodily, 'Not that she'd listen to me if I tried. *I* wouldn't have. Love is a terrible thing, but then . . .' she glanced at Tessa again, 'what would you know about it?'

Tessa looked at her sharply. 'What do you mean?' she asked. I won't, won't, won't let her upset me, she thought, but she could feel the anger within and knew there were two bright patches on her neck which always flared up when she was disturbed.

Clemmie looked at her and laughed. 'You know very well what I mean,' she said softly. 'You've never been in love, Tessa Masters, it's as simple as that. You've never felt the pain, the agony – sharp, like knives . . .'

'I won't let you talk like that, Clemmie,' Tessa said heatedly.

'Oh come on, you know it to be true.' Clemmie reached for her bag. It was a soft grey suede to match her dress. She took out a slim silver cigarette case, opened it, put a cigarette between her teeth and lit it. 'Trouble is, we paint this impossible picture of how it *should* be. All those romantic novels, all that poetry we're fed. Mothers, fathers telling their sons and daughters about love. Moon, June, spoon. Listen . . .' She cocked her head and took the cigarette out of her mouth, blowing out a cloud of grey smoke that made Tessa press her handkerchief to her nose and put down her plate of food. 'Listen . . . "I'll buy that dream". Hear it? Sure it's a dream! It's illusion. We feel it for a while when our glands are over-active, then one of two things happens: it dies, or at very best it changes. The fizz goes out of it. Sad people wake up one morning next to a stranger they never really saw before, don't really know, and find faintly irritating. Or we are betrayed. It's funny how that keeps love alive. You never find the husband who is having an affair irritating – you want him more than ever.' Her face had an intense and ugly look, then she shrugged and sighed. 'We women have to keep young and lovely or the men in our lives will start playing the field with girls young enough to be their daughters. Oh Christ, it's so unfair!'

'Clemmie, it's not always like that,' Tessa told her firmly. 'Rogan and I . . .' Clemmie brought her gaze to rest on Tessa's face, raising one eyebrow.

'We are perfectly happy,' Tessa said.

'You were never in love with the man for him to be able to hurt you or betray you,' Clemmie told her impatiently.

'Clemmie!' Tessa protested.

'Well you weren't. And I'm not sure it isn't the best way. At least this way you'll not be wounded and humiliated.'

'But Rogan would never . . .'

Clemmie turned her face to Tessa; her eyes, narrowing in a cloud of smoke, had a malicious gleam. 'Wanna bet?' she asked, smiling.

Tessa stood up. 'That's enough, Clemmie,' she said briskly, shaking off a wave of dread. 'Really, you go too far.'

Clemmie stared up at her and laughed. 'I speak the truth, Tessa dear. And you *should* warn poor Fliss. She's in for a nasty awakening one of these days.'

Tessa decided enough was enough and turned away. 'I must see if everyone has everything they want,' she murmured calmly.

'I'm sure no one here has everything they want, Tessa, and they never will,' Clemmie chuckled and Tessa left her alone under the chestnut tree.

It's true, she thought. Everyone here, except maybe me, wants more. Wants to be wealthier, prettier, happier. Fliss and Derry want to be married. Derry keeps saying he'll never be happy until they are. Meriel wants to be thinner. She turned her face to the lilac blossom and looked at Rogan. What did he want? More money? More power? As if he didn't have enough already. She stared at him. Portly. That was what he was. A serious, portly man. Opinionated. Lacking in lightness, lacking in humour.

Oh no! No! How disloyal of her. But it was true!

And what did she want? A fantasy. Clark Gable. Cary Grant. A gorgeous man, a man who stopped her heart the way they said in books, a man who would make her feel the way her daughter looked: eyes dazzled, lips ardently apart, breathless, expression stupefied. Was that what Clemmie was making her feel she'd missed? She looked over at Fliss and Derry on the swing. Every time he looked at her his love for her spilled over into gestures of affection. He touched her, kissed her, said he loved her; it was a chorus, a background to everything. It was as if his love for her poured from the very centre of his being in a tide. It was remarkable to behold. Well, she would never feel that violent surge of emotion. Even if Errol Flynn or Clark Gable arrived here in her home in Dublin and improbably fell in love with her, what would happen then? As Clemmie had once remarked cynically, 'But what are his politics? What is his taste in music? And has he got good manners? How happy would you be with a womanizer like Flynn? Oh, we have to understand that life is real and dreams don't come true. There is always an awakening.'

Tessa crushed the lilac between her fingers and heard Meriel call to her: 'Mother, did I tell you I'm going to the dance in the Gresham? Bobby'll be coming to fetch me.'

'Oh, Bobby, is it? Bobby Mitchell? Oh golly, Merry, why him? He's wet.'

'Shut up, Fliss.' Meriel was stung by her sister's jibe. 'You don't know him. You've never even talked to him.'

'Girls, behave!' Tessa cried. 'That's nice, darling. Bring him out here to see us when he comes.'

'Oh, we'll be inside by then, I hope,' Rogan said. 'It gets chilly this early in the year. I don't want your mother catching cold.' He glanced at her and Tessa felt her heart warm. He might not be dashing and romantic but he always showed concern for her well-being and that was very important.

It's all right, she thought as the lilac fell crushed to the ground. It's all right.

Her heart leaped as her son ran out of the house, arms open, blond hair tousled, face flushed from his nap.

'Mummy, Mummy!'

Her throat closed over a lump of gratitude and she felt a shiver of pure joy overwhelm her as her arms closed about his small warm body.

'Robbie. Robbie, love,' she whispered into his soft curls, and knew it really *was* all right.

CHAPTER SIX

He could hear them talking as he hid, concealed by the thick green foliage of tree, shrub and bush. He watched them come out of the house through the French windows, plates of food in their hands, that expression of sweet anticipation on their faces that said, 'I've got something to eat that I like, something delicious I'm going to enjoy and the world is a fine and comfortable place and I'm a big guy in it.' That's what they looked as if they were thinking as they emerged into the sunlight.

Each one of the men, as he came out, surveyed the territory as if he alone among men was monarch of all he surveyed. They each took a deep breath, let it out on a long 'Ah-h-h-h'. Each one of them did exactly the same thing, then chose a seat beside a table under the trees.

And waited for the women.

Lonny was sure that was because the women were helping to serve the food. Looking after the men. Women always went last. They waited. They knew they were inferior. Second class.

There were three servants; the fat one called Nora, bossy and sharp-tongued, Trixie and the man Colm who set up the tables in the garden. But the people were helping themselves. He could see them, shadowy figures in the room, moving about, mysterious, separate. Then they came out, emerged into the sunlight; 'Ah-h-h-h,' they went, smug. Satisfied. The world was theirs. They owned it.

Trixie was awkward. She tilted forward and dropped things. She covered up well, but Lonny saw her pick something up from the ground and replace it on one of the men's plates. No one noticed, except the lady under the chestnut tree who smirked and shook her head.

Trixie interested him. She was the one who took Bette McAlister's place after she got the sack. Now it was his turn to smirk, in the bushes where he crouched, concealed.

He had followed Bette, watched her in case she talked. Like the Shaughnessy girl. Split on him.

It would be awkward if she talked after that court case. It was a frightening thought. He might have to go through that again. Jee-sus! That would not be fair. Standing up, listening to all that dirty and embarrassing stuff in front of people he had never met. He nearly died! Stuff like that shouldn't be *talked* about. Not out loud, that way, in public.

He liked sometimes to hide like this in the bushes and watch girls and talk dirty to himself. That was exciting. But out in court in front of all those people! He would never forgive that cow Arlene for putting him through that.

Boy, had he made a mistake there. She was a real slut, a . . . Then he said the word softly, saliva at the corners of his mouth. 'Bitch. Fuckin' cunt. Bitch.'

He whispered it, not wanting to be heard. Hiding – secret here, buried in the bushes, the earth mouldering, smelling damp and pungent beneath him.

Sometimes when he had concealed himself the scent of roses came to him on the breeze. Or the mixed smells from the herb garden: parsley and thyme, mint and comfrey and the sharp smell of fennel.

He had never meant to do it again after the court case but he had seen Bette in a shop in Ballsbridge and, force of habit, he followed her. To this house. It turned out she was a maid here. That made him despise her even more. A maid. Jeez! Then he laid his plans. He liked that, setting the trap, planning. Then doing it here, in the bushes. Following her in here, getting her, and afterwards the perfect peace that came, that always came, that never let him down.

Then the worry, creeping in. Spoiling it. Would she talk? Would she squeal like Arlene? Would he have to go through that humiliation again? That terrible embarrassment?

But no. She kept silent. And Mrs Masters sacked her. He chuckled noiselessly to himself.

He had chosen her, Bette McAlister, followed her for a few weeks like he usually did, to see when and where best to trap her, catch her, then push her down and do it to her. So she suffered like he did. So she paid good.

Once something was started it had to run its course. He liked to know their names. He asked shopkeepers – postmen. People in Dublin loved to talk, to tell you things. Give you information. They liked to let you see they *knew* things. He'd find out all about the girl, knowing she had to be taught. He'd follow her. And teach her.

Bette was easy. Most were. People – women – went around blithely thinking nothing could happen to *them*. They lived behind garden walls and fences, doors – front doors, bedroom doors. He could get through doors and over fences. He could climb the walls easy and wait. He was in no hurry. Half the fun was waiting. Like stalking an animal. Hunting. Only they were cows and you didn't stalk cows. Don't hunt cows, Christ sake!

Well, in the end, Bette McAlister didn't talk and Mrs Masters told her to go and that was that. He had heard the fat one, Nora, tell the man, Colm, about it in the garden.

'Some man at the bottom of it, I'll bet,' she said. He had smiled to himself. Well, she was right in a way, silly old cow. And that was all.

By then he had got into the habit of lurking in the Masters garden. When he had followed Bette and found the place, here at the bottom of her employers' garden, it had been so easy to climb the wall and hide in the trees and bushes that grew thickly there. Sometimes the servants left the door open – they came into the house via the back door. So did the delivery men. Drove up the lane and sauntered up the path, through the vegetable and herb gardens, past the roses, up to the kitchen by the side of the lawns. There was a lot of activity there and he liked to watch, laughing at their stupidity in not noticing he was there.

He kept coming back after Bette had been sacked, to watch and wait and see. Curious. At first he did not know what he was waiting for. He just kept coming here and watching. That family. The Masterses.

They were always excited, as if life were some wonderful party. He hated them and could not understand why he nevertheless kept coming here.

Then another thought occurred to him. Why not have someone else from here? Punish someone else? He knew the place, felt safe here. Why not Trixie? Or – he suppressed a shiver of excitement – one of the girls who lived here? One of those stuck-up bitches? One of them should pay. Why not? The victory would be greater.

But which one? The plump one? Or the stuck-up one, the thin one with the boyfriend? That'd show her. And him. Soppy eejit. Oh shit, yes! That would wipe the uppity look offa her face. And his too. But the plump one would be more like . . . No, he didn't want to think about that now.

No, what he'd think of was the rest, the quietening in his head, afterwards. If it came to a choice he knew he could really get that peace from the bigger girl, get that surcease of irritation, the end, for a time, of that jerky discomfort that plagued him. Yes, Lordy, yes!

He ran his hand over his hair, smoothing it down. He could feel the grease, his hair oil, on his palms and he grimaced. He did not want to wipe them on his suit so he bent down and patted them on the grass.

He was getting hungry. Watching that lot eat made him aware that he had not had any food since eight o'clock that morning. He'd been up all night with old Mrs Delaney. With her remains. The only way fuckin' women were bearable was when they were dead. Then he felt very tender towards them, liked to touch them gently. They couldn't do anything to him. They just lay there, helpless.

'Home to bed, sonny,' Mr O'Laughlin had told him. Instead he had come here. It was such a beautiful morning. You could smell the sea.

His mother would be waiting. If he went to bed who knows what would happen. It was bad enough at night. The days were infinitely worse. He could see then. Seeing was terrible. A nightmare!

If he had his way people would only die at night and get their bodies attended to by daylight. Then he'd not have to work out the night with Mr O'Laughlin, then he'd never have to go to bed in the morning or afternoon. But Mr O'Laughlin liked to work at night. 'It's peaceful, sonny.' No phone calls. Nothing to disturb you. Just you and the corpse, and the corpse don't bother you with arguments, no sir. And you can make it beautiful for the relatives – see, they like to remember their dear one healthy and robust. So's our job to groom that corpse till it looks a treat. A treat, sonny. Whatever happens it must not look as if it suffered. Then they feel free to have a grand wake—' here he usually winked at Lonny '—an' include us if we're lucky.' Some of Mr O'Laughlin's corpses looked very rosy indeed but only the very brave complained about his liberal use of carmine.

Lonny watched now at the bottom of the Masters garden, eyes glimmering like a cat's through the lattice of the leaves.

'Eeny, meeny, miny, mo.' He wagged his finger between the sisters, giggling. The finger came to rest on Meriel. The plump one. She was calling something about going to the Gresham for a dance. But no. It would be the thin hoity-toity one. Or then again, no.

He was getting cramped. His leg was going to sleep. That was because he had been up all night, working. He always got cramp when he was up all night. Oh well, he had lots of time to decide. That was such an intrinsic part of the excitement; the fact that *he* was in control. Like God, he was in charge. He was boss. He would decide.

It would all happen when he had made up his mind. So he'd take his time. Do it when . . .

When he decided.

CHAPTER SEVEN

They were sitting sprawled in their chairs, lazy now in the warm afternoon sun, full of good food and wine. The servants had cleared away but most of the guests had retained a half-full glass or a cup of coffee within their reach.

Meriel sat on the grass, her head against her mother's knees resting and Robbie stood beside her, his head resting on Tessa's shoulder. Rogan sat beside his wife on the white wrought-iron bench, a glass in his hand. Fliss and Derry whispered to each other, laughing every now and then while Clemmie contemplated the spectacle with some irritation, sitting alone still under the chestnut tree. Valentine rambled on about golf to a deaf Bigger who was deep in his own thoughts. Agnes smiled at the young people in a benign, uncritical way.

Rogan was talking about women, holding forth as was his wont after a good lunch. He was saying, in effect, how perfect God's creation was, how beautifully He had arranged everything, quoting the Book of Genesis rather freely and inaccurately viz women being the weaker vessel and man the Lord of Creation.

It all began, as usual, with an innocuous remark. Agnes Devlin was saying to Fliss that she had seen the cutest two-piece swimsuit in Switzer's in Grafton Street.

'It's white, wonderful with a tan. There's a frill just over the bust and around the lower half.'

'I adore bikinis. They are so much more stylish than the boring old one-piece—' Meriel began.

'I forbid any daughter of mine to wear a bikini,' Rogan said with calm finality.

Tessa glanced apprehensively at her husband. 'Fliss and Merry are grown up now, dear,' she murmured.

'I don't care,' Rogan cried in a tone that brooked no argument 'While they are in my charge, living under this roof, they'll not sport about half naked.'

'Fliss and Merry will marry and then they can do as they like,' Agnes said complacently.

Rogan nodded. 'Then they'll belong to their husbands,' he agreed. 'And it will be appropriate that *they* will make the decisions regarding how modestly their wives disport themselves. But until . . .'

Agnes looked at him with something like contempt. 'You're a shocking old prude, Rogan Masters, so you are,' she said. 'Wouldn't they look gorgeous in bikinis?'

'Ah now, a man should keep his house in order,' Bigger Devlin nodded perhaps a little enviously, Tessa thought. If Agnes was a sweet woman she was also a strong-willed one and managed to get her own way most of the time. 'He's entitled,' Bigger added, catching his wife's eye. 'Entitled,' he added feebly.

'Women are not wise enough to know what's best for them,' Rogan informed them. 'No steel in them. Pliable, all of them. Not leaders, ever. Not creative in the arts or sciences. That is territory reserved for men.'

'Oh, Daddy, you are old-fashioned! Women have achieved lots! Lots!' Meriel hunted for an example. Whenever her father pontificated on a subject she became angry and argumentative and she did not know why. He just made her cross and contrary. Her mother always asked her to be diplomatic and not to rise to the bait but she did not seem to be able to keep her mouth shut.

He also made her forget all she knew. It was as if the accumulated knowledge she had locked in her mind refused to emerge when she tried to marshal an answer to his sweeping statements.

'Look at Marie Curie,' she cried triumphantly.

Her father laughed, that unworried, slightly superior smile on his face. 'Everyone knows that Pierre Curie, *not* Marie, discovered radium, only he was gentleman enough to allow his wife to take the credit.'

Meriel hooted in disbelief, speechless for a moment, and Tessa shook her head in warning. 'Don't upset your father, dear,' she whispered.

Fliss came to her sister's rescue. 'And Branwell Brontë wrote *Wuthering Heights* and *Jane Eyre*?' she asked sweetly. Not Charlotte and Emily?'

'Probably. Probably,' Rogan agreed, not one whit put out. 'Or maybe their father.'

Meriel squeaked and Tessa, holding Robbie to her side, smiled at her daughters. 'Don't argue with your father, girls. You know he is always right.' She smiled and winked at them, then dropped a kiss on the top of her son's golden hair

'I'm amazed, Rogan, that in a houseful of women you haven't been downtrodden yet.' Agnes Devlin laughed. She was so small, Tessa thought, such a sweet woman, yet so strong. Not even a wee bit afraid of Rogan.

'Oh, Agnes, you must agree, or at least accept, that men are the strong ones, the inventive ones, and it is no slur on the ladies. We are here to defend womenkind. Women are weak. That is a fact. It is our job to look after and protect the weaker sex.'

'Oh! Is that so? Well all I can say is you have a funny way of show-ing it. That judge for instance didn't do a very good job of protecting Arlene Shaughnessy.' This was Clemmie, loud and clear, 'throwing her spanner in the works' as Bigger phrased it. There was silence as they all stared at her.

'What the devil has that got to do with it? Sure that was ages ago. Besides, the girl was a floozie.' Valentine was flippant.

'Oh, so there's only one kind of woman men protect?' Meriel asked.

Rogan nodded. 'It was always so. There were always good women and bad women.'

'And the bad women were the ones who involved themselves somehow in sex?' Clemmie asked. Rogan nodded, a bit uncomfort-ably. 'Sex does involve two people? Or am I wrong? It does take two, doesn't it? Then what about the man's part in it? Does he get blamed at all? Hum?'

'Oh, Clemmie, don't be so ridiculous. Some women put them-selves outside the pale, you know that.'

'Some men put them outside the pale, you mean. Oh, at least be honest about it.'

'If they *do* put themselves outside the pale, Daddy, as you suggest, does that mean they don't deserve protection?' Meriel looked up inno-cently.

'You can't win,' Agnes laughed, trying to lighten the tone of the conversation, for Rogan was becoming distinctly prickly.

He shrugged. 'No one has to. You, my dear, will never be in that position. You are not that kind of girl, so you don't have to bother your head about the rights and wrongs of it. Life, I'm afraid, is very unfair.'

'To women! Not to men in their invincible position. Only us poor weaker sex.' Fliss was smiling.

'Indeed'n I've never known a woman wasn't stronger than me, cleverer and braver.' Bigger smiled fondly at Agnes. 'What about having children? Birth pain is terrible, so they say.'

'*They* say! *They* say!' Rogan was triumphant. 'Women make a terrible fuss but a doctor told me it's really like a difficult bowel movement, that's all.'

'Really, Rogan! Must you? Do we have to be so specific?' Clemmie asked acidly.

'And you'd know, Rogan, would you, having experienced it with Meriel and Phyllis and Robbie?' Agnes remarked good-naturedly, but there was a serious undertone to her voice.

Rogan was not to be discouraged. 'Women feel pain more intensely than men. That's another thing,' he said. 'They are the softer, as I said, weaker sex.'

'You're very sure about us, aren't you?' Clemmie blew out a cloud of smoke. 'Have you asked Tessa how she feels?'

'I *know* how she feels,' Rogan said complacently.

'How does she feel about that?' Clemmie persisted.

Tessa started to protest but Rogan answered firmly, 'Why, like I do, of course.'

'Is that how you feel about women, Tessa?' Clemmie asked.

Tessa was disconcerted, but she smiled and nodded. 'Of course,' she replied firmly. 'Of course.'

'Traitor!' Clemmie looked at her and shook her head. 'Oh, Tessa!'

Everyone looked at Tessa but she paid them no attention. The sun shone in her eyes and she raised her hand to shield them and thereby set her son free. He galloped down the garden path and they all turned lazily and watched his little legs pumping as he ran.

He stopped suddenly. He stood, perfectly still, at the bottom of the lawn where the lime and apple trees grew and the privet and laurel clustered. He stared at the hedge, and seemed transfixed.

To Robin the bushes were a place of mystery and fear. Anything might be behind the massy verdant hedge. No one knew what lurked in the green heart of the shrubs. To him they were as vast and impenetrable as a jungle and just as dangerous to enter.

He stood, or rather hovered, on his plump little legs, poised for flight and the safety of his mummy's arms should Fe-Fi-Fo-Fum or the Wicked Witch of the East or Bluebeard burst forth suddenly from the thicket.

But all he saw were the eyes. Wide eyes, staring.

He turned and, pointing to the bushes, he called out, 'Mummy! Mummy, someone's there. Eyes. There's eyes.'

Rogan laughed. 'It's the cat, Robbie. The cat.'

There was a great ginger cat called Grizzle who stalked the garden and kept the house clear of mice.

Tessa called, 'Come here, darling.' Her voice echoed down the path.

Lonny froze where he was in the shrubbery, absolutely terrified. His stomach lurched and he wet his pants, shivering as he crouched. But he kept staring at the child, his eyes watering. Their eyes were locked, the child's wide and curious, fascinated. Lonny felt cold now, panic in his chest, little squirts of urine saturating his pants.

'No!' the boy said, taking two cautious steps forward. 'No. Not a cat!' Lonny swallowed. The child was only a couple of feet away from him, staring right at him, near enough to touch. He was petrified. Suppose they found him? Suppose they got the Gardai and he was arrested? He could be sent to prison. His heart was hammering against his ribs. Not like it hammered when he was doing it to the cows, the bitches, not like that, but with a terrible fear. Bang – bang – bang! Against his ribs.

'Come here, darling,' Tessa called and there was sudden caution in her voice, the beginning of alarm.

'He's imagining things,' Rogan said calmly, dismissively. 'Children have such imaginations.'

'He's not an imaginative child,' Tessa replied with some asperity.

The boy still stared at Lonny and Lonny wanted to kill him. Full of murderous rage he wondered what to do. He felt as if he was shrinking, growing smaller, down to a Tom Thumb size and the child was huge now, towering over him. This must be what the bitches felt when he loomed over them. But he must not think about that now, what he had to do was get out of here without being discovered. The child had huge innocent hazel eyes. They were unblinking. He had that tall, gracious mother who held him in the circle of her arms and kissed his hair. He dwelt in one of those rooms above with their windows open and the gossamer curtains billowing out. The child had soft sisters who played with him and surrounded him with affection and warmth. Soft arms, soft smiles, soft kisses. He must not think of that now. He dared not think of that now. If he did he would either burst into tears, hysterical sobbing, or he would strangle the boy. And enjoy it. Choke the life out of his sturdy little body.

The boy was standing still, and now suddenly he moved cautiously forward, spurred on by who knew what spirit of adventure.

'Mummy, there's a man here,' he called.

'Come here, Robin,' Tessa shouted back, rising, lilac blossom falling from her skirt.

Lonny opened his eyes, full of murderous rage, opened them to the full, and glared at the boy, intensely, venomously. He widened them until they were enormous and staring, hate-filled. The lad drew in his breath, jumped back as if he had been stung, then ran back to the group under the trees. Lonny could see him through the rainbow drops of the fountain which had blocked him from view for a second.

'Colm!' Tessa called, drawing the adored child into the welcoming circle of her arms, cradling him, soothing him, petting his body as if it were part of her own. 'Merry, get Colm. Tell him to scour the bushes. Make sure.'

'I saw him, Mummy, I did, I did. I saw him,' Robbie insisted, twisting and turning in his mother's arms, yearning to run back down the garden but too frightened to actually do so.

'Hush, my darling, my own.' She pressed him to her breast, something he usually disliked for her arms were strong and her buttons scratched, but this afternoon he welcomed it.

'It's daft to think anyone could be there,' Rogan said impatiently 'This is what I mean by women's nerves. Don't mollycoddle the boy, Tessa, God's sake.'

'Whether he saw someone or imagined it isn't the point,' Agnes said. 'He's had a fright, that's obvious.'

Colm came out minutes later and searched the garden but found nothing.

Rogan said again, 'He imagined it. There, you see, just as I said. No one there.' Tessa gave him an impatient look but said nothing.

'Someone *was* there,' Robbie insisted doggedly.

The leaves above them shivered and quivered, trembling in the soft breeze, and the sunlight dappled them in shifting golden patterns. The myriad multi-coloured leaping drops of fountain spray shimmered in the afternoon brightness.

'I'm going to change now, Mother,' Meriel said, rising and stretching.

'All right, dear.' Tessa loosened her grip on Robbie. 'Don't forget to bring Bobby to us before you go.' Then to her son: 'Like some lemonade?'

'Ooo, yes!'

'Nora, give him some lemonade and a cookie.'

'But, Mum, you said he was never to—'

'Oh, it's Saturday, Nora. And he's had a fright.'

Nora's dough-like face broke into a smile. 'All right, Mum. Come on, little fella. Come with Nora.'

'You mustn't spoil him, Tessa,' Rogan murmured.

Tessa ignored him. Her heart felt such relief, such love, she needed to *give* her son some token, some gift. The lemonade and cookie were just the ticket and she had no intention of allowing Rogan to stop it. I'd die if anything happened to Robbie! The thought slipped swiftly through Tessa's mind and she watched her son disappear in the direction of the kitchen with Nora. He was trotting along, keeping up with her adult strides, hand in hers, and he turned to look over his shoulder at his mother, nearly falling over as he did so. The little face was so open, guileless, trusting, that she felt a fierce pain stab her heart and she caught her breath. That was love. Could women feel the same for a man?

She wondered. Meriel ran and caught up and took her little brother's other hand. He gave a squeal of delight and lifted his legs in the air.

'Need anything, Merry?' Fliss called to her sister's retreating back.

Meriel thought of the gloves and blushed. 'No thanks, Fliss,' she cried and hurried through the French windows.

'Oh well. We better go.' Agnes Devlin rose reluctantly, brushing down her skirt. 'Come on, Bigger. It's time.'

Fliss and Derry stood also, without words, in unison.

'We're going to play tennis now,' Fliss said with sudden energy. She kissed her mother's cheek and ran in after Meriel. 'Come on, Derry.'

'Thank you, Mrs Masters, Mr Masters. See you later.' Derry bowed slightly to them.

'Have her home in good time,' Rogan instructed him and he nodded and hurried after Fliss.

'Wonderful thing, love,' Bigger Devlin said, smiling.

— 40 —

Clemmie and Valentine thanked the Masterses too and left the garden, not touching, separated by an invisible wall of animosity.

Colm showed them out.

It was still in the garden now, only the birds could be heard, and the splash of the fountain and suddenly the sun went in and it was cold. Tessa turned to her husband. 'We should put an alarm on that back door,' she said. 'Just in case. Perhaps get a dog.'

'We have a dog.'

'But Benjy is a lapdog, dear. Jack the Ripper could come in that door and Benjy wouldn't bark.'

'Oh, Tessa, you're not still on about that imagined intruder? Really, dear, you are impossibly fanciful. Impossibly. Honestly, you only confirm my argument that women are weak, totally dependent on us men.

'As you say, dearest,' Tessa smiled, his insistence beginning to convince her that perhaps it had been imagination.

'Yes, my dear, you women are imaginative and fanciful.' He smiled at her fondly. 'And who would want you any other way?'

Tessa, much later, was to remember the conversation.

CHAPTER EIGHT

The tables were scattered in a circle around the Gresham Ballroom, spilling out into the lounge. The hotel was packed. The chandeliers glittered and the tables were laid. White damask table-cloths and napkins, silver spoons, fragile china, miniature sandwiches, small soda scones full of sultanas, butter-pats moist and dewy the size of Meriel's thumbnail, dainty little cakes; food for the little people, Meriel thought, awaiting their pleasure at a ringside table at the edge of the dance-floor for the *thé dansant*. Geraldo and his orchestra played 'You Are My Lucky Star' strict tempo. Every so often he turned around to the dancers and flashed them a tooth-filled smile.

Bobby Mitchell held her hand tightly. His hand was sweating. Her glove – Fliss's glove – on her right hand was wet. Sopping. They would never be pristine-white again. Fliss would murder her. Oh well, she'd worry about that later.

'I'd like to get you on a slow boat to China, all to myself alone . . .' Slow tempo now, Bobby's cheek on hers, wet too after the quickstep and the foxtrot, beads of perspiration running down from his thick brown hair, hair that made you want to run your fingers through it.

' 'S hot in here,' he said apologetically. He had big brown spaniel eyes and nice teeth but he wasn't much on the conversation. He was shy. She knew that and liked it. She loathed the 'I know it all' boys; they didn't appeal to her.

Her father had given Bobby strict instructions. He had doled out a small Paddy on ice for him in the drawing-room before they left – before Meriel made her grand entrance in her pale-blue cocktail dress with the heart-shaped neckline and the puff-sleeves and the wide skirt over three layers of petticoats.

'What time does it finish, this dance?' her father had been asking Bobby when she came into the room.

'It's over early, sir,' Bobby told him. 'It's a . . .' Nervous of Mr Masters, trying to look him in the eye man-to-man and not managing it, he couldn't pronounce *thé dansant* – was worried how it would come out – so he stammered to a halt, then managed finally, 'It's a tea dance, sir.'

'Well, what time's it over?'

'Should be finished by eight o'clock latest. It's three hours.'

'Well then, have her back here by nine. Give you time for the journey.'

Bobby cleared his throat and shifted from one patent-leather foot to the other. Then, catching Meriel's eye, he plucked up courage. 'We wanted . . . that is, I hoped we could go for a milk-shake at the soda fountain in O'Connell Street after. I'd have her home at ten, latest, sir.'

Rogan nodded his head benevolently. 'Very good then. It's a deal.' He smiled at Bobby. 'You take good care of her now, laddy,' he said, patting the young man on the back.

Bobby had come in his Riley and brought her a corsage. It was a large, unrealistic-looking purple orchid, quite spectacular. It did not suit her delicate dress, but she wore it nevertheless and was touched and flattered that he was treating her like a real grown-up date. As if they were doing a line. Like Fliss and Derry. It gave her a warm glow inside.

He parked right across the street from the Gresham, in the middle of O'Connell Street, down from the taxi rank.

The sound of music had greeted them as they entered the hotel. There were priests having tea in the lounge with their families, relatives up from the country meeting Dublin family or friends, girls from offices and shops sitting around drinking tea and eating scones and talking. A buzz of conversation and a clatter of china vied with Geraldo and his Big Swing Band from the ballroom.

Meriel left her coat in the cloakroom and entered on Bobby's arm. There was a big beefy fellow on the door taking tickets. He wore a uniform that would not have disgraced the Commander-in-Chief of the Allied Forces in full regalia. His job was to see that no one but ticket-holders entered the ballroom. Students from Trinity College were notorious for gate-crashing.

The tickets were expensive. Twelve shillings and eleven pence each. You could get the best seats at the pictures for two and six.

Meriel loved dancing. She sped around the floor in the circle of Bobby's arms, light as a puffball in the wind, twirling, dipping, bending, leaning back over his arm, hair flying, graceful as a bird on the wing.

Bobby was very gallant. He told her she looked like Laraine Day and had lovely hair. She told him so had he and giggled at her temerity. They did a samba, rumba, tango, 'Mini From Trinidad', 'Jealousy' and 'Ko chi-ko-chi-ko-cha, Ko chi-ko-chi-ko-cha, Ko chi-ko chi-ko there's a cuckoo in my clock'. Even Geraldo was sweating now.

They looked at each other and laughed. They were full of vim and happy to be alive, tingling with excitement and trembling anticipation. They devoured their tea, not giving it the attention it deserved, not appreciating the care that had gone into the cutting of the sandwiches, the delicate moulding of the butter-pats, just hungry from exercise. Healthy youngsters full of a joyous celebration of life.

'Blue Moon, I Saw You Standing Alone . . .' Cheek to sweating cheek but neither aware of the perspiration, dipping and gliding, her body like part of his own. 'Take me in your arms and hold me, like I've been holding you in my dreams . . .'

Sitting down after the slow foxtrot he complimented her obliquely: 'My mother says your mother's chic.' He pronounced it chick as in chicken but she didn't mind. She glowed.

'Your mother is too, Bobby. She's very pretty,' she told him generously, aware that they were not talking about their mothers.

He was not sure where to go from there. If he contradicted her it might seem like he thought his mother was plain. If he accepted it she might think him conceited. So he said nothing, popped another cucumber sandwich in his mouth and nodded.

The table was now littered with the debris of the finished meal. The butter-pats that remained were melting in the heat. The silver knives were jammy. So were the crumpled napkins. There was a tea-stain on the damask cloth.

Bobby looked at her, his brown eyes soft with a new expression of tenderness brought about by the music, the words of the songs, the dancing and the lights.

'*You're* very pretty, Merry,' he told her, then, staggered by his audacity, he blushed and popped a miniature éclair into his mouth, realizing too late that it was in there with the cucumber sandwich. She smiled at him. He really was terribly nice, she thought. A gentle person. She was not nervous of him and never felt apprehensive in his company the way she did with some of the other boys at the tennis club. The way she did with Derry. Awkward and gauche. As if she wasn't pretty enough or svelte enough and they were measuring her up and finding her wanting. She felt comfortable with Bobby Mitchell. Accepted.

'You and I do a line?' He blurted it out, swallowing the mixture of cucumber and éclair, astonished at himself. She could see he'd been steeling himself to ask her and was desperate now for her reply.

She couldn't think of anything she'd like more. To be his exclusive girlfriend. She nodded, eagerly. 'Yes,' she told him. 'Yes.'

It would be such a relief. Not to have to stand at the wall at the tennis-club hop and hope someone would pick her, ask her to dance. Not that she was often a wallflower, she was too good a dancer for that, but it meant she would be with Bobby now. They would always dance together. She would not have to wait to be chosen any more.

They would belong together now. Everyone would know this. It would mean she was a success – she had a boyfriend. Like winning a prize. She had proved herself. 'Bobby and I are doing a line,' she would tell everyone. That would put Patsy O'Brien's nose out of joint. 'Bobby and I are doing a line' or was it 'Bobby and me . . .' She wasn't sure, but it sounded so sophisticated. They would be a couple. He'd escort her everywhere, be responsible for her. In his Riley. He'd be her boyfriend. Her fella. And she'd be his girl.

'Yeah,' she breathed again. He pressed her hand, looking relieved. He held on to it.

'I can't say "Good night" because, folks, it's still early evening,' Geraldo told them over the mike, low-voiced, trying to sound sexy with his Cockney accent, which was impossible, beating the air with his baton, strict tempo, all the while he spoke. 'But it's farewell here, then over to the Hibernian for the Sodality of St Philomena Annual Dance. Hope I'll see you all again soon. So it's . . .' and he turned to the band and the music swelled as 'Good night, Sweetheart' filled the ballroom with its ultra-sweet sound. Everyone clapped, then rose and turned into their partners' arms for the last dance. Meriel laid her cheek on Bobby's shoulder. She would leave a panstick stain on his black dinner-jacket but she didn't care. She was too happy. She didn't want the dance to be over.

Coming out into the semi-dark was always surprising after a tea dance. Usually after a ball it was midnight or one or two in the morning and the streets were dark and deserted, no traffic, no people. Now it was dusk, a slow tranquil fading, like dying – day slipping away into night. But her heart rose. They would go to the soda fountain. The evening was not yet over.

O'Connell Street was crowded. Next-door to the Gresham in front of the Savoy Cinema people queued for the last show. There were two queues. The right-hand side was for the expensive seats and the people were well-dressed, smart, beautifully behaved. At the other side, for the cheap seats, pushing and shoving was the order of the day, the gurriers horse-playing, doing their Jimmy Cagney or their Errol Flynn. They whistled at the girls passing by in their new-length dresses. They bought ice-cream from the vendor and consumed it there, in the street, when everyone knew only the most ill-bred ate in the streets. They puffed on fags, cupping smouldering butts in their palms, showing off. Their comments were loud, raucous, insulting:

'Hey, Missus, if ye follow yer nose ye'll go straight to Heaven', 'Ooo, lookit her, thinks she's a film star', 'Will ye lookit the legs on that one – like a heifer, so she is', 'Hey you in the purple silk, that's a great uplift yer wearin' under yer gansey'.

They called out to the dancers leaving the Gresham but no one deigned to reply. Superior, they cast sidelong glances of withering scorn on the taunters.

The pubs were still full, laughter spilling out into the street, the windows glowing amber in the falling twilight. There was the sound of accordian and flute from the buskers and Mother Macree being sung with nasal proficiency. The birds were gathering for the night, chirping harshly, the pigeons cooing throatily in the glimmering dusk.

Bobby guided her down the busy street. It was nice to feel his firm hand steering her. Made her feel feminine and delicate. The soda fountain, Luigi's, was brightly lit, one of the few places in Dublin with the new neon lighting. They perched on high stools and ordered lime sodas with a scoop of ice-cream in. The proprietor, who was Italian and therefore exotic (there were few foreigners in Dublin), stood now behind the white imitation marble counter, wiping it with a damp cloth.

Bobby smiled at Meriel as Luigi took a bottle of lurid green liquid off the shelf and began to mix their drinks.

'Looks like the stuff Spencer Tracey drank in *Dr Jekyll and Mr Hyde*,' Bobby whispered, sending her into gales of laughter. 'It was good? The dance? You enjoyed it?' he asked her.

'Yeah!' She nodded, smiling into his eyes. He looked nice in his black dinner-jacket and tie. She thought again how thick and soft his brown hair was and tentatively leaned over and touched it. The close curls at his forehead. He was not sweating now, his skin felt cool under her fingers. He kept his eyes lowered and a slight darkening of his ruddy cheeks was all that signified he had noticed.

Lonny stood outside under a lamp-post and watched them. The place looked bright and clean, spot-lit in the evening dusk. Its decor was white with clear blue contrast, new fresh paint, tall chrome stools and a white and blue tiled floor. The girl's dress matched, flouncing out over her stool, and she hooked the heels of her shoes over the silver bar of her perch.

He had heard Meriel say she was going to the Gresham so he had made his way there, taking his time, mingling with the Saturday-night crowds outside the Gresham and Savoy. He had not followed Fliss to the tennis club because there was no way he could have concealed himself there, no way to get in without signing, nowhere to hide. He would be conspicuous there while here he was simply one of the crowd. So he went to the Gresham and waited in the vicinity, smoking cigarettes under the O'Connell statue, gawking at the nobby audience filing into the Gate Theatre to see a play called 'Traveller Without Luggage'. There were students with patched tweed jackets, no overcoats and scarves around their necks.

He watched the queues outside the cinema, all in pairs. Always couples. Only he was alone. Always alone. Even the tramps and beggars, the scruffy-looking travelling man playing his accordian outside the queue for the Carlton opposite – 'Oh Dan-ny-boi-boi' he sang through his nose, 'The pipes are call-ll-ll-in' mea' – even those men had each other. Every so often they would collect near the water-trough and share out cigarette butts, a gulp of Johnny Walker, half a can of beer, or the sinister, clear contents of a milk-bottle that Lonny was sure was not water.

When they came out of the dance they stood for a moment at the top of the Gresham steps, looking at each other. He followed them to the soda fountain. He hoped the fella would put her on a bus from the Pillar. He could get on behind her, follow her. He was not sure how they got to the Gresham. He had left abruptly after Mrs Masters had called Colm, telling him to search the bushes.

He had been sick with fear, scrambling over the wooden fence at the back of the garden. He could get off rape lightly, but not trespass. Judges were hot on trespass, even he knew that.

He got the bus to O'Connell Street and went to the Gresham and waited. He saw them go in, asked the doorman what time the dance was over. The puffed-up, over-dressed official pretended not to hear him so he said it again very loudly. The doorman told him eight o'clock so he went down O'Connell Street, round the corner to Grady's and played a few games of billiards, mooched back then at ten to eight, saw them come out, smirking at each other, holding hands.

At first it looked good, them walking down O'Connell Street towards the bus stop, but they didn't join the line for the bus. They went instead to the soda fountain, sat in there, giggling, smiling at each other like eejits. It irritated him the way they kept smiling at each other, not seeing anything else, not even noticing him standing there, nose pressed to the window.

So he waited under the lamp-post, smoking, watching them, feeling the tension, the beginning of excitement. Any time now the fella would take her to the bus stop, put her on the bus, maybe kiss her in a shop-door porch, but anyhow put her on the bus or tram and he'd follow her. If she went upstairs he'd stay down. If she stayed down he'd go up. Watch her. He knew where she lived, where she'd get off. No problem. Part of the game was the following. Stalking. Waiting his moment.

It would not be tonight. He would shadow her for a while, take his time, savour it. Following her would be an absorbing occupation. He got to know so much about the girls he had done the business with. Shown them who was boss. It was like becoming part of their lives: knowing what they bought in shops, where they went, who they visited. Bette McAlister had a postman boyfriend in Cabra she visited on her day off, and Arlene Shaughnessy liked to go to McGuire's pub in Donnybrook and have a few jars and a sing-song on a Saturday night.

He became alert, stubbing his cigarette out under his shoe as he saw through the plate-glass window the girl look at the big clock on the wall, put her hand to her mouth, eyes wide, point at it. The fella looked too, and, suddenly galvanized, paid the bill, took her elbow and they came out on to the pavement, within arm's reach of where he stood.

But they didn't go to the right as they should have for the bus. They retraced their steps towards the Gresham. Lonny decided they were getting a taxi. Fecky, fecky, fecky. He couldn't follow her. Only they didn't get a cab. Guy had a car! They got in a smart shiny black motor, him holding the door for her. Fella had a stupid car.

Lonny watched helplessly as the guy backed the car out, turned its nose south and varoomed away into the night, leaving Lonny gawking where he stood, angry and frustrated.

CHAPTER NINE

Bobby Mitchell stopped the car outside Meriel's house. They looked at each other for seconds then he suddenly leaned over and pressed his lips hard on hers. So hard he could feel her teeth.

They sat there a moment, locked rigid, mouth-on-mouth, then broke apart, breathless, not from passion but rather from the lack of air.

'Good night, Merry,' he told her, nervous, flushed.

' 'Night, Bobby,' she replied.

He leaped from the Riley, hurried around, opened her door and she got out and ran inside with a half-turn and a wave to him.

Her parents always left the front door slightly open until everyone was home. Last in locked it.

Rogan and Tessa sat in the drawing-room. The wireless was on and they were listening to Valentine Dyall, 'The Man in Black', 'bringing another story from the other side of darkness'. The deep velvet voice filled the comfortable room with tales of horror, screams, creaking doors and blood-curdling shrieks.

Meriel kissed her father's cheek. He was reading the *Herald* and didn't look up but grunted 'Meriel!' as if to say 'you're home'. Her mother was crocheting a tiny baby jacket, a matinée coat for one of her friends' daughters who was expecting. The jacket looked delicate as lace, minute, a doll's garment.

The lamps were low. Tessa put her finger to her lips. 'It's the exciting part,' she mouthed, pointing to the radio, eyes glowing, and Meriel hugged her, then sank down at her feet, head against her mother's knees, her favourite position. Her dress billowed out about her, her legs surrounded by the frills of her petticoats, her feet sticking out, tired from her dancing. She slowly eased off her shoes.

Valentine Dyall's rich voice was getting lower and lower, being terrifying about a ghost or a ghoul, and Meriel stared at the Japanese screen in front of the empty fireplace. It was at her eye-level, the strange oriental world depicted there – geisha ladies, men in sleeves that seemed as big as the garment they wore sitting on huge carved chairs – but tonight she did not see the screen. Her mind was full of Bobby, his face, his smile. She sighed deeply and settled more comfortably against her mother's legs.

The programme was just drawing to a close, Tessa not crocheting now, holding the crochet-hook in the air in one hand, poised, the delicate little coat in the other, listening intently for the *dénouement*, when suddenly the door burst open and Fliss rushed in, Derry in tow.

'Mother, Father, Derry gave me this tonight. Under the elm in the tennis club, in the moonlight. It's official. Ma. Pa. Ooo, I'm so excited.' She held out her hand and they could see a three-stone ring – diamond, emerald, diamond, three perfect stones surrounded by pavé diamonds glittering on her hand.

Tessa let the crochet fall, forgetting Valentine Dyall as she rose and Meriel screamed excitedly, 'Oh, Fliss, congrats! Oh, Derry, it's gorgeous.'

'Oh, darling, it's beautiful.' There were tears in Tessa's eyes. 'Oh, my precious.' She hugged Fliss then stood on tiptoe to kiss Derry's cheek. 'It's lovely, Derry. Lovely. Father will put an announcement in the *Irish Times* tomorrow, won't you, dear?'

Rogan stood and shook the young man's hand. 'Well, well, well, can't say I'm surprised.' he said. 'Welcome to the family, Derry.'

He rubbed his hands together. 'This calls for a toast.'

'Champagne, darling?' Tessa cried.

'Champagne is for cissies! No, we'll all have a brandy. The Napoleon.'

'I'd prefer a wine,' Tessa said feebly but Fliss had obediently taken out the fat cut-glasses and the brandy bottle. Rogan poured.

'Happy life, Fliss. Happy, happy life.' Meriel hugged her sister. 'Oh I'm so glad for you.' Then she whispered in her sister's ear, 'Forgive me for the gloves.'

Fliss burst out laughing. 'Don't be silly, Merry. Oh gosh, I'm so happy. What do I care about your thieving habits? I won't be here much longer, then what'll you do?' Meriel joined in her sister's laughter.

'When do you plan getting married?' Tessa asked as they all settled down around the empty fireplace. They always sat there, in a circle, even when there wasn't a fire. Derry sat on the arm of Fliss's chair. She tilted her head and looked at him every now and then or laid her cheek on his thigh.

'We thought—'

'Sooner the better,' Rogan said heartily.

'Oh no, Rogan!' Tessa intervened aghast. 'No. We must have time. There's so much to do. Invitations. Reception. . . .'

'We can have that here,' Rogan decided.

Tessa looked at her husband as if he'd lost his reason. 'There'll be at least two hundred guests. Where'll we put them?' She spread her hands and glanced around eloquently. Their drawing-room was large but not that large.

'We can have people here – the music-room, the dining-room, the garden.'

'Suppose it rains?' Tessa asked calmly.

'I don't *know* two hundred people,' Rogan protested.

'Of course you do. Then there's Bigger and Agnes's friends.'

'Derry's father and mother's friends are *ours* too. The same.'

'And the relations, theirs and ours. No. We'll have to go to the Royal in Bray or the Country Club, Kilcrony. Or the Grand in Portmarnock.' She turned to her daughter. 'Well, Fliss? When were you planning on?'

'September, Mummy.'

'Oh, Fliss, that's perfect. Perfect. Oh, we'll have such fun.'

'Well, I don't know,' Rogan muttered. 'I'd like the reception here. In our home. More cosy. More personal. I *hate* hotels.'

Tessa smiled tolerantly. 'It's only one day, dear. You don't want all those people tramping through here, now do you? Caterers? Visitors? People and guests that won't go home? Crowds around all the time, no privacy. Relatives from Galway! People we've never really encouraged but who will have to be invited. They'd want to stay. They'd be under our feet all the time and you couldn't just ask them to leave. In a hotel, they'd not be our responsibility.'

'Well . . . put like that . . .' Rogan sounded doubtful.

'Dear, you leave it all to me. I'll arrange it so that everyone is comfortable and we can all come home here to peace and quiet when it's over.'

'Yes . . . I can see your point, Tessa . . .'

'Of course you do. It will be perfect. We'll order Fliss's wedding gown from Paris? Or get it made? What would you like, Fliss?'

'Mrs Flannery, Mother. She'll do it perfectly. I don't want it to be a show-offy fashion-plate of a dress. I want a simple old-fashioned gown: lace and satin and orange-blossom.'

'Mrs Flannery it is then. She can do the bridesmaids as well.'

'I'll be one?' Meriel begged, suddenly aware of her role in the forthcoming celebrations.

'The most important one. My maid of honour.' Fliss told her.

Meriel squealed. 'Yellow – oh, let me wear yellow. Yellow taffeta.'

'What a splendid idea, Merry,' her mother cried. 'We don't want pink or blue. It would be too banal. Every Tom, Dick and Harry has pink or blue.'

'I sincerely hope not!' Rogan said, winking heavily at Derry. 'If every Tom, Dick and Harry wore pink or blue bridesmaids dresses, well – I ask you!'

Derry laughed obediently.

They settled down to discuss the wedding. They drank their brandy and talked of dates, invitations, dresses, flowers, food, caterers, churches, cars, decorations, lists, suitable and unsuitable guests, ushers, bridesmaids, relations, business associates, pages, organ-music, hotels, honeymoon, and so on and so on.

They did not realize that this was the last evening they would ever be so carefree, so happy. They could not know that this gathering, all of them together, hearts light, full of delighted anticipation of a joyful event, was the last time they would be so united, that laughter would spring unbidden to their lips – that the closeness and love they felt, uncomplicated and taken for granted, would be destroyed, their lives damaged for ever, beyond repair.

CHAPTER TEN

She was overwhelming; a huge monolith of a woman. In the dusk of the room she seemed larger than life, looming over him, Gargantuan.

When she put her hand on him it was with sick horror that he felt himself grow beneath her manipulating fingers and he knew what would happen next. It always did.

He responded. Or rather *it* responded. Against his will. He had nothing to do with it really. It was like a god that had to be appeased. Up it went at the touch of this obscene hand and the ritual had begun and would not end until Nature had taken its course.

He lay in the dark room which, though it was his own, smelled of her and she crouched over him, murmuring in the dark, doing those things to him.

Lonny had thought he would escape it tonight. It was so late. By the time he took a bus from the Pillar to the bridge over the Tolka it was pushing midnight. He had stayed out as long as he could, avoiding it. Avoiding her.

The house was a small four-roomed lopsided cottage beside the river. River! That was a laugh. It was twelve feet wide, its nettle-infested banks right on his doorstep. River rats sometimes poked their noses into the kitchen and the house which had once been painted white was grey now, the paint peeling, the roof leaking, the gutters rusty and ineffective. There was a slimy fungus over the kitchen walls, a sort of grey mucus in the corners.

It had not looked like that when his father was alive. Tom Clebber was a jolly man, a plumber by trade, and he kept the house in very good nick, painted it every other year, mended things, repaired and maintained. But since he died *she* had not done a thing, made no effort.

— 54 —

Before he died! Oh, everything had been different then. It seemed to Lonny that the river had been more manageable then. How could that be? Had the river obeyed his father? Stayed obediently within the confines of its banks for him?

There had been a wall around their pocket-handkerchief garden, but after his father died the wall, like the house, had crumbled. Eventually it collapsed and was washed away. Now only the ivy crawled over the stones scattered here and there, and grey plants grew, and slithering things crawled, grey-bellied and frightening.

The house had been a cheerful place when Tom Clebber was alive. His mother had been a plump, rosy woman then. He remembered her, a different person, someone he loved, someone he had trusted. Her skin had been pink, her arms fat, her eyes smiling.

Oh, those days had been marvellous. His father had taken young Lonny to football matches and the hurling, and when the circus came to town what a grand time they had. Tom Clebber was something of a child himself and he got as much fun out of Walt Disney, the dodgems, candy-floss and ice-cream as Lonny, and he held his son's hand, skipping along with him, jumping puddles and the hell with what anyone thought.

And then he died and with his death everything changed.

First of all Tom's mother, his Grammy, became very peculiar. She had spent her days in a rocking chair in the corner by the fire, beaming at her son, whom she adored. He was the light of her life, her sun, moon and stars. To Lonny she was a benign old body, a nodding, toothless creature rocking perpetually in her chair in the inglenook. Now she developed a vicious streak. Lonny was sure it was his fault, just as he blamed himself for his father's death. If he had been a good boy, if he had always done as he had been told, then his father would not have died and Grammy would not pinch him every time he passed her rocking chair.

Lonny used to lean against that chair listening to some far-fetched tale Tom Clebber told them; some story of heroes and heroines who waited to be rescued, or an adventure in the South Seas, with lotus blossom and lagoons (such magical exotic things) or a battle in the frozen North with huskies and screaming winds and vistas of ice and snow. Tom Clebber would cry out in a rich full-throated baritone:

'There are strange things done in the midnight sun
By the men who moil for gold;
The Arctic trails have their secret tales
That would make our blood run cold . . .'

And they were a spellbound audience, unable to move, enchanted and thrilled. Lonny would never forget his father, never forget the magic he wrought.

Old Grammy Clebber missed her son too. She kept thinking he would come back: any day now he'd open the door and fill the room with his jovial presence, his stories and his songs. But he never did and she took to pinching Lonny when he stood near her, bewildered by his loss, confused and grief-stricken at the sudden absence of the huge man he had adored. She would choose a sensitive part of his anatomy and squeeze it hard, to cause him pain, as if she too blamed him for his father's death.

'You're the little man of the house now,' his mother would say and Grammy Clebber would catch a piece of his upper arm and nip it fiercely. An agonizing nip to a boy of nine years.

And then his mother seemed permanently angry with him. She lost her rosy glow and became a grey thing. She let her appearance go, stopped wearing a brassière or girdle, did not bother to wash or dress, didn't shop but had the grocer deliver. She didn't go to the hairdresser any more and didn't wear lipstick but slouched about the house in an old tartan dressing-gown and spread outwards, becoming over-ripe and overblown.

Then one night she came into his room, weeping. She had had a few whiskies; he could smell the alcohol on her breath. Often nowadays she took a drink. She was tearful, self-pitying that night. She said, 'I'm so lonely, Lonny. So lonely. I guess you are too.'

'Oh, Mammy, Mammy, I miss him so.' He had turned to her for comfort, arms out, the tears, so long bottled up, flowing now, flowing like the river used to when his father was alive, unimpeded.

His mother had cried too, great harsh sobs tearing her chest. They had fallen asleep in each other's arms, relieved and exhausted. Then the next night she had come again to his room, snuggled down with him in her arms.

He was happy. He needed her warmth, the bulk of her was a

consolation. The reassurance of her presence there, close to him made him glad. Soothed him.

After that she had returned each bedtime. It became a habit.

Then one night she had touched him. Turning away from her he tried to avoid her hands, but he had nowhere to escape to. He pretended to be half asleep but he didn't fool her.

And to his shame, his embarrassment and disgust his body responded. Of its own volition. It was then he learned that that thing hanging between his legs, that soft little rosy muscle, could harden and stiffen and become an instrument of horror, and one of infinite release and power.

As time passed, every so often he tried to leave home, to escape, but he found he could not. He had heard of drug addicts and he knew he was like them, that he couldn't do without the thing he hated most. He was hooked.

He turned away from God. He could not go to Confession and tell a priest about what was happening to him. No priest would believe him. How could he explain? It was all so confusing. Anyhow, the priests always said avoid the occasion of sin, and how could he do that?

He stayed out late, volunteered for night work, but that did not stop her. She looked upon it as her right now. She would come to his room daytime as well.

Sometimes he managed to avoid her for days but eventually she got him. They never talked about it. But always when she had used him she gave them two teaspoons of syrup of figs. 'That will clear you out,' she said. And it did. He would sit on the outside lavatory and evacuate his bowels, wincing at the curling, griping pain that twisted his guts.

Once he said to her: 'Why don't you leave me alone?' but she shook her head. 'I don't know what you're talking about,' she said and stared at him coldly.

The tiny cramped house was a dark place, and she, like a spider, sat inside and devoured him.

'Your father said you were to look after me,' she told him. 'My little man.' And soon he was. Grown up and not able to break away. No will of his own; he was like a puppet and she pulled the strings.

But not when he was stalking a bitch. He was in charge then.

He thought now of the thin one they called Fliss as his mother groaned on top of him, grunts of primeval satisfaction shaking her. He thought of the plump one, Meriel. He narrowed his eyes as he came, as saliva ran from his slack mouth down his chin and his manhood squirted down his leg.

Which one, which one, which one? Fliss? Or Meriel? Fliss or Meriel? Oh Jesus, oh! Oh Jesus, no!

CHAPTER ELEVEN

The next day was Sunday. It dawned over Dublin fair but drizzly. A soft lilac mist hung over the purple and olive mountains and rose in plumes from the Liffey. It slipped in pearly scarves over Dublin Bay, veiling the coves around Dun Laoghaire harbour and Dalkey, and hung in wisps over the church spires.

The Masters household rose late. Nora sounded the brass gong in the hall which meant they had slept it out. The sound wakened them and the smell that tickled their noses and encouraged the drowsy family to get up was a delicious aroma of bacon, fresh-baked soda bread and coffee. Only Robbie was up, playing in his room, absorbed in his electric train-set.

Fliss and Meriel squabbled.

'Not content with my gloves you sneak my best petticoat,' Fliss was complaining.

'Aw! Please lend it to me,' Meriel begged. 'Mine tore last night when you told us your news. I caught my heel in it when I stood up. I was so excited.'

'That's no reason. And you can cut out the blarney.'

'Aw, Fliss, you'll be getting a trousseau, c'mon. Don't be mean.'

'Do I ever ask you for *anything*? Do I? Why is it you're always on the scrounge?'

Meriel lifted her hands, palms forward in a helpless gesture. 'Dunno,' she said pulling the corner of her mouth down in a deprecating grimace..

'I'll tell you why. You're careless. You never think of anyone but yourself.'

'That's not fair, Fliss, that's beastly, *and* it's not true.'

There was a knock on their door.

'Stop quarrelling, girls, and get a move on. We have to make twelve mass and it's nine-thirty already. You know how your father hates breakfast eaten in a rush. So if you want any you'll have to pull your-selves together. You can't go to church carelessly dressed.'

Fliss sighed. 'Damn,' she said to herself. 'Oh, I suppose . . .' She glanced at her sister, then grimaced, casting her eyes to heaven. 'Oh, have it,' she said.

Meriel's eyes sparkled. 'You mean it?' she breathed. 'Oh, you angel.' She hugged her sister, who struggled away. 'It looks perfect with my yellow,' she said.

'Oh you! You're mad about yellow.'

'It brings out the auburn in my hair,' Meriel retorted.

Fliss shrieked. 'Auburn? Auburn! About fifteen reddish hairs doesn't make auburn! Brown, Merry. Your hair is brown.'

'It's got auburn glints,' Meriel replied grandly. 'Mother said,' she added, clinching the matter.

It was a scramble that morning. Only Robbie moved serenely through the chaos. People rushing in and out of rooms, calling to each other.

'Where's my beige stockings, Nora?'

'Trixie, can I have orange juice? I'm parched and the jug's empty.'

'Nora, get Colm. I need him to go for petrol.'

Fliss screaming, 'Merry . . . Merry, you took my best gloves!'

'I told you last night. You *said* it was okay. You *said*!'

'But not those ones. I never thought you'd take my best ones. My pearl-button ones with the frill. If I'da known I'd never let you have my petticoat.'

'Well it's too late now. I've got it on. I can't change now.'

In the breakfast-room the rain pattered against the glass.

'They say it's going to clear up later,' Rogan told them, as they fil-tered in, one by one. He was reading the papers. *The Irish Times*, the *Sunday Independent*.

Tessa absently admonished her children's lapses in good table man-ners as she mentally worked out arrangements for the day: how they would get where they were going and back and how many would be in for what and so on.

'Would Derry like to come to dinner with us tonight?' Tessa asked Fliss.

— 60 —

Fliss shook her head. 'No, Mother. I haven't seen Mr and Mrs Devlin yet to tell them the news. We told you first. We thought we should.'

Rogan glanced up from his paper. 'That was nice of you, Fliss.'

'So we'll tell them at cocktails this evening, if Derry hasn't told them already. Derry felt he should spend the evening with them. Privately. So I'll be back here for dinner.' She glanced up. 'Are you going there for cocktails, Mother?'

'Of course, dear,' Rogan said. 'I wouldn't miss it. A Devlin cocktail party is ace.' He smiled at her. 'It's so suitable, Fliss dear. I'm so pleased Derry chose you. My best friend's one and only son.'

Fliss flushed. 'You talk as if I was a blend of tea or coffee. We chose each other, Father.'

Tessa sent her daughter a warning glance. But she was thinking how lovely she looked in her slim-skirted suit, navy-blue with a pure white piqué collar. Fliss was always so perfectly turned out. But even as she thought this she also admired Meriel in her wide-skirted buttercup-yellow grosgrain, neat little jacket top with peplum and tiny buttons up the front. Meriel loved that dress, its snug little waist, the peplum disguising her wide hips.

Yes, both of her daughters were a credit to her and she felt justifiably proud of them.

They sat in their places and laughed and chatted, munching their corn flakes or porridge, bacon and eggs, sausages, black and white pudding, toast and marmalade, drinking coffee, tea or orange juice.

'Anyone coming for lunch?' Rogan asked his wife.

'No, dear. We're eating at the club,' she replied. 'What are your plans exactly, Fliss? So that I'll know.'

'Well, we thought we'd go to the Devlins' after mass and break the news. Or if Derry thinks it better, wait until the cocktail party.'

Rogan shook his head. 'I don't think that's a great idea. Someone will blab. I think you should telephone Derry and let his parents know as early as possible. We don't want anyone miffed about this, do we?'

'Your father is right, Fliss,' Tessa agreed.

'Then we'll do that. At any rate we thought we'd go to the club with you. Then the cocktail party and then I'll be in for dinner. As I said.'

'Perfect,' Tessa smiled. 'And what about you, Merry? Will you be with us for supper?'

Meriel shrugged. 'Bobby Mitchell said he'd phone me.'

Fliss glanced at her sister. 'Bobby Mitchell? That dumb cluck . . .!'

Meriel screamed and stood, shivering with rage.

'Fliss, I will not allow you to talk to your sister like that. Suppose she called Derry a dumb cluck?'

'But he's not,' Fliss replied tranquilly.

'He's not to *you*. But beauty is in the eye of the beholder,' Tessa said calmly. 'Bobby Mitchell is a charming young man—'

Fliss hooted and Meriel, to her surprise, felt tears spring to her eyes.

'Fliss!' Tessa's voice had become cold. It was a tone everyone recognized and dreaded. She seldom became really angry but when she did it was not agreeable. Everyone glanced at her nervously.

'Sorry, Mother,' Fliss cried hastily.

'I'm not the one you should apologize to,' she said crisply.

'Sorry, Merry. He *is* nice actually. Sorry.'

'That's better.' Tessa glanced around the table. 'So. You all know we're lunching at the club? Good.'

Nora came in with a fresh pot of coffee and Tessa turned to her, 'Nora, we'll be four in to dinner tonight. It can be cold. Some of the left-overs from yesterday. We're all out to lunch. Tea for Robbie as usual. None for us. We have cocktails at the Devlins' at five. We should be back here by seven thirty or eight. Serve at eight thirty to nine. All right?'

Nora nodded. Her mottled face was full of urgent good-will and she stayed after she put down the silver pot. Tessa looked at her, surprised. 'Is there something else, Nora?'

'I must, Mum, I must . . .'

'Well, what must you?'

'I must . . . Miss Phyllis, congratulations. I'm that pleased, that delighted. Bless you, Miss, and Master Derry. Oh, it's grand news, really grand.'

Rogan looked up from his paper. 'How the devil did you find out, Nora?' he asked in a baffled tone.

'Trixie told me, sir.'

'How did Trixie find out? Did you girls tell her?'

They shook their heads negatively.

'She might have heard us talking,' Fliss said.

'Damned if I know how things get out around this house,' he muttered.

'How clever of you, dear, to advise Fliss to let Derry's parents know as soon as possible,' Tessa said.

Rogan looked pleased. 'Well . . . you know . . . we don't want anyone offended,' he said.

Nora nodded and Tessa smiled at her. Men are such boys, her eyes said, and the two women understood each other. There was a sudden spurt of activity in the eating department. Marmalade was spread swiftly on toast and crunched hurriedly and the last of their coffee or tea was gulped down as the church bells began to chime and they all got going, collecting missals, rosaries, lipsticks, powder compacts, handkerchiefs. They checked that their stocking seams were straight, peplums were fluffed out, gloves were on, hats at the right angle, veils over powdered noses and everything in order.

Tessa put Robbie's cap on and tied his shoelaces, hunkering down over them as he made faces at his sisters over her head.

And they left the house, piled into the car and drove the three blocks to the Church of the Holy Redeemer and midday mass.

'We must let Father Hegarty know about the wedding,' Tessa whispered as they knelt. 'Set the date.'

'Let's wait until the Devlins know, Mother, then I'll go in to see Father Hegarty with Derry. It'd be nice if we could get the Papal Blessing.'

'How sensible you are, dear. Of course.'

Tessa patted her daughter's hand and thought how lucky she was. Her family was healthy, happy and good-looking. Her husband a pleasant companion. Her home comfortable and well-appointed. She had what she wanted and life was incredibly enjoyable. And now Fliss was engaged to marry their best friends' son, a most suitable young man. Her younger daughter was dating another eminently well-bred boy, perhaps not the most intelligent young man, certainly not a University First material, but he came from a wealthy and socially acceptable family and he was good-looking. A most desirable catch, if things came to that. And if it didn't it showed Merry's taste lay in the right direction. What more could any mother want?

Tessa made up her mind that she would say an extra decade of the rosary in thanksgiving for her good fortune.

CHAPTER TWELVE

Lonny had no work on that Sunday. Unless there was a rush and several people snuffed it, which often happened in the depth of winter, he would not have to check in. If something unexpected happened Mr O'Laughlin would send a message and he would then go down to Capel Street.

But there was no message today. Lonny looked at the mat under the front door. Nothing.

The linoleum was torn in places and it curled up in frayed edges near the walls. There was a new outcrop of grey fungus near the dado or where the dado had been, long ago when his father was alive. The house this morning was particularly damp. It was always clammy but this morning, with the mist from the river and the rain, it was shrouded in grey fog. Even inside an evil vapour seeped under the door and through the windows and down the broken chimneys. The windows and doors didn't fit properly and had shrunk and contracted over the years. There was this morning an unhealthy pall hanging over the interior of the rickety dwelling place.

Lonny shivered. He sported an imitation Ronald Coleman dressing-gown that he had bought at Cleary's sale. It was wine-coloured, simulated silk and it tied at the waist – very sophisticated, very debonaire.

He went into his room. It smelled of *her*. He shivered again and went to his wardrobe. He opened it.

There were about twenty outfits in there. All copies of what the film stars wore. He had his Jimmy Cagney gangster-type pin-stripe in an imitation flannel; a white Humphrey Bogart jacket with a black shirt. A Basil Rathbone navy-blue with an imitation silk scarf worn knotted nonchalantly at the throat and an artificial carnation in the buttonhole; a Fred Astaire dinner-jacket. He had a Clark Gable smart but careless gabardine with a drape and a John Garfield raincoat to be worn over a black polo-necked synthetic-wool sweater and baggy trousers, and that was the outfit he selected for today.

The room was tiny and it was difficult to dress, but Lonny, quiet as a feline, was meticulous. He shaved, trying not to see himself. He saw instead Cary Grant looking back at him from the mirror, smiling his deprecating and stunning smile.

The room was full of postcards from the stars pinned on the walls. James Cagney. Clark Gable. Cary Grant. Errol Flynn. Tyrone Power. No women.

Best wishes to Lonny Clebber.

He had written for the postcards, written to those huge, larger-than-life idols of his and *they had replied. To him*. To the cottage by the Tolka. Unbelievable!

He had sent his request and his dignified letter of admiration: 'I admire your acting so much. I think you are very talented.' Not fawning. Man-to-man like, inferring he was a mate, on their level, delivering a well-deserved pat on the back. And they had all replied! Sent him pictures of themselves. Signed. From Paramount Studios. Warner Brothers. And Metro-Goldwyn-Mayer. Culver City, California, USA. America. He imagined them sitting at their desks, like you saw in the films, staring at his letter to them, thinking about him, choosing a photo, signing it. Fab-u-lous. America was not like Dublin. That land people were all rich. They must have thought he was too. He had fixed the postcards to the walls with thumb-tacks, but because of the slimy damp surface they kept falling down and became curled at the edges. Like the linoleum. He kept fixing them back up again and added stills from his favourite movies, stills that he begged off the distribution houses in Abbey Street. The largest one was Burt Lancaster in *Rope of Sand*. And there was one of Charles Laughton and Maureen O'Sullivan in *The Big Clock*. Both films he had seen a couple of times and both films he had lost himself in. There were small stills of *A Foreign Affair*, Burt Lancaster and Kirk Douglas in *I Walk Alone*, and Alan Ladd in *Chicago Deadline*. These he cut from *Film Fan* and *Film Weekly* and *Picturegoer* magazines.

He did not look at them now as he dressed. He took them for granted, part of the background as he was pretending to be John Garfield in the mirror. Turning nasty – Cary Grant was gone.

He giggled. John Garfield was always nasty. He called women *babe* and his mouth turned down, as if he'd tasted something sour.

Lonny decided he'd go to mass in the pro-Cathedral. Candles, lights, intoned Latin and incense. Then he'd find those cows and make up his mind which one.

He parted his hair carefully, took a dab of Brylcreem on his finger and rubbed it over his palms, then smoothed it on his head. Then he put on his raincoat over his black polo-neck and hunched his shoulders in a John Garfield way.

He heard his mother stirring. 'Lonny . . . Lonny. . . c'mere . . .' She wanted tea, a cup of tea. Well, let her get her own tea. He hurried out of the house, giving the door a vicious bang as he went, then smiled mirthlessly and walked up the riverbank to the main road.

CHAPTER THIRTEEN

The Devlins were as delighted as Tessa and Rogan that Derry had for-
malized the understanding that he and Fliss had, that the engagement
was now official. Their fears that Derry or Fliss might wander from
each other, become infatuated with some unsuitable person, not in
their *milieu*, not their 'sort', were allayed and the fairy-tale would
have a happy ending.

Bobby Mitchell gravitated to Meriel's side in the church and no one
was able to dislodge him that day.

'Well, we have to go to the club now, boy,' Rogan informed him
outside the Holy Redeemer, but he ignored the hint and, pulling
Meriel into the Riley, followed the Masters car to Portmarnock.

'We're doing a line, Daddy,' Meriel informed her father, who was
bewildered by the boy's barnacle tendencies. The information
enlightened Meriel's parents as to the exact nature of the association
and they then accepted his shy, silent presence among them with
equanimity.

Lunch was a huge celebration that spread. Everyone in the golf
club lunching that day or arriving back to the bar after a game toasted
the young couple and wished them well. Fliss and Derry reminded
them of their own youth and the hopes and dreams they had had, and
they remembered, fleetingly, the sweetness of romance and great
expectations. Everyone there felt a warm rush of affection and a slight
stab of pity for the young couple who were so sure that the magic
would never diminish, the dream never be betrayed.

Lunch was a cacophany of half-finished sentences, plans,
arrangements and thoughts, excited conversation with little eaten.

Everyone had a suggestion to offer, an idea to contribute, a reminiscence of a disaster that could be learned from. There was little disagreement. The two families were at one regarding tastes, preferences, social mores and what was suitable or not for what would be a society affair.

They sat all together on the terrace of the club, looking out at the rain-swept sea and the golden sand dunes, talking all at the same time, laughing a lot, faces beaming, hearts light. It was a perfect match, they all agreed.

Fliss and Derry held hands, smiling modestly. He dropped an occasional kiss on her softly blushing cheek, the back of her hand or her hair, breathing in the sweet fresh scent of her. They accepted congratulations; Fliss showed off her ring; gasps, exclamations. A stiff breeze blew from the sea and the curling waves crashed on the slipper-satin-gold sands and Meriel stared out at a fat seagull taking a dip while Bobby Mitchell worked up enough courage to take her hand, squeeze it till her eyes watered, then hold it hotly in his own. It was great, doing a line.

Tessa and Agnes put their heads together, nattered about colours and venues, lilies and orangeblossom, the respective merits of hotels, marquees or home. The men talked about the fact that they would be ruined by the expense, not meaning it, talking with the confidence of the rich who knew no anxiety. They made ribald jokes, out of earshot of their wives, and nudged each other. Champagne was served although Rogan protested it was a cissy drink.

'Ah now, Rogan, the ladies like it,' Valentine Bushell cried. 'So quit bellyachin' and order it. You can stick to your brandy, no law against that. We're not forcing *you* to drink it.'

The Bushells had come over to offer their felicitations and as Valentine sorted the argument about the champagne, Clemmie glanced over at the happy couple.

'God help them!' she was muttering, so Tessa rose and steered her firmly away. She had no intention of allowing Clemmie to spoil the general joyfulness of the occasion with her doom-and-gloom predictions.

'Fliss raises the tone any place she is,' Agnes remarked. 'Oh, isn't this a grand day!'

It was four in the afternoon when they returned home.

'We'll have to hurry,' Tessa called to the girls. 'We can't be late for the party.'

The men were in the drawing-room, waiting while the women changed. They were wearing their formal church clothes and so they did not have to change for the cocktail party.

'It's from five to seven, lads, so we're not in evening togs,' Rogan said. 'Now what'll you have?'

Bobby Mitchell was trying not to show his unfamiliarity with and dislike of the strong drink Rogan served him with. He was glowing with a sense of achievement at this acceptance into the bosom of the family and did not want to sputter and cough and thereby reveal his *gaucherie*. What he did not realize was that what he saw as acceptance was in fact a polite inability to get rid of him. Rogan was not quite sure how to tell the lad to go home.

Upstairs Fliss sat on her bed and sighed. 'I don't think I'll go to Derry's,' she said, stretching. 'I'm tired.'

'You'll *have* to. You just got engaged,' Merry protested.

'Well, I think we covered that in the club, Merry. The whole of Dublin must've congratulated me.'

'Oh gosh, Fliss, it'll look funny if you don't go.'

Fliss shrugged. 'I don't care how it looks. I'll talk to Mother.'

Tessa agreed with Meriel. She felt that Fliss ought at least to put in an appearance. 'You don't want to start on the wrong foot with Derry's parents, love,' she said. 'I know if it was my party and Derry didn't show I'd think it odd.'

Fliss gave in graciously and they joined the men and drove to the Devlins'.

'I'm bushed, darling,' Fliss told Derry. 'It's the excitement, I think.'

He patted her hands, folded in her lap, without taking his eyes off the road. 'I'll drive you home whenever you want,' he told her. 'Mother and Father won't mind. Just put in an appearance.'

Fliss frowned. 'I don't want to give the wrong impression. You know, like your mother might think I was being flip.'

Derry shook his head. 'She'd never think that,' he said and smiled at her. 'She dotes on you.'

She looked up at his face. He was frowning, intent on his driving. He had a lovely face, she thought, the kind of face she loved to look at. The bones were clear under the skin and there was a sensitive curve to his mouth. His lashes were long and he kissed wonderfully. He would be a great lover, she could tell. Her skin, every nerve in her body, responded to his touch.

It had been tough. They had gone as far as they could, further than they should, petting. She had felt herself pliable as hot wax in his arms and did not know whether she admired or hated his refusal to 'take advantage of her' as he put it. Nice girls were virgins on their wedding day and heaven knew that she didn't want to do anything to change his love for her or diminish his respect. Boys were brought up to put girls on pedestals and she did not want to topple from hers. Was she abandoned that she panted with desire for him? Was she a floozie that she ached to 'go all the way' when he kissed her and fondled her? Sometimes she felt so guilty about the strength of her feelings but she hoped it was normal nevertheless. Still she kept how she felt to herself, just in case it was *not* all right. The boys she knew said such derisive things about girls who allowed them to take liberties. A girl with a tarnished reputation in Dublin would never get a desirable husband. Men with prospects played around with that sort, but they didn't marry them, that was for sure. Fliss sighed and told herself that she had not much longer to wait. September wasn't that far away and then they would be married and she could wrap herself around Derry's gorgeous body, let him in and her love pour out to him, the man she adored.

All the same people were at the Devlins'. It was as if they had been transported from the club to Agnes and Bigger's home. Fliss and Derry were greeted with renewed hoots and whoops of congratulation, winks and nods and more champagne. Fliss didn't want a drink but accepted a glass which she held without tasting in her hand.

It was the same conversation. Wedding plans, organ music.

'I favour Mendlessohn myself.'

'But that's old hat.'

'If you think that, you should have Tony Doyle and his swing band playing "Blue Moon". Connie McGuire did that in Drimnagh.'

'And the priest allowed it?'

'Ah sure, Father Doodie loves a bit of modern. He's mad for Benny Goodman.'

'Well I think there's nothing like Gounod's "Ave Maria". It tears the heart out.' This was Agnes, dabbing her eyes.

'Should be "The Last Post".' This Clemmie, scathing.

'Mrs Devlin, I'm jaded.' Fliss looked at her mother-in-law-to-be, her big eyes pleading. She found only sympathy and understanding in Agnes's faded blue ones.

'O'course, love. You slip away now, off home. Derry will take you.'

'Oh, it's all right. I'd quite like to ride on top of the tram. Blow the cobwebs away.'

But Agnes Devlin would not hear of it. 'No. He'll take you to the door. It's only right. His job from now on. Look after you.' She nudged Fliss and gave a conspiratorial grin. 'Husbands are useful for that – you'll never again have to cadge a lift or wonder how you're getting home.'

And for other things, Fliss thought, gorgeous other things. Kisses and love and holding hands and doing things now forbidden. Being admitted to the grown-up women's group. She moved towards her mother to tell her she was going home.

In the car she said, 'I never felt happier, Der.'

He smiled at her possessively. 'You're mine now, Fliss,' he said. 'You'll be my wife and we'll belong together. No regrets?' He looked at her half joking, half earnest, his eyes vulnerable. She reassured him. Touching his cheek gently she smiled and shook her head, then softly kissed his lips.

'I thought maybe you got tired because you were sorry . . .'

'Shush. You know that's not so. Shush.' She put her finger on his lips.

'Yes, I knew,' he replied. 'But at the same time I was afraid.'

'Well don't be. I'm tired because it's been a long day and I'm excited.'

'I'm so lucky, Fliss, you going to marry me. I hope I'm worthy of you.'

'Darling, darling, darling.' She snuggled close in his arms.

He was tired too. She could see it in his face. She wondered briefly if he felt the weight of the responsibility he was assuming, taking her on for life, providing for her, losing his liberty, then knew he would never regret that. She gave a secret little smile of contentment, kissed him good night and went indoors.

It was still early. The clocks were chiming six and the church bells tolling the angelus.

The house seemed empty and strange with the rest of the family out. Only from the kitchen came sounds of supper in preparation. Fliss went to her room and slipped out of her cocktail dress. She unhooked the uplift and pulled her roll-on down over her hips, then flexed her body and stretched. Wrapping herself in her terry-towel robe she padded down to the kitchen. The silence in the house unnerved her, made her tense. It was so unusual.

Nora yelled when she suddenly and noiselessly appeared.

'God bless ye, Miss, ye startled me. Put the heart across me, so ye did.'

'Oh, Nora, could I have a coffee? Please? I'm that tired and I know Mother and Father will want me to chat and talk things over at dinner. A cup of coffee would do the trick – help me stay awake.'

'It'ud be my pleasure, lovie. You just go into the dining-room and I'll bring it to you.'

'Thank you, Nora. Where's Robbie?'

He exhausted himself earlier so he's in bed now.'

'Oh, I see. The house is so quiet . . .'

'Yes, Miss, I know. It always makes me nervous when ye're all out together. It echoes, like.' She bustled about, talking as she worked. 'I'm that pleased about you and Master Derry. I know you'll be very happy, so I do. Sure you're made for each other.'

Fliss gave her a hug and went to the dining-room.

The table was laid for supper. The room was dark, quiet. Only the ticking of the clock could be heard. Like a slow heart-beat. Tick, pause, tock.

Fliss sat at a vacant place and stared at her hands. Her ring gleamed in the dark. Glowing green fire. White fire. So pretty. She smiled again, tranquil. Content. The others would return soon filling the house with activity, displacing the silence with noise and bustle.

Nora brought her coffee on a small silver tray. 'I put it in a breakfast cup for you, Miss Phyllis. So you can have a good slug.'

Fliss sipped her coffee, felt the jolt it gave, replacing her lassitude with a nervous energy almost instantly. Nora made strong coffee. She finished it, swallowed the dregs, then rose and went to the French windows which stood open.

It was very still out there, the garden full of shadows. She was about to close the windows when she thought she saw some movement at the end of the lawn.

'Grizzle?' She stepped out. 'Grizzle, that you?'

The smell of the lilac at dusk was intoxicating. She breathed it in, then moved down to smell the alyssum and night-scented stock. All the perfumes of Arabia don't compare with an Irish garden, she thought, touching the petals of the roses, listening to the nightingale.

Nora glanced out of the kitchen window, saw her figure, ghost-like in her white robe, gliding down the path. She glanced down at her dough for tomorrow's bread, then looked up casually again but Fliss was not there any more. She had gone. Nora shrugged and continued with her pounding as day lengthened into night.

CHAPTER FOURTEEN

Lonny watched her, in the house. He saw the light come on in the upstairs room and he stared as she lifted her dress over her head. He saw her naked back as she unhooked her bra, he saw her stretch. It made him angry. Then he thought, yes, this is the one. It would be this one.

He had been to Capel Street, put in three hours' unexpected work for Mr O'Laughlin, then come here. It felt like coming home. The bushes welcoming him, his place here, the small clearing just big enough for his body, ready, waiting.

There was no one in; they were all out except the little boy. The little boy played in the garden. He had fat little legs and was stupid, Lonny thought. The plump cook stayed with him all the time, then set up a table and they sat at it together whilst he had a meal. There was a lot of laughter that irritated Lonny. He nearly went home. But he remembered his mother and knew he could not face that at the moment. So he made himself comfortable and settled down to speculate. Which one? The thin one? The plump one?

He fell asleep there, face near the soft, loamy soil. He had not slept properly for a long time and he was quickly dead to the world. The church bells awakened him. Then he heard the girl's voice. Light, cheerful. She was calling: 'Nora. Nora!' He was instantly alert. 'Nora!'

Then the figure at the window. Then she went away and he could just faintly make out her form at the table downstairs. Sitting. Patient as a leopard he crouched, waiting. Then she came to the window, half closed it and he thought he'd lost. But she changed her mind and came out into the garden.

Again she was calling. 'Grizzle. Grizzle!'

The suspense was unbearably pleasurable. Would she reach him? Wouldn't she? He knew the servants could see the garden in this light and he didn't dare take any chances.

But she pressed inexorably on, plucking a flower here, smelling one there, moving towards him slowly, slowly. She held a bunch of white lilac in her hands; bunches of sweet-smelling blossom that she brought to her face now and then as she idled along. Every so often she made a little clicking sound in her throat – 'Grizzle. Grizzle,' she called, bending down. Looking for the cat. He shuddered mirthlessly to himself in the undergrowth. The fucking cat was perched on the roof of the little outbuilding, probably the larder, next to the kitchen, watching her, just as he was. Cat didn't give a shit. Just sat there as she moved closer and closer all the time. 'Grizzle. Grizzle.' And the cat sat there silently on the roof, blinking.

Lonny's sharp expectant joy reached peaks higher than ever before as she came nearer and nearer. Close. He could almost smell her now, see her skin, the shadow of a smile on her face. Nearer. Nearer. He would pounce any minute now.

Now.

She did not scream. So deep-seated was her serenity that, even then, grabbed roughly like that she did not anticipate harm. Her nerves, her reflexes were not prepared for violence. She had not an apprehensive bone in her body, so when her alarm system went off it was too late. His hand was across her mouth.

'I have a gun. I'll shoot if you scream,' he whispered, but she barely heard and he hit her.

What happened next was beyond any nightmare, any traumatic imagining. Beyond experience and knowledge. Beyond any foul concept. A violation of her most spiritual centre, of her innocence, her modesty. She was lucky she lost consciousness quite soon after, her face bleeding, for he struck her repeatedly as he raped her, spitting, 'Bitch. Fucking bitch.' Spitting on her face, defiling her.

He took his time but she was unconscious. The red demons pounded in his head, reaching a crescendo, sulphur smell in his nostrils, her blood on him; stained in her blood.

And he would crush, maim, destroy. He was all-powerful. He could violate, desecrate and turn her into nothing. Nothing. An empty shell.

Then, at last, peace. Total peace. An emptying of all the horror into this receptacle. Then peace. Lassitude. Drugged forgetfulness.

At last to feel nothing at all. To move in a trance. To glide bodiless on his way, forgetting her, the thin one, lying smashed, desecrated, damaged beyond repair on the bare mud under the bushes.

He went to Synge Street baths. In the dark no one noticed him. There were lots of poor sods, God help them, reeling out of the pubs with bloody noses and mouths who had had a few too many, got in a fight and dared not face the missus, so he did not look out of place.

He didn't even have to act sloshed, he felt sloshed. He felt no pain, just numb. Full of love for the whole of mankind.

He would not go home that night. He felt so peaceful. He would wander over to Capel Street to O'Laughlin's. He had his own key. Mr O'Laughlin had gone home and in any event it had never occurred to him that anyone would want to spend the night with the dead on his premises.

Lonny would not mind the dead. He loved their company. They were so still, so peaceful, easy to sleep with. He would lie in Mr O'Laughlin's best satin-lined coffin and sleep there. He would not dream now. There would be no nightmares, no terrors in the dark. He might even close the lid on himself, then he would be alone in the soft satin night.

CHAPTER FIFTEEN

Meriel was thrilled with herself. Bobby Mitchell's mother was at the Devlins' for cocktails and she had been *so* sweet to her son's girlfriend.

'I'm so *glad* you like him, Merry dear. You will do him the world of good. He's such an awkward boy – needs a girlfriend.' Then she added hastily, 'But he's strong. A very strong character. So the Jesuits say. You'll be a great influence on him, dear.'

His father had said to her, 'The boy's got good taste,' and gave her a roguish grin. 'I suppose the pair of you will follow your sister and Derry's example.' And Mrs Mitchell wrinkled her nose and cried, 'Oh, honey, don't be daft! It's much too soon to get serious.' And Bobby whispered in her ear, '*I'm* serious, Meriel. I hope you know that.'

She had giggled. It was a stupid, childish thing to do and she despised herself for being awkward and gauche, but they didn't seem to notice.

He drove her home in the Riley. They left about half an hour after Fliss and Derry and they sat together in the car, lights off, engine cut, outside her front door.

'Mother and Father will be after us in a minute,' she said as he put his lips on hers, cutting off whatever else she might be going to say in a clumsy kiss that didn't quite hit its target.

He jumped back almost as soon as his lips touched hers as the import of what she had said dawned on him.

'Oh yes!' He glanced into the rearview mirror as if he expected to see Mr and Mrs Masters looming right behind them. 'That wouldn't do,' he said.

'Oh, don't be silly, Bobby. We're doing a line and they know that. It's okay for you to kiss me.'

'I don't want to do anything to spoil it,' he said 'Turn them, or you, against me.'

His voice was cautious but she could see in the glimmering evening that he was sensitive and worried about what she would think.

She took his face between her hands. 'We're going out together,' she whispered. 'You're my boyfriend,' she said and kissed him squarely, her lips soft and infinitely tender against his.

When she broke away he looked at her with clouded eyes. 'That was . . . nice,' she said.

'Nice!' he gulped. 'Nice. Oh gawney mac, *yes*. Do it again,' he asked but the headlights of the Masters Bentley swept a spotlight into the Riley and they quickly moved apart, the mood broken.

'Gotta go,' Meriel said and opened her door, not waiting for him to do it for her. She was not yet sophisticated enough to wait for the man to help her. ' 'Night.'

' 'Night, Merry. I'll ring you tomorrow. Maybe we could go to the flicks?' He had a broad grin on his face.

'Sure.' She laughed, waving at him as she slammed the door, and she was gone, running up the drive to catch her parents.

Rogan was closing and locking the garage gates. Tessa saw her daughter, stopped and turned to wait for her and, slipping her arm in Meriel's, they went inside the house together.

When they reached the hall Tessa called, 'Fliss? Fliss? Nora?'

That good woman, whose sharp ears had caught the sound of the car, was there as she spoke.

'Yes'm?'

'Supper ready?'

'On the table'm.'

'Oh good. We really haven't eaten properly today, have we, Merry? People kept interrupting us at lunch, Nora, and I didn't manage a mouthful. I'm starving.' Then she glanced upstairs. 'Fliss here?'

'I got her coffee'm. Saw her in the garden twenty minutes or so ago. Or mebbe half-an-hour. Time flies. I bin busy'm. Could be she's in bed by now. Said she was tired.' Nora hurried back towards the kitchen. 'You sit down'm and I'll bring the salad.'

Tessa and Meriel went into the dining-room. There was a bowl of lilac on the damask table-cloth. The cutlery and glass sparkled and a bottle of white wine lay in a cooler. A cut-glass decanter of whiskey sat beside Rogan's place. Everything was just as it should be, Tessa noted with satisfaction.

'Come on, let's simply sit and eat,' she urged her husband and Meriel. 'I don't know about you but I'm pooped.'

'Umm. It's been a long day. Terribly tiring,' Rogan agreed and seated himself at the head of the table, Tessa at his right. Meriel sat one down at his left leaving the empty chair between them for her sister. It was an automatic action; that was Fliss's place.

There was a moment's silence then Tessa asked, 'Where is Fliss? Merry, go see if she's fallen asleep. It's not like her to go off to bed like that, not saying good night.'

Nora had arrived with the salad and Rogan was carving some meat off the joint of cold roast beef when Meriel returned shaking her head, but unperturbed. 'She's not there. Bed's empty,' she said and reseated herself, taking the proffered salad-bowl from her mother.

'She must have stopped off somewhere with Derry. Maybe to break the news to one of their friends.' Rogan piled the cold meat on plates and passed them around.

Meriel put the servers down abruptly. 'But her dress is upstairs. On the bed,' she announced. 'And Nora said she saw her. Got her coffee, remember?'

Her parents looked at her.

'Her dress . . .? You say her dress . . .'

'Yes. And Nora said she made coffee.'

'Then where is she?' Tessa looked serious now.

Nora came into the room with jars of chutney and pickles on a tray. As she placed it on the table Tessa asked her about Fliss but Nora was looking out into the garden. Through the open French windows a figure appeared. It rose from the bushes, unsteady in the wavering light. Nora stopped and stared, perplexed. It was the figure of her employers' daughter and the girl seemed strange, like a spectre, swaying, hovering. Then as Nora watched she turned and vomited into the bushes. She looked, Nora thought fleetingly, like a mad child wandering alone and lost, and there was something alarming about her.

'Mum . . . Mum . . .' She pointed out of the window. The others followed her gesture and turned and stared out at Fliss who had been bending over, retching. As they looked she straightened, staggered forward a few steps, fell on to her knees. They could hear the thud in the room and they winced for it must have hurt. She slowly pitched forward on her face and lay there motionless, a white wraith in the dark garden.

Tessa rose, dropping her knife and fork, rattling the glasses. 'Fliss . . . what . . .?'

She ran out through the windows and down the garden path, followed by Rogan and Meriel.

'Oh my God . . .' Rogan lifted his daughter in his arms. 'Oh my God . . . Sweet Jesus. Oh my God . . .'

She was battered beyond belief, her lovely face pushed out of shape, as if it were made of putty; swollen and caked in blood and filth, but at least she was alive.

'Fliss, my baby, Fliss,' Tessa cried aghast.

At first the full extent of her injuries was not obvious.

'My darling, my baby,' Tessa moaned, holding the hand that fell limply, swinging in space as Rogan carried her to the house. Tessa turned to Meriel, white-faced, tight-lipped. 'Phone Doctor McCawley, Merry, quickly, quickly, run.'

Meriel had never been so frightened. Never in her life had she seen such a sight. She was terrified she'd fail her parents and faint clean away in shock. She was breathing as if she'd been in a race, but she pulled herself together and the wave of blackness that threatened to engulf her slowly diminished. Drawing in deep breaths that tore her chest she dialled the doctor's number which was on a card by the phone in the hall along with the Fire Brigade, the Gardai, and Mr Dent, Rogan's solicitor.

She replaced the receiver as her father, carrying Fliss, went up the stairs.

'Phone Derry. He should be told. She might need him,' her mother instructed as she passed Meriel, still holding her daughter's hand. Meriel told her Dr McCawley was on his way.

She noticed her hand was trembling as she dialled the Devlins' number. The party seemed to still be in full swing when Agnes Devlin answered the phone.

'I can't hear you properly, Meriel. Derry? Yes, he's here. He's staying in tonight, at least I thought that was the arrangement. What? You want to talk to him? Just a moment . . . hang on . . .'

There was a pause that seemed endless to Meriel. She could hear the distant thunder of voices all talking at the same time and the sound of laughter made her wince. At last she heard his familiar voice. 'Yes? Meriel, is that you? What's up?'

'It's me, Derry. Fliss's been hurt bad. Mother said to let you know. You better get over here . . .'

'What you say? What . . . the noise here is . . . hurt? You said hurt?'

At last she made him understand and he plonked the phone down with a crash that made her jump. He had shouted that he was on his way and she dialled Bobby's number, biting her lip and trying not to think of Fliss's mashed face. All she knew was that she wanted Bobby with her now.

Bobby answered the phone himself.

'Bobby, it's me. Something awful's happened to Fliss. I can't . . .' And suddenly it was all too much and she burst into floods of tears, sputtering and hiccupping. Sobs caught her chest and she could feel herself trembling uncontrollably. She picked up the phone to talk to Bobby, teeth chattering, but the line was dead and she let it fall again, too out of control to replace it on its cradle.

She stood in the hall shaking from head to foot, clasping her arms around her trembling body, unable to move. How long she stood there she never knew. Nora passed her several times with basins of hot water and towels, and at last the doorbell rang and Nora opened it. Dr McCawley hardly saw her as he hurried past clutching his black bag, following Nora up the stairs two at a time And still she stood, her arms tight around her body, trying to hold herself together, keep herself from falling apart.

Nora was praying audibly as she rushed to and fro. 'H'Mary, full of grace, Blessed art thou 'mong women, an' Blessed is the fruit of thy womb Jesus, Holy Mary, Mother of God . . .' On one of her trips downstairs she tried to steer Meriel into the living-room but gave up when Tessa called down to her in urgent tones, 'Hurry, Nora, hurry.'

When the doorbell pealed again Meriel remained rooted to the spot, trying to move to answer it, but she was paralyzed, her teeth rattling like castanets. Trixie, who had been running around the kitchen for Nora, came to her aid and let Bobby Mitchell in.

Bobby asked no questions. He held her tightly in his arms for a moment then guided her into the drawing-room, half carrying her, his arms firm as steel around her. He put her down on to the sofa and poured a large brandy, forced it through her chattering teeth. When she had finished it he cradled her until the shaking slowed down, became a small shuddering, then stopped.

'What is it, Merry? What happened, dear?' he asked her softly, still keeping a tight hold on her.

'There's the door again,' she told him as the bell rang, clutching his hand now in a fierce grip. 'I couldn't get there . . . I couldn't move . . .'

'I know, love. I know.'

'I couldn't move . . .'

'You rest there. I'll get it.'

He took over and she felt his strength, and the release from responsibility left her weak and relieved. In a moment he brought Derry into the drawing-room, saying, 'Merry is in here. I don't know yet what's happened.'

She told them what she had seen, all she knew. She tried to tone down, under-dramatize Fliss's state in order not to alarm Derry. She did not succeed and Bobby had to pull him away from the door several times.

'I think we should wait until Mr or Mrs Masters or the doctor comes down,' he told the agitated young man. 'You can't just go barging up there.'

'But Meriel says Mrs Masters told her to ring me.'

'Yes, well, letting you know doesn't mean that you should charge in before the doctor is finished.' Bobby was stubborn.

'But what happened? What on earth *could* have happened? She was fine when I left her home, just fine.' He turned to Meriel. 'You say she was sick?'

Meriel nodded. She felt light-headed, a little unreal, as if she was floating. It did not occur to her that she had consumed a large brandy and so was probably a little drunk, not being used to alcohol.

'Yes. She threw up,' she told them. 'In the bushes. At the bottom of the garden. But, her face . . . her face was . . .'

'What was the matter with her face?' Derry asked. He was bewildered and looked it.

'It was beaten . . . she looked as if she'd been beaten.'

'But that's impossible! Who could have done it? And I left her at the gate. I watched her go into the house . . .'

'We don't *know*, Derry. We'll have to wait and see.'

It was a long time before the trio in the drawing-room heard any news of Fliss. The clock ticked, its slow monotonous sound filling the vacuum left by unanswered questions. The silences grew longer and longer and the queries, what happened? why? how? quivered on the air.

Eventually the door handle turned and the three of them looked apprehensively towards it as if they expected some strange or shocking apparition to enter.

It was Dr McCawley. He looked old and tired and strangely vulnerable. Meriel knew him as a brisk, good-humoured, no-nonsense physician, but as he came through the door her heart sank. His normally jolly red face was pale and serious and he avoided their questioning eyes.

'How is she?' Meriel asked urgently as Derry cried, 'What happened?'

'She's . . . she's . . .' The doctor paused and swallowed. He seemed to have difficulty speaking. 'Get me a drink, Merry love, God's sake.' His voice held a mixture of dismay and exasperation.

'Doctor, please tell us what happened. Can I see her?' Derry pressed.

'I've given her a shot of morphine. She's sleeping now. At least I hope so. I profoundly hope so. I cannot bear to think what that child's nightmares would be like.'

Meriel went obediently to the cabinet. She was better now, having something to do, a chore to perform. She kept her mind firmly on the job in hand, glad that Bobby was here with her. She could leave her turmoil with him, do only what she was asked, not think too much. She poured a generous brandy and gave it to the doctor.

Derry was asking, 'What is wrong with her? I have a right to know. I'm her fiancé.' He sounded frightened.

The doctor wiped his brow with a large handkerchief he had pulled from his pocket. His face was creased and wrinkled with concern.

He shook his head again. 'You better speak to Mr Masters,' he said and Derry sighed impatiently. 'It's terrible,' he continued. 'Terrible. Poor girl. Poor girl.'

'For God's sake, Doctor, tell me what's wrong.' Derry was begging now.

'I brought her into the world, God help us,' the doctor went on as if he hadn't been interrupted. 'Delivered her. Saw her through mumps and measles, chicken-pox and influenza. For what? For this! Never thought I'd live to see the day.'

'What day? What are you talking about?' Derry was nearly in tears. He had picked up the doctor's despair. It echoed shrilly in his voice although he remained in total ignorance of what had happened to his beloved.

'We live in a wicked world when such things happen,' the doctor continued.

At that moment Rogan came into the room and the three young people fell silent. The doctor drank his brandy and continued to shake his head. They watched Rogan nervously, dreading what he might say. He crossed in silence to the drinks cabinet and poured himself a large whiskey. They saw his hand tremble as he lifted the glass to his lips. He took a gulp, then banged the heavy glass down on the cabinet.

'Meriel, go to the spare room,' he said. 'Your mother told me to tell you. Fliss must be by herself just now.' His voice, like the doctor's, was harsh and sad.

'Can't I see Fliss? I want to see her, Mr Masters,' Derry said.

Rogan shook his head. He looked distracted. 'No. No. She's in no condition. Your mother says go to bed now, Meriel. In the spare room.' It was an order. He was like a sergeant repeating a command given him by his commanding officer.

'But it's only about eight o'clock,' Meriel protested.

'It is eight-thirty,' Rogan said irritably, glancing at the clock.

'Well, eight-thirty then! You can't expect me to go to bed at this time. I'm not a child.' Meriel felt near to tears again and Bobby hurried to her side and put a protective arm over her shoulder.

'We want to know what happened to Fliss.' Derry spoke firmly now. 'I have a right to know. What is all this secrecy about? I don't understand. Why don't you just tell us what happened? I'm going to be her husband, for Christ's sake.'

'Yes, Father. I'm a big girl now . . .' Meriel turned to Bobby who nodded in agreement.

Rogan Masters looked at the doctor who said, 'All right. The truth is, poor Phyllis has been attacked and r—'

'Brutally attacked,' Rogan Masters voice cut the doctor's voice off. 'Brutally attacked,' he repeated loudly, shooting the doctor a warning glance. 'Brutally attacked,' he reiterated as if confirming what he had just said. 'Her face is horribly bruised. She has a broken rib . . .' He faltered and paused.

The doctor took up his cue. 'She is bruised and generally in a bad way. The man must have been a savage.'

Derry gasped and sat down abruptly. Meriel could see tears in his eyes. 'Poor Fliss,' he whispered. 'Poor Fliss.'

Rogan took a deep breath then continued, 'A bone in her wrist is broken. She is covered in . . .' He paused again, then, glancing at the doctor, '. . . all over and she is badly shaken. Very badly shaken. She's in shock. That's all.'

'That's enough,' Derry said coldly. 'Why didn't you just say that?' he asked incredulously. 'When you came in? Why didn't you just tell us that immediately?'

Rogan removed his fierce gaze from Dr McCawley and looked at the boy. 'We didn't know what happened, the extent of the damage. We still don't.' There was something shifty in his expression as he said this, but he hurried on. 'She has not regained consciousness, not real awareness. She is raving, in shock. Tessa—' he glanced at Meriel— 'your mother is with her. She mustn't be disturbed tonight.'

There was another lull, questions buzzing around their brains, an uneasy feeling that the information they had received was incomplete.

'Let's go for a drive to Dollymount Strand and get a breath of fresh air.' Bobby Mitchell's loud pronouncement startled them all.

'At a time like this?' Rogan demanded. 'I'm shocked, Bobby, I really am.'

Bobby's face flushed but he held his ground. 'Merry'll be alone in the er . . . guest room. Not her own. She'll be anxious.' He glanced at her. 'Won't sleep this early. She gets worked up,' he explained. 'Walk'll do her good.' Surprising everyone with his common sense. 'And the sea air,' he finished, then cleared his throat, raised his eyebrows and glanced around.

'That sounds like a very sensible idea, young man,' Dr McCawley remarked.

'Be careful,' Rogan said doubtfully. 'Although I don't suppose . . . be careful.'

'I'll not let her stray an inch from my side.' Bobby's voice was purposeful. 'I'll guard her with my life. I'm Senior Boxing Champion at UCD.'

Meriel was warmed and consoled by this display of protective concern and practical help. But she was confused and not a little perplexed. There were questions to ask and answers she needed. However, it seemed her mother was unavailable, Fliss's need being greater than hers, and her father, so tense and on edge, was either unwilling or unable to help her now. Meriel recognized what she called his Victorian father mood and when he was like that there was no communicating with him – he treated herself and Fliss as if they were two-year-olds. Explanations would have to wait and in the meantime a walk by the sea would help to calm her. Bobby had thought of just the right thing.

The strand at Dollymount was cold and grey under the clear light of the moon. They drove on to the sand then left the car, took off their shoes. Meriel pulled down her stockings and Bobby pulled off his socks and rolled up his trouser-legs. He took her arm through his and they walked along the shoreline.

Sometimes the chill black water edged in and foam broke over their bare feet in icy wavelets. The sand felt like wet fish beneath their toes. In some strange way Meriel found the discomfort therapeutic and the brisk salt breeze off the sea a consolation.

'Here, let me put my jacket . . .' Bobby took off his jacket and draped it over her shoulders.

'There's something they're not saying,' Meriel said, holding on to his waist, shivering, but not in shock now, glad to be here with him, near the sea.

'Yeah.' He drew her nearer him as they walked along. His body was warm, the heat of it lovely to her, reassuring.

'Why, Bobby? What would they lie about?'

He turned her to face him. 'Don't you know?' he asked. 'Can't you guess?'

It was so dark. She couldn't see his face. The moon was behind him, spotlighting her. He was in the dark. She was somehow aware that his eyes were full of gentle sympathy though she couldn't see the expression. She slipped both arms around his waist and rested her cheek on his chest. The heat came like energy through his shirt and made her draw even closer.

'No,' she mumbled against him. 'Tell me. Please.'

'I don't think you'll want to hear.'

'Why do you say that?' she asked, surprised.

'You *know*, Merry. Deep down you know. Just as I know and Derry knows. Only none of us can bear to face it.'

'What?'

He broke away from her, picked up a stone and flung it as far as he could. They didn't hear the plop. The sea shushed and murmured incessantly and he turned around and now his face was clear under the moon.

'Fliss was raped,' he said. 'It's what your father and the doctor couldn't say. Fliss was raped.'

She knew then that he was right. Deep in her mind she had suspected something dark and terrible, something unspeakable. Something no one wanted to say aloud. But rape?

She gulped at first, not taking it in. Rape. It was an alien word, a word that belonged in ancient literature: *The Rape of the Sabine Women. The Rape of Lucretia*, a word whose meaning had nothing to do with her or hers. A word that had no place in the lives of nice people. Rape was something hilarious the Danes did on their forages from the North Sea to large ladies, Angles, Saxons and Jutes. Rape was something Roman maidens resisted and so became saints.

She had never actually thought about rape, never examined it as a possibility. Now, for a fleeting second, her biology lessons, the awkward talk her mother had delivered about the 'facts of life', a seedy flasher she had once seen in a lane off the Rathmines Road, all these things, combined in an obscene image of male genitalia and brute force, made her cry out in horror.

'Bobby. Oh, Bobby.'

'Sorry,' he said. 'Sorry.' He hugged her and they stood awhile watching the endless sea and the cold, pale moon. Then he took her arm and they walked back to the car in silence.

There was an awkwardness suddenly where moments before they had been so close, an embarrassment where there had been none. Something they had both taken as lovely and sacred had been defiled and besmirched and had, for the moment, created a division between them.

CHAPTER SIXTEEN

It was to be like that afterwards: half-truths, evasions, secrecy. No one spoke openly of what had happened to Phyllis Masters. It was never discussed. Tessa listened to her daughter's ravings and ground her teeth in impotent rage. She too felt violated, her body too shrank from her husband in a sort of automatic revulsion against the whole male sex. Only men were capable of such bestiality. When he laid his hand on her shoulder or kissed her cheek she shuddered and moved quickly away, out of reach. They did not have sex any longer but even so his maleness repulsed her and he recognized this and felt sick.

Fliss couldn't bear to be conscious. Couldn't live in her head. She quickly became, if not addicted to morphine, certainly dependent on it. Every evening when he came to see her she begged Dr McCawley for something to make her sleep and she was in such a state of distress and hysteria that he reluctantly administered a dose. On opening her eyes she tore the air with piercing, unremitting, horror-filled shrieks, like a Banshee, Nora said, blessing herself. Every time she regained consciousness and remembered what had happened to her, some of the terror, the obscenity she had endured returned and she screamed and moaned and tried to get out of herself, flee from the prison of her defiled body.

'We're not going to tell the police,' Rogan Masters told Dr McCawley that first night and he remained adamant. 'I'll not have her subjected to any publicity.' Then he looked at his wife. 'Where did we go wrong, Tessa? Where?' She pressed her lips together and remained silent.

Dr McCawley would have liked Fliss to make up her own mind about going to the police but she refused to discuss it and Tessa went along with her husband.

'I couldn't bear it,' she told the doctor. 'Everyone knowing. Everyone looking at Fliss. Gawking. She'd become a freak. No, best not involve the police.'

'But he might harm someone else,' the doctor said.

Tessa turned to him, her face almost ugly with anger. 'I don't *care* about anyone else,' she hissed. 'I just don't care. There is enough to worry me here.' She pointed at her daughter's distraught face, pale on the pillows.

Rogan spoke as if it would all go away if they ignored what had happened altogether. 'It's over now!' he said firmly. 'Over and done with. She was attacked, most brutally. But it is over. She has to be cared for and nursed back to health. Naturally the poor child has had a terrible shock. But time cures all ills and she'll recover.'

'But don't you want that bastard caught and punished?' Dr McCawley asked him.

'Think of what that would mean,' Rogan said, appalled. 'Publicity! The papers. People scrabbling over the story. Fliss's name bandied about by every Tom, Dick or Harry. Oh no. It's over and done with and the sooner we can put it behind us and get on with our lives the better.'

'But it is *not* just an attack, Rogan,' McCawley insisted. 'It's rape and rape is a terrible thing. It has a terrible effect . . .'

'Don't use that word!' Rogan yelled at the doctor. 'I'll not have it uttered in my house, y'hear?' Then calming down, 'Enough said,' and he reiterated, 'It will pass. She'll recover and time is a great healer. We'll get back to normal and it will be as if it never happened.'

But things would never go back to normal and the only people to realize and accept that seemed to be Meriel and Bobby Mitchell. 'She'll never be the old Fliss again,' Meriel told him. 'She's, like, crazy half the time. She keeps washing her hands – like Lady Macbeth.'

'How could she be the old Fliss, Merry, that happen to her? It's stupid to expect it,' he told her matter-of-factly.

She wouldn't see Derry. He moped about the drawing-room evening after evening but the summons never came.

'She'll be back to normal soon, m'boy,' Rogan told him. 'Have patience.'

'But why won't she see me, Mr Masters? Why? I don't mind how bad her face is. She must know that.'

'He just can't face up to what he subconsciously knows,' Bobby told Meriel.

'Should *we* tell him?' she asked and he looked at her thoughtfully and frowned.

'I don't know,' he replied. 'I just don't know.'

After the hysteria and acute shock had lessened, Fliss began to eat a little. She relied heavily on the morphine the doctor prescribed for her. She still could not sleep unless she was helped artificially. In a month she ventured out of her room and downstairs for the first time. Derry was there to greet her.

In that month their relationship had changed drastically. He had been badly hurt that he was forbidden to share whatever she had been suffering with her. She was an invalid now; the dancing laughing girl had gone and in her place a tormented woman found it difficult to function. Derry unconsciously slipped into the role of minder, nurse, treating her as if she were old or fragile – certainly unhealthy.

She could not bear him to touch her. She shrank from even the most casual contact. He did not notice this at first, but little by little he became aware of it and was desperately upset and worried by her revulsion. He tried to make allowances for her, wanting to do the right thing, behave properly. Someone who had been so brutally beaten up must, of course, feel instinctive reluctance to be handled. But caresses? Soft loving gestures? Surely they should not be briskly rejected. She wounded him deeply and he could not rid himself of a profound unease about the whole affair. He despised himself for what he thought of as lack of sympathy and an idea that she had over-reacted to an attack. Not knowing the full story he could not understand the gravity of the damage that had been inflicted upon his fiancée. Whenever, through the fog of unease and pain, a glimmer of the truth tried to penetrate he hastily pushed it away, convinced that he had a foul mind and that such an idea was preposterous in connection with a girl of Fliss's upbringing and breeding.

Fliss vomited constantly. At first Dr McCawley thought it was a result of the disgust and loathing she felt for what had happened to her. As time passed another more terrible fear caused the doctor to do tests. He found to his horror that his guess was correct. Fliss was pregnant.

CHAPTER SEVENTEEN

Lonny Clebber did not return to the back garden. He had no desire to. For him, it was finished. The Masterses were a memory. In fact, a week after the violent release of all his frustration and anger, a week of tranquillity such as he had rarely known, he forgot all about that house. It eased itself from his memory, slid away. Like a hurricane destroying all beauty, leaving havoc behind, he was indifferent to the damage he had caused and went his way, cleansed. The inmates of that house, who had been an obsession for so long, vanished from his mind and their faces were forgotten. He felt wiped clean, new-born. All he could properly recall was that he had rid himself of his bad dreams, his demons. That he was not carrying the black dog on his shoulders any more. That the crawling shadows of his nether life were dormant for a while. Even his mother's night-time visits did not shake him as profoundly as usual. He was cut off, unavailable; his body there, inert, himself elsewhere.

Where? In another ether. Floating. At peace.

He stroked the corpses as they lay in the Chapel of Rest, then took them off to the mortuary with such tender care. He talked to them in whispers and smiled so much Mr O'Laughlin got worried. 'I hope yer not gettin' like Stephen – grin splittin' his face alla the time,' he muttered.

But Lonny was not getting like Stephen, whose sole desire was to charm a bird into the back of the hearse on a Saturday night and indulge in a marathon of heavy petting, getting as much relief as possible in holy Catholic Ireland whose female population was ruled by a terrible fear of pregnancy and fear of being blasted out of the Confessional.

Lonny spent those weeks at rest, in a state of peaceful mindlessness until May had passed into June and June drifted by. His nerves came slowly to life again, imperceptibly waking from their slumber, jingling to awareness. Snapping a little now and then, making him jump. Sharpening his senses, scraping his consciousness, becoming once more an obstruction in his life, demanding to be fed, attended to, shouting once more for peace.

And Lonny began to look around again.

She had to be the right one. She had to interest him. She had to possess a special light, a happiness about her that he could smash. Destroy. That was the only thing that would bring him surcease, set his soul quiet.

He did not fear being caught. It never entered his mind. Nothing had happened after the bitch called Fliss was smashed, and the court case was so long ago and far away he had forgotten it. Like it happened to someone else in another country. There was no apprehension in him, no fear of discovery. It was not wrong, after all. Someone had to be punished. It was only right, only fair. He was like Gabriel the Archangel with the flaming sword, or Moses before the Golden Ram, righteously angry. The Avenger. *They* had to suffer and only *he* could choose.

He chose Imelda Manning.

CHAPTER EIGHTEEN

He had always been patient before, took his time, did not rush. He had always followed the same scenario. First he got restless, nervous tension rising, then the search, the picking and choosing. Then the stalking for days, weeks, sometimes months. Enjoying it. Relishing the hunt. It had all been part of it.

But this time his nerves screamed urgently, louder and louder, demanding, NOW. NOW. He could not understand it. Then he worked out that the last bitch, the annihilation of her, had soothed him so, had been so beneficial, had brought such *real* peace, that his body felt the need more urgently than before and his mind ran round and round stuck in a groove, pleading for that peace again.

When he saw Imelda he knew at once she was the one. How come he knew that? Perhaps he was divinely guided. It could be. Perhaps the Avenging Angel had chosen that special one for him. Perhaps that was her fate, written in the stars. It had to be something like that, else how was he so sure *this* was the one?

She had a cute little ass that swivelled right then left when she walked. And she glowed. Like a dragonfly. Buzzing about, flitting here and there in Moore Street market, buying fish, Dublin Bay prawns, salmon steaks, vegetables, lettuce grown in the sand in Rush, tomatoes, carrots and beetroot, stuffing it all into a string-bag. She wore a cute little polka-dot summer dress, red on white, with a wide red patent belt cinching in her waist. She hummed as she flitted here and there and her breasts in her uplift jutted and bounced as she moved. He ground his teeth and thought he'd like to cut them off, put them for sale on one of the stalls there.

He shivered then, aghast. His thoughts had become more violent recently and that frightened him. His old mum had begun to bother him again, and the syrup of figs, the taste of it, the effect of it weakened him. Bit by bit his mother had begun to reassert her presence, overcome his mental absence, pull him back from wherever he was to the damp little bedroom so that he had to steel himself again against the reality of her.

The black dog was back and his presence heavy and dark on Lonny's shoulders.

He had wanted so badly to kill her. At first the thought alarmed him, then it became an idle idea that slithered in and out of his mind mainly in daydreams. Recently he had actually weighed it up, the pros and cons. But she never left the house and if he killed her there he was bound to be suspected. The odds would weigh heavily against him, then the police might take him away and put him in a cell. It left him sweaty all over to think of that.

And beneath that fear lay a powerful deterrent. He did not know what it was, but it was there, a command inside him that said no. You cannot kill your mother. Perhaps it was his father's voice. Perhaps it was the Angel.

Sometimes when he was with her he felt himself still a little boy. She was so huge, so strong, and when his hand closed over the green crystal his father had bought him in Howth, a big shining piece of rock green as a shamrock, and she lay like a beached walrus on top of him puffing and blowing, he longed to crush it into her skull, longed with all his might to pound her with it, to let loose all the violence within him. But he resisted, frightened of having to leave his home, having to get out from under her, quit his job, frightened of being on the run, of the demons taking over.

And something else. Losing her? No. Not that. Surely not that. And yet. . . and yet . . .

Imelda. Imelda would erase the fears, the terrors, the unnatural inclinations. Imelda.

He followed her down Moore Street. She twinkled, she glittered like a bright star. She pushed back her hair that seemed to have a life of its own, she laughed, greeting people as she passed. 'Bedad, Imelda, yer lookin' great today!' 'Aren't you the fine girl, Imelda Manning!' 'Yer a sight fer sore eyes, Imelda darlin'!' followed her as she passed, leaving a trail of broken-toothed smiles behind her. And he followed her.

He followed her down Henry Street, then when she turned right into O'Connell Street. He followed her over the bridge down Nassau Street to College Green, down Grafton Street, along St Stephen's Green and into Leeson Street.

He followed her and no one saw him. He felt less cat-like, more wolf-like now as he trailed behind her down the crowded Dublin streets until she got to a tall Georgian house and, keys in hand, let herself into it.

He stood beside a lamp-post opposite, watching until the door had closed behind her. It would be difficult here, he thought. Not like the Masterses' with its large garden, the yew hedges to hide behind, the dark shadows even on the brightest day, the space. The Leeson Street houses were flat on the street, no gardens, bushes or trees, no yards or gates or steps to the front door, no nothing. However, the house she entered had a mews beside it. An arch connected it to the next house and through the arch where there had once been stables were now garages used by the professional dwellers of the street. It was a cobbled courtyard surrounded by closed doors which had to be unlocked to park the cars that were left there. It would help.

He decided not to worry about it now, relying as he was used on opportunity and chance. But he noticed over the next few days that there never seemed to be anyone around the mews. No one hung around the cobblestoned courtyard.

The houses in Leeson Street were used by doctors, dentists and lawyers as surgeries and offices. So the street was only crowded during office hours and then mostly by strangers who would not notice anything amiss. It was mainly deserted at night. Once dusk came and the surgeries closed and the offices shut up business the street tended to be sparcely populated, the garages in the mews empty of cars. Who would notice through a window or a passing vehicle a boy and a girl tussling in the dark? Slip up on her, catch her and pull her into the mews.

It would be hard on the cobblestones but what did he care for that? It would be her back, not his, that hit the pavement.

He found out things about her. She must be an actress. People in the market were always asking about it.

'How's rehearsals, pet?' the fishwoman inquired, wiping her hands on her scaly apron.

'Lovely, Maisie,' Imelda sang out, happy. There was an edge to her voice like laughter all the time. Full of life. Joyously expectant.

She went to the Gaiety Theatre off Grafton Street, the stage-door entrance opposite the back door of Neary's pub, each morning. Lonny thought of doing it there. It was a dark lane but he quickly scotched that idea because it was constantly busy with actors and stage-hands, nipping across for a drink.

In the afternoon she sometimes took a dance class in a big room on the second floor of a building overlooking the Green. He could see the girls in black leotards criss-crossing back and forth. They would disappear and reappear, arms up over their heads or stretched out gracefully. Their faces looked hot, even from the street where he stood. Another afternoon she went through a small door squeezed between two shops in Georges Street. It had 'Fencing Academy' over the entrance. She always left these places with eyes sparkling, a bouncy spring to her step, her carry-all slung over her shoulder.

In the evening she went to the theatre, then came back to the apartment in Leeson Street.

He worked out that she lived on the top floor of the tall house. After she had gone out one morning he scrutinized the bell-board and saw that the ground floor was occupied by a dentist, a Mr Owens, the next floor by two gynaecologists, Dr Levy and Dr Mason. Then top bell: Miss Imelda Manning.

He saw her name, low on the cast list outside the front of the Gaiety Theatre. Opening next week. She was not one of the stars whose pictures were large, as were their names, but she was there, a small picture on the side: MISS IMELDA MANNING. And another one, in a group, smiling, showing her teeth, their names underneath, among them, hers.

There seemed to be a musical comedy on at the moment. *The Boyfriend*. But Imelda Manning, whose name was not in that cast list, went there each evening except Sunday. He decided she must be rehearsing the play she was going to be in, *The Seven Year Itch*.

On Sunday she stayed at home. An older man and a woman came to visit. They always carried a bunch of flowers and a shiny gift-wrapped present. When she answered the door she threw herself into their arms and for a moment on the front step, to his disgust, every-one would be hugging and kissing and laughing. He would leave hurriedly, not wanting to watch, but he was there again first thing Monday morning. He did this for two weeks.

He figured that the best time would be after the show on a weekday when she returned home. He figured there'd be fewer people around in Leeson Street, less risk. Yes, he decided at last, that would be the plan. He'd get her there. Stop her smiling forever.

CHAPTER NINETEEN

Dr McCawley told Rogan and Tessa that their daughter was pregnant.

At first Rogan laughed, saying it was impossible and that Derry was totally trustworthy and would never behave in an ungentlemanly fashion.

'No, no, you're wrong, Doctor. You've made a mistake.'

'But we've done tests. And double-checked to be sure,' Dr McCawley said, looking at him incredulously.

'Then the laboratory made a mistake,' Rogan Masters said firmly.

Tessa and the doctor looked at him open-mouthed, unable to think of anything to say. Tessa knew Rogan refused to discuss the rape but that he had decided it had not happened astounded and appalled her.

'I think, Rogan, you'll have to come to terms with the fact that your daughter was raped and is now, tragically, pregnant.' The doctor was as firm as Rogan had been.

Rogan leaped to his feet in the drawing-room, shaking with violent emotion. 'Don't *say* that,' he cried. 'Don't say that.'

'Shush, oh shush.' Tessa rose and took her husband's arm. 'For God's sake think of Fliss upstairs. The slightest thing upsets her. She'll be frightened to hear you shouting. Oh, Rogan, Rogan, surely her well-being is more important than your pride.'

Rogan's legs suddenly gave under him and he sat down abruptly and buried his face in his hands.

'It didn't happen. It didn't happen,' he moaned. 'It couldn't. Not to Fliss.'

'It wasn't your fault. It wasn't hers. She feels you are somehow blaming her. Oh, Rogan, face up to it.'

'Yes. You've got to face up to it, old boy,' Dr McCawley insisted. 'There are decisions to be made.'

He looked intently first at Rogan, then at Tessa. Tessa put her fingers to her breast, then bit her lip, unsure whether she was reading the good doctor correctly. She gave a gasp.

'You mean . . . but you can't . . . it's not . . .'

Dr McCawley shook his head. 'Not me personally, no. But there are doctors, em . . . not here, of course, it's against the law, but in England . . . oh, it is against the law there, but not in some cases . . .'

'Back-street butchers . . .' Tessa shuddered.

'No. Clinics. Private places. For the treatment of nervous breakdown. Or a curette. From what I've seen Fliss is well on the way to needing treatment for both. Put it that way.'

Rogan opened his mouth to speak but the doctor held up his hand. 'You must *not* think that I condone such, em, a method of solving such a problem, but in this case . . . rape, the girl's state of mind; she is distraught – we have to make an exception, think of the long-term consequences for Fliss, for Derry, for the families.'

'Get rid of it,' Rogan cried fiercely. 'I'll pay. Anything. Just get rid of it.'

Dr McCawley looked at Rogan's closed face, his lips a thin line, eyes cold, and he shook his head. 'No, no, Rogan. It can't be done like that. You cannot just rub something like this out. You must discuss it between yourselves. Fliss has to be consulted; her feelings are vitally important.'

'I *know* how she feels,' her father stated angrily. 'I think we should tell her nothing. I think she shouldn't know of the baby's existence. She doesn't know yet, does she?'

'No.' Dr McCawley looked at Rogan, a frown on his forehead. 'She may suspect, dread it. Subconsciously she may have some idea. But no. She does not know for a fact, not yet.'

'Then, God's sake, why should she be burdened with such knowledge? Why should she have to cope with such a decision?'

'What are you suggesting, Rogan? Surely you can't mean . . .?'

'I mean that she has had enough horror, enough misery, enough to contend with without ever having to find out that that . . . *loathsome* creature left her with . . .' He could not finish his sentence and shook his head slowly from side to side. Then he looked up, glancing from the doctor to Tessa and back. 'Don't you see? We can save her at least from that. Send her to England. Tell her it is for a thorough check-up and to help her get well. She need never know.'

'Dear one, we can't do that. We just can't. Fliss has to make up her own mind.' Tessa looked at him, her eyes wide with sympathy.

'What is there to think about?' Rogan looked at her as if she were insane. 'She hasn't anything to make up her mind about!'

'It's her body, Rogan. Her life!'

'Tessa's right,' Dr McCawley interpolated. 'You cannot take that kind of decision *for* her.'

'I can't see why not. She's my child. It will save her from so much pain, so much heartache. Don't you see, if I take the responsibility from her shoulders I'll save her at least some agony. It is not a decision someone so vulnerable, so young should have to make.'

'I was her age when I gave her birth,' Tessa said quietly.

'No, Rogan,' the doctor said. 'It is out of the question. There'll be papers she has to sign. The doctors there will talk to her. They will have to satisfy themselves that they have her full consent.'

Rogan looked at him narrowly. 'But it *could* be done? With documents to say her mind would be unbalanced . . . or that her mind was unhinged . . . by the shock . . .?'

Dr McCawley nodded. 'Yes, Rogan, it *could* be done. But I'm not your man. I don't believe in abortion. I'll only tolerate it under the most extreme circumstances. And I believe this is such a time. But not without Fliss's knowledge. I have come to the decision – not lightly mind – that Phyllis should have one if she so desires, and there are a hundred extenuating circumstances in her case. It is a mature decision: the fact that it was a most terrible rape, a brutal attack, that is my overriding reason. The situation here, Fliss's personality, her relationship with Derry. How impossible it would be if they had the child, her delicate disposition, all these things conspire to make me overcome my most deep reluctance. The climate in this backward country *vis-à-vis* illegitimate children makes me doubly convinced that in this case I am doing right. The struggle for Fliss would be long and hard if she was placed in such a position. And she is not strong. She has led a privileged and protected life and she has not the stomach for such a battle. And lastly, this:' he cleared his throat, 'I am sure that Derry will stand by her, but not if she has another's baby. Oh no, sir. That's asking too much altogether. So, Rogan, you'll have to tell her. *I'll* have to tell her. Fliss willy-nilly will have to make up her own mind.'

CHAPTER TWENTY

Imelda Manning was excited. All her life she wanted to be an actress and at last it was happening. She was careful to inform her parents, her friends, her tutors, her teachers at the Abbey School of Acting, especially Ria Mooney, the head, that she wanted to be a *serious* actress, *not* a film star, *not* a movie queen; no, a real, one hundred per cent, Leichner stick make-up 5 & 9, tread-the-boards, working actress.

Ria Mooney had recommended her for a tiny comedy role in *The Seven Year Itch*, an American play that was following *The Boyfriend* into the Gaiety Theatre that summer. Milo O'Shea was playing the lead. It was a comedy naturally for summer and a wonderful start to her career.

She got on well with the rest of the cast and the director liked her. Everyone liked Imelda and she felt sure that she was set fair for work.

She had little time for anything else. There were no boyfriends in her life – she had no room for them. All that would come later. She simply did not think about men, so busy was she with elocution lessons, fencing, ballet classes, voice production, singing and mime. Her whole mind, heart, soul, body was geared to work at anything that could help her gain her ambition.

She kept her little apartment at the top of the house in Leeson Street impeccably neat and tidy. Her shelves were laden with volumes of Shakespeare, Stanislavski, Michael Mac Liammoir, Joyce, Synge, Yeats (poems and plays), Ibsen, Chekhov, Strindberg (when can I play Miss Julie? Oh when?) and such books as might be helpful to her.

There were always flowers in the apartment, sometimes one carnation, or a rose Manny McMahon at the flower stall in the market had thrown away. She would pull off the outside leaves and put the bud in a jug, Japanese style. The sight of it satisfied her soul. Although she did not spend time sitting looking at it, it was nevertheless always in her consciousness, pleasing her. Sometimes she thought that Manny discarded the flowers just as she passed so she could pick them up. He would call after her, 'I'll send you a grand bunch on yer opening night, Imelda, see if I don't,' and she was sure he would.

They were due to open in two weeks' time, and she was filled with excited energy fit to bust. Sometimes she could barely keep her feet on the ground and sometimes she gave a little skip and a jump and smiled to the right and the left as she walked down the street. People smiled back at her. They couldn't help it, her smile was contagious.

She watched *The Boyfriend* from the wings each night. She knew it by heart now, every note of music, every word of the lyrics. 'It's Never too Late to Fall in Love', 'Nicer Much Nicer in Nice'. She loved it. When the orchestra struck up the overture she could feel the adrenalin start to pump and she had a hard time sitting still and small beside the ASM with the prompt copy in her hands.

On Sunday her parents came to see her. They were proud of her and she adored them. She knew they would back her no matter what. She was their only daughter and very precious to them. They lived in Bray, County Wicklow, just too far out for her to get home after the theatre without making it a worry for her in case she was delayed. So they had got her this tiny apartment so she could stay in town. They always brought her flowers and a box of candy or a scarf or shawl or a pot or pan or a cushion. Something that she instantly adored.

The first time they noticed Lonny was the weekend before the show opening. Mrs Manning, out of breath after the long climb up the stairs that Sunday night, said as she collapsed into the comfortable chintz-covered armchair, 'Jim and I noticed a funny-looking boy leaning on a lamp-post across the street from you.'

Her husband nodded. 'Yes, love. Funny geezer. In an outlandish suit. Terylene, I think.' Imelda's father was a draper, import and export – fine cloths and tweeds from Ireland, Scotland, Italy and Hong Kong. He knew about cloths. Always told her: 'You can tell a person's character by what he or she wears, by their taste. You can see at a glance, love, whether they are rich or poor, have good taste or are *nouveau riche*, whether they care what you think about them or are indifferent. Oh, you can sum up a person pretty well by how they dress. And it's not as obvious as you would suppose. If a fella is wealthy he may dress like a tramp, but you can bet the fabric will be quality. That's what you look for, the quality. Never forget Imelda, the dearest is the cheapest in the end. Good bit o' cloth will last a lifetime, guaranteed.'

'Maybe Imelda doesn't want her coats or suits to last a lifetime, Daddy,' Imelda's mother said.

'Maybe not, but she can pass it on, can't she?' Mr Manning snorted. 'To someone less fortunate. That way everyone benefits.' He smiled at his daughter. 'Always remember to help the next one down. That way you'll be helped. What goes around comes around. And remember, Imelda, what I said about clothes. When you act. Remember what the character wears is of paramount importance. It tells the audience so much. Saves you some effort.'

'Oh, Daddy, get away with you. Imelda knows what she is doing. What would you know about the stage?'

'No, Mama. He is right. I'm grateful, Daddy, for the hint.'

'Well that fella down below is, I can tell, a most unhappy fella. He has no taste but thinks he has. He wants to be a big shot but is a poor imitation of one. And there is something not quite right about his mind. I don't know, but it takes a huge ego, somewhat distorted and maybe . . . well, *odd* to wear such inappropriate colours and such a gaudy tie. Yet he lurks behind the lamp-post as if he was a nonentity. Be careful, Imelda.'

'What's he look like, Daddy?'

'Terylene, like I said, awful cheap texture, blue. A yellow shirt that would make a canary weep. And that tie. Hawaiian.'

They went to the window and looked out. The boy lurked there across the road, trying to seem as if he was part of the lamp-post.

'Yes. He seems to be watching your flat, Imelda. Standing there leaning on the lamp-post. Looking up here.'

'Must admit it's funny,' her father said softly. But he wasn't really worried. Imelda was a sensible girl, responsible, and knew how to look after herself.

'You phone the police if he goes on doing it.'

'Yes, Daddy.' She kissed his cheek then stared out of the window at the figure under the lamp-post. She opened the window, threw it up and leaned out, over the sill, looking down. Yes, she could see him there, his shadow on the ground, the white moon of his face looking up. She made a face, crossing her eyes, pulling her mouth down. It was a funny face and it made her parents laugh when she turned to them. She leaned out of the window again, and called out, her voice echoing in the deserted street, 'Oh, he's just a weedy little yobbo!' Then she turned back to them, closing the window. She moved her face about the way she did in mime and they laughed.

'But you must be careful,' her father told her.

'He couldn't see me, Daddy, not really. Or hear me.'

'Oh well, you be careful.'

But he had seen her. He had heard her. And her voice, what she said, the face she made sealed her fate. It had sent an arrow of pain through his heart and made him very, very angry. Bitch. Cow. He would punish her soon, very soon. He'd make her sorry.

CHAPTER TWENTY-ONE

Fliss said, 'Don't tell Derry.' Then she looked at her mother with large, haunted eyes. 'Why should I say that, Mummy? Why should I even *think* it? Derry's supposed to love me.' She turned her head away from Tessa, squeezing her eyes shut, trying to readjust thoughts, beliefs, and morals that had been handed down to her, resentful that she had to. All the promises had been broken – her parents' pledge that nothing would happen to a 'nice' girl, that if she did certain things, behaved in a certain way she was safe. It was difficult to understand. Nothing would ever be the same again. Ever. She would never be able to trust in the same way.

She sighed. What she had to do now, what she *must* do was adapt. To the circumstances, the change in her life. What had happened to her could not be undone. It was a fact of her life now. She thought wistfully of her engagement day; under the lilac trees, the smell of the blossom, Derry's face close to hers. The wonder of it. How peaceful she had felt, how joyful and content. How little she knew then, how innocent she had been, not realizing there was such evil in the world. She winced. The pain was now psychic. But she must not dwell on the past, must not dread the future. She must live in the present.

At first that had been impossible. She had been incapable of accepting what had happened to her. Even now her mind shrank away from even tiptoeing near the memory. Her flesh crawled and she would wring her hands and tear at her skin and moan. As for *down there*! No one would ever touch her down there again except maybe the doctor. Only dear old Dr McCawley. Dr McCawley was different. Like her priest. She did not think of either of them as men. No, she thought of them only as dedicated professionals, almost sacred and quite sexless. The one for the body, the other for the soul. No. No one except the doctor would *ever* touch her there. That she was sure of. The mere sliver of recollection about that part of the horror drove her out of her mind, made her whole being shrivel, made her vomit and shake, made her bowels turn to slush.

Now her mother had told her she was pregnant. In a way it did not surprise her. With the huge change in her body it seemed just one more thing. Out of chaos life is created. Out of evil cometh good.

'Your father and Dr McCawley feel you should, under the circumstances, and at this point in time, get rid of it.'

'Have an abortion, you mean?' Fliss looked at her mother squarely.

The room was full of cowslip-yellow light. A bowl of tea-roses on the vanity table scented the air and now and then a petal fell in slow motion. The windows were open to the balmy day in late June. White curtains billowed in a soft breeze. Fliss lay in her bed, propped up by pillows, surrounded by the paraphernalia of the childhood she and Meriel had shared. In this room they had grown, been loved, cosseted, taken care of. Priceless toys surrounded her – battered dolls wearing carefully mended clothes, bald heads hidden under bonnets, the odd glass eye missing. Old books, carefully preserved, of the fairy-tales their mother had read them at night in the lamp-lit room. Other books – Beatrix Potter, *Alice*, *Heidi*, *The Swiss Family*, all there, then Jane Eyre, Austen, C.S. Lewis. A snow-storm in a glass globe, a cuckoo clock, a music box with a ballerina on top that played 'Für Elise', a gondola with a bottle of Cologne; girlish objects all. And now, surrounded by the innocence of her past, she felt alien, ill-at-ease.

Their room, she had pondered, was quite different from her little brother's. Robbie had trains, guns, cowboy outfit, police uniform, rough, rough, rough. Teaching him to be violent? She could not imagine that; her sweet little brother a predator? But would he become one? Eventually? Learn to attack. Learn to fight. Learn that force solved things.

Tessa tenderly smoothed back her daughter's hair from her brows. 'It seems shocking,' she said. 'I know, but you've got to think about it.'

'It's against the laws of the State and the Church, Mummy.'

'But it seems the only way out,' Tessa sighed.

There was silence in the room. Fliss could hear people call to each other outside. She winced. She did that a lot now in the face of others' carefree unconcern, wincing as if they were pressing on a bruise. It was a new thing, Tessa thought, an expression suitable for someone far older, part of Fliss too soon.

'I want to have the baby, Mother.' Fliss spoke quietly, almost in a whisper.

'What?' Tessa thought she had mis-heard and stared at her daughter in astonishment. 'What did you say?'

'Something good *can* come out of this, Mother, if a baby is born.'

'I don't see that, Fliss. I don't see that at all. What about the father? That loathsome, vile . . .' She couldn't finish, the thought that came into her head was too unbearable to entertain. So she rose and walked to the window to still her agitation. She looked out on the lawn, the trembling leaves on the trees, the serenity of the scene. But it did not soothe her. She plucked the curtains. 'No, no, no. Best put it behind you. Best get rid of anything that will remind you . . .'

'But don't you see, Mother, I *can't ever* put it behind me. For the rest of my days I'll remember what happened. It will be a part of me and maybe, just maybe, having a baby will turn it from a terrible evil to a terrible good.'

Tessa turned and stood, back to the window, twisting her pale hands together. 'Suppose you hate the child? Suppose it takes after the father? Suppose . . .'

'Mother, suppose not? Think about me. Think about how *I* feel.'

'I *am* thinking about you, Fliss. You don't know what people are like. They'll despise you. They'll ostracize you. They'll be quick to blacken your character. Unmarried mother! they'll call you. Bastard! they'll call the child. Derry won't marry you if you have it, I hope you realize that. And I can't say I'd blame him. It's bad enough . . .'

'Me not being a virgin? Is that what you mean?' The anger in her daughter's voice forced Tessa to look at her.

'What happened to you was vile . . .'

'But I'm not a virgin any longer and Derry might, just might, big-heartedly forgive that,' she couldn't keep the sarcasm out of her voice. 'But he cannot forgive the fact I'm pregnant, even though it is none of my fault, Oh, it's a wonderful world, Mother, where men make all the rules.'

'But Fliss, my dear, we cannot change that. It's the way things *are*.' She drew a deep breath. 'What we've got to take into consideration is that the *child's* life will be horrible. Someone will tell him, perhaps even *you* will, in a moment of temper or frustration, that he is the result of a rape. Think what that will do to him. Think how that will effect him. It is a terrible thought, Fliss.'

'Nevertheless I want to have him – her. Maybe *because* of that. Maybe because it will be so difficult. It is a challenge. Something to devote my life to.' She pulled herself up on her elbows in the bed, interested for the first time, unconscious of herself for the first time since the rape. 'Don't you see, Mummy, I can't marry Derry now. There, I've said it!' She clasped her knees, both arms around them. 'We've all pretended it will go away, that things will go back to the way they were. Well they won't. They'll never be the same. Derry and I are over.'

Tessa gasped. 'But, Fliss, he loves you. And he'll get over this. So will you.'

'Yes, he'll get over it. Big of him. I've done nothing. I'll always resent that he has forgiven me for something that is none of my making. What has he got to get over, I'd like to know? Something terrible has happened to his fiancée and he has to recover. He feels I'm tainted, Mother. I've done nothing but he looks at me as if I was recovering from some horrible disease, something he might catch.' She shook her head. 'Oh, Mummy, Derry idealized me. I was his princess, his mediaeval maiden, and he was my knight in shining armour. He failed to protect me and he cannot forgive himself. That would always be there, between us. He didn't save me, Mummy. He'll never let on he knows, he'll pretend everything is fine and he'll quite happily live a lie if I get rid of the baby. We'll both live a lie. Pretence, dissimulation, deceit. A life built like that is an appalling prospect.'

Tessa thought of her life, of her dissembling, the lack of truth between herself and Rogan. Try as she would she could see nothing wrong with it and she simply didn't understand her daughter.

'Well I won't live like that, Mother. And I won't get rid of the baby. And I'm *not* against abortion . . . it is not a moral decision. In another situation I'd have one, no problem. But having this baby is my only chance of survival, the only thing that makes sense of what happened to me. Believe me, Mother, I know what I want and that's it.'

CHAPTER TWENTY-TWO

Imelda did not bother to look for Lonny next morning. She was too anxious to get to the theatre.

They had a line call that morning, then a make-up call, then tonight, dress rehearsal. Oh bliss! Oh joy! She was excited, but like a sensible girl she was not going to get panicked or frightened. Stage fright would have to go. She would channel her energy and simply do her best.

She would eat in Neary's. If she had time. If she could get a sandwich and a Gaelic coffee down.

When she got there they sat around in the Green Room throwing each other lines. Milo O'Shea carried the play, a marathon task, and they all supported him, a group mutually dependent on each other. If he was a success, they would be.

Now and then they heard the director's voice yelling instructions to a stage-hand or the set designer or the lighting director. There was an air of purpose, the sense of a deadline nearing, a frisson of intense excitement in the air.

The line call ran over but make-up and costume was fast. Imelda shivered in her swimsuit. It was tomb-cold backstage and hanging around had made her come out in goose-pimples. A walk-through was suggested and then suddenly it was time for the dress rehearsal.

The music, the lights. 'Am I all right?', 'You look fine', 'Good luck', 'Good luck', 'Good luck'.

It was better than she had dreamed and even more terrifying than she could have imagined. And then, abruptly, it was over. No audience to applaud. That would come tomorrow.

'I want everybody here tomorrow ten o'clock sharp for notes.' The director's voice from the stalls, disembodied.

Milo shaded his eyes against the lights,

'Was it okay?' he asked anxiously.

'Brilliant, Milo. You'll feel better when the house is in and the laughs come. All right, everybody, home to bed. Have a good night's rest. See you bright-eyed tomorrow. Jerry, that flat masks Imelda in the second scene. Get it fixed, the position. Exactly, y'hear?'

Imelda in the second act! Imelda in the second act! It was a reality. She was going to be on tomorrow night, the director was watching over her. She had arrived.

They went back to the dressing-rooms and took off make-up. They changed, chatting, asking about the performance, making minor suggestions, tired. They left, dawdling, going over bits, laughing about slips and mistakes. Reluctant to leave the theatre, yet dying to hit bed.

'I can give you a lift, Imelda, I'm going your way.' It was Denis Martin, one of the young actors whose first play it was too, catching her at the stage door. His father sometimes gave him the loan of his car. She shook her head. She was too excited to accept a car ride. She'd chat with him, then go into the house wound up tight as a drum. She'd never sleep unless she walked a bit. She wanted to clear her head, wind down.

'No thanks, Denis. I'll walk,' she told him, and sealed her fate.

CHAPTER TWENTY-THREE

He nearly gave up. She had broken the rhythm of her routine and it confused him. She had stayed at the theatre much later than he expected, not appearing at the usual time. But he had become dogged and persisted because she had irritated him the night before.

Mr O'Laughlin had given him the day off. No one had died in a week, things were slack and there were no corpses. Work always dropped off in the summer, picked up again in September.

He followed her to the theatre, then hung about. She didn't come out all day! He got bored waiting. One of the stage-hands said it was a dress rehearsal and they wouldn't be finished until late. Could be ten, eleven, twelve, or one or two or three. That's what the stage-hand told a man he called Mr Martin, a man who said oh, in that case he'd leave his car for his son Denis and would the stage-hand give him the keys? The stage-hand said he'd be glad to, pulling on a fag, his eyes squinted up against the smoke.

Lonny was going to slope off home, then he had a bet with himself. He'd go see a flick in the Green Cinema around the corner and then he'd return and if they'd gone home, then okay, he'd drop it, for that night, maybe altogether – this girl was dangerous, seeing him like that, out the window. He preferred the anonymity of a victim who was totally unconscious of his presence. He could always get another bitch. Find another quarry. But if, when he got back, she was there, well then, that'd be a sign. That'd be a signal. Like a message from the Avenger that it was the right thing to do.

He slipped into the cinema. It was showing John Garfield and Lana Turner in *The Postman Always Rings Twice*. He loathed Lana

Turner. She had no business behaving the way she did, like a bitch on heat, a slut. He squirmed in his seat, righteously angry. Incensed. Cecil Kellaway, her husband, was a nice old guy. Good to her. His smiling old face was all trust, but she sashayed around in those shorts and clickety-click high heels even on the sand! She wore a clinging sweater and had shiny lips and she and John Garfield killed the old guy who'd done nothing but be kind to them. Which was a lousy thing to do but typical of a woman. John Garfield wouldn't have done it on his own, no siree. He needed that blonde bitch to put it in his mind, and she coming on to him all provocation.

Lonny was still angry when he left the cinema, a little tight knot inside him for poor old Cecil Kellaway. That's what they're like, he murmured to himself out on the pavement, that's what the bitches are like. Deserve to be punished. Deserve it. People looked at him, muttering to himself.

He stood still, the cinema emptying, the crowd swirling around him, irritated by him blocking the flow. He hunched his shoulders and a long swatch of his greased hair fell over his forehead. He pushed it back, then walked to the end of King Street and stared down at the Gaiety. There were no lights; the theatre was dark and there seemed to be little activity. A couple of men stood on the corner of King Street and Grafton Street talking. One of them said: 'Make sure the table gets struck quickly in that scene, Sean, *before* Deirdre enters. It's a hold-up and Milo is left hanging, so I want it done quick as lightning. And tell Steve to get those goddamn notices up.'

'Okay, Squire. Will do.'

The men parted and Lonny sloped past to the corner of the alley where the stage door was. Almost at once he saw her coming. She walked briskly down the lane, and she was alone.

He jumped back into a doorway. Waited. It was all now in the hands of fate. He would not rush, he would take his time and what would be, would be. But he could feel himself trembling and he knew it was anger and excitement. Rage at Lana Turner in the film filled him with a righteous and blinding fury; and excitement at what might happen next: the expiation of that fury, the wonderful time of peace to come.

He watched her cross the road and head down the Green towards the Shelbourne Hotel. He tailed her. She didn't notice. She seemed absorbed in her own thoughts, but the plump little ass swivelled to the right and then the left. Giving people ideas.

The night was dark purple, not many pedestrians about. A couple in evening dress emerged from the Shelbourne, laughing and talking loudly. The man wore evening dress and the woman had a long pink taffeta frock, and around her neck and in her ears diamonds sparkled. The uniformed porter gave a piercing whistle and a taxi materialized and the couple got in, still laughing and talking, unaware that the girl and Lonny had both stepped back to allow them right of way.

Lonny merged into the shadows while Imelda glanced at the pair and she too smiled. Lonny didn't smile. Bloody rich! They whistled and got what they wanted, whilst the likes of him . . . He watched Imelda move away and he wondered, what did he want? Then in a moment he knew. He wanted his mother dead. Not by his hand, but like an accident. He wanted her removed. Erased. He wanted her to disappear from his life completely. Je-sus H. Christ!

He let Imelda get well ahead of him then thought he had lost her. Oh well, again the bet: if she got into her house then, okay, he'd give up. But if she didn't then he'd look on it as a sign that it was meant to happen. He was in a state of total acceptance. He was but an instrument of fate and events had been decided millennia before by the Winged Avenger, the Deity of Vengeance.

She didn't notice him at all and that was another sign. Even when she turned down Leeson Street and his heels echoed half a beat after hers, she seemed deaf to the sound. She seemed lost in a world of her own.

Then suddenly, for no apparent reason, she seemed to catch on, pause infinitesimally, then walk along with her head cocked, alert. She was aware of him, he could feel her awareness. She was getting nervous, hurrying. The beat of his excitement increased as she stopped in front of her door and got her keys out of her handbag, fumbling.

He had never been so exposed before, out in the street, in the lights, no cover. But he didn't care. He felt reckless and full of purpose. He quickly unbuttoned his flies, leaving only the top hooked – be ready. She glanced over her shoulder at him, real panic in her eyes as he came up on her and grabbed her, she like a wild animal, trying to get away. He was not adept at doing it this way and she easily slipped from him, falling up to the door, fumbling with the keys, making little whimpering noises as she tried to insert one into the lock.

His anger fuelled him. Bitch. Bitch. She could see him, clearly see him in the light of the street-lamp. It made him pause, and a fleeting memory of the court case flashed into his mind and his anger accelerated and he pounced again. She had her back to him, keys in the door now, and he grabbed her right arm with both his hands. She swung around at him, left shoulder bringing her to face him, fighting like a tiger, yelling, 'Leave me alone, you pervert. Get off! Get off!' Screaming it so loud it terrified him so that he pulled and twisted viciously, ripping her arm from its socket, holding on like a vice. With all his furious strength he dragged her around the corner to the mews. She dug in her heels, like a child pulled by an angry parent, but he had her now, overpowering her, his rage exploding in him. He threw her brutally down, crashed on top of her on the cobblestones.

She screamed on and on – where did she get the breath? – shrieking like a mad woman, a Banshee, struggling wildly, but he straddled her, pinning her left arm behind her for her right one hung useless, seriously damaged. There would be no opening night tomorrow for Imelda Manning.

Lonny was now in charge. He was proficient at the next phase of his operation. He twisted her wrist and that meant the left arm was out of action and he went to work, flipping open the top clasp of his Terylene trousers.

He pushed into her. Her whole system resisted. This one fought madly, and he hated that. But overpowering her, he found to his satisfaction that the obstacle was there, this bitch also was a virgin. He breached the obstacle, smashed into her dry, unwelcoming vagina. The shriek she let out was like something from a Peter Lorre film, some movie about witchcraft or voodoo. 'Shut-up!' he hissed but she didn't and he grabbed a bunch of her hair and, holding it in his fist, lifted her head by it and smashed it on the cobblestones. He did this a couple of times more as he belted into her, then he got his release, grunting, falling over on her. He lay there a minute, panting, feeling the peace steal over him, feeling all the agitation go, the anger subside, the hate diminish.

Over. It was over. Nothing. He was empty.

He lay on her a moment, worn out, the darkness whispering around him, and he became aware of his hand on the cobblestones. His hand was wet and there was a lot of hair between his fingers. He didn't know what it was. He did not seem to be able to assemble his thoughts.

All he knew was that he was grateful to her now. Very grateful. He raised himself to say thank you, thank you, ma'am. He'd tell her she could take herself off, go home, go and sleep, but her head lay in a pool of blood and she was dead.

CHAPTER TWENTY-FOUR

Rogan was totally unnerved by his daughter's refusal to have an abortion, or, as he put it, to 'wipe the whole affair out of their minds and put it behind them'. He had had a vision of her being taken, first-class naturally, to London, checked into this fashionable clinic, her condition rectified, by professionals of course, and thus dealt with she would return home, his old Fliss, happy once more, quite cured.

But she remained obstinate, refusing to listen to him or her mother, repeatedly talking twaddle about it being her body, and now the whole sordid mess would become common knowledge.

Everyone knew that she had been attacked. That was all he wanted anyone *to* know. He had hoped that that was all they would find out, but pregnancy and babies were not things you could hide and people would put two and two together and come up with the only answer available to them. Then the gossip would begin, the side-taking, the condemnation, the pity.

'I have money, my dear,' he told her. 'You'd have no worries, the best attention. You'd be comfortable. It would be safe. And soon you'd be home, like your old self again, and you could have the wedding in September.'

'Oh, Father, if it was only that simple. I have to live with myself, Father. What about me? What about Derry? What about truth?'

Rogan hung his head. At one point he had toyed with the idea of putting about the rumour that it was Derry's doing, but he realized it just wouldn't wash. Derry's character was above reproach, they were due to marry anyway and the timing was too convenient. People were not idiots. Fliss gets attacked, gets pregnant – there was only one conclusion to come to.

Fliss had broken the engagement. She told her mother she wanted to let Derry off the hook.

'He'll stand by me and die,' she said. 'He will not let anyone think he'd desert me. So he'll kill our love slowly. I want to sever it now. If he really loves me he'll stick around. He won't accept my rejection. We'll see.'

Derry didn't stick around. In her heart Fliss did not blame him. A romantic young man, in love, faced with a pregnant girlfriend who had been brutally raped, was naturally aghast and unable to cope. It would have been nice, though, if he could have been man enough to deal with it. However, she knew that it would be a rare young man indeed who could survive such circumstances.

Dr McCawley reported a great improvement in Fliss's condition, and indeed her life appeared to have a purpose once more. Unfortunately for Rogan and Tessa that purpose seemed to be dependent on her having the baby. She was still given to fits of depression and fell occasionally into nervous bouts of panic, but she was at least fighting it off.

Then one morning the papers arrived with the news splashed across the front page that a beautiful young actress, one Imelda Manning, had been brutally raped and beaten to death. Rogan tried to hide the paper but Nora mentioned it as she served the hot toast and jam at the breakfast table. 'No one's safe these days, Miss. But at least you are alive.'

She dropped the bombshell and left the room, her innocent remark having caused havoc.

'My God, do you suppose it was the same man?' Meriel breathed. 'How *dare* he! How *dare* he! How dare that bastard get away with this! How dare he!'

Fliss was totally unprepared for her sister's reaction. She grabbed the paper and read it. 'Look what it says, Mother.' Fliss pointed to the page. 'It is the same man! Loud suit. Slicked-back hair. See? Her parents describe him. They saw him out of the window of their daughter's house the night before she died. See that description? It matches.'

Rogan grabbed the paper. 'Leave it *be*, Fliss. It's no use getting worked up about it . . .'

'"No use getting worked up"?' Meriel cried aghast. 'Father . . . a girl's been beaten to death! Suppose Fliss had . . .' She gulped and put her arm around her sister. 'Oh God, Fliss, I can't bear the thought.'

'I've got to go to the police,' Fliss said calmly.

'You'll do no such thing,' Rogan commanded. 'No such thing, my girl. No member of my family is going to make our affairs public.'

'Father, the police won't do that, I'm sure,' Meriel ventured. 'I'm sure they'll keep it quiet if asked. Fliss could help them find this man. We might help find him before he hurts someone else.'

'I don't *care* about anyone else, I only care about us,' Rogan told them calmly now. 'If I could, Phyllis, I'd *force* you to go to London and have that operation. You have no idea what you are letting us all in for. You have no conception of how this is going to affect the rest of your life. You'll live to regret your decision, my girl, you mark my words. I think you are being selfish and inconsiderate, placing your whole family in jeopardy. Meriel and your mother will have to bear a lot of unpleasantness on your behalf.'

Tears spilled down Fliss's cheeks as she sat there listening to her father berate her for a decision she had found intolerably difficult to make.

'For it is not just you but the whole family that suffers. Scandal always sticks. For ever more people will talk of you as the rape victim, or the girl who got raped, and they'll talk of Meriel as the sister of the girl who got raped, and your mother as the—'

'Oh, don't go *on*, Rogan,' Tessa pleaded. 'Please don't go on.'

'But what have I done, Daddy? What?' Fliss begged.

'You refused to take my advice, refused to do as I asked and now you expect to go to the police and air your dirty linen in public. And you ask me what you have done.'

'What dirty linen, Father? What has anyone in this house done that's dirty?' Meriel's face was hot and flushed with righteous indignation.

'He blames me for this – this atrocity that happened to me. He blames *me*.' Fliss clasped both hands, wringing them in a gesture that had become familiar to them all since the rape. It heralded depression or the hysterical weeping they were now used to.

'People will behave like Derry and run from us. And he was one of our dearest friends and your fiancé.'

Tessa shot a warning glance at her husband.

'You agree with him, Mother, I know you do,' Fliss sobbed.

'Fliss, calm down, dear,' her mother said. 'But as you ask, I think your father is right about the, er, operation. I think he knows best. It can help no one to have a weird little baby in the house, constantly reminding us about your terrible misfortune . . .'

'Oh, Mother!' Meriel cried reproachfully.

'Well, that's what I think, Merry, and it's no use my lying. I can't help myself, and I'll not apologise for my feelings. It's not nice.'

'What happened to Fliss wasn't nice,' Meriel said.

'Don't be facetious, Merry. Have you thought how your father and I would feel about having a baby in this house? Have you? The upheaval in our lives?'

'There'll be no baby here. I will not have it in this house and that is final.' Rogan rose. 'If you have this baby, Phyllis, you'll have to move out. Hear me? You have ruined my breakfast, ruined my digestion, I hope you are satisfied.'

CHAPTER TWENTY-FIVE

'If it was you, Merry, and I was Derry, I'd never leave you. No matter what!'

Bobby's voice was firm, unhesitating. He meant it, Meriel knew, meant every word. She glanced across at his pale face by the driving wheel. In the dim interior of the Riley, speeding along the Howth Road to Sutton, the line of his jaw was set firm and Meriel thrilled to his reaction at the news of the broken engagement.

'It's such a feeble thing,' he muttered.

'What, Bobby?'

'Loving someone when everything is sweetness and light. That's not what love is, Merry.'

'No. I know.'

'It's about being there, like it says, sickness and health. It's people sticking together fair weather or foul. It's knowing that there is someone on your side no matter what.' He hit the wheel with his fist every now and then. 'God, he's not worth much, Derry Devlin, running off like that at the first trouble. Not a man to have with you when you need a friend.'

'But you can understand it, Bobby, can't you? Fliss says it's too much to expect . . .'

'*Nothing's* too much to expect!' He banged the wheel again.

'Even betrayal?' she asked.

'Even betrayal. But Fliss didn't betray him. Caring about the other's feelings. That's what marriage is about. That's what it's all about.'

'But the baby? That's a bit much to expect a man to put up with.'

'A baby is a tiny creature, Merry, no harm to anyone. Can't do any damage unless you let it. No, in my book Derry Devlin is a lemon!'

She felt very honoured by his devotion, his support of Fliss, his love. Sometimes she lay awake in the guest room and tears would fill her eyes at the thought of his passionate partisanship. He had pledged himself to her and hers and only death or she herself could change that. It was awesome and it thrilled her.

Sometimes in the night she was awakened by her sister's sobbing next door, muffled crying into the pillow, and Meriel would get out of bed and draw back the curtains and look at the stars. How remote and tranquil they were, indifferent to the creatures on this little planet so far away. Up there in the purple sky, cold as ice, they cast their serene gaze upon the world and Meriel thought of all the others crying into their pillows about some lover, a desertion, an act of violence, a death.

Rogan wept too, in his room, alone since the birth of Robbie. Arm flung over his eyes, the tears saturated the hair at his temples and the pillow he lay on. He wondered what exactly he had done to cause this banishment from his beloved wife's bed, her room. He had always been so careful not to offend, to treat her gently. He remembered her as a bride, her fear, like Fliss in the face of man's brutality, her innocence. Surely it was different? But he didn't know what women felt about all that sort of thing. All he knew was that she had never liked it and he was asked not to come back to that warm sweet nest after the birth of their son and that he was lost and lonely now.

His mistress couldn't make up for that. She satisfied his appetites, appetites that he was now ashamed of and considered foul and sinful. She could never console and comfort and he felt ostracized and anchorless, desperate for understanding, isolated in his pain.

He thought of Fliss, his first melting sight of her at her mother's breast, the mystery of it. Often he had wanted to hold her, play with her, but it was not done and he was barely tolerated in the nursery. However, he had carved out a comfortable and happy way of life for them all, doing his job in the creation of family life, making an affluent setting for them to be cosy in. He had done that and now that was destroyed. How he had loved his daughters, both of them, cherished them, and now this terrible outrage within him, festering like a huge boil, made him hate them, separated them and alienated him from them, his dearly beloved family. Because of what happened to Fliss. It had happened to all of them. He saw his family split, angry with each other. Distressed and lacking in understanding. It was a terrible time, and he was very afraid that, like Humpty Dumpty, they would never be whole again.

And so in the night he wept, silently. He wept for his daughter, he wept for the tranquil past, he wept for himself.

Tessa in her room next door tossed and turned, restless. She did not cry; she was lonely and puzzled and vaguely aware that there was something hugely important here that she had missed. There was an ache in her heart for love lost, betrayed, never experienced, and a bewildered feeling of incomprehension. What was it that she did not understand? She did not know. Each day that passed made her more and more aware of how little she knew of the ways of the human heart. She thought this had something to do perhaps with her limited understanding of passion; she had, after all, decided to stick to the safety of friendship and not risk the danger of romance, of love. Had she missed so much then? Was she less wise because she did not understand? She was hot and bothered, unable to find peace or rest, yet it never entered her head that all she sought might be only a room away.

And Lonny slept. Slept like a log, dead to the world. When his mother had come to him he told her, 'Get offa me!' When she came into his room that night after Imelda Manning: 'Get offa me,' he said fiercely, coldly.

And she did. There was something new about him, some authority he had not possessed before.

'Get offa me,' he spat at her and she obeyed. He did not beg her, he *told* her. He commanded her and his tone brooked no refusal. 'Get offa me,' and she slunk away like a shadow into the filth of the back of the house and he slept. Alone. Quiet. So quiet, such peace.

The Gardai were putting things together, but he did not know that. So he slept.

CHAPTER TWENTY-SIX

The Gardai were putting things together. Slowly. Imelda's distraught mother and father gave them the description of the youth they had seen. The police were patient, waiting, allowing them to take their time.

'She was such a dear, lovely little girl. Such a joy. She never gave us any trouble. None at all. We never lost a wink of sleep over anything she'd done, did we, Daddy?'

Mr Manning shook his head, unable to speak, his Adam's apple riding up and down, up and down.

'But the man?' the detective prompted her softly.

Mrs Manning nodded. 'Oh yes. That man.' Wrinkling her forehead, eyes destroyed with weeping, face contorted with grief. The light had gone out for them, never to be rekindled.

'Yes. She was to open Tuesday in *The Seven Year Itch* . . . all she ever wanted to do . . . be an actress . . .' The mother gulped, unable to continue.

'She was very careful to explain,' Mr Manning said huskily, 'the difference between a stage actress and a star. Very careful to tell the difference. She wanted to be a hard-working actress . . .' His voice cracked and Detective O'Malley looked back at Mrs Manning. 'The man?' he said softly again, patiently.

'We had supper with her. Mother brought her two lovely Waterford cut-glass tumblers. For when she had visitors. I brought her the flowers . . . Daisies. Big white ones with a yellow centre . . . her favourite . . .'

'Margueritas,' his wife supplied. 'Those flowers are called

margueritas. She fed us, lovely it was – salad, steak and "tossed" salad, she said it was called, lifting and shifting it in the salad bowl, telling us how excited she was about the play . . .' Again the faltering, the pain shooting almost visibly through their eyes.

'And we looked through the window . . .'

'We saw this fellow beside the lamp-post opposite the house—'

'He'd been there when we arrived at eight—'

'Looking up at the house—'

'Looking up at the flat—' Faster and faster now, their words tumbling over each other. 'Lurking . . . only we thought nothing of it—'

'Some lounger—'

'But when we saw him again we told Imelda he was watching her flat and that she was to tell you – the police, if he was still there—'

'Looking up—'

'You *told* her?' the detective asked, jotting down notes, unobtrusively so that they wouldn't feel self-conscious.

'I think so.' Mrs Manning looked at her husband for confirmation, worried, trying to get it right.

'What then?' The detective had a nice homely face, a face that elicited confidences. They knew he was on their side, they felt he would help them. He knew that and he knew he couldn't. She was gone. Their beloved little girl was lost forever. Even if he caught the shit, that wouldn't bring Imelda back. Detective O'Malley knew that no one could heal the limitless loss ahead of them. Nothing, no one could do that. Still, he'd like to get his hands on the little pervert. Like to . . .

'His appearance? What'd he look like?'

'In this suit. Blue . . . Awful modern fibre . . .'

'Yes. American-like. Hair greased down. Slicked back with hair-oil. You'll find him?' This, the mother. As if that would mend things. As if that would bring them more than a moment's brief satisfaction, these gentle loving people whose lives had been blasted forever.

'We'll find him,' Detective O'Malley assured them calmly and unemotionally.

They had leads. People had seen him. He had been around the Gaiety all day. A stage-hand spoke to him. Said he asked a lot of questions. An usher saw him in the Green Cinema.

Detective O'Malley decided nothing would be lost by publishing an artist's impression of the man. *Have you seen this man*? Put that in the papers and though it always brought out the loonies, still they could shift through all the oddballs and creeps and maybe, just maybe, there might be one or two genuine replies. Where did they all come from, Detective O'Malley pondered, those weirdos who came out of their holes when the police advertised? What dark corners did they dwell in?

Well, it was worth it if it threw up a genuine witness. Or even someone who knew this perv. You never knew. But one thing he did know. He was going to get this bastard, come what may. He had seen the girl, the mask of horror on a face that must have been lovely. Her actor friends said she had been 'full of hope'. They used words about her like 'enthusiastic', 'vital', and she lay there on the cobblestones, her skirt over her waist, her arm broken and her skull smashed in, brown blood dried into the glorious masses of hair that framed her face.

Poor Imelda.

Yes, he'd bust a gut to get that fucker, that was a promise.

PART TWO

CHAPTER TWENTY-SEVEN

Breeda Deegan pushed the pram down Gardiner Street and yelled at Minny to hold on. She was the eldest of the Deegan clan and as usual in charge of the tribe. She had Deesy, Lizzy and Mackey on one side, Fosey, Minny and Charlie on the other and Babs, the babby, in the pram. The bunch comprised of her half-brothers and sisters, her job to look after them. Minny kept slipping away, running out into the street. She'd duck under Fosey, the nervous one, and skitter on to the road and into the traffic, putting the heart across Breeda.

'Why de ye do it, Min?' Breeda asked her, but Minny did not reply. She just yelled in frustration. She had somewhere in the back of her head the idea that as Breeda was so firmly opposed to her escape there must be some wonderful discovery to be made in the midst of the hurly-burly of the Dublin slum street.

Breeda admonished them energetically. She was in a state of constant irritation with the six of them: Minny, Fosey (Frank), Charlie, Deesy (Delia), Lizzy (Elizabeth) and Mackey (Mark). Little Babs in the pram was too young yet to tax her anxiety. She was a messy little creature of just under a year who leaked copiously from both ends.

And her mam was pregnant again.

Because Breeda was the eldest it fell to her to look after them. Breeda's da had died when she was seven. Toppled from the roof of a building. Wouldn't wear a safety belt, refused utterly, and doing the roofs in Cabra, on the housing estate, he fell after lunch and several pints and broke his neck. Snapped like a twig, one of his mates said. Died instantly.

Breeda had been busy idealizing him ever since. Her mam had married his brother Sean soon after and you'd never know the difference except that Sean, learning from his brother's tragic mistake, made sure he wore a safety harness.

Breeda didn't like men. She resented Sean, all beer-gut and hanging around the house watching them work. 'He doesn't even know where to find the tay or the sugar,' her mam said with withering scorn. 'Couldn't look after himself if he tried.'

Big lazy lout. Got all the pleasure in life, avoided the grief. No one could tell her that a day on the building site with the lads wasn't better than being cooped up in two rooms with seven childer. Sean went out of a morning, when he was working, and slapped on the cement and mulched the bricks down into it, then leveled off the excess cement, like the girl in Moriarity's levelled the ice-cream. Then he put it on top of the brick, ready for the next one. Like making double-decker sandwiches, only easier. Then he went for a beer with the boyos. 'Deserve that one, fellas. Down the hatch. *Slainte*.' All of them gulping, wiping the foam off their mouths with the backs of their hands. 'Ah-h-h-h! That was good. Set 'em up, Sean (or Bill or Gerry). Same again, fellas.' Then back to the building site, not so energetic by this time, not so much back into it, the bricks sometimes slightly askew. Then the pub again, lunch there; a plate of beans and a sausage and another pint, then back on the job, then back to the pub after work, another libation slipping smoothly down the gullet and then home to Mam. 'Where's my tay, woman?' Then bed and humping so Breeda and the kids could hear through the wall, then grunting, satisfied, and roll over asleep. Some hard life! Breeda snorted to herself when she thought about it and when her stepfather complained about how none of them understood about work, them being at home all day.

Breeda thought about her mother. There were no breaks for beer during her day, no let-up from work for a little rest, let alone a pint and pay. She was lucky if she got a pair of shoes for one of the children in a year. And Breeda would listen in disgust as she told her husband, 'Ah no, Sean, *you* need a pair mor'n us. Sure I hardly ever go out an' the childer is young an' aren't you the workin' man.' As if she lounged around all day twiddling her thumbs! No, there was no letting up at all for Nuala Deegan. None. She washed, cooked, cleaned, scrubbed, nursed, a babby always at her breast, a child one on each side, a great tiredness in her eyes, an air of total defeat in every line of her body. She was a no-hoper. There was no way out for her, no chance of fortune turning. Breeda often wondered what her mother dreamed of or if she ever dreamed. The very, very best that could happen to her was if one of her children made a fortune, took her out of it. But by then it would be too late. She was already physically beyond redemption – the toll of seven children and grinding poverty had left her, at thirty-five years of age, prematurely old, exhausted and, worst of all, in Breeda's opinion, without hope.

Breeda knew that although there was no escape for her mother there was for her. She had no intention of frittering her life away, wasting it on some swillin' smirkin' fella from the slums who fancied his chances and who'd do to her what Sean had done to her mother.

She wanted a proper job in a store, a big store like Deary's, with a pension at the end of it. She'd get one too. Eventually. It was just that she hadn't passed her Inter and she needed that certificate to get any work worth having. These days you needn't bother to ask if you didn't have *some* qualifications and she had nothing. She'd missed too many days at school helping her mam with the kids. One of them was always sick. It was inevitable with a diet that lacked the vitamins and protein they needed to keep them healthy. They never saw fruit or fresh vegetables and an egg or cheese was luxury. Homework was out of the question in two rooms, with their cold water basin, shared bath and lavatory that stank like the black hole of Calcutta on a hot day and not much better on a cold one, and seven brothers and sisters always around. No, homework was impossible.

Breeda didn't know what her mam would do without her and she had to steel herself to face the fact that she would have to desert her mother if she did not want to end up exactly like her.

She was reluctant to leave Nuala in the lurch, even though her mother urged her to go, get a job and find a way out of the trap she was in. Her stomach churned when she thought about it: leaving her mother without her help would remove the only life-line Nuala Deegan had. Breeda loved her mother in an overwhelmingly protective way. Her mother was, in her eyes, braver than any decorated soldier, more virtuous than a saint, more patient even than Job.

But Breeda didn't want to be like her. She had no aspirations to virtue or sainthood. She wanted to own a long dance frock and high-heeled shoes and wear those little white gloves. She wanted to giggle with other girls and talk about boys and flirt. She wanted to look pretty and have a full bath once in a while, all of her immersed in water – hot! And maybe to top it all, scented soap – Gawney! She dreamed of handsome faces, like the men in films, Gregory Peck and James Stewart, and them dancing with her, holding her in their arms, looking at her with admiration in their eyes. She wanted to be wearing skirts and petticoats that flew out when they twirled her in their arms, and she wanted to be taken to the soda fountain in O'Connell Street and sit on a high stool and suck sweet drinks through a straw. She wanted to rock 'n' roll, and to have more than one pair of shoes. She wanted to be able to go into the chemist and buy Purple Passion lipstick and Dorothy Grey powder, get Max Factor Panstick and Midnight in Paris perfume.

But the dilemma loomed, the awful choice: if she wanted freedom – any kind of life of her own – she would have to leave her mother and do it soon.

She was pretty, she knew, eliciting whistles from the boys on bikes down the back streets and the men who loitered outside the pubs of a Saturday, with nothing to do but yell and whoop at passing talent. Gurriers called out compliments as she passed and the toffs eyed her as she crossed O'Connell Bridge. Even the University students reacted to her and called out the latest American come-on learned from the movies.

'Hey ya, doll-face, whatcha doin' later?'

'Jeepers, you can shine anytime in my eyes, baby!'

'Hey, baby, whatcha doin' tonight?'

Sometimes a car drew up and a guy inside offered her money. She told them to piss off, but played with the idea. She would go on trying to get her store job, go for interviews, interviews she always failed, and if her luck continued bad then she'd think about it.

She was tempted. It was a card up her sleeve, if the worst came to the worst. Not in a car though. She knew she was worth more than that. But a nice room in a hotel, money up front and she got to pick the guy. It might not be too bad. But whenever she began to visualize it she flinched and told herself, on the other hand . . . on the other hand . . .

She liked her body, wanted to have enough money to groom it. Decent shampoos, Schaperelli Shocking Perfume, depilatory cream, Elizabeth Arden red nail varnish on her toe-nails. Stuff like that. She knew her bust didn't need an uplift and her legs looked as good as Betty Grable's any day. Her hair was thick and red, a bright copper colour and it curled and men loved it.

Yeah – she had the equipment all right, only opportunity was missing. And the gift-wrapping without which she couldn't expect to raise herself from her slum origins. Oh, if a guy looked close he could see her potential, but if she wanted to get anywhere worthwhile she needed money for packaging. So, she had to get a job.

She had another interview tomorrow, but she did not expect it to be any more successful than the others. 'What qualifications do you have?' 'None, Miss.' 'Sorry. Good day.' And out.

Tomorrow she was going to Deary's. One of the biggest stores in town. The idea excited her as she crossed the street, pushing the wheezing pram, trying to keep the kids together. She'd leave it to fate. If she got a job then it meant that she was *supposed* to leave her mother to cope on her own. If she failed, then she was *meant* to stay home.

Mackey and Lizzy were racing ahead, barefoot, little patched smock on Lizzy, little patched cut-down pants on Mackey.

There was a square of grass, or what was supposed to be grass, across the road, and there were two benches riveted to the balding earth. Some of the locals called it a park but nothing grew there, there were no flowers or trees and the odd patch of grass that survived was a curious lead colour, not green at all.

Breeda sank gratefully on to one of the benches and took six different coloured lollies from the sagging pocket in her pinafore. They were small discs of pure sugar, violently coloured: red, purple, yellow, green, on sticks and sold at a farthing for the six. They were all the Deegans could afford in the way of a treat and the children clambered around Breeda now, making the serious decision which colour they should choose

'Ui wan' yaller,' Deesy screamed.

'No, me. Yaller me,' Fosey echoed. He always wanted what someone else had chosen.

Charlie grabbed it and fled chortling, 'I gorrit, I gorrit, I gorrit!'

'Okay, the red.' Lizzy settled for the brightest colour. Like a magpie she was attracted to brilliant things and often purloined what was not hers. Whoever got red could play jokes about bleeding.

'Here, dear, you have another yellow, you bin so good.' Breeda took another lolly the shopkeeper had given her. She popped it into Minny's mouth, which she always held open, expectantly. Fosey tried to grab it from her but Breeda took his hand away and shook her finger at him, 'Now be good boy, Fosey, or you won't get one at all.' Fosey started to wail like a banshee so she hastily put a green one in his mouth, and the sweet taste stopped him in full cry.

Breeda groped in the pocket of her printed cotton dress under her pinafore, her fingers feeling for a small packet of Woodbines and a box of Swan matches. She lit a cigarette by igniting a match with her thumbnail, and sat puffing and dreaming on the bench.

The sun did not reach this street ever and there was a chill in the air even in midsummer. But she was impervious to the weather. She knew the children wouldn't stray now. So she dreamed, leaning her elbows on her knees, cupping her chin in her hands, thinking about pretty clothes, bopping, boys, freedom.

Across the dirty square on the only other bench Lonny watched her, wondering. He had never been here before but Mr O'Laughlin had pushed him out of the room where a mouldering corpse had been found by a neighbour. They had been sent for by the police.

What had happened was that a Mrs Clancy who lived above the Deegans had not seen Mr Brophy who lived one floor up from her for a couple of days. So she had gone up to check. She was not too worried as he was reclusive and bad-tempered most of the time anyway. She had banged at the door and when she could get no reply she had sent for the police who found poor Mr Brophy dead in his bed. He had been there for some time.

'You wait outside, son,' the undertaker told Lonny in Gardiner Street. 'This is not something you should see. Mouldy body is a shockin' sight an' I'm a man considerate of the sensibilities of others.'

So Lonny's sensibilities were protected and he waited outside the tenement building while his boss went upstairs and dealt with the corpse.

Lonny saw Breeda come out with the kids around her, like a

school. He was standing on the pavement outside the house when she emerged. He paid little attention, noting only that her flowered cotton dress was too short and skimpy, terribly old-fashioned. Then he noticed that her legs were long, shapely and smooth-skinned, but she wore darned socks and her sandals were the cheapest and in a fierce awful state, straps tied together with string.

When he looked again she was sitting on a bench across the street and he was struck by the purity of the profile turned away from him and the aureole of glorious copper hair that fanned out around her head.

He crossed the street, dodging a dray piled with beer barrels, and mooched around the edge of the square, eventually sitting on the bench opposite hers. He stared at her. There was something about her – an insolence, an undefeated defiance in the face of hopelessness that fascinated him. She had a devil-may-care attitude about her that caused him to shudder and aroused his intense interest.

She looked, he thought, like a left-over from the last decade, like someone in a Greer Garson film. Her dress had puff-sleeves. And it was so short. No one wore skirts that short any more. She looked as if she was one of those heroines who defied the Germans and didn't give way under torture.

The children screamed and yelled and quarrelled and pushed each other and she rebuked and admonished them firmly and with authority, yet she seemed to be elsewhere, dreaming. There was nothing cowed about her in her tatty dress and darned socks sitting beside that pile of rusty parts that passed for a pram and surrounded by squalling kids. No, she was sassy as hell and to judge by her remarks to the children her humour was sharp. She tossed her spectacular hair and pouted and crossed her long legs, the socks pushed down under her ankles, and stared into space, winding a curl around and around her fingers. He was definitely interested.

It would be difficult, he thought, very difficult. This was a dangerous neighbourhood, moreover a neighbourhood whose inhabitants were famous for sticking together and meting out their own rough justice when necessary. There were stories in these parts about fingers amputated, castrations and executions, and everyone knew that though the people here never cooperated with the police crime against one of their number was *always* punished.

Lonny shivered again. He was not worried about that aspect too much – it added spice to the endeavour – but was filled, since the episode with Imelda Manning, with a vague free-floating dread. He found himself constantly anxious and he was not sure why.

Yet things had improved so much for Lonny. His mother left him alone now. Since that night – 'Get offa me, Mother' – she had stayed away and things between them were easier. She was jollier and she didn't dose him with the syrup of figs any more either. He didn't have to sit on the bog emptying his bowels in agonizing pain and discomfort. Punishment. Punishment.

Mr O'Laughlin had given him a half-crown a week increase. He said Lonny deserved it. He told his son Stephen that Lonny never had to be begged to do overtime.

'I don't have te bow the knee and *plead* wi' Lonny Clebber now, do I? Oh no! But wi' my own son, my own flesh an' blood I have te *beg* te get him te do *anythin'* at all! Stephen O'Laughlin, ye have not worked one full day this summer, galavantin' around, an' it's pushin' autumn now, near winter, so that's why I've decided to award Lonny Clebber wi' an increase and ye wi' none!'

Stephen had winked slyly at Lonny and grinned. His mother gave her son as much money as he wanted and Stephen cared little about Lonny's half-a-crown extra. Lonny had wished, for a moment, that he could be like Stephen – so carefree and good-humoured. But he could not. Despite his mother leaving him alone and the rise Mr O'Laughlin gave him he more and more felt this terrible worry within him. Worry, worry – little spasms of terror clutching at his innards, thrilling over his skin and giving him a headache.

He had been very upset at what Imelda Manning had done – dying like that. It was mean of her and very unfair. He had not intended that to happen at all and blamed her and the cobblestones. It would not have happened in the Masters garden. She shouldn't have put up such a fight. What did she *expect*? No, he did not blame himself for her demise and in any event he did not feel that death was a bad thing. Not at all. All the dead he had seen had seemed so peaceful. He envied their peace – their freedom from the complications of this world.

But he had decided not to 'do it' to anyone else. The chances of him being caught and sent to prison were increased ninety per cent by that death. No one minded rape. Even the police didn't mind rape. But they minded death. (He refused to call it murder, that was the word the press used and they were lying.) So he decided he would give up now, now that his mother left him alone. He would stop. Finish.

But, looking at Breeda across the square of bald earth, he thought: one more. Just one more. Perhaps he could get rid of this anxious feeling. Perhaps it would exorcise the terror not just for a while but for ever. Perhaps he would be released from the gnawing worry in his guts and the throbbing in his head. Perhaps.

CHAPTER TWENTY-EIGHT

The street was long. It contained two blocks of the worst slum dwellings in the city. Beautiful Georgian mansions once owned by the English overlords, deserted by them when Dublin ceased to be fashionable, and fallen since into disrepute and decay. The buildings were owned by absentee landlords and as the state of them worsened the tenants who were prepared to put up with such conditions became the poorest of the poor. They were all crammed together so that the landlords could make a few bob out of them while the buildings crumbled around them.

Breeda shoved the pram up the rickety stairs. Once fashionable ladies had floated down in evening dress to greet their guests. Now the wood had been used for firewood and replaced by boards of doubtful safety, rat-infested and cockroach-ridden.

She had to bring the pram up to their rooms because if she left it outside it would be stolen in a matter of seconds. Nobody left anything in the hall. They may have been fiercely partisan when threatened by outsiders, but within the community it was every man for himself and trust elicited a sarcastic 'more fool you' and no sympathy at all.

The children milled around their mother, who shoved her damp hair from her forehead and sighed. If it was chilly across the sunless street it was boiling in the room. Condensation ran down the walls and on the range a pan full of water with a bone in it bubbled incessantly, sending up clouds of steam. There was a line of wet clothes drying, this being Monday, stretched across their heads, and on the far side of the table, which took up most of the space, the mattress Mrs

Deegan shared with Sean was rolled up, its insides sticking out, an irresistible target for little prying fingers. Folded carefully and balanced on top of the rolled mattress were a much-patched sheet and a greying Army blanket.

If she lacked Breeda's notion of herself, Breeda's mother had nevertheless once been lovely. Time and the life she led had rectified that.

'I don't care what Father Deesey says, Breeda. Life's not meant to be like this,' she cried as she bustled about putting a damp rag quickly over the children's faces, ignoring their shrieks and grimaces. 'This is no way to live. There's been a foul-up in the scheme of things, you ask me, 'as landed us an' the kids in this.' Breeda noticed she never included her husband in their plight. 'In the great tapestry of life, Breeda, you 'n' me have been unravelled. That's for sure.'

Nuala Deegan knew what happiness was, that state so often depicted in the cinema and in magazines. She had known it once in another dimension. She remembered what it tasted like.

Charlie Deegan had been her darling. Love had come down the mean paths she lived on and made her heart soar for precious moments, fly like a swallow, beat hotly in her breast and compelled her eyes to fill with tears. It caused her to marry him and gladly embrace a life of struggle in a hostile world.

It had not lasted long, the euphoria. It had died quickly, been brutally murdered actually, when Breeda was born. Charlie had been otherwise engaged when her body had been ripped open in agony and the fruit of that happiness was born. He had not surfaced for a week. He had left her in the public ward of the National Hospital, unvisited, alone with her new-born babe.

She had been bewildered, feeling unloved and afraid as she stared at the strange mite in her arms in puzzlement. Charlie had not surfaced from his particular womb – the snug in his local and the company of his beery buddies – until she had got herself home from the hospital on public transport, Breeda wrapped in a hospital blanket in her arms.

She had returned to the two small rooms they occupied since he brought her there as a bride. Oh yes, her happiness had been short-lived, but she *had* felt it and she had not forgotten what it was like.

She was well aware of Breeda's dilemma but they were not an eloquent family – had neither the time nor the energy to sit around exchanging conversation, and Breeda did not realize her mother too had once had dreams.

'Set. Set at the table, alla ye, an' quiet,' Mrs Deegan ordered and they obeyed. They were not quiet exactly but they sat, hair tangled, thin arms and elbows busy poking each other, desperately hungry, and greedy in the knowledge that there would not be enough food to fill their empty bellies.

'Mam, I'm goin' to Deary's tomorrow after a job.'

She expected to be discouraged. She expected her mam to complain. But Nuala Deegan did not react as expected.

'Good on yerself!' her mother cried. 'Go for it, girl.' She smiled tiredly at Breeda. 'An' I'm that sorry ye didn't get the others ye tried for.'

Breeda gulped. 'I . . . I . . . I didn't know ye knew, Mam . . . I didn't tell ye because . . .'

'I know, dear, I know. Yer a nice girl, so ye are.'

She was serving the liquid from the pot with the boiled hambone and the children were sopping it up with white doorsteps moistened with dripping.

'Mam, Mackey's after eatin' all the bread!' Deesy wailed.

'I dinnot, I dinnot! Anyhow I'm bigger'n you an' I . . .'

'Shut up the lot of yiz! Shut yer gobs. I'm talkin',' Mrs Deegan chanted without much feeling or much hope that her children were really listening. She turned to Breeda.

'You deserve some luck, darlin',' she said. 'Ye can't stay here the rest of yer life. Ye'd rot!'

'But, Mam, I hate te leave ye with the kids. Ye've enough to do . . .'

'Nonsense, girl. Lizzy's near big enough to take over from ye. An' she's bossy enough! No, Breeda, only thing I'd mind – ye stayin' in this dump gettin' old afore yer time lookin' after *my* kids.'

She wiped her face with her apron. 'Only how'd ye get an interview in Deary's an' you havin' no Inter?'

'I lied, Mam. Said I'd Inter. Figured they'd not look too close an' I said Inter. Who's goin' to lie about Inter? Only Leaving they'd think it worth to lie about an' so have to check.'

'Well, I hope ye get it, so I do.'

Nuala Deegan looked across to the mantelpiece over the range where, next to a picture of the Sacred Heart, there was an old faded photograph of her grandmother and grandfather outside their cottage in Ballylickey, Bantry, County Cork. Neither of them had teeth, their faces were lined as a crocodile's, their knuckles swollen and they must have been in pain with arthritis yet they looked impish in their happiness. Mrs Deegan often thought that her daughter Breeda showed that same gleeful zest for life and she did not want that stamped out of her.

'I'll steam out the dress,' she said now to Breeda. 'Though 'twon't be difficult in here. Sure it's like a Turkish bath. I'll rinse out the collar and cuffs. Thanks be to Jasus it's the warm weather and ye'll not need a coat. Fancy if it was December!'

'Thanks, Mam.'

The dress was navy-blue georgette. It had big box pleats from the yoke and a wide white belt at the waist. It had a neat white piqué collar and cuffs and Mrs Deegan had worn it at both her weddings and now she lent it happily to Breeda. Her daughter had worn it at her Confirmation and when she had to go to the doctor when her chest was bad. Though it was not the kind of dress Breeda ached for she was nevertheless very grateful to her mother for giving it to her, otherwise she would be wearing the ancient print dress she had on now, a dress her mother had got at a St Vincent de Paul jumble sale ten years ago.

'How'd ye feel, Mam?' Breeda asked her.

Mrs Deegan sighed. 'I'm okay, considerin'.'

'Don't ye mind, Mam? Ye have so many childer. Another'll wear ye out.'

'Ah sure, if it's the Lord's will, who am I to dispute it,' her mother said with resignation.

'It's *not* God's will, Mam, It's Sean's. If my father'd lived ye'd not have so many babbies hangin' outa you, exhaustin' you.'

'Ah now, don't talk like that, Breeda love. Sure I wouldn't part wi' one of ye. Not one. I love every hair on yer heads, so I do. An' yer father was the same as his brother, God rest him – two peas in a pod.'

'I don't believe ye, Mam. You'da seen! He'da treated ye like a princess.'

Nuala Deegan thought of that first birth and the memory scalded. But she said nothing. Let Breeda dream her dreams. They were such reasonable dreams yet they would soon be dead, Deary's or no Deary's.

They were all in bed when Sean Deegan came home that night roarin' drunk. Breeda was in the other room with the children. They lay two by two on mattresses on the floor. Breeda's dress – pressed, steamed, white collar and cuffs laundered – hung by the window and Breeda lay, eyes open, staring at it, dreaming her modest dreams. She heard her stepfather's feet on the stairs, his cheery slurred greeting to her mam who lay on the double mattress on the kitchen floor. Her feeling was one of relief. He was in a good mood. He would not beat his wife. She heard him shout, 'Oh, Nuala, me darlin'. I'm a man in need,' and then the inevitable followed. Her stepfather made a lot of noise when he claimed his conjugal rights, as he called this act of self-gratification. He puffed and huffed and grunted like a pig, Breeda thought, knowing she would not have to listen long, and very quickly his grunting turned to a banshee moan, then with three or four cowboy whoops he was finished. It was over and she and her mam could sleep.

CHAPTER TWENTY-NINE

The next morning Breeda was up at the crack and washed every inch of her body in cold water at the tap over the sink in the kitchen. The shared bath was hopeless. Mrs Clancy, never one to miss a trick, had purloined the plug and unless you paid her two pence halfpenny you couldn't get it and the bath was rendered useless. Someone else had broken the lock, so anyone desperate enough for a bath and who had paid for the plug and was prepared to manage on an inch or two of water in a dirty tub risked having the local gurriers, hooligans and degenerates (of whom there were legions) burst into the bathroom and you starkers. No, thank you! Breeda would not risk that. The mere thought of it and she broke out in a cold sweat. No, a cold, segmented wash at the kitchen basin was infinitely preferable.

So she washed in the sink at six o'clock in the morning, listening to her mam groan as she returned to awareness. God, her mam's soul must shudder and shrink when she came to life of a morning at the prospect that confronted her, the unremitting toil. Dragging herself out of bed, Babs yelling and mizzling for food, she'd draw her black skirt on over the petticoat she slept in and, pulling her matted and darned jumper over one shoulder and arm, she left the other free and with it placed the babby at her breast. There was a little silence then as she bustled about preparing breakfast. Then at six thirty Sean Deegan, master of the house, would rise up off the mattress, and, without even rolling it (he left that for his wife to do), shave in the basin, pull on his dudes, and sit down to the breakfast Nuala had prepared for him – doorsteps liberally spread with bacon dripping, a rasher if he was lucky, and a large mug of tay. Then he'd leave –

seven, seven-thirty – and with him the tension left the two small rooms and the family relaxed. It was as if he was a stranger who blundered into their midst late each night and while he was there they were nervous, constrained and uncomfortable and when he left next morning they could return to normal.

'Ye look as if ye've stepped outa a bandbox,' Mrs Deegan told Breeda, looking at her daughter, eyes full of admiration. 'Oh, Breeda, ye look a treat.'

Breeda did indeed look good in the navy georgette with the white belt, collar and cuffs; neat and pretty, her marvellous hair framing her face like a sunburst. 'Oh, darlin', they'll take ye, never fear. They'd be mad not to.'

'Oh, Mam, I hope yer right. Say a prayer, will ye?'

'Sure o' course I will, child. What time are ye goin'?'

'They said eleven-thirty.'

'God'n' yer early.'

'Well I wouldn't a' got the basin to wash otherwise. Isn't it full of nappies now and won't you be needin' it for the rest of the day?'

The sink was indeed full; Breeda was right. Mrs Deegan sighed. She spent a lot of time at the sink: washing nappies – or the strips of rags that did for nappies. Washing Sean's work clothes. Washing the kids' stuff. Washing, washing, washing. And all in cold water, or tepid if she could get the water to boil and not have to take the stock they lived on off the range for half an hour.

Nuala Deegan was only grateful that for some reason the sink had been placed under the front window. This was, she often told Breeda, a real miracle. 'I can look out while I work, see the world pass by. None of the other rooms has a view. Mrs Clancy above and Mr Brophy above her and the Cahills below all have sinks against the back wall an' they starin' at it all day! The bloody wall! Can you imagine? Gawney Mac, I'da gone mad by now. Isn't it great now an' I can look outa the window an' see all the comins and goins.'

Breeda sat bolt upright on her chair at the table, careful of her dress. When the little ones got up, pulling darned cardigans on over the clothes they had worn when they fell into bed last night she fixed them with a hypnotic glare. 'If one of yiz comes *near* me in me best dress I'll *murder* ye, y'hear?'

They nodded, round-eyed, too awestruck by her smart appearance to disobey.

'God'n' ye look gorgeous,' Lizzy sighed enviously. 'Pure gorgeous, Breeda.'

'Ye look like Maureen O'Hara,' Charlie breathed in awe. He had seen Maureen O'Hara in a pirate film he'd got into for a jam jar at the local flea-pit and she'd reminded him heavily of Breeda. He was very proud of his sister and many was the fisticuff he had engaged in behind the pub in defence of her virtue.

'She looks like a fillum-star. She looks like a fillum-star, she looks like a fillum-star . . .' Deesy chanted and was soon joined by the smaller members of the family. But Breeda remained aloof, thinking her own thoughts, the taunts bypassing her completely.

'The undertaker is back,' Nuala Deegan remarked without expression. She often described what she saw in the street, making pertinent comments about the goings-on down there. She had done this for Sean's mother's benefit when that poor lady had sat for three years by the range, dying, coughing her lungs out after a lifetime of toil at the flour mills, and Nuala had never got out of the habit.

'Can't be. They took poor Mr Brophy away yesterday, Mam,' Breeda said.

'Well, that little weed of a fella is over across the square. I wonder what he's doin'?'

'Mebbe he lives here,' Breeda suggested indifferently.

'He's settin' on the bench you sat on yesterday,' Nuala Deegan rambled on, not paying much attention to what she was saying. She pulled the chain and the plug shot into the air and the dirty water gurgled and groaned down the drain.

'Who're ye talkin about, anyhow?' Breeda asked.

'A fella. Dressed snappy. Cheap though. Not a gentleman . . .'

'Oh, Mam! A gentleman in the square outside, sittin' on the bench! That'll be the day.'

'Well he's not a gentleman like Mr O'Laughlin. But he came with him yesterday. Oh, there's not much I miss, lookin' outa this winder. Mr O'Laughlin buried yer granny, remember?'

' 'Course I do,' Breeda protested.

'Well he sent this young whippersnapper outa the house. His assistant, I take him te be. Said poor Mr Brophy was in a shocking condition – well, what'd he expect an' the ould fella dead nearly a week. Said it might upset this fella in his Jimmy Cagney outfit. I thought to meself at the time that what that young fella-me-lad needed was to spend a wee spell wi' us here in Gardiner Street an' he wouldn't be so squeamish. Toughen him up mebbe. He looks wet to me. Gormless.'

Her mother had refilled the sink and was pounding the nappies now in fresh cold water. Slap, bang. Slap, bang against the sides of the stone sink and her hands the colour of beetroot. Breeda shifted her eyes. She wanted to cry when she noticed things like that, like her mother's hands, red and raw. Sometimes she did cry. But not today. Today she had to stay calm and happy and hopeful. Otherwise they would not want her. If they thought she was a little gurrier from the slums they wouldn't touch her with a barge-pole. She must not get upset over the state of her mother's hands.

'You musta seen him.' Slap, bang. Slap, bang. 'He sat opposite ye on the bench yesterday. Wonder what he's doin' today?'

'Mebbe he likes it here, Mam. Mebbe he's thinkin' of comin' to live here. Wants the view. The gorgeous surroundings. Ye never know.' She smoothed a pleat between her fingers. 'Well, Mam, I don't remember him. He made no impression on me. An' I've got more important things to think about than fellas.'

CHAPTER THIRTY

Lonny sat on the bench across the road wondering why he was there. He had never felt like this before. It was as if his body was programmed, obeying some force other than his mind, and had brought him here and told him to wait.

He could feel no excitement. There was none of that wonderful anticipation, simply a compulsion. He *had* to do this. There was no way out. And there was no emotion, no sense of justification, no wild flutterings of the heart, nothing of what he had always felt before. There was only tired resignation.

He clasped his hands on his head, pressing on his skull as if there was something in there trying to escape. Then he let his body go limp and stared at the house. To his horror all he felt was a dry certainty of the outcome; like one of those movies where the camera shows you events out of time – flash-backs and flash-forwards. He saw Arlene Shaughnessy with her Lana Turner sweater and her shocked eyes. He saw Bette McAlister with her dimples and smiles and heard her wild screams. Then Fliss Masters, her buoyant movements and her loveliness and then her horror; and Imelda Manning, her sassy vivacity and then her terrible stillness. And he saw Breeda Deegan, yes, Breeda, her face below him, her mouth open, screaming like a madwoman, like the Thuatha dé Danann, like the Gorgon. They all became Gorgons. They all became ugly. Women were all ugly underneath.

But he had not 'done it' to Breeda yet so how come he could see her, hair spread on the hard, caked clay at his feet, mouth open, screaming. Just like the others.

And then peace. Even to think about it gave him that tranquil feeling. Which would not last. There would have to be another. And then another. Would it ever end? Would he only find the peace he sought in one of Mr O'Laughlin's coffins?

He was weary of it all, weary unto death. He sighed heavily, looking up, and glimpsed the moon-shadow face at the window looking out at him. He caught his breath. He *knew* that face. That was the face he called the Angel. That was a face that saved him. It was a face he had seen in his dreams. A youngish face, prematurely aged, kind-eyed, red hair streaked with grey. It was a face diametrically opposite to his mother's; lean where his mother's was plump, strong where his mother's was weak, kind where his mother's was selfish. Often he had seen her come to help him in the night when he was in despair and had no one to turn to. In his dreams she soothed him, in his dreams she brought him peace.

He stared now in amazement at the face floating like a mirage in the second-floor window. Behind the dirty glass it was like a beacon. It moved up and down, bobbing, and he couldn't make out if it was real or a vision, some figment of his imagination. Oh yes, he knew it from his dreams.

In his dreams he would find himself in this peaceful place (oh, why was it never like that in reality?). There was water there, he could hear it gurgle. A river and reeds. And she came from the water and he saw her face, looking at him. In his dreams his mother was always after him with a knife. Like 'Three Blind Mice'.

Three blind mice, Three blind mice, See how they run, See how they run (the song spiralling upwards, always higher and higher, like fear mounting). They all ran after the farmer's wife, She cut off their tails with a carving knife, Did you ever see such a thing in your life, As three blind mice?

His father used to sing it to him but he was never afraid then, not when his father was alive. Even when he rolled his eyes and chanted fierce and low: *'cut off their tails with a carving knife!'*

But after his father died his mother became in his dreams the farmer's wife carrying a huge knife, running after him, brandishing it in the air, chasing him to cut off his willy. That was what he dreamed, that was what he saw vividly as he tossed and turned and sweated.

Then *she* would come, from the water, that face that hovered and moved in the second-floor window. She would rise out of the reeds and he would run to her at the waterside. She would hold out her arms to him, her red hair curled at her temples and stranded with silver, her tired face bestowing that infinite peace upon him. In the grey mists, as she stood, arms outstretched, she seemed to him everything a mother should be: tranquil and loving, kindly and warm and welcoming, and as his enormous mother chased him, knife extended, grey hair straggling and wild, stockings torn, he would flee to the other woman who stood, her feet in the water, promising him peace, and when he ran into her arms they both fell into the water, into peace, deep peace, and he awakened. Always he awakened at that point. With a start. Just when he had reached his goal and wanted to drown in the peace she brought him, he awoke.

The face had vanished from the window and with a start he saw that Breeda Deegan was emerging from the slum dwelling. There was no front door. It had been dismantled and used for firewood years ago and Breeda materialized in the foggy day from the shadows of the hall into the street, neat and pretty in a navy-blue dress. He sighed, stood, shook himself and followed her down Gardiner Street, aware always of that joyous spark she seemed to exude, that wonderfully contagious vitality.

CHAPTER THIRTY-ONE

The Retail Manager, Desmond O'Keeffe, saw her move through Cosmetics, past Hosiery and Haberdashery, and like Lonny Clebber admired her vitality.

'That's the type of girl we need,' he said to McGillicuddy, the Head Cashier.

They sat in the glass-fronted Cashier's Office, high up over the heads of the shoppers. It was a small room, like a lighthouse, and Mr McGillicuddy, lofty above his fellow workers, loved it. It made him feel like God.

Every now and then they were interrupted by the zip and clang of the little brass containers arriving with payslips and cash up the electrified cable from the customer below. The salesgirl would pop the bill and money into the canister, screw it with a twist into its holder, then pull the cord and, like a mini-funicular up the cable, the little container flew to Mr McGillicuddy in his glass cage. He would take out the bill, detach the receipt, initial it and put it and the change, if any, into the canister and send it flying back down to the sender.

Deary's was gradually getting rid of this system, much to Mr McGillicuddy's alarm, and newfangled cash registers were being installed in the department store. Mr McGillicuddy waited hopefully for the collapse of efficiency and the financial mix-ups the installation of these modern fal-de-rols would, must, bring in their wake. After all, it meant leaving *women* in sole charge of money, and everyone knew how that would end up! Women dealing with cash! Surely this was tempting fate? Women were notoriously bad at ready-reckoning and even if they were honest, Mr McGillicuddy reasoned–, and everyone

knew that women did not have the same standard of honesty as men –
even if they were honest their brains would surely scramble and there
was no doubt they would lack the ability to add guineas and half-
pennies and nineteen shillings and eleven pence!

At the bottom of all that in Mr McGillicuddy's brain was the gnawing worry about the security of his job. If the whole store changed and
adapted to cash registers then he would be superfluous. He would be
made redundant. The thought made him shudder and he was a little
more waspish with Mr O'Keeffe the Retail Manager than he normally
was and that was unwise. It was inadvisable to be sharp with the all-
powerful young upstart Retail Manager but sometimes he couldn't
help himself. O'Keeffe was young and handsome in a cheap film-star
way, and in with Mr Graham de Vere, the General Manager. Thick as
thieves they were, and sure to take each other's side in any argument.

McGillicuddy glanced now at the Retail Manager and heard the
admiration in his voice.

'That's the type of girl we need.'

'Hussies! That's what her kind are, Mr O'Keeffe, you mark my
words. Hussies!' he said, staring down at Breeda Deegan. He did not
really dislike young girls like Breeda, but he feared all young or new
things, feared them dreadfully. They represented modernity and
progress and change and he feared modernity and progress and
change. It was change and updating that brought about the advent of
the cash register and that could make him unemployable – a candi-
date for the scrap-heap.

Mr O'Keeffe disliked Mr McGillicuddy intensely. In the Retail
Manager's opinion he was dry and ungenerous and had not a humor-
ous bone in his body. Also he blocked any changes Mr O'Keeffe tried
to push through in his efforts to make Deary's the Store of the Future.
That was what he was employed to do. Mr Graham de Vere had
employed Mr O'Keeffe to do just that and he expressly told him he
could have his head, but had added in his crispest tones that he was
to be careful not to upset the feelings of the older members of staff
and that he did not want to be bothered about petty differences or
squabbles.

'Be tactful, O'Keeffe,' he instructed his new young manager. 'Handle
them with kid gloves. They must not be given cause to strike. After all,
it was the likes of them that built this store to its present eminence.
We must remember that.' He caressed his Ronald Coleman moustache

lovingly and added, 'But be that as it may, we have to tiptoe into the twentieth century. It's a matter of supply and demand, O'Keeffe. Supply and demand. Ladies nowadays want nylon, not lisle or silk, more's the pity. Nylon's not at all good for them.' He tapped his nose. 'But we mustn't tell them that. Oh no. We must provide them with nylon if that's what they want. They want roll-ons, not corsets. Poor Mrs Crookshank will have to retire soon. It's inevitable. And they don't want to wait for their cash to travel up to heaven and back when they pay a bill. No. They want a cash register. That'll give Mr McGillicuddy a heart attack. But do it tactfully, O'Keeffe, for heaven's sake.'

Desmond O'Keeffe found that the best way to deal with the old-timers was to make the changes without consulting them, dropping hints that complaints just might lead to redundancy and leave it at that. They usually adapted without complaint. Except Mr McGillicuddy.

'You know Mr Graham de Vere will not fire anyone who was here in his father's time!' O'Keeffe told them. 'Unless they rebel and refuse to go with the flow. He does not like rebels. Or so he says. Oh I know, Miss Pilkington, you've never dealt with uplifts and padded bras but you'll soon get the hang. Ladies now like divided cups. The old all-in-one just won't do. But Mr Graham de Vere said to me only the other day, "Desmond," he said (Mr Graham de Vere had never called him anything but O'Keeffe but how were they to know that?), "Miss Pilkington will get the hang of cups," he said, "you mark my words. Otherwise I cannot bear to think of the consequences for that poor woman and her aged parent."'

O'Keeffe would leave the thought dangling and usually had no more problems with the old dears. Except Mr McGillicuddy.

Mr McGillicuddy was a real smartass. He could not leave well enough alone. He had to have his say. But O'Keeffe was determined to show him who was boss and drag this store screaming and kicking into the fifties.

'Mrs Lepner'll never have her,' Mr McGillicuddy said now, a smirk on his lips, delighted he could get a rise out of his young boss. O'Keeffe glanced at him. He sat at his desk, unscrewing canisters, his skin dry, dandruff on the shoulders of his work jacket, his grey crinkly hair cut short and greasily combed across his bald pate. He was correct, the young man thought. Mrs Lepner, a dragon of the old school,

FOUL APPETITE

would never employ this vision of youth and freshness with the halo
of red hair like a mortal sin around her. Mrs Lepner would be appalled
by her vitality and brightness. Mrs Lepner, like Mr McGillicuddy,
would see her as a threat.

Well, they'd see about that. They would see who was boss here. But
tactfully. Remember tactful.

He left the glass-fronted office without a word, a tall, personable
young man with good teeth, and took the lift to the ground floor. As
he did he dreamed of escalators. He had heard that some London
stores had them. Escalators! He envisioned smiling customers being
wafted upwards and downwards, no problem, and they standing still!
Not having to wait. Not having to press buttons. Smooth as silk. How
wonderful that would be. He'd have problems with Grandad
McGinley, the elevator boy who had been Mr Graham de Vere Senior's
batman in the Boer War. But he'd get around that.

He waited impatiently for the lift doors to open. They took ages.
Then he turned to the right of the store, walked past Men's Neckties,
Men's Scarves, Pipes for the Discerning Gentleman and nearly crashed
into the redhead on her way out from a door marked 'Offices'.

He could tell at a glance she had not been successful. Mrs Lepner
had rejected her. It made him furious. He looked into the woebegone
face. 'Hey – whoa-up! What's your hurry, Miss? What's up?'

Her eyes filled with tears and he distinctly felt his knees go weak.
Her eyes were velvety like shamrocks, bright green and soft. Dewy
now. He swallowed violently. No one had ever looked at him in such
a melting fashion before.

'Oh, Mister, sorry. Didn't see ye.' She blinked and looked up at him
and the tears trembled on the long, dark lashes. 'I, em . . . wanted a
job so bad . . . so bad. . . . but . . .' She let out a little sob, a little hic-
cup of misery. 'But . . .'

'Listen, Miss . . . what's your name?'

'Breeda. Breeda Deegan, sir.'

'Well, Miss Deegan, all is not lost. You stay right there. Don't move
an inch, y'hear? I'll be right back.'

The nice young man glanced upwards as he said this and Breeda
could see a little grey-haired man watching them from his glass office
in the sky. His malicious little eyes were fixed on the beautiful young
man who seemed to want to help her and who was obviously a person of importance.

— 153 —

'Wait here,' the young man instructed her again and went through the door marked 'Offices'.

Mrs Lepner sat at her desk shuffling papers. She glanced up and pursed her lips when she saw him. She was a tall woman dressed in unrelieved black with jet trimmings and an eyeglass on a velvet string around her corded neck. She bore a striking resemblance to a tortoise Desmond O'Keeffe had once owned and had the same watery eyes. Eyes that looked like oysters.

'Everything all right, Mrs Lepner?' O'Keeffe, charm itself asked, wondering for the millionth time what Mr Lepner was like.

'Perfectly, Mr O'Keeffe. What can I do for you?' Her voice spoke volumes and O'Keeffe read correctly all that had been left unspoken. What are you doing in my office, O'Keeffe, wasting time? I am perfectly capable of managing the firm's affairs and have been doing so since long before you, O'Keeffe, were born.

He gave her a wide smile and was rewarded by a blank stare. 'Mrs Lepner, Mr Graham de Vere advised me that he was sending a young girl, a Miss Breeda, er . . .' he screwed up his eyes, thinking, '. . . Deegan, yes, that's it, Deegan, to be interviewed. He hoped you would find her suitable.'

Mrs Lepner went pale. That is, paler than she normally was. He decide she looked faintly green.

'She is the daughter of one of his servants and he particularly asked me to look out for her. He feels her family deserves to better itself . . .' Had he gone too far?

'But Mr O'Keeffe, the girl lied about her Intermediate Examination saying she passed with honours when it appears she never sat the exam at all!' There was a world of scorn in Mrs Lepner's voice. It dripped contempt.

O'Keeffe thought fast. 'Ah! Well, you see – we knew about that. It was a mistake. A Government Departmental error. They wrote about it to Mr Graham de Vere. They let us know . . .'

'But the girl admitted it,' Mrs Lepner shrilled. 'She did *not* contradict me . . .'

'She wouldn't. Mrs Lepner, Mr Graham de Vere said that he particularly wanted her – he told me she was such a nice young woman . . .' He shrugged and turned away. 'Well, I'll inform him that you disagree. It can't be helped, I suppose.' He gave her a rueful smile. 'I just thought I'd tell you what he said – save you embarrassment. He gave me to understand that in spite of your long years of service, Mrs Lepner, he, er, Mr de Vere was sure that you had not lost your touch. That you did not suffer from the silly prejudices some of the others here are prone to.' She was smiling a little anxiously now. 'He said to me, "Desmond, I know Mrs Lepner will not let this one get away. Her judgement is too acute." He added not to tell you. I think it was to be some kind of a test. He was sure you would employ Miss Deegan, but I thought it kind to let you know . . .'

He left it hanging there. Mrs Lepner was beginning to get the full implications of what he had said and he gave her time to let his words sink in. The heinous fact dawned on her that she had boobed. Mr Graham de Vere, the Great White Chief, retirer of people on small pensions, had placed his confidence in her and she had let him down.

'I just told her we had nothing for her,' she blurted out.

'Oh, did you, Miss Lepner? That was most unfortunate.' He looked at her sorrowfully as she sat, tearing her handkerchief apart in her bony fingers. Then he brightened up. 'Perhaps I could catch her for you.'

Mrs Lepner never emerged from her office once she was settled in for the day. Daisy McCawley, the tea-lady, brought her a cup of tea at eleven, another at one to have with her packed lunch, another at four precisely, and at six she left the store as she came in, sweeping through the main concourse, looking neither right nor left, as befitted the Employment Manager, a faint superior smile on her thin lips. For her to rush out seeking Miss Deegan was too much to expect, and here was Mr O'Keeffe offering to do it for her. 'Don't worry. She cannot have got far. If I'm lucky – if *you're* lucky – we can catch her. You can say you had her papers mixed up with someone else's.'

'Good Lord, Mr O'Keeffe, I would never do that,' Mrs Lepner cried aghast. 'What will I tell her?'

The humiliating fact that she would have to recant some scathing remarks about hussies from slums made her swallow in distress, but O'Keeffe laughed lightly.

'Tell her you changed our mind. Tell her, as I said, *someone else* mixed up her papers. Whatever you do, don't mention her mother or Mr Graham de Vere. He doesn't want anyone to know.' He rolled his eyes. 'Can you *imagine* how *shocked* he'd be if he knew . . .'

'Oh yes. Oh dear, oh dear. Oh, Mr O'Keeffe, please hurry! Hurry! Get her back here quickly, please.'

He left the room, closing the door softly behind him, and stood there a while waiting, shaking with silent mirth. He did not want to return too soon or she might suspect something. He did not mind if she suspected something later, or discovered from McGillicuddy the truth of the matter. By then Miss Breeda Deegan of the glorious red hair would be employed and once signed on could not be summarily dismissed. Not without his say-so at any rate. He hugged himself with glee, straightened his face, pulled down his jacket and at last came out into the store. He knew McGillicuddy was watching. He touched Breeda Deegan on the shoulder and said a few words to her and her face lit up like Christmas-tree lights. She followed O'Keeffe back through the door marked 'Offices', and McGillicuddy slammed a receipt into the canister so hard that he nipped a piece of flesh out of his thumb, swore, then sent the canister back with such force that poor Miss Vincent had to duck.

'Damn hussy. Damn hussy,' he cried to himself alone in his glass office. Then fiercely, 'Damn O'Keeffe.'

CHAPTER THIRTY-TWO

'Mam – Mam, I've got it! I done it! I got into Deary's. I gotta job.'

She was breathless, cheeks glowing, eyes dancing, a grin as wide as the Liffey splitting her face.

Nuala wiped her forehead tiredly. She smiled fondly at her eldest. 'God love ye, Breeda, now isn't that grand. Sure didn't I say a prayer to the Holy Virgin and didn't it pay off.'

' 'S nuthin' to do wi' the Holy Virgin, Mam. 'Twas a real nice man called Mr O'Keeffe. He took me back to see the ould wan and she changed her mind and gev me a job an' I start Monday. Dressed sober, they said. Could I wear this, Mam?' She indicated the navy georgette. 'I'll get ye a new one . . .'

'Of course ye can, me darlin', ye don't haveta ask. How much'll ye get?'

'Two pounds ten shillings a week, Mam.'

'Mother o' God, isn't that a fortune. Gawney, Breeda, yer rich!'

'I'll take ye outa this, Mam, so I will. I promise.'

'An' where would I go?' Her mother smiled. 'Lave the babbies an' Sean? Don't be daft! No. Ye can buy me the odd luxury, sure, I'd be glad of a bit of help wi' the food. The childer don't get what they need. But if ye want to please me ye'll save all ye can an' get *yerself* outa here. That'd make me happy. What I want is a bright future for you, me darlin'.'

'Oh, Mam, I'll get me a full-skirted dress in sage-green to match me eyes, an' a pair of stiletto-heeled shoes, an' cami-knickers an' Evening in Paris.' She clapped her hands together in breathless joy. 'An' you an the kids can have Hafner's sausages *every* day.'

'Sure wouldn't that be grand,' Nuala cried enthusiastically. 'Ah Breeda, mebbe things is lookin' up.'

Across the street, shoulders stooped in his funeral-parlour suit, Lonny stood staring at the window, wondering if the face from his dreams would appear. Wondering if Breeda Deegan would come out without the children. They were a definite drawback – little terrors would have no qualms about shouting for help, running for aid. He could do nothing with them around. They wouldn't be terrorized by a wide-eyed glare like the nice little Masters boy had been.

Ten to one though she'd go out by herself at some point. Stood to reason. She wouldn't want to be lumbered with those kids morning, noon and night. Thing was to wait and watch and see. She had no boyfriend, or friends other than the family. He had found that out from the old crow called Clancy, an inveterate gossip who was only too happy to tell everything she knew about her neighbours.

She had no routine. One minute she was streeling across the dirt-patch, a trail of kids behind her, and the next she was sashaying out in a smart dress to the big store in O'Connell Street, right opposite the Pillar. Deary's.

He had not wanted to follow her in there. He hated places like that. The assistants grabbed a hold of you and rattled on nineteen to the dozen about stuff he didn't understand in what seemed to him a foreign language and he felt trapped and terrified.

So he had waited outside for her, under Nelson's Pillar, in the shade, around the corner from the raucous flower-seller who screamed her wares loud enough to wake up poor Mr Brophy.

He lit a Craven A, lurked there, and to his surprise the old hunter's instincts, that excited anticipation, crept back into his being. He began to feel elation grow and as he sucked on the fag he was flooded with a sense of vast relief. He had been going through a bad patch, that was all. He needn't have panicked. Ever since his father had died Lonny had felt that there was some dreadful vast region within him where unimaginable horrors lurked and if ever he let them out, those nightmares, those phantoms of evil, they would engulf him and drag him down into their hell. He had been afraid for the past month – since the peace bestowed on him by Imelda Manning wore off – that this was what was happening to him. He was being sucked into the vortex of a terrible hell. Now, he realized with relief, it had only been a black phase, some might say a depression, a dark mood he could not seem to shift.

It was all right now. What he had needed was a quarry. He felt the weight fall off his shoulders and he hunched them like Bogart, then shifted them up and down a couple of times like Cagney and felt much better.

When he saw her again he knew he was right. She had that bounce, that eager-rushing-forward-into-life aura about her and she practically danced down the street. He followed her home. And waited.

When she left the house next she had on the short cotton dress with the puff sleeves and the kids were with her. She crossed the street and sat on the bench just like she had before. She didn't even notice him, couldn't have cared less. Well, he'd change that, never fear. The bitch would be sorry.

Meanwhile he'd wait, patiently. It was good for him, waiting. Revved up the excitement. He sat on the other bench staring at her. Against the darkness of the slum street that formed a backdrop her hair was a violent splash of autumnal colour. Her pale, neat profile was still, immobile, and her eyes, half concealed by drooping, shadowed lids, were full of dreams. As he stared he became aware of someone staring at *him*. His neck prickled and he turned and looked up and saw once more the disembodied face in the window above. The small white face floating behind the dirty glass, sad, tired, watching. His Guardian Angel. The Lady from the River.

He smiled. A warm contented feeling circled him and held him in its embrace and he turned his attention back to Breeda with a serene calm.

CHAPTER THIRTY-THREE

Mr and Mrs Manning sat in their small front room in their two up, two down and stared at the fitful flames licking the brickettes in the tiny grate. Like everything else in their lives at the moment the fire was half-hearted.

Through the window they could see the bay and the Wicklow Mountains gloriously arrayed for autumn before them. The cooling sun turned the water greyish silver and the broom-starred, heather-splashed mountains warmed themselves under the glowing rays. A chill little breeze ruffled the water and shook the leaves off the trembling branches of the trees.

They saw nothing. They were totally unaware of the shimmering beauty of the bay where so often they had walked on either side of their daughter, each of them holding one little trusting hand.

There was no laughter in their house now. They would never hear her laugh again. They remembered, so in tune that each of them thought the same thing at the same time, glancing at each other and nodding without words; Daddy pushing her in her pram, Mother checking every now and then, leaning over, peering at the bonny little face smiling back at them. They remembered in unison her flying legs and hair, her cheery greeting as she arrived like a whirlwind home from school, aching to divest herself of the uniform she always managed to make look second-hand even though it was Deary's best. They remembered seeing her shine in the school play and realizing it was not just parental bias and pride that made them think her exceptionally talented, for the audience reaction and the comments of the other parents and the teachers confirmed that she was a star. Gifted, they said. A born actress.

How had they managed to produce such a glowing creature? Dull, middle-class (or lower middle-class), ordinary people, they had begotten a bright flame, a gloriously talented girl who shone. How had they managed it? And now she was gone, leaving behind her an impossible emptiness. A vast unfillable darkness without light.

They looked at each other and now their thoughts separated and took different paths. He bit his lip and felt his heart swell within him as he held close the memory of a little face, lovely as a summer rose, turned to him. 'I love you, Daddy.' And she thought of all the riches her baby had missed: a boyfriend, timid and shy as Daddy had been, or glamorous and gallant as Aiden Grenell had been in *The Recruiting Officer* in the Gate Theatre. She would never have a boyfriend.

Her first kiss. Never that either. Her first child. That too was a non-event. Her opening night – the applause, the flowers, the notices – she had missed all that too. And that was the worst. To have worked so hard for such a long time for success, to have it so near, within her grasp, all nipped in the bud.

Father Connell had tried to comfort them. 'Don't talk to me about love, Father,' she had told him bitterly and her husband nodded in agreement. 'Don't. Just don't.'

'She was all we had,' he told the priest. 'What was the point of it?'

'Why should such a hideous thing happen to someone who never hurt anyone in her whole life? Someone who was only starting out? Oh, why didn't it happen to me?' she asked in anguish.

The young priest tried to answer the questions but could find no words; all that came out were platitudes. They didn't listen anyway and went home after the funeral and sat staring into space. They were motiveless, uninterested in anything, deprived of energy.

Time passed and it was autumn now. The leaves, copper and gold, russet and purple, fell to the ground in drifts. Another year was dying.

There would be no rebirth for them. They knew it. Darkness had fallen forever.

'I've lost my faith, Daddy,' she said, a vast emptiness in her voice.

'I know,' he answered, sighing. They were in tune as always. They had known without having to discuss it what they would get for her, what their offerings would be. They always knew. While she lived in Leeson Street, her short time there, Mother would look at something and know it was right. Daddy would catch her eye and nod. Knowing it was for Imelda. 'Has her name on it,' she would say. And he would nod.

He did this now on this misty, moisty autumn day, leaves tapping the window-panes as the wind picked them up and whipped them. He looked at his wife and nodded.

No word was said. No words were needed. He rose and shuffled slowly from the room. All the elasticity had gone from his step since she died. In a moment she could hear him put on the kettle. First she heard the tap spraying into the tin kettle, then the pop as he lit the gas, then the rattle of china. Their best cups.

She looked around the room. It was spotless as always. The Tintawn carpet was wall-to-wall, the sofa and chairs covered in the best synthetic fabric, new in Deary's, in yellow and brown. There was a nice carved imitation walnut table between the easy chairs in front of the fire, a radiogram on one side and some books on a shelf on the other. There was a bowl of everlasting chrysanthemums on the mantelpiece beside the cup Imelda had won at the Feis. A clock ticked between the cup and the chrysanthemums and broke the silence in the room.

She liked this room, had always been content here, proud of its neat cleanliness. Until . . . until . . .

He returned from the kitchen and she smiled at him. It was a smile of understanding. He returned it. He had already poured out the tea He always made it in the pot then let her pour it when he brought it in here. Let her milk and sugar it. But today he had broken a lifetime habit and brought in full cups. Milked and sugared.

Yes, she knew and approved. The thought had flown without speech from one to the other and back since that morning when they had had to identify the body of their beautiful young daughter and they had seen what had been done to her.

She sipped her tea. It tasted awful but obviously that was because of what he had put in it. The rat poison? she wondered. Something he had bought? Whatever it was it would not hurt much, she knew that. He couldn't bear her to suffer.

The Gardai had been around a few days ago. Detective O'Malley. They said they were 'getting there', whatever that meant. Well, they would have to 'get there' without them. Detective Inspector O'Malley said, 'You're very important to us. Only you can identify him. The other witnesses *saw* him, sure, but that doesn't *prove* anything. But you can place him at the scene of the crime.' Well, he'd have to find another witness to help him. Another witness to identify that pathetic little weed of a human being who had destroyed their most precious love. What did they care about him? Catching and punishing him would mean nothing. It would not bring their darling back to them.

They'd be with her soon. They'd be with Imelda.

They did not believe in Heaven, Hell, Death and Judgement. Eternal Life hereafter did not seem realistic to them any more. But they knew they'd join her. They knew she was somewhere out there and they'd find her, or she'd find them. You couldn't extinguish such a pure bright flame forever. They knew that much.

They sat opposite each other and drank their tea and stared into space. Then Mother gave a strangled little cry, like the sound of the seagulls outside, one raucous call and the cup fell from her hand on to the floor and cracked and fell apart. Her hand relaxed and went limp. Daddy watched her, suddenly remembering her young and pretty, like Imelda. Trusting him to protect her. And Imelda. She had trusted him too. And he had let both of them down.

He was suddenly very alone, very frightened. He said a prayer. How odd that was, praying to a God you didn't believe in any more. Then he felt a sudden spasm, like an electric shock. Mother must have felt this too, he thought, and it was not too bad. But Mother had always been better at pain than he was. Something to do with her being a woman. He stretched out to her, trying to reach her. She was lying in the other chair, face and body rigid, a funny purple ring around her mouth, and he felt himself fall forward, and the cramp tore at his body, wrenching the life out, then all went dark, darker, darker than the darkest night.

CHAPTER THIRTY-FOUR

Detective Inspector O'Malley turned the key in the lock of his front door and, pushing it open, was instantly attacked by his eleven-year-old son Seamus.

'Da . . . Da . . . Da . . . ju get the bike fixed? Ha? Ju get it fixed?'

'Hey, hey, hey! Hold yer horses! God's sakes, Seamus, hold on!'

'Let yer da in the door, Seamus,' Mary O'Malley called from the kitchen.

'Ju get it fixed?'

'Yes, son. It's outside again' the hedge.'

'Welcome home, love,' Mary called, same as always.

The kitchen was at the end of the hall facing the little back garden where he grew his vegetables. His heart lifted at the sound of her voice. It always did, never failed. Since they married not a day passed that he didn't thank God for her presence in his life. And Colleen. And Seamus. They were part of the both of them, of their love for each other, and he loved them and Mary as himself.

His daughter Colleen, pretty, fair and seventeen, came out of the parlour where she had been studying and put an arm on his lapel and kissed his cheek.

' 'Lo, Da,' she said and softly smiled at him, and he felt a lump in his throat as big as an ostrich egg. He gave her a hug, lifting her off her feet and swinging her around in a burst of love, and she, used to his expressions of tenderness, laughed and cried, 'Oh, Da, put me down. The hall's too narrow.'

She was studying to be a nurse and he was so proud of her he could not contain it sometimes. This evening more than ever before he was grateful, for the pictures of Imelda Manning that he had been looking at that day haunted him. Her murder had left an appalling and indelible print on his mind and he could not help personalizing it. Imelda Manning was not unlike his daughter and if this ever happened to Colleen . . . he felt sick at the mere thought.

He was determined to find her killer before any more damage was done. Before he destroyed another life.

The case kept him awake at night so that he had to get out of his warm bed and leave the dear presence of his wife and go downstairs and suck on his briar pipe and think and think and think. In his mind there was nothing worse than the destruction of a young and innocent person. Nothing. Even if they lived after his attack it blighted their whole lives, crippled them mentally, and there was no place on earth foul enough in which to consign the perpetrator.

He would get the bastard. If it took him forever. And in the meantime that weasel had affected their lives. He took away, with his violence, other people's peace of mind. Even though they'd never met, even though the monster was unaware of their existence, he had affected the O'Malley family and the families of young girls everywhere in Dublin City.

He had become over-protective of Colleen, nervous if she went out alone, worried about her if she was five minutes late. It put pressure on her and it put pressure on him. And that was not good. The old freedom was gone. It made her nervous when she should not be. It curtailed her spontaneity and her independence. And he had communicated that tension to his wife and she in turn was anxious.

Oh, Colleen was very cooperative about it. She understood his anxiety. But she was also burdened by it and he was unhappy that she should have to carry that weight on her young shoulders. And Mary was burdened too. All because of that little shit. All because of a little turd who liked violence and was mentally sick.

They had supper in the kitchen.

'Good day at school?' he asked Seamus.

'He got four stars for History,' Colleen told him, eyes shining.

'Oh . . . it was nuthin'.' Seamus shrugged deprecatingly.

'Well congrats, son. Well done!'

Colleen glanced at her mother and Mary cleared her throat and glanced at him. He knew what was coming and felt a vice grip his heart for a moment.

'Can Colleen go to the hop in Bective tonight?' Mary asked.

'Oh, love, you shouldn't even have te ask,' he replied and pounded his fist on the table. 'You shouldn't have te ask.' Then he collected himself. 'Who's takin' ye?'

'That's it, Da. No one. Gerry's car is broken.' Gerry was her friend. He was not a boyfriend, she told them, but someone she enjoyed being with.

'Ye mean yer goin' on yer own?'

She nodded. He tried to keep calm. It was difficult.

'No,' he said. Then, seeing her disappointment, 'No,' he repeated, rising and coming to a decision. 'But I'll take ye.'

'Oh, Da, would you? That'd be grand. Then Mam needn't worry either.'

She was so thoughtful. What a burden to have put on you, he thought.

'I've quite made up my mind,' he said. ' 'Twon't be any bother at all.' He'd do it for his own sake, he thought.

'I'll get ready, Da,' she cried happily and ran upstairs to dress.

'Stupid hops! Why do girls like dancin'?' Seamus muttered. 'Rock an' roll an' all that. Gawney Mac!' He rolled his eyes heavenwards.

'Oh, love, you sure you don't mind? I know you were dyin' to put your feet up and sup a pint.'

'You know I don't mind, Mary. She's more important. I'd die if . . .'

She laid a soothing arm on his. ' 'Twon't. Don't worry, love. We're taking every precaution. Since poor little Imelda Manning every mother in Dublin is doing likewise.'

'Jasus, I must get him. I *must*. That guy has to be put away. Hanged.'

'Are ye any nearer?' she asked.

He shook his head. 'Further. Imelda's parents . . .' he lowered his voice, then drew her into the hall, glancing at Seamus who was deep in Dan Dare. 'The Mannings committed suicide. Spiked their tea with rat bane. Or some such. The pathologist will tell us exactly what.' She shivered and he put his arms around her protectively. 'They died almost instantly. Cahil went to ask them some more questions, check the details. Had to force the lock. Found them cold. God, the repercussions of a thing like this, Mary, it's terrible.'

'I know, dear, I know.'

But she didn't. She hadn't seen Imelda Manning's body. She had not seen the violence done to it. She was not haunted by the horror of that young girl's face. Thank God, he added to himself.

'So now you've got no one to identify him?' she asked quietly.

Mary was quick. He kissed her hair gently. 'Not really,' he said. 'But there must be someone out there who can. There must be.'

'What'll you do if there's not?' she asked.

'Wait till he strikes again,' he said grimly. 'An' he will. You mark my words, he will.'

He drove his daughter to the dance. She smelled young and fresh beside him, like a bouquet of spring flowers. She looked like that too. So bright. So feminine. He gripped the wheel. Anyone lay a hand on her! A red haze enveloped his brain when he thought of it. She should have gentle boys in her life, loving, flirting. Until she found the right man, a good man, a kind man, then he would walk up the aisle, proud as Punch with her on his arm and hand over the responsibility, give her to her best-beloved. That was the right and proper way. Not abused, in the street, violated on the cobblestones.

He sat in the car outside when she went into the dance. Gerry was waiting for her. He came to the car and greeted him, a nice boy with honest eyes. 'Hello, Mr O'Malley. I'll take good care of her, never fear. I'm sorry about the car, sir.'

'That's all right, Gerry. See you do.' He grinned at the young man. 'Take care of her, I mean. I'll call back for you at what time?'

'Twelve, Da – if that's not too late? I don't mind if you have to come sooner.'

'No, twelve would suit me fine,' he grinned at her out of the car window. 'Cinderella.'

She laughed. 'Oh, Da! Well, see you later.'

He peered out at Gerry, eyes narrowed as she walked away. 'Now, keep an eye on her, Gerry, won't you?'

'Sure, Mr O'Malley. Sure.'

But he didn't go home. He stayed there in the parking lot, thinking. He turned off the engine and the car lights, left the window down and lit his pipe and thought.

He never got a chance to do that, think in peace. At home there was always Mary and the kids and in the station there were his colleagues. It was an opportunity and there was something on the periphery of his mind that he had not been able to catch. Something bugging him.

It was dark and there was nothing to distract him in the car park. He could hear the music from the clubhouse – 'Who's sorry now?' and 'I wonder who's kissing her now'.

He was very still, listening, but not to the music; to the inner voice that made him such a good detective. Something, somewhere, he knew, had to be linked up. There were two facts in his brain and they needed to be tied together and then he would know something crucial. What was it? What in God's name was it?

He thought it through. Went over and over again in his head every possible fact they had concerning the Imelda Manning case. The time. The place. The rape. The – wait – wait – it was coming – a voice. A girl's voice, not connected to Imelda Manning at all. A girl's voice, tremulous, almost mumbling, full of horror.

'He kept hitting me and hitting me. All the time he was . . .'

'Having intercourse?'

She, nodding, ashamed. 'Hitting me across the face. And he spat on me. He spat while he did that awful thing to me.'

'Raped you?'

So softly, so frightened. 'Raped me.'

Arlene. Arlene Shaughnessy. Of course! The rape case nearly a year ago. The girl who made a gallant attempt to bring a rapist to justice and who had been humiliated for her efforts, Arlene Shaughnessy.

It was the same. Imelda Manning had been hit repeatedly while being subjected to that onslaught, and according to the pathologist she had been spat on. He felt a surge of triumph as he realized it had to be the same guy. What was his name? He could visualize him now, in the dock, a sharp, shifty little greaser with nervous eyes and snappy clothes. Lonny Clebber. That was it. Lonny Clebber.

He thought about it for a while. Lonny Clebber.

Lonny Clebber lived down beside the Tolka. Worked in O'Laughlin's the undertaker. Lonny Clebber.

He smiled to himself in the dark. 'Got ya!' he said and hit the driving wheel with his fist. Oh, they had no proof. As yet. But they would. They'd watch him.

'Outa thousands I've got it down to one,' he whispered. 'Lonny Clebber. Well, Mr Clebber, I'll be havin' ye. I'll have a tail on you from now on, he thought. We'll know when ye tie yer shoes. We'll know when ye piss and when ye sneeze. An' we'll know where ye go. There'll be no more sport for ye, ye slimy little git, so there won't, an' that's a promise.

CHAPTER THIRTY-FIVE

'Can't you all stop talking about her as if she were contagious?' Clemmie cried as she sat in the armchair, slightly separate from the others as usual. Meriel sat with her mother on the sofa.

'We're *not* discussing her,' Tessa protested. No one asked who they were *not* talking about – no one had to.

'You're all so po-faced about Fliss,' Clemmie continued. 'It's not as if she has committed a crime. A crime was committed *against* her.' The others looked at Clemmie uncomfortably. She always managed to disconcert them. Tessa cleared her throat. Bigger had explained that Agnes could not come to tea. She had a head cold and did not want to risk catching a chill.

'In *this* weather?' Clemmie hooted derisively and Bigger looked embarrassed. Agnes had not set foot in the Masters house since Fliss and Derry had broken up.

'Oh, it's all too bad,' Bigger said now. 'So unfortunate!'

If Bigger and Agnes had not been to the Masters house since the tragedy, Rogan had not set foot in the golf club, so he had not laid eyes on his two friends since that day so long ago when their son had announced his intention of marrying Fliss. There was a terrible awkwardness between them. Even Valentine seemed ill-at-ease in their presence and only Clemmie had not changed.

Not that Rogan or Tessa had done much to give them a lead. But then neither Tessa nor Rogan knew precisely how to behave. They felt they were in limbo. There was no manual on prescribed behaviour for a situation like this and Rogan simply opted out rather than face the wagging tongues in the club.

They loved their daughter but were acutely embarrassed for her. It was not an attitude she liked or encouraged. They could not understand her decision to have the baby and found her situation untenable. They had been relieved that the Devlins had kept a low profile and it was only Tessa's inability to cancel the yearly tea-party held in their home to discuss Christmas arrangements that precipitated this meeting.

Meriel was disgusted. She was horrified at her parents' awkwardness and had little time for their friends' total inability to behave naturally in the face of Fliss's decision. For it was her determination to have the child that stuck in their throats.

All except Clemmie. That perennially awkward woman had earned Meriel's respect and admiration over the last months.

'Goddammit, Bigger, the girl's going to have a baby – what could be more natural than that?' Clemmie said now, gulping down tea and wrinkling her nose at it.

'Well, yes, but it's not . . . well, it's not *like* other babies,' Bigger began, then stopped.

'Couldn't you say she'd been married secretly and her husband died? Unexpectedly?' Valentine asked, and Clemmie snorted loudly while Tessa and Rogan stared at him incredulously.

'I think you're all dumb. So dumb! You're so afraid of what other people will think.' Meriel jumped up, cheeks flaming. 'Don't you see it doesn't matter? Have none of you any courage at all? Oh you make me sick.' She turned to leave the room.

'Merry,' Tessa protested. 'Darling, don't be rude.'

It seemed her world, ordered and calm, was falling apart, and every time she spoke now Tessa detected a note of uncertainty in her own voice.

'Oh, Mother, all I can do is thank God I've a boyfriend like Bobby. He doesn't judge. He's on Fliss's side, no matter what. He doesn't sit around and wish it would go away or blame my sister for the awful thing that happened to her.' Meriel was nearly in tears.

'But then, my dear, *you* are not the one who was—' Valentine glanced at Rogan's tight face— 'brutally attacked.'

Meriel gave him a withering glare as Bigger turned to her with a face of thunder. 'I *hope* that was not a slur on my son,' he cried.

'Oh no, Bigger, of course it was not,' Tessa cried, distressed. 'You mustn't think that . . .'

'I sincerely hope that remark was not aimed at Derry,' Bigger insisted, staring at Meriel.

'And what if it was?' she said, her voice dripping with contempt. 'If you must know, I think your golden boy behaved feebly. Like a soppy boneless class of an eejit—'

'How dare you, girl!' Bigger's voice could barely control his fury. 'Why, you little whippersnapper, talking like that about Derry. My son behaved impeccably, d'you hear?' He was beside himself, waving his finger under Meriel's nose, his face throbbing with rage. 'My son insisted on keeping his offer open to Phyllis after that unfortunate affair. Against my wishes. Against Agnes's.'

'Calm down, Bigger. That's enough,' Clemmie ordered. 'Stop before you say something you'll regret.'

'He already has,' Meriel said coldly. But Bigger Devlin had no intention of stopping. Fretting for months over the whole affair, as he called it, feeling vaguely uncomfortable as if he were somehow to blame, all his bottled feelings rose up within him in volcanic unstoppability. Furious with himself and the Masters family, angry at the way Meriel and Bobby Mitchell seemed to view the whole *contretemps* as something to be cheerfully dealt with, frustrated by the unexpected twist of fate that broke his son's engagement to the daughter of one of the wealthiest and most powerful families in Ireland, genuinely grieved at being separated from his friend, he had been simmering for months now and had suddenly reached the boil. Besides, in his deepest heart he blamed the Masterses for the whole thing. He knew it was unreasonable but he did not seem to have any control over this conviction.

'You speak to your elders with respect, young lady,' he hissed now at Meriel. 'You surprise me, you really do. I didn't know you had such unpleasant characteristics and all I can say is if your sister has the same tongue on her that you have, then I'm not at all surprised she got herself into trouble.'

There was a gasp, then Tessa rose, face paling. Meriel stepped back from him as if she'd been hit and for once even Clemmie was speechless with shock. But Bigger Devlin showed no repentance. He turned on his heel and marched to the door. 'And my wife does not have a cold,' he announced. 'It is just that she prefers not to set foot in this house. I bid you good-day.' And he left, slamming the door behind him.

'He's going to regret that little outburst,' Clemmie said, then looked at Tessa's ashen face. 'He didn't mean it, Tessa, you know he didn't.'

'He may not have,' Tessa said softly, 'but he's broken something. He can never go back.' And she began to weep softly, dabbing her eyes with her handkerchief. Rogan looked bewildered. Meriel was shaking.

'Well, it takes a bit of trouble to show who your friends are,' Clemmie continued. 'Come with me, Meriel. Valentine, go get the car. I'll be out in a minute. Rogan, your wife needs you.'

Rogan looked at her bleakly. 'What?'

'Tessa needs you,' Clemmie said. 'Come along, Meriel.' She steered Meriel out of the room and into the dining-room.

'Now you sit down there, and listen to me.' Clemmie pressed her on to one of the tall dining-room chairs. 'But first a drink. I need a drink.'

Meriel pointed to a decanter on the sideboard. It was half-full of brandy and Clemmie poured herself a generous measure then added a splash more and sipped it undiluted with obvious relish, smacking her lips and taking a second sip before she turned to Meriel.

'Now listen to me, my girl. You seem to me the only one in this house with any sense, but that doesn't mean you have *carte blanche* to go about upsetting everyone. Society is run on balance and it is a delicate balance. If we all went around telling everyone what we thought a lot of us would be dead. None of us, my dear, can afford to say everything we think and feel. If we do we'll find ourselves firmly alone. On the outside looking in. That's what friends are, Meriel – people who see your faults and tolerate them.'

'But, Clemmie, you of all people—'

'I know. I do not take my own advice. But you see, my dear, I'm already on the outside and I know how cold it gets out there. I don't want you to find yourself out in the cold too. You're too fine and nice a person. And your sister needs you.' She smiled at the girl and touched her cheek. 'So do your mother and your father, child. They need your strength badly. They are bewildered and you can influence them, you really can. Help them to understand Fliss's predicament. And Merry . . .'

The girl looked up. 'What, Clemmie?'

'Bobby needs you. He's a lucky fellow, is Bobby. And you, my dear, are lucky too. So many people need you. Don't let them down.'

'I'll try not to,' Meriel said.

'Your mother and father must have done something right to have produced someone as intelligent as you.'

Clemmie swallowed the rest of the drink then turned once more to Meriel. 'And remember, Merry, however it seems now, this will all blow over. And it's up to you to help. Don't bear grudges. Forget harsh words. Tell your mother and father to forget too.' She laughed. 'That pair will, Agnes and Bigger. They'd lose too much. It would be too inconvenient to remember, so they'll forget. And you must let it go. All right?'

Meriel nodded.

'Good girl,' Clemmie smiled. 'Now, I must go. Join Romeo in the car.'

She put down the glass and went to the door, gently touching Meriel on the shoulder as she passed. At the door she turned. 'Merry,' she said and the girl looked up.

'Yes?'

'You're a very special person. I hope Bobby knows that,' she said, and then she was gone.

CHAPTER THIRTY-SIX

Fliss did not come down to see the visitors. She saw few people these days. She was fed up with the constant awkwardness, the self-conscious silences when someone slipped into a reference that *could* be construed as an allusion to the 'unfortunate incident', as they all insisted on calling the rape. She also found references to her present condition, laced as they were with implied criticism, very hard to bear. She felt herself cast in the part of a scarlet woman, a marked creature, an oddity, and she hated it. She longed to belong to the human race again, simply to be an indistinguishable member of the social circle she had grown up in. But that same society, she found to her cost, had consigned her to another role, a part she was expected to play: damaged goods, a handicapped and suffering victim, and she did not want that under any circumstances, so she did not see them.

But she wanted, oh so much, to laugh and dance again, to sit with friends and chat about inconsequential things – fashion, films, who was doing a line with whom. But on her arrival, she had found people's faces became long and serious and silence fell.

If only she could be the Fliss she felt inside – still Mr and Mrs Masters' little girl, who went to school at the Sacred Heart Convent, who had her coming-out party at Portmarnock Country Club, who played tennis and danced and was engaged to Derry Devlin. Instead everyone's, including her own and the family's, perception of her had changed, and suddenly she was this pathetic creature who had to be pampered and whose presence demanded a censored conversation.

She was isolated suddenly from the family she loved in a way she would never have been had she simply left home and travelled to the ends of the earth – say Borneo. In Borneo she would have felt the family's support, their unconditional love, but not here, not now, not any more. She discovered their love had never been unconditional and that was a shock.

Even Meriel, so fiercely on her side, was fighting a crusade brought about by what had happened and the general reaction to it. Meriel was treating her like a figurehead, a cause. She was no longer so shocked by the rape as by how people had behaved to Fliss afterwards and she had turned it into a personal war.

Gone was the easygoing bickering. They never quarrelled now and even when Fliss knew herself to have been sharp or unreasonable her sister bit her lip and kept her mouth shut, restraining herself in a fashion that was unnatural.

Fliss sat on her bed looking out of the window. In the distance she could see through the soft autumn mist the curved back of the rust-coloured mountains. Leaves flurried, bronze and gold, carpeting the gardens, dancing along the street, scudding in perpetual motion and collecting themselves into little piles for the children to kick. She wished she could go away. Far away where no one knew her. Borneo? She laughed to herself. If only she could relieve the family of the burden of her problem. But where could she go, realistically? Her baby needed security far more than ordinary babies born to married couples. She had felt, or thought she felt, vague stirrings within her. The movement consoled her. There would soon be someone else to fight for, to give her courage. There would be another human being who knew nothing of guilt and sin, someone she would bring up to be strong and brave and loving. Unafraid of the opinion of others. Boy or girl, what did it matter? As long as they understood that what he or she *was* was more important than what others cast them to be.

She knew her father believed she had somehow shamed him and that her mother was bewildered and acutely embarrassed, that Nora thought she was a tragic, spoiled female and said double prayers for her employers' daughter. And Meriel looked on her as a woman marching in the forefront of a battle that had begun with Emily Pankhurst.

None of this was true. She was a girl who had been raped and brutalized and she was pregnant. Soon she would be a mother, like any

GENEVIEVE LYONS

mother, anxious to do her best, but vulnerable because there was no
husband for her to turn to for help.

She knew too that she would never be treated like that. She would
not resemble in their minds any other young mother. She would be
different; she would carry a stigma.

Thinking about it all, mulling it over rationally, one leg tucked
under her, she came to certain conclusions. She would not be forced
into leaving home. Not yet. She would not go until she was ready. But
she would go eventually. The child stood no chance here. Someone
would reveal to him/her the shocking manner in which he or she had
been conceived. Someone wouldn't be able to resist breaking that
confidence. She could explain it in a different, more gentle way. If she
stayed someone would brutalize her child's tender mind. So she
would have to leave. But not until the baby was born and was, say, six
to eight months old. Yes. About then she would go. To London
maybe. They would protest, her father, her mother, but they would be
relieved. Life would be tidy again. 'Ah yes, Fliss is fine. She's in
London now. Teaching.' Yes, that was it. She'd do a teacher-training
course. While her little boy or girl was still small. Then she'd have the
same schedule when they were at school.

Her father would give her money, she knew that, and was grateful.
He'd only be too glad to. It would salve his conscience. She would be
okay.

Did people realize the terrible repercussions of this rape? The
break-up of the family? The disadvantaged life she would be forced to
lead, away from her family, the people and friends she had known all
her life? Even if she stopped having the nightmares, the terrible haunt-
ings she was subject to, the disgust she felt, she still had lost so much
more than was fair. And Derry. Dear, darling Derry.

Her heart had broken over Derry and it would never be properly
mended She would never again trust in the same way. It had been a
terrible spoiling of love. And no matter what happened to her the rest
of her life, there would always be moments, seconds even, before
and during the most intimate moments of her life when unbidden
memories of that vilification she had been subjected to would insin-
uate themselves between her and whoever was beside her. She and
Derry had had something pure and bright and lovely, a warm innocent passion that would have grown to deep and abiding love over
sweet years of marriage. An unspoiled life, unpolluted, advantaged,

— 176 —

privileged. They would have had happy pregnancies and legitimate, welcomed babies. Welcomed by everyone, that is. The blessings of both families would have been bestowed upon them.

But the rapist had come between them, defiled not only her but Derry and his family and her own. She had been soiled in Derry's eyes and as a consequence he was diminished in hers. And her heart had been broken.

There had been a moment when she had thought they might be able to surmount the tragedy, but he had unconsciously let her see how unrealistic that hope was. His mother and father had avoided coming to see her. They had stayed away, sending a clear message about how they felt. But Clemmie came and held her hand in a fierce, sympathetic grip. And she had turned on Derry one day, in her forthright way, and demanded what was the matter with Agnes and Bigger. 'They're not very good around sickrooms,' he had answered. 'And it shocks them that Fliss has been through such an experience. It *is* very shocking after all.'

'Does it worry you too, Derry?' Fliss had asked and he had looked at her with those warm kindly eyes, sorrowful now, and nodded. 'I'll get over it,' he said. 'I'll get over it.'

And it was gone. Vanished in that sentence. The foundation upon which that sweet love was built crumbled and was swept away forever.

She sighed, wrapping her arms around her knees, staring at the mountains and the leaves, and decided she had no more time for regrets and might-have-beens. She had a small new life to consider and no one was going to turn that into a tragedy or a cause. No. She had her plan now and she would stick to it. She smiled to herself and wondered if it was going to be a boy or a girl.

CHAPTER THIRTY-SEVEN

Breeda's first day at work was a huge success. Somehow the girls on the floor had found out that she and Mr O'Keeffe had one-upped the dreaded Mrs Lepner and they welcomed her with enthusiasm.

As soon as she entered the back door of Deary's around the corner in Abbey Street and down a lane behind the big old Victorian building that housed the department store, she was greeted by a bright, slightly gingery blonde called Mavis Harper.

'You're Breeda Deegan? I bin told to look after you, yer first day. I'm Mavis Harper.'

Breeda had on her navy georgette but Mavis gave her a pink overall, knee-length with a high Russian neck, patent fastened at her throat.

'You can wear it over yer dress, or you can wear a skirt an' take off your blouse and jacket, leave them in your locker and just wear the overall in the shop. Whatever you like.' Mavis stared at her helpfully. 'That's what I do. Saves my clothes.'

She had huge brown eyes fringed top and bottom with heavily mascara'd eyelashes which she blinked rapidly every so often. 'This is your locker. We each have one,' she told Breeda and gave her the key.

'We sign here,' she instructed when Breeda had fastened the fasteners, patted her red hair and locked up her meagre belongings. She looked in the mirror and saw that the pink overall suited her, was in fact startling with her hair, and she looked very nice indeed.

Mavis showed her the big ledger on a stand outside the cloakrooms where the staff signed in and out. Mavis told her to sign her full name and add the exact time. 'After it, to the minute. Whoever comes in next will be furious and have your guts for garters if you put it down wrong. An' if you have to make a mistake, for God's sake make it early rather than late. See?'

This seemed logical to Breeda, so she made no comment, simply nodded and did as she was told.

'We're docked for lateness,' Mavis said. 'Awful. Like the bloody Army.' She batted her eyelashes. 'So Terry says.' She glanced at Breeda who looked blank. 'Me boyfriend,' she explained.

Next they ascended the back stairs, old stone steps with no covering. 'That's only for the store,' Mavis explained. 'Behind the scenes we're very basic. Except for Mrs Lepner. She does all right. Old battle-axe. So does Mr McGillicuddy. They both started in the store when old Mr Graham de Vere ran it and young Mr Graham de Vere, the boss now, was in his pram.'

'I thought Mr O'Keeffe was the manager,' Breeda said and Mavis giggled and shook her brassy curls.

'Oh no. Mr Graham de Vere is the General Manager and chief shareholder. Mr O'Keeffe just manages *us*. He's Retail Manager. And Mr Adare is Wholesale Manager. Mr Graham de Vere is head bottle washer. Owns the whole shebang.' She leaned forward confidentially. 'But tell us, what happened between you and Mrs Lepner? Ah g'wan, tell us.'

Breeda told her, honestly, how much she had wanted the job.

'Ye must be mad,' Mavis remarked.

'An' Mrs Lepner turned me down – said I was common, a little chit from the slums.'

'God'n' she's awful!' Mavis breathed and Breeda continued, 'So I was just lavin', thinkin' I'd missed me chance, when up comes Mr O'Keeffe, smiles at me like an angel an' says, "You stay right there!" Then he disappears for five minutes, comes back and tells me to go into that ould harridan again. I didn't want to, Mavis, but I wanted this job so bad!'

'Starkers! Bonkers is what you are,' Mavis sighed.

'Well, wasn't she as nice as pie this time, when before she was like a weasel. I dunno what made her change her mind, deedn't I don't, but I'm here now an' I don't care.'

'I bet it was him. Mr O'Keeffe,' Mavis said.

'Why should he care?' Breeda asked her.

'To get at them both. Mr McGillicuddy an' Mrs Lepner, that's why.' She looked at Breeda speculatively. 'An' mebbe he likes you.

Though every girl in the store's been after him – with no luck – no luck at all.'

They emerged into the store. Everything was completely covered. An army of men and women arrived with them, surging into the store, the women in their pink overalls, the men in dark suits. They scattered to the various counters and within minutes all the covers were whisked off, revealing a million treasures to tempt the affluent. Jewellery sparkled on black velvet. Hosiery was smoothed on to elongated glass legs. Colourful scarves were draped over brass hands with fingers curled to hold them gracefully. Perfume in exotic bottles tempted the buyer: Cardin, Worth, Chanel – French names that sounded exciting on the tongue. Cosmetics made by Max Factor, Dorothy Grey, Elizabeth Arden, Coty and Pond's displayed on the counters of a department that was growing all the time. Up a curved marble staircase carpeted in green, model dresses were draped on dummies and hung side by side on racks. Gossamer lingerie lay on satin pillows. Hats balanced on stands, feathered, veiled, artificially flowered or beribboned. Furs were at the back behind the coats, a reminder that winter was nigh. Sweaters – angora, cashmere, lambswool, Aran in marvellous variety – tempted the customer to buy, buy, buy.

Breeda to her delight found she was assigned to Perfume with Mavis.

'You can dab some on from the samplers,' she told Breeda. 'First week I was here I smelled like a whoor in a cat-house I wore so much. Kept dabbin' it on. Then Mr O'Keeffe said they could smell me up on the second floor in Furs an' did I really want people to pass out in my presence? I learned my lesson, so go easy.'

The work was, Breeda thought, wonderful. She had never been so happy in her life. All she had to do was charm the customers and if she made a sale ring up the price and give change. It was all so simple. Perfume didn't have to bother with Mr McGillicuddy up above in his glass box of an office. They had the new till.

'Gawney it was awful before. You just knew he *hoped* you'd make a mistake,' Mavis whispered to her, rolling her eyes up to the glass office above. 'And him always in a state of high dudgeon,' she added. 'That man was *born* in a state of high dudgeon.'

Breeda loved chatting to the customers and they liked her, she could tell. Mavis confirmed it. 'You're genteel, see, Breeda. I'm not.

I'm better suited to lipsticks and make-up, or swim-wear. You're what my mam calls one of Nature's ladies.' She giggled and rubbed her nose with a long scarlet-tipped finger. 'I admire Mr O'Keeffe for putting you here. Shows good judgement. He's smart, is Mr O'Keeffe.' She smiled at Breeda and continued explaining. 'The customers in Perfume are wealthy. Ladies who are used to luxury. No Cabra matrons here, Breeda. No Biddy Mulligans from the Coombe.'

Nor anyone from Gardiner Street, Breeda thought, but did not say.

'Anyone who can afford these prices to smell good has got to have money to burn,' Mavis finished.

'The smell is gorgeous though, Mavis, so it's worth it, an' one day I'll buy meself a bottle, you see if I don't.'

'An' ye'll get it at wholesale price,' Mavis said smartly, imparting this news with pride. 'Anythin' you want in the store ye get discount.'

Breeda's eyes widened. 'Really?'

Mavis, pleased at the new girl's awe, added, 'An' we get set lunch cheap and tea and coffee free. Oh, we don't do so bad here, deedn't we don't.'

'Gawney!'

'An' I was tellin' you about the customers. Ladies—'

'Wi' money to burn . . .'

''Zackly. An' gentlemen, ditto. Husbands getting a present for their wives. Young buccos buyin' a gift for their girlfriends. Gormless young eejits wi' no money sometimes come in. Ye give them short shrift. You can tell them by the way they dress. You send them scarpering outa here when they see the prices, point them in the direction of Woolworth's down Henry Street.'

'For Evening in Paris?'

''Zackly. But Mr O'Keeffe says to do it nicely. Let them down gently. Mr O'Keeffe says, "Every millionaire was once a poor man in this country anyway. Never forget that. The young gurrier tryin' to buy a bottle of Chanel for a shillin' shows good taste and he'll remember if he's treated nice in Deary's an' if he makes it to the top he'll come back and spend here." That's what Mr O'Keeffe says. Po-ten-tial customers, he says.'

At that moment the Retail Manager, neat as a pin, his tall young figure immaculately clad, appeared at the counter and gave them a charming grin.

GENEVIEVE LYONS

'And what was it I said, Miss Harper? I hope it was something wise?'

'Oh, Mr O'Keeffe, I didn't see you there! Oh, o'course it was. Everythin' ye says is wise,' Mavis twittered.

'That's extravagant, Miss Harper. A slight, very slight exaggeration.' He flashed a grin at Breeda. 'And how are you this morning, Miss Deegan? Everything going okay?'

'Oh yes, Mr O'Keeffe. Thank you, Mr O'Keeffe.'

'Good. Anything you don't understand, ask Miss Harper. I'm sure you couldn't find a better teacher,' he said, and he was gone.

'He's gorgeous!' Breeda breathed. 'He's the most gorgeous fella I've ever seen.'

'All the girls say that,' Mavis replied, smiling cynically. 'Every single one of them set their caps at him and he's never once asked anyone here out. I had a go myself. That was before I met Terry, of course. But it was no use. An' he's not a poof! He's not married. I think he's just very ambitious.'

'So am I,' Breeda said calmly.

'Mebbe you might have luck with him. Ye never know unless ye try.'

Mavis leaned her elbows on the counter and cupped her chin in her hands. She slid her hip to one side and, slipping her foot out of her shoe, rubbed it on the back of her leg. 'It's the feet get you on this job,' she muttered. 'Janey, they're killin' me already. Mebbe you *could* snaffle O'Keeffe for yourself, Breeda, yer pretty enough. I wish you luck.'

I wish, I wish, I wish! Breeda leaned her elbows on the counter beside Mavis and speculated. If she was single-minded, if she put everything into being what he wanted in a woman, maybe, just maybe she could, as Mavis put it, snaffle him. But no! That would never happen. It would be the most marvellous, magical thing. Beyond her wildest dreams. Oh God. A moment before this thought entered her head, before Mavis gave her the idea it was possible, just barely possible to 'snaffle' Mr O'Keeffe, she had been gloriously happy because against all odds she had landed this job in Deary's. Without Leaving Cert, without even Inter she had landed the career of Perfume Counter assistant. Now, suddenly shifting gears, that was not enough! Now she wanted Mr O'Keeffe as well. Gawney, she *was* ambitious!

— 182 —

But she knew nothing about him. Just that she wanted him with a hopeless craving, with all her might. But she knew divil a bit about him!

Well now, hold on. She knew he loved his job. They had that in common. It was a start. He was ambitious and he loved his work. It was something to go on.

They had lunch in the canteen. At twelve-thirty a plump, freckled girl who had a body odour problem came and said Mr O'Keeffe had told her to come and relieve them so that they could go to lunch. 'He said you'd want to take her – the new girl I mean – wi' ye. Said she wouldn't want to venture into the lunch room alone her first day.'

'Thank you, Miss O'Reilly,' Mavis batted her thick lashes at the girl who, Breeda saw, had a nice smile. 'That shows consideration,' she whispered to Breeda.

'Not at all,' Miss O'Reilly slipped in behind the counter, over-whelming them with a mixture of ripe perspiration and menstrual scents. 'Only happy to help. He said that for today ye should go together.'

'Shows he was thinking of you,' Mavis said to Breeda, giggling. 'I *wish* Miss O'Reilly would take the hints about Immac cream and get rid of that pong!' she added *sotto voce*.

The canteen was a huge hangar-like room, vast and echoing. The furniture was basic and cheap: plywood tables and benches to sit on. At the bottom there was a counter, and white-aproned women with chef's hats served them such a plentitude of food that Breeda gulped and stared as she followed Mavis's example and took a tray and a knife, fork and spoon. She was open-mouthed and going to say something about the magnificence of the feast when Mavis, seeing her expression, grimaced. 'I know,' she said. 'It's awful, isn't it? 'Zackly like school. Meat an' gravy, peas an' mash every day 'cept Friday when we get plaice. Plaice an' peas an' mash,' she said, rolling up her eyes and sighing, and Breeda shut her mouth and nodded.

There was a lot she had to learn. To her, from the slum and the boiled hambone-broth, this was a feast. But, she quickly realized, to the more sophisticated Mavis it was pig-swill. That was what Mavis called it: pig-swill.

'Gawney, they'd feed pigeons better,' Mavis cried, winking at a lad from Fabrics. Mavis was very popular in the canteen, Breeda saw, and she kept her mouth shut and listened and learned as the crack and the banter swirled around her. The complaining was good-natured and there was a sense of escape from the discipline of the store, a feeling of school's out. They had a half-hour of freedom as they ate and it was a time to relax and be as silly as they pleased. They acknowledged her presence casually, some of them congratulating her on what they termed 'the incident' the day of her interview.

'They haven't a clue,' Mavis whispered, 'not a clue, but they know something happened to upset Mr McGillicuddy and Mrs Lepner, the scuds, and you did it an' that's enough to make 'em like you.'

'But I don't think I did it,' Breeda protested. 'I think it was all down to Mr O'Keeffe.'

'Never mind. Let them think it. 'Twill ease you into Deary's. They usually give new bods a hard time. At least you'll escape a ragging.'

Breeda saw Mr O'Keeffe sitting at a separate table with a group of other well-dressed, superior men. They were the big noises, Mavis said. There was a cloth on the table and the men laughed loudly not caring who heard. Lords of the Earth.

She stared at him so hard, admiring the back of his neck, smooth and tanned, his hairline neat as a manicured lawn. He must have felt her gaze for he turned, masticating and swallowing, and he saw her, and he smiled at her, a warm smile, then turned back and forked another mouthful.

'Gawney! He smiled at ye,' Mavis breathed.

'You saw?' Breeda's heart had stopped and now was knocking at her ribs ten to the dozen.

'I see *everything*,' Mavis said complacently. 'Didn't I see you comin' outa the office lookin' tragic and Mr O'Keeffe catchin' you and you going back in *and* I served two customers at the same time. Oh, I'm a genius, I am.'

Then a bell rang and they went back to the store. 'The one o'clock crowd will be comin' in now,' Mavis told her. 'We better get back and relieve Miss O'Reilly. Otherwise she'll be banjaxed.'

'Why?

'The bell rings at one-thirty and lunch is over. I mean *over*. It's like everything stops. Dead. And you have to *race* back to your post. God help ye if Mr McGillicuddy sees you come back late. He can report you an' ye're docked. Time lost.'

Breeda made a mental note as they took the stairs two at a time back to Perfume. As she ran, to give Miss O'Reilly her full half-hour, she gave little whoops of joy. Silently. This was the life! The job was great! Mr O'Keeffe smiled at her! What more could a girl want? This was what she had dreamed of. This was freedom. And she would be paid for doing something she loved. Being charming to customers, squirting the glorious fragrances on to their wrists.

And Mr O'Keeffe worked here and he had smiled at her. The impossible might become possible. Indeed what more could any girl want?

CHAPTER THIRTY-EIGHT

Lonny Clebber had had a bad day. They had had two funerals, both in the ProCathedral, then Glasnevin to bury them which meant a lot of running around. But funeral directors, as they were now being termed in America, could never be seen to rush and there was no way one could whizz the hearse down a back street to O'Laughlin's in order to get the second coffin to the ProCathedral *fast*. They did not finish up until one p.m.

'Off home, boy. There's nothin' for ye until tomorrow. I want ye here at the crack. Two corpses comin' in. Aye, tomorrow'll be busy.'

Lonny took the eleven bus to Findlater's Church, got off, then meandered up Dorset Street to Gardiner Street, then slowed and sat down on the bench opposite the slum dwelling where Breeda Deegan lived. He watched the shadowy hallway through slitted eyes but she never emerged. Once he saw the woman's face floating behind the window, but no Breeda.

She never came. One of the other kids pushed the dilapidated pram, a tall skinny kid, already old. He heard one of the little tykes call her Lizzy.

After a while, watching her struggle to maintain some order, Lonny strolled over to her. Dressed in his black funeral clothes he had an air of prosperity, of authority in this part of the world where most of the males were either layabouts or wore workman's overalls.

'Hey Miss – Lizzy, isn't it? Where's the other one, Breeda?'

'What's it te you?' the girl snapped, sharp as a razor.

He knew this was wrong. Knew he shouldn't talk to these kids. They could identify him and he had never done it before. He knew he should stay in the shadows, part of the scenery so no one ever really *saw* him. But he couldn't help it. Although the old hunter's instinct was once more firing him, he felt himself sometimes to be acting under constraint.

'I wanted to talk to her,' he said, nervously glancing around.

'What's it worth te ye?' Lizzy asked. Her eyes were slits and she winced up at him, her old/young face calculating.

'I'll give you half-a-crown if you don't say I talked to you. Not to anyone. I'd find out, mind.'

'That's a *fortune*!' the young part triumphed. 'Half-a-crown? Give it here an' I'll tell you.'

'You'll not tell a soul?'

'Cross my heart.' Her fingers closed around the coin, warm from his hand. She turned to run, to leave the children stranded on that patch of earth and tell him nothing, but he grabbed her shoulder in an iron grip.

'She's workin' now in Deary's,' she told him crossly. 'An' take yer hands offa me or I'll *scream*.' She yelled the last word, her face red, and he let her go instantly and turned and hurried down the street.

Deary's! That was why she was so pleased when she came out of the store the other day. She'd got herself a job. Little slum girl bettering herself. Bright sassy little bitch. With a smart-ass sister. So, he'd have to plan accordingly.

Daytime was out. No more hanging around that parched square of earth. Well, that was no loss. So, it would be Deary's after six. They closed at five thirty or six so she would have to come out not earlier than six, not later than six-thirty, or thereabouts. A few minutes here or there would be allowed for. It suited him just fine. There were no funerals at that time and when Mr O'Laughlin wanted help with a stiff it was usually at night.

'It's more peaceful then,' he said, 'and you don't mind workin' overtime, do you, boy?'

Lonny didn't. And he was in no hurry about Breeda. He had plenty of time. He could wait. He liked waiting. Watching and waiting his moment.

The next morning he reported for duty feeling good now that he had a plan of action. Now that he knew where he was going. He reported for work bright-eyed. The first corpse was no problem. All went smooth as silk. But the second was a hunchback and they had a terrible time getting him into the coffin. Mr O'Laughlin had done a powerfully good job on him and all was well until they found that when they pressed his knees down in the box he popped up in a sitting position and when they squeezed his top half down his legs flew up like a rugby player kicking a goal for Ireland. It took them the Dickens of a time to get it sorted but at last they had the poor ould fella under control and the coffin lid on.

'All I pray is he won't sit up in the middle of the service tomorrow,' Mr O'Laughlin breathed, wiping his sweating brow after the struggle. 'It'll be more than my job's worth if he Jack-in-the boxes during the service. Lonny, it might be a good idea to hammer a few nails in the coffin just to be on the safe side. He's powerful strong for a corpse, so he is.'

Lonny didn't care what the corpse did one way or another. He left the undertaker's at five and made his way to the Pillar.

It was a cold day. There was a snap in the air and the leaves rustled as they blew along the pavements. There was a smell of bonfires wafting on the air from St Stephen's Green and passersby had glowing cheeks.

He waited, as he had before, under the Pillar, his collar turned up as time passed and the wind sharpened. The flower vendor with her raucous voice that sawed the air screamed her wares and was soon joined by the paper seller shouting the evening papers: 'Heddlermail. Heddlermail.' Herald or Mail. Herald or Mail.

Soon the evenings would draw in and the flowerseller would be joined by the chestnut vendor and the lamps would light up at six.

He waited and still she did not come. The banks closed, the offices emptied and there were queues for the buses. The trams for Dun Laoghaire departed regularly from the Pillar and the cafés began to buzz and the cinemas started the evening's business. The lights went out in Deary's and still no Breeda.

Over his shoulder he saw the soda fountain slowly fill with young, eager-eyed couples and he remembered watching . . . who? Who was it he watched there? Imelda Manning? No, not here. Who? Oh yes, it was the thin one's sister. He could see the thin one's face now. Screaming. He pushed the thought aside and turned his attention to Deary's.

Where was she? He couldn't have missed her. It wasn't possible. Anyone with hair her colour stood out, flame-like, in a crowd. He watched and waited but still there was no sign of her.

Suddenly he felt very angry. Swamped with anger. He looked at the cigarette between his fingers and saw his hand was shaking. His knees felt weak and his temples throbbed. There was a red mist before his eyes. Where was she? Where the fuck was she?

'You waitin' fer someone? Haw?' The voice beside him made him jump. He hesitated. The fella was standing close, thin as a whippet, lean and stooped with a red nose with a drip on the end. 'Haw?' he repeated and sniffed. The drop quivered but remained pendent.

'Well, I'm waitin' for my girl. She works in Deary's.'

'She must be your new girl. Ye can't have come here before. Haw?'

'What do you mean?' Lonny was irritated, yet this fella seemed cognizant. Lonny waited, knowing the chap would have to speak soon.

'Sure they go out the back!' the fella said, knowing it all. 'Didn't ye know that? Yiv missed her. They've gone hours.'

Lonny turned on his heel and strode away up O'Connell Street. The fella yelled after him but Lonny was too angry to hear what he said.

He was in turmoil. Why had he spoken to that guy? Why? He must be mad. He was getting careless. The secrecy was going. He was asking the world and his wife about his quarry. Je-sus! The rules of the game were changing and he was scared.

He remembered the dark lonely places he had waited for others – the lane by McGuire's pub for Arlene, the Masters garden for Bette and Fliss and the cobblestoned alley for Imelda. All places where he was unlikely to be seen, yet with the tension of doubt about it; someone could show unexpectedly. Like the boy that day, staring at him in the bushes. But to hang about here, in the crowded city centre at rush hour, talk to some guy, having already spoken to that zappy child, Breeda's sister. Oh God, was he losing his mind?

For a moment he hesitated. He thought of going to Gardiner Street, watching there for a while, but decided against it. In the mood he was in he didn't trust himself.

He'd never felt like this before and he wondered what to do when before he had always been certain. He had been outside life, apart from others. But he had broken his rule and talking with that fella had somehow become part of the human race. And he didn't want that. Not at all.

He'd go to the Public Baths and immerse himself. Stay there for a while. Then he'd go home. He felt the usual lurch of fear, then reassured himself. 'Get offa me, Ma.' He'd tell her to piss off if she came anywhere near him. It would be okay. Mr O'Laughlin had a funeral tomorrow. The hunchback. He grinned mirthlessly. He'd be free after that. He'd wait for her tomorrow and this time he'd know where to position himself. He'd wait for her at the entrance at the back. Yes. He'd do that. No problem.

CHAPTER THIRTY-NINE

'Commenced surveillance this morning, sir.'

'Good.'

'I follied the suspect to the undertaker's, from his home, where we started,' the young red-cheeked garda told O'Malley, 'then he went to the Pillar. Waited there – oh – ages. Then walked away. Went to the Public Baths in Pearse Street. Then home. Nuthin' else.'

'Did he speak to anyone?' O'Malley asked.

'Yep. One fella. I asked him after. He shouted something after Clebber – "No honkey tonight" – and I said, "What was all that about?" Fella, real know-it-all, said, "Fella told me his girlfriend worked in Deary's. Eejit didn't know the staff came out the back way in the lane off Cathedral Street." I said, "Gawney, he was an eejit." Asked him, "Did you tell him they came out back?" He said, "'Course I did." Then he laughed and said, "He'll be in trouble. Poor fella. No honkey tonight." That's all, sir.'

'What's honkey, McGuigan, do you know?' O'Malley stared at the young policeman under bushy eyebrows.

The boy looked enquiringly back. He couldn't make up his mind if he was being quizzed or not. He went burgundy and looked at his feet. 'Well . . . hanky-panky . . . you *know*, sir!'

'I see. Yes. I suppose I should have guessed.' O'Malley looked squarely at him and gave him a faint smile. 'Well done, my boy. Very well done. Is Rahilly on duty? At the Tolka?'

'Yes, sir. Though how anyone can live in that cottage I just don't know. It's covered in moss and ivy and slime. It's slipping into the river. Halfway there, I reckon. It must be damp as a beaver's set, so it must. It's like *Macbeth*, sir.'

'Really?'

'Yes, sir. A shambles of a mud-hut.' O'Malley didn't ask the garda where he got his idea of *Macbeth*. 'But I'm to take over duty at eight a.m., sir.'

'Good.'

'And should I follow him if he goes to Deary's back entrance, sir?' A note of excitement entered the young man's voice. He had just seen a movie with Broderick Crawford as an undercover policeman following a murderer and saw himself in the part. That was why he had joined the Gardai. And he bore a striking resemblance to Broderick Crawford. Although his mam didn't think so. She thought he was more like John Garfield. But she was the only one. His girlfriend thought he was like Broderick Crawford. *He* thought he was like Broderick Crawford.

'Yes, McGuigan. I'll be there too. I want that bastard. But we have nothing on him. No evidence at all.' He glanced at the young man. 'I can trust you to be careful, I'm sure.' McGuigan nodded his head vigorously. 'We have to be careful. We mustn't scare him off. We must not arouse his suspicions. And we mustn't arrest him without due cause.'

'You mean we have to let him attack the girl?'

'Precisely. That is why we cannot afford to lose sight of him for a second.'

'Yes, sir.'

'You did well, McGuigan,' O'Malley said again. 'We know now, thanks to you, that he is after one of the girls from Deary's. Well, I'll see you tomorrow.'

'Yes, sir. Thank you, sir.'

Things were hotting up and O'Malley felt jubilant. He tried to tell himself that he *might* be wrong, that this might *not* be the perpetrator of the terrible rapes and the murder of Imelda Manning, but in his bones he *knew* it was. He knew too that Mr Lonny Clebber had chosen another victim. That was why he waited outside Deary's. The girl, whoever it was, worked there. How many others had there been? Defiled and pillaged, bestially attacked, unknown victims of Lonny Clebber's foul appetite. God alone knew. O'Malley shuddered. Lovely young girls, flowers in their first bloom, blighted by that scum. He was sure that Imelda Manning and Arlene Shaughnessy were not the only two. A lot of victims of rape never reported it. They would never tell what had happened to them. They were too ashamed. They would not contact the police, could not face up to the public's scrutiny, the inevitable ordeal, so they said nothing, licked their wounds in private and never recovered. He thought of Arlene Shaughnessy and shook his head. She had had the courage. She had such gumption, but society had failed her.

'Lonny Clebber, I'm going to get you,' O'Malley whispered to himself. 'With luck, you little scud, tomorrow night.'

CHAPTER FORTY

'He's gorgeous, Mam, really gorgeous, like someone in the films!'

'That was quick off the mark, Breeda,' her mother said. 'Meetin' a man yer first day.'

'What does it take, Mam? Only a minute! A second! I looked an' I knew.' She was excited and Nuala Deegan was excited for her. It reminded her of hope. She was buoyed up by her daughter's excitement.

'Well apart from yer fancy man how was the job?' she asked, able to crack a joke.

'Great, Mam, great. Pure lovely. I love customers. I love showin' them the scents, tryin' it out on them. Oh, Mam, I'm really happy there.'

'Well then, see ye work hard an' keep yer nose clean and everythin' will be hunkey-dorey.'

Her mother pulled the plug and chain out of the sink and the water gurgled down.

'That fella's not there tonight,' she said.

'Which fella?'

'The one that was there the other night. The one with O'Laughlin the undertaker.'

'So what?' Breeda was indifferent.

'He spoke to Lizzy,' Nuala said. 'I saw him.' She looked over her shoulder at her second child. 'What'd he say to ye, Liz?'

Lizzy looked blank. 'Nuthin',' she said flatly. She had learned early in life that if you denied anything firmly and persistently enough eventually they believed you. It was politic to deny everything.

'Yer lyin'. He did. I saw him,' Charlie snarled. He liked to think of himself as a hard man, did Charlie, so he snarled.

'I din' hear him then.'

'He gave her money,' Charlie growled at his mother but she was not listening.

'I'll get you lovely flour from the Blanchardstown Mills an' butter from Kerry instead of drippin', an' rashers on Friday,' Breeda was saying.

'We can't eat rashers on Friday. It's fast!' Lizzy cried, shocked out of her silence by this suggestion of sacrilege.

'I meant I'd *buy* them on Friday. When I get paid. You don't have te eat them till Saturday.' Breeda rolled up her eyes as she had seen Mavis do, appealing to Heaven to witness her sister's stupidity. Lizzy, not to be outdone, poked out her tongue and made a horrible face and Breeda said calmly, 'You'll get stuck like that, Lizzy, an' you not careful.'

Nuala Deegan looked worried.

'What's the matter, Mam? What's up?' Breeda asked her. Breeda always sensed her mother's changes of mood.

'Yer da was talkin' about you givin' him yer pay-packet, for the house,' Nuala said, then she turned to Breeda and took her by the shoulders. 'But don't ye listen to him, Breeda dear. Eh? Don't.'

'Yer da was what?' Sean stood in the doorway, smiling benignly. He had reached just the right level in drink, the booze comfortable on his stomach.

'God, I could murder tay. Where's my supper, woman?'

'Sure I'm just poppin' it on,' Nuala said placatingly. 'The kettle's on the hob. I'll pour you a nice strong mug instantly. Set down, Sean, set you down an 'twill be in front of ye before ye know it.'

'An' what were ye sayin', I said, Nuala love?'

'Sure nuthin', Sean. Nuthin'.'

'Oh yes 'twas! You were tellin' Miss Breeda here not to give me her pay-packet an' I distinctly ordered ye to tell her it was to go to the housekeeping.' His equanimity was fast evaporating.

'Down yer throat, ye mean,' Breeda said coldly.

'An' what if it does? Amant I the master here? Amant I yer father? Good as?'

'No! Ye'll not touch it, Sean, an' yer *not* my father, never were.' Breeda's voice was calm.

Sean banged the table suddenly with his clenched fist, making them jump. 'Ye'll give it me or ye'll lave this place.'

Nuala, behind his back, nodded vigorously. She wanted Breeda to find herself a nice room in a better area but she couldn't say that in front of her husband. So she nodded her head and hoped Breeda understood.

'Well, an' I'll leave then!' Breeda said unperturbed. 'Or we can make an arrangement an' I'll give Mam, *only* Mam, money for board and lodging. Or it can go to a stranger – ye take yer pick.'

She wasn't afraid of Sean. Like most bullies he was insecure, all bluster and puff.

'It's up to you, Sean. Mam gets the money an' the conditions are that ye don't touch it. Ye'll probably get a better class of food, but ye don't touch it or it goes to some landlady in Harold's Cross or Drimnagh and this house doesn't benefit at all. Up to you.'

'Why, ye little whoor.' He lunged across the table at her but she stepped back and he stumbled and sat down precipitately, a startled expression on his face. Lizzy sniggered.

'Clean out yer mouth, Sean. I'm not a whoor. An' ye can take my offer or I'm off this night, never fear.'

She smiled at Nuala, put an arm around her mother and gave her a gentle squeeze. 'I'm off to bed now, Mam. Tell the little ones to be quiet. I'm knackered, so I am. It's been a long day.'

She needn't have worried, she was too tired for them to disturb her. No one could keep order like Breeda, and Nuala, her hands full with Sean and the supper, was quite unable to check them in the other room, so the rafters rang with their shouts and teasings and quarrels and sudden tantrums and bouts of crying, but Breeda heard not a sound. Her eyelids did not even flutter as the children leap-frogged over her. She lay still as a corpse until morning.

CHAPTER FORTY-ONE

The next day unfolded like the one before and Breeda was just as content. It was slightly more stressful insofar as she had to face the canteen alone. People nodded but no one spoke to her. Intent on their own affairs, in obviously friendly pairs, they had a million things to catch up with since the day before and no time for her, a stranger.

She didn't mind. She could hear them,

'An' so I said to him, I said, "If ye don't take us to Killarney this year I'm leavin' ye. I'm sick of bloody Rush. It's Killarney or ye can kiss me goodbye!"'

'"Take yer hands offa me," I told him, "I'm *not* that sorta girl." But, Angie, tell ye the truth,' (sigh) 'I'm that sorry he stopped . . .'

'It's a lovely shade of vermilion an' I read in *Woman's Own* that it's the colour of the year. Teamed with grey or black.'

She sat alone. It wouldn't be long before she too would be sharing the events of the previous evening with a friend. And her hopes. Her dreams. But not yet. It was too soon yet. She was patient, she could wait.

She chewed her mince and stared at the wall where huge Deary's advertisements from bygone years hung, showing corsets, bonnets, Liberty bodices, chemises, men's long johns (that one had a man in a boxer's pose with a huge handlebar moustache).

As she gazed at the wall she felt a hand on her shoulder and she turned and looked up into the twinkling eyes of Mr O'Keeffe. She gulped and the meat went down the wrong way and she choked and sputtered and gulped as if she was being strangled.

He handed her a glass of water and she drank it down gratefully, emptying it in seconds. The coughing subsided.

'I'm sorry, Miss Deegan. I didn't mean to startle you.'

Oh God! Her face must be red as a beetroot. Like her mother's hands. Vermilion, the colour of the year. Damn, damn, damn.

'Are you all right?' he was asking her now, sitting beside her. A sudden hush fell over the canteen. A lot of heads turned. Most of the girls in their pink overalls were watching. O'Keeffe sitting beside one of them!

'I'm fine now thank you, Mr O'Keeffe.'

She stared up at him, holding his blue eyes with hers, her lip trembling.

'Miss Deegan,' he said slowly, 'will you come to the pictures with me one evening?'

It was so unexpected that she nearly choked again. She said nothing for a moment, just stared at him.

'Will you? Don't keep me on tenterhooks. Have I offended you?'

She simply nodded. 'Yes, sir. I will. I'd love to.'

'Not sir. Mr O'Keeffe here. Desmond outside. Des.'

'Yes, Mr O'Keeffe.'

He was gazing at her, smiling. 'We're very formal here, Miss Deegan. It's good for business. Makes the customers think we're sober, serious people.'

'Yes, Mr O'Keeffe. Mav . . . Miss Harper told me.'

He stood up. 'Okay!' His eyes were sparkling. 'Hunkey-dorey! Friday then. Pay-day. Let's celebrate. There's a grand film on at the Metropole, *Roman Holiday*. I'm sure you'd like it. Have you seen it? Gregory Peck and Audrey Hepburn?'

She shook her head, 'No, Mr O'Keeffe. I haven't seen it. I'd love to.'

'We'll have tea there first. We'll go from here. I'll meet you outside. Okay?'

'Okay.'

How could she tell him he had nearly killed her with excitement? She sat there, letting it simmer inside her. The rapture! She tried to keep the worries away, at least for the moment. What would she wear? He'd want to take her home afterwards, it was what polite people did, and how could she let him see where she lived? She'd lose him for sure if he found out she lived in a slum in Gardiner Street. Oh Janey!

No, no. She'd not think of that now. She'd just let this glorious feeling ripple over her – Jasus, I could drown in it, she thought.

The freckled little O'Reilly girl shook her arm. 'Miss Deegan, hurry back or poor Miss Harper'll miss lunch altogether.'

'Oh golly. Thanks, Miss O'Reilly. I forgot.'

'Sure wouldn't Mr O'Keeffe put the Day of Judgement owa anyone's mind,' a Miss Doyle from Cosmetics remarked archly in passing.

Breeda grinned but said nothing and hopped it back to Perfume.

'Mavis, Mavis, I'm sorry, Miss Harper, I'm sorry, I'm sorry . . .'

'Hey . . . hey . . . what's the matter? Calm down. Where's the fire?'

'Your lunch . . . I forgot . . .'

'Yer not late, God's sake.'

'Mr O'Keeffe's after askin' me out.'

Mavis let out a piercing scream, then when two customers turned and stared she pretended she hadn't.

'Ye mustn't tell,' Breeda pleaded.

'I won't! Cross my heart I won't,' Mavis swore.

'Yer lunch. Ye'll be late for it.'

Mavis looked at her with amusement. 'Honest, ye'd think ye were starvin' the way food is important to ye,' she said. 'I'll have a piece of pie – it should be apple today. And a coffee. Take me quarter of an hour. Easy. This is much more interesting – go on, tell me all.'

'Well, we're goin' to the Metropole Friday. It's *Roman Holiday*.'

Mavis let out another scream. 'Oh it's gorgeous!' she breathed. 'So romantic! You'll love it.'

'And we're having tea in the Metropole first.'

Another squeal. 'Oh, they have a band there. Soft lighting and romantic music. Oh Janey! You'll be toasted, so you will.' She nudged Breeda. 'Don't let anyone know. Otherwise the whole staff'll be there. In the Metropole. Watching.'

Breeda was aghast. 'Oh no, Mavis . . . Miss Harper . . . no!'

'Don't worry. I'll not breathe a word.' She looked at Breeda's worried frown. 'What's the matter wi' you? You've won the Sweep an' ye look all troubled. What's up?'

'Oh, it's just that . . . I've nothing to wear and it'll be too late to buy anything Friday, and . . .'

'Simmer down now, simmer down.' Mavis took her hand. 'Listen to me. Tonight, after work, come home with me and we'll go through my

wardrobe an' you can take yer pick.' Breeda stared at her. Such gen-
erosity was outside her experience. She started to protest but Mavis
continued. 'Listen. Terry, me boyfriend, is a car salesman. He works in
Ginty's in Dawson Street and he drives a Caddy like the Yanks. He'll
pick us up in front in O'Connell Street, five forty-five on the dot. Hell
take us home. My rooms are in Harcourt Street so it's not far. And you
can pick a dress. I've got thousands. I spend all me spare on clothes
and me mam spoils me an' so does Terry. He likes me in nice things.
He likes me to look snazzy.' She batted her eyelashes. 'We're getting
married next spring.'

'Well, Mavis, if you're sure . . .'

'I'm sure. I like you, Breeda. We're going to be good friends.'

'Oh yes. We are already. Now go . . . go get your lunch.'

Mavis smiled at her. 'I won't starve,' she said and trotted off to the
canteen.

Maybe Mam's prayers to the Virgin do work after all, Breeda
thought and turned to a stout lady in a swagger coat and a fox-fur tip-
pet across her shoulders. The fox had his tail in his mouth and looked
at her with glazed eyes. Some of the fur had worn off his cheeks and
the lady kept nervously rubbing her finger on the bald spot.

'Er, Miss . . . I wanted . . . could I see . . . smell something . . .
em . . . well . . . a bit . . .'

'You'd like something spicy with an undertone of musk,' Breeda
offered fluently, remembering what Mavis had taught her.

The woman looked at her gratefully. 'It's so modern you know,' she
said. 'Wearing scent. We always wore eau-de-Cologne or lavender
water as gels. It's only recently that a lady . . . well, my husband
wouldn't like it at all if he knew, and I'm a bit at sea when it comes to
buying. He goes by what his mother told him, but when he smells it
on me . . .' She blushed and looked coy, 'Well . . .' Breeda smiled sym-
pathetically and the lady confided: 'He likes the smell,' she said. 'He
thinks it's natural.'

Mr O'Keeffe passed by, nodded in approval and Breeda busied
herself looking after her customer. She sold a bottle of *Je Reviens*,
large size, and was congratulated by Mavis on her return from the
canteen.

They were at the main entrance of Deary's, under the clock, at five
forty-five. At five forty-six a car drew up, a huge car, light beige, and
the passenger door was thrown open. Mavis hurried over, said

something to the driver and opened the back door. She beckoned Breeda, who ran to the shining, purring monster beside the pavement and slid into the rear seat. It smelled of leather and luxury, and she curled up in its ample roominess then turned expectantly to be introduced to Mavis's boyfriend.

'This is my friend Breeda,' Mavis told the jolly-faced young man in the driver's seat. 'This is Terry, Breeda.'

'Howdy-do an' all that jazz, any friend of Mavis, etcetera. How'd you like being one of Deary's slaves?'

Mavis giggled. 'She's mad!' she replied, indicating Breeda. 'She loves it.'

'Never!' he cried.

'Yeah! Guess what, Ter? O'Keeffe's asked her out Friday. Can you believe it?'

'Sure! 'Course I can. You're a smasher, Breeda,' he said, glancing over his shoulder and easing out into the traffic. 'Mavis already told me. Hey, you can have any man you want, hair like that! Beats the band. Rita Hayworth watch out!'

'Oh, Ter! He's terrible, Breeda. Don't pay any attention.'

Breeda liked him. He was easy to be with, an uncomplicated sort of fellow with an open face and a happy-go-lucky nature. Quite unlike any of the men in Gardiner Street.

They drove up Nassau Street and turned into Stephen's Green, the huge car drawing some attention as they passed.

'It's as big as a hearse,' Breeda told Terry, who laughed and said, 'Yeah! They think I'm a Yank, so they do. Does me no harm.'

When they arrived at Harcourt Terrace Mavis said, 'The canal's there in front of the house. God help us, it's a tip, it really is. In hot weather it stinks. An' it could be lovely. But the rubbish that gets dumped there! God, ye wouldn't believe what ye'd find there on a bad day.'

'Come on, Mavis. I'm dyin' for a drink. Ye can give the tour-guide later,' Terry said and turned to Breeda. 'She's a very tidy woman is Mavis. Likes everything neat and pretty, so she does.' There was admiration in his voice and Breeda could see them as a totally compatible couple.

'Well I like an orderly existence,' Mavis said, lips pursed. 'After all, we're not animals.'

Terry, when he got out of the car, revealed himself to be a stocky young man with black hair tightly curled, like a sheep, over his head. He had a charming grin and was neatly dressed. He suited Mavis, like they were composed by the same creator, like book-ends, incomplete without each other. Mavis had a soft femininity, and she looked up to Terry as her mentor and guide. He responded to this by being masterful and masculine, taking charge and looking after Mavis as if she was china.

The apartment reflected their joint personalities, and it quite took Breeda's voice away. She couldn't believe it. Sure, she had seen gracious rooms, grand rooms in films, but it had never occurred to her that they existed in real life. They were flickering images in fantasy up there, peopled by the unreal. That real people could live in comfort she knew, but that people could have knick-knacks, cushions, frilly curtains, pictures, vases of flowers, candlesticks, fancy lights and lampshades, ornaments, lace tablecloths, pouffes, books and magazines and, would you believe it, a bowl of fruit, Gawney Mac!

Mavis's two rooms on the second floor possessed all these treasures. They were big, spacious, and the walls were painted apricot and there was a wall-to-wall carpet. There were great heavy apricot curtains drawn back and the windows were draped in snowy net with frills. The furniture was covered in a shiny beige fabric and there was a large sofa and two armchairs. There was a table with four upright chairs around it in an alcove and some bookshelves and a drinks cabinet.

'Got it all from Deary's on the never-never,' Mavis told an open-mouthed Breeda. 'That sofa opens out into a bed.'

The apartment was a revelation to Breeda. She was learning so fast, so fast. She had never in her life seen anything like Mavis Harper's apartment and was grappling with that and the knowledge that Mavis was after all only a counter assistant in Deary's, and if she had an apartment like this what would the homes of the staff higher up be like? The mind reeled.

The bedroom was like something out of the movies and Mavis told her, 'I got pictures out of *Picturegoer*, this room Deanna Durbin had in *Three Smart Girls*, and I copied it exactly. See the drapes around the bed? 'Zackly the same.'

A further revelation was the way Mavis and Terry behaved towards each other. They were so obviously loving, so good-natured, so aware of each other. They *listened* to each other, often laughed before one or other finished a sentence as if they could read each other's mind.

Terry went to the drinks cabinet. It played a tune when he opened it. He poured them a drink, or, as he put it, 'Mixed them a Martini'. Breeda had never heard of Martini. Alcohol to her was a pint in a pub.

And they sat on the sofa and chatted. Terry and Mavis held hands, Terry played with her fingers. It was amazing, another kind of life. No 'Where's me tay, woman!' No clutter. No laundry drying overhead. No children screaming. No shouting from the neighbours. No smells. No rows. No decay. Just well-dressed people sitting in a quiet room, sipping a cocktail. That was what Mavis called the Martinis, cocktails. And with each lesson Breeda learned she knew there was no going back. Now that she knew what was available she could not return to squalor and deprivation. As each new aspect of decent living was revealed to her the more revolted she was by her poverty-stricken environment at home. She knew she would have to leave it behind her very, very quickly. Knew she would adopt new standards very quickly.

'Listen, Breeda, why don'tcha move in here with me?' she heard Mavis asking. Like it was nothing. Breeda was nonplussed. Things were moving too fast. She was not used to change and she took a deep breath in order to keep up.

'Wha . . .?'

'Listen, don't make up yer mind in a hurry. It's just a thought.'

'Gosh, it'd be great though!' Terry exclaimed, lacing his fingers through Mavis's. 'We're savin' up to get married. It'd help if ye shared the rent wi' Mavis.' His good-natured face was turned lovingly towards his girlfriend and he leaned over and kissed her temple as Breeda watched, fascinated.

Mavis, ever businesslike, said, 'I wouldn't charge you the full half. 'Twouldn't be fair. I have the bedroom all to myself an' you wouldn't have privacy during the day, so what if I said, say, one pound ten shillings a week – thirty bob? If you wanted to share, I mean?'

Breeda was listening engrossed. She had never sat in a lovely room, sipping a drink, chatting about moving house as if it was the most ordinary thing in the world, as if everyone had a choice.

'Tell you what,' Mavis suggested. 'Why don't you give it a try.' She leaned forward. 'See, I'd like the company as well as the money.'

'Can't bear to be alone, my Mavis,' Terry smiled fondly. 'Loves someone to talk to.'

Breeda remembered her date with Desmond O'Keeffe. It would be great to live here, have him bring her home here, introduce him to Terry, offer him a drink. Not have to bring him to the slum. She frowned. Maybe he wouldn't bring her home at all. Maybe the evening would be a disaster. Oh no. She wasn't going to think like that; it was unlucky. But whether he did or he didn't it would solve all her problems, moving here. Help her so much not having to give Gardiner Street as the address where she lived.

'Mavis, I'd love to. I only hesitate because . . . me mam . . . me mam . . .'

'Well, ask her.'

'Yeah! She'd like me to. I know that. She's always urging me to get out of . . . But I haveta ask her. To explain.'

'Tell you what. I'll drive ye home now an' ye can ask her,' Terry offered. 'When she sees me she'll know it's respectable.'

'Oh no!' Breeda protested. They both looked at her, the vehemence of her protest startling them. 'Oh no! I'll ask her when . . . when . . .'

'Don't rush her, Ter,' Mavis smiled at her boyfriend. 'Real get-up and-go is Ter. Quick on the mark. He'll get along. And he's that keen to get married, aren't you, dear? He doesn't understand that people don't always move as fast as he does. An' he's anxious for you to say yes.'

'Well, every penny counts,' Terry said. 'An' you're a cute kid, just the sort Mavis gets on with. Have another Martini?'

'He's determined to have enough to get married in the spring,' Mavis said.

'Doesn't that . . . forgive me, but isn't that expensive . . . the Martini?'

Terry had his back to them at the musical drinks cabinet. He looked over his shoulder at Breeda, grinned and winked. 'Sure is. Canny girl. I know what you're saying. If every penny counts how come they're spending money on drink?' He turned, cocktail shaker in his hand. 'But see, Mavis and I talked about it.' Mavis nodded vehemently. 'Discussed it fully, an' she agrees with my philosophy of life. I believe the quality of our lives is most important. There is a standard below which I will not go. I *won't* save by giving up all the little luxuries that make our lives so enjoyable.'

Well for some, Breeda thought, shifting gear again. God, she was learning.

'It's what I tell our customers: "Do you want a car like any other car? A Ford, or a Volkswagen? Or do you want to pay a few quid extra and have luxury?" Well, most of 'em go for the safe and sound. Most people opt for security, but I figure that if I aim to provide myself with the best I'll achieve it. By hard work, but in the meantime I'll not deprive myself of life's little luxuries. Oh no! Every day for Mavis and me there is abundance. That's how I see it. Comfort and abundance.'

Mavis smiled through this and nodded her head. Breeda listened riveted. 'I make a comfortable livin', see. A very comfortable livin'.' Terry waxed eloquent. 'An' when Mavis an me marry, we won't live in a poky little apartment like this, will we, Mavis?' Breeda gulped, and Mavis shook her head. 'Not likely! We'll have a snug little bungalow in one of the new developments. That's what we'll have. Newly decorated. Everything fresh. Dandy. Eh, Mavis?'

Breeda felt shell-shocked. Having found herself in this fabulous place she now discovered she was supposed to despise it. Terry was shaking the cocktail mixer and he replenished their glasses, warmly expanding his theme and glancing every now and then at Mavis for affirmation. 'See this place?' he asked. 'See the drinks? Look at Mavis. She wants for nuthin'. Look at her, groomed as good as Lauren Bacall any day. No. It's my way, Breeda. Each day should be lived as if it were your last . . .'

'Oh, Ter . . .' Mavis rolled her eyes, then looked at Breeda conspiritorially. 'I hate it when he gets to this bit . . . talkin' about death!' But Breeda could see she was proud as Punch of her fella and his ideas.

'Suppose I died tomorrow?' Terry asked dramatically. 'I'd be able to say I'd not missed much. I've driven the best. I've eaten good food in Jamet's, the Hibernian, the Red Bank, the Bailey. Mavis an' me both.'

She nodded eagerly as he expounded his theory, 'Gorgeous meals,' she whispered to Breeda. 'Smashing food. So glamorous.'

'I've had cocktails in the Shelbourne and Davy Byrne's. I've gone to tea in the Gresham and the Metropole . . .' Breeda gave a little squeak and Mavis giggled and nudged her, but Terry didn't notice. 'No,' he continued, 'I have no time for those doom-and-gloom merchants who warn you all the time about ending in the gutter and talk non-stop about pensions.' Breeda's mouth was open and she drew in her breath sharply. What he was saying was sacrilegious! She had ached for that: a safe job, save up, pension at the end. How wonderful that seemed to her. Now this fella was saying it was all wrong. She listened breathless. 'The way I see it, what's the point of a life that's lived solely to survive? Work, work, work. Save, save, save. It's struggle, that's what it is, struggle.'

Breeda thought of Sean whom she despised. The way he lived his life was nearer to what Terry advocated than her mother. Was her mother a fool then to be so unselfish? Breeda's mind was in a whirl.

'No. I think every day should be pleasurable. Treats. Have fun in it, otherwise what's the point of life? Might as well be dead.' He sat down and looked at Breeda intently. 'Mavis said you loved Deary's? Hum?' She nodded, still breathless. 'I think that's great. I think that's smashing. You *should* enjoy your work. I think everyone should.' He looked around. 'I enjoy mine.' His brown eyes sparkled. 'I *love* mine. Mavis doesn't.' He smiled at her ruefully. 'But that's all right. She's longing to be a housewife. She'll love that.'

'That's what I was made for,' Mavis said, sipping her drink, little finger extended in genteel fashion. 'I can't wait, Breeda.'

'But in the meantime,' Terry interrupted, 'in the meantime we must enjoy life. We can't mark time. It's not on. Save your dough, sit on it – have a lovely funeral – that's not the way I think. See, every day should be a fun day. Well, that's how I see it.'

Breeda had never heard such talk before. The ideas crowded into her head, jostled about with a lot of hows and whys and reallys. She couldn't think straight, couldn't get the jumble in order, didn't know what she thought. She was so bemused that she forgot about where she lived and allowed Terry to steer her into the car and close the door behind her and when he asked 'Where to?' she was so embarrassed she stammered an incoherent 'Gardiner Street', so softly he could not hear.

'It doesn't matter where you're from, Breeda,' he said, sensing there was something wrong. 'It's where you're going to that counts.'

All her shame about the slum disappeared. What he said was right. It was not her fault that she had been born in penury. It would only shame her if she did not try to escape it. She told him where she lived in a clear voice and without comment he drove her across town and dropped her in front of the doorless tenement building. He got out of the car and opened the door for her as if she were a princess. She got out, glanced at him uncertainly. He gave her an encouraging wink and said, 'See you, Breeda. Think about what we discussed,' and watched her as she went into the dark open mouth of the house and disappeared. Then he turned around, bounded back into the car and glided away.

He did not see the figure lurking in the shadowy street, the figure in his John Garfield polo-neck and raincoat, pulling sulkily on a Craven A.

CHAPTER FORTY-TWO

Lonny Clebber was confused and angry. He smouldered resentfully as Breeda proved a far from satisfactory quarry. All the others had a routine or he had access to information about where they were going, where they would be. Breeda Deegan was turning out to be an exasperating and slippery customer.

He had waited for her at the rear entrance of Deary's, holding back, a shadowy figure blending with the background. But she never came. That bastard had said the employees all emerged from this door but Breeda never showed. Others streamed out of the building, men and girls laughing louder in their release from supervision, chatting, hurrying home or off on dates, or making a dash for the pub opposite for a drink.

But no Breeda. He waited until they were all gone, the last few stragglers had left, then drove his fist into the brick wall behind him in his rage.

Where was she? Where could she have gone? Infuriated he walked right around the block, not once but three times, passing the firmly closed doors of Deary's, walking under the clock whose hands now pointed to seven o'clock, and around the square again. No sign of her. None at all. Where could the bitch be?

He was restless, burning with anxiety and frustration, enraged as a big cat deprived of its prey. He could not let it be, let it slide until the morrow. The rage was inside him and he tossed and turned mentally until he thought his head would burst.

So he went to Gardiner Street. He walked as twilight fell, coat collar turned up, kicking out viciously at the piles of leaves and the tyres of cars parked beside the pavement, and now and again he took a swipe at a tree or a lamp-post.

And behind him another walked, inconspicuous, following at some discreet paces, watching him.

And waited with him outside the tenements in Gardiner Street. Lonny Clebber did not register in any obvious way Breeda Deegan's arrival home, nor did he leave the street once she had gone inside. He had watched all the comings and goings in the street equally intently, crouched, as if ready to spring, so McGuigan could not have told O'Malley who in particular Lonny Clebber had come to see. There were a lot of people about: drunks, workmen drifting home, some weary from work, some slightly relaxed from a few pints in the pub, others legless. There were women sitting on the doorsteps gossiping, women leaning out of windows shouting to each other, women nursing babies, women rocking prams, women trudging home from factories or service. There were pasty-faced children playing hop-scotch, swinging out of ropes tied to the lamp-posts, puffing on fags in the area basements or simply hanging out around corners. Corner-boys, they were called. There were a lot of young girls about, flirting with the boys or hurrying home from work, but which of them worked in Deary's the policeman could not guess.

O'Malley next day set in motion discreet enquiries in the neighbourhood but his men came up with nothing. The tenement dwellers closed ranks and would not talk to the Gardai. They were certain the polis were interested in what was going down and were not prepared to divulge any information at all about the Deegan family or let them know Breeda had landed a job in Deary's. Sean might have been up to his old tricks nicking the odd quota of stock from the building site. Or they might be checking up on Breeda herself, who, you never knew, might have been palming stuff from the store. At any rate it was them and us and no one was taking any chances. You didn't grass in Gardiner Street. And if Breeda or Sean was involved in a scam so much the better an' good luck to them. Didn't Sean stand his round in the pub like a gentleman.

'Look, we just need to know which of the lassies here works in the department store,' Rahilly asked and was rewarded by blank stares.

'Don't know.'

'Never heard no wan was workin' there.'

'Haven't a clue.'

'It's for the lassie's own good,' Rahilly told them.

Grins all round. 'Oh'n' I'm sure of that. Oh yes! For her good. I suppose whoever yer lookin' for is in mortal danger an' only the polis is goin' to save her?' And a burst of derisive laughter.

Constable Rahilly looked severe. 'You could say that,' he told them seriously, being as honest as he dared within the parameters of how much he had been told he could divulge. But they only jeered him and would not listen.

Rahilly and McGuigan followed Lonny Clebber around for the next few days and all Lonny did, when he was not working in the undertaker's, was wander around Deary's, go to Gardiner Street, and generally appear either furious or dejected. He never seemed to find what he was looking for and the policemen said there was no one person they had seen at either place. An extensive search revealed no one in the employ who had an address in Gardiner Street. O'Malley had to reluctantly concede that his hunch was erroneous. He was still sure that Lonny Clebber was his man, but could not work out what Gardiner Street had to do with Deary's.

'I think,' he told his by now bored men, 'that the girl lives somewhere else. We'll have to find out where.'

'Do we still keep up surveillance?' Rahilly asked.

'Of course,' O'Malley replied, glancing at the man irritably. 'And remember Rahilly, McGuigan, we are trying to prevent another rape. Another murder.'

They followed him with less and less enthusiasm. From O'Laughlin's to Deary's, the back entrance, the front entrance, around and around, then to Gardiner Street. Waiting there in the now chill weather. Waiting in the evening while the populace sneered, well aware of their presence. Then they followed him back to his miserable little hovel beside the Tolka.

CHAPTER FORTY-THREE

Breeda Deegan had told her mother that night on her return from Mavis Harper's all about the offer she had received.

'An' it's wonderful, Mam, such an apartment you wouldn't believe. All modern. Gorgeous. Like the filums.'

'Ye must go, Breeda. It's better ye do. It's the only way ye can escape outa here.'

Breeda, sitting at the table, lifted an anxious face to her mother.'But, Mam, I want te help ye. It's more important than anything.'

Her mother turned from the sink, sighing and pushing back her hair with her forearm, a damp cloth of dubious colour clutched in her hand. 'Listen to me, darlin'. Get outa here while ye can. I'm tellin' ye. Don't get trapped here. An' don't worry about me. I'm all right. I *chose* this for meself, so I did. I know ye think I'm hard done by, Breeda, but I'm not tryin' te escape, am I? I'm here, amant I? Because I want to be an' ye'll never understand that.' She sat down opposite her daughter and continued earnestly, 'Ye'll help me most by takin' that offer and goin'. Ye can help me wi' the finances later.'

So Breeda took her mam's advice and left.

She hated Gardiner Street even more now since she had o'erleapt its boundaries and made her first sorties into the big world outside. There were so many obstacles to overcome, so many fences to jump and it was both stimulating and daunting. She had to re-weave her life and she greeted the challenge with a mixture of excitement and fear.

Some of it had been made easy for her. Mavis Harper's offer and Terry's encouragement coupled with Desmond O'Keeffe's interest all gave her a spurt of the necessary energy. Her mother's encouragement was the final spur. Especially as she realized that even though she was paying Mavis, if she was careful with her money she could still afford to give her mother some help. That discovery made up her mind for her.

The next day she moved in with her co-worker. The invitation had been sudden, her acceptance precipitate. She had nothing to bring so she just brought herself. Mavis, though taken aback at the swift and impulsive acceptance of her offer, asked no questions. It did however strike her as odd that her new tenant did not seem to realize that people usually arrived at least with towels, face cloths, soap, toiletries, nightdresses, slippers and other such bibs and bobs, but Breeda seemed unselfconscious about her lack of worldly goods, not even possessing mementos of the past, such as books, photos or favourite pictures. Mavis said nothing and it was because of what Terry told her that she remained silent.

Terry had returned the previous evening with news of where Breeda lived.

'You shoulda *seen* the place, Mavis. Gawney Mac, it's the sink of the world; the drain of Dublin; the sewer of Ireland. How'd she manage it? How'd she get herself outa that place? How'd she get herself fit to show herself in Deary's? Mother o' God, that took some doin'!' His voice was full of admiration, but Mavis was a little put out at the news. 'Are we sure we want her, then?' she asked Terry, batting her eyelashes in concern, running her fingers through her yellow curls. 'She might not be honest. She might nick things if we let her drop her slipper here.' She caught his eye and added defensively, 'Well, ye know what ye read about those places and the people there. Dens o' thieves, they say. Everyone a villain.'

Terry took her face between his hands. 'Listen, Mavis,' he said firmly, in the masterful way she loved, 'Breeda's okay. Ye know I'm never wrong. I can tell a wrong 'un a mile off. I can smell 'em, they come into the showroom. Breeda's okay. An' the money would be nice. An' ye know how ye hate bein' alone. Ye love company.' He laughed, 'An' ye have any worry, ye can stand beside her, she gets her pay-packet an' take it offa her then and there.' He looked at her, encouragement in his eyes. 'An' the kid deserves a break. No wonder she was gobsmacked when she saw this place.'

Mavis nodded. It was nice to get a reaction like Breeda's to what she considered a beginning. These rooms in Harcourt Terrace were for her the bottom rung on the housing ladder. She planned that when she and Terry married they would get a bungalow in Whitehall furnished cost-price from Deary's, everything new and fresh and pretty. She'd leave these rooms behind without a glance over her shoulder.

'She'll never go back to that slum,' Terry was saying. 'Not after she's left it behind. She'll never feel comfortable there again. So mebbe she'll take this place on, after we're married, I mean. Share it with someone else.'

Mavis shrugged. She didn't care what happened to this place after she left. She saw herself in a Deanna Durbin apron in a Deanna Durbin kitchen in a Deanna Durbin bungalow, flowered curtains fringed with frills, looped back, blue and white check kitchen dressings and table-cloths. She saw a double bed with satin covers, two pillows each side over a bolster and a living-room with flowered chintz and scatter cushions and bowls of flowers and rustic paintings. She knew what she wanted and if Breeda came to live in Harcourt Terrace they would be able to afford it sooner, so she decided to make her co-worker feel welcome and overlook the little matter that she came from an area heavily populated with criminals. Mavis was nothing if not practical.

Breeda settled in next day and in a few days she had become used to the comfort and, to her, the luxury of Mavis Harper's flat. It was as if she had never lived in the slum. She adapted, shifted gear so fast, became accustomed so quickly to hot water, uninterrupted baths, a calm atmosphere undisturbed by children's gabble and demands, the sweet smell of cleanliness, music on the radiogram, and all the other pleasures she had never tasted before. And the miraculous space – space to move, to stretch, to breathe. Within a week it was as if she had never been without these benefits.

Her routine changed completely. At closing time, five twenty on the dot, after she and Mavis had covered everything on the counter and shelves behind with canvas sheeting, after they had done the tally on the day's takings, matching the receipts to the cash, after they had delivered the cloth bags to Mr McGillicuddy whose disgruntled acceptance made them drop the bags and scuttle away giggling, after they had signed out, they went to the cloakroom to titivate. It was something Mavis was very good at. Then they made their way to the underground passage which led to Deary's car park for employees where Terry awaited them.

Terry had sussed out this car park ages ago but never ventured to use it. It was, or had been, a concrete loading area arrived at by the tunnel from Cathedral Street, and the directors and management found it convenient to park their cars there when they had business in the store. So it had gradually become a car park with allotted places, and very convenient it was too.

The day he picked up Breeda for the first time, before they had emerged from the store, a garda had sauntered over to tell Terry that he could not wait in front of the department store. ' 'T'ain't allowed,' the cop said. 'Ye can see yerself why.' He indicated the stop in front of the store just under the clock. 'An' this is not the first time, is it?' he asked Terry wearily. 'You're a constant hazard here. Every evening, five-thirty.'

'But I'm waitin' for me girlfriend,' Terry informed him, man to man. The garda rolled his eyes in mock sympathy. 'Janey – she won't take kindly to ye not bein' here when she gets out then!' The polis leaned against the Caddy, lifting off his hat and scratching his head. 'You'll have te move on, sonny. Sorry.' He paused, then leaned down till he was face to face with Terry. 'Ye said she works in there? For Deary's?' he asked. Terry nodded. 'Well, why don't ye use the Deary's car park?'

'Didn't think I'd be allowed,' Terry told him, the question in his eyes.

'Sure how'd they know? The big noises in there leave at four-thirty – avoid the traffic, God help them! You could hop into one of their places, no problem. It's not as if ye work for them. They couldn't sack ye.'

'Ye think I could?'

The policeman nodded. 'Sure why not? Anyone asks, just tell them you're passin' through. Pickin' up an employee. Or better still—' he winked at Terry— 'Say yer waitin for the head bottle-washer, the top brass. No one'll check. Would, if I were you.'

At that moment Terry had seen Mavis and Breeda emerge and he thanked the cop for the information.

He told Mavis about it and she thought it a good idea. 'You can try it anyhow. See how it goes. They can't eat ye! If anyone objects ye can light out! Scarper.'

No one objected. No one seemed to care very much. So from that evening on Terry waited for Mavis and Breeda in the underground car park and drove them both out of the cavern-like entrance directly to

Harcourt Terrace. So the girls left the store by car and never appeared on the street at all. And Lonny flapped about outside, bewildered as to where he had gone wrong. He was thwarted, furious, unable to find Breeda anywhere.

Evening after evening as the days got shorter he made his way in irritable anxiety from the Pillar to Gardiner Street and back, combing the area, determined to find her, obsessed now by the elusive Breeda.

And Rahilly and McGuigan followed Lonny Clebber and came privately to the conclusion that their boss was on the wrong track altogether. They became bored and discontented with this assignment and wanted nothing more than for it to be over, thus allowing them to get on with the real business of policing.

A series of smash-and-grab raids had startled Dubliners over the last weeks and the young gardai wanted nothing more than to have a go at catching the culprits. Devil-may-care thieves, they were, buccaneers who threw a brick through the windows of shops with valuables enshrined therein and, bold as brass, grabbed what they could and sped away, cocking a snook at the populace as they watched in awed fascination They had so far 'done' a jeweller in O'Connell Street, a furrier in Grafton Street and a pawnbroker's down Nassau Street. Bold, audacious, they were asking to be nabbed with their daylight robbery and Rahilly and McGuigan ached to be allowed in on the case, wipe the grins offa the robbers' faces – instead of hoofing it around the back of Deary's department store and bleedin' Gardiner Street following an insignificant little loafer who worked in an undertaker's.

'Weird little creep,' Rahilly told O'Malley. 'But he's not made a wrong move, sir.'

'Well I want you after him for a little while longer at any rate,' O'Malley barked gruffly. He understood their feelings, sensed their frustration, but could not shake off his conviction that Lonny Clebber was the murderer of Imelda Manning. That shifty-eyed schoolboy face he had seen in the witness box haunted him. 'I simply want to be sure about this, boys. So,' he said with finality, rising to his feet and shuffling some papers together, 'so another few day, please.'

They reluctantly obeyed.

CHAPTER FORTY-FOUR

Desmond O'Keeffe was waiting for Breeda outside the cloakrooms on Friday evening when the store closed. He did not seem in the least disconcerted when most of the staff saw him there. He greeted Breeda unselfconsciously and warmly when she and Mavis emerged from the ladies locker-rooms. Staff passing by gawped and giggled and nudged each other and the more foolhardy whistled. But Desmond remained perfectly composed.

'You look great, Breeda. Lovely!' he said, smiling at her.

Mavis had given Breeda free access to her wardrobe and Breeda had chosen carefully, circumspectly. She had restrained her natural desire to wear the most spectacular outfit she could find. Instead she selected a black jersey dress, gracefully draped Grecian-style, and a matching black swagger coat trimmed with black fox-fur on the sleeves. Mavis had insisted on lending Breeda her three strand graded imitation pearls and matching earrings and they lay on Breeda's white skin elegantly. Her hair like a nimbus framed her small pale face and her eyes were feverishly bright with excitement. It was her first date ever.

Desmond steered her to the car park, helped her into the passenger seat of his roadster and, when he had settled himself behind the wheel, told her, 'Hope you don't mind but I thought we'd drive to the Grand in Dalkey. We'll have tea there and come back for the nine o'clock show.'

'Of course I don't mind,' she smiled, her cheeks pink. She wouldn't have minded if he had asked her to sit in the car park all night.

'I thought you'd enjoy the view of Dublin Bay while we have tea,' he said. 'It's gorgeous. I thought you'd appreciate it.' He tucked a rug around her knees. 'Don't want you cold,' he remarked. 'I've booked for the film so we won't have to queue The manager of the Metropole is a great friend of mine.'

'Oh, it sounds lovely, Mr O'Keeffe.' Nodding acquaintance with the manager of a cinema! Booking tea in the Grand in Dalkey! She felt overwhelmed but determined to keep calm.

'Des, please,' he laughed. 'We're not at work now, Breeda.' He backed the car out and Breeda noticed Terry slumped down in the Cadilac pretending he wasn't there. She giggled. Desmond didn't seem to notice and looked over his shoulder, steering the little two-seater out into O'Connell Street, then around Trinity College and out towards Blackrock and Dun Laoghaire. He chatted all the time, inconsequentially, and she was very grateful, for she was suddenly overcome with shyness and self-doubt. Why was this gorgeous, well-dressed young man with a car taking her out? She who came from Gardiner Street? She who talked like a gurrier? She who knew nothing of style and polish and such like. Why? Was he sorry for her? Did he pity her so much that he was anxious to bolster her confidence? But why bother? Was he going to take advantage of her? Her blood ran cold for a moment and she was overcome with fear. Was the reason he was taking her to a hotel in Dalkey because he intended, oh Jasus, Mary an' Joseph, to have his way with her?

'The view in Dalkey is spectacular,' he was telling her, 'and there is nothing like a sea-breeze for blowing the cobwebs away.'

As he manoeuvred the car through the traffic he occasionally turned and smiled at her. It took her breath away and she smiled tremulously back. His blue eyes were so gentle, so sweet, that she was suddenly sure there was no malice in the man.

As they came into Blackrock it suddenly began to rain and he asked her, did she mind? 'Not that there's anything I can do about it,' he laughed. 'Most things I could change for you, Breeda but not the weather.'

She simply shook her head. She wanted the drive to go on forever.

' "The best laid plans of mice and men",' he quoted ruefully. 'Oh, I'm sorry. Do you mind?'

She shook her head again. If only he knew.

Maybe we should have had tea in the Metropole,' he remarked. 'Stayed in town. Would you like me to turn around and go back?'

'No. Let's go to Dalkey.'

'It's not much of a view you'll see through this rain.'

'I'm happy,' she told him. 'I like the drive. I like the rain.' I like being with you, she wanted to add but restrained herself. He glanced at her again and nodded satisfied then lapsed into silence as he drove the car onwards through Dun Laoghaire.

Breeda had never been so happy. She had never before been so free from care, from anxiety, so totally in the moment, wanting to savour every second, wanting to hold on to time, dare it to rush past and steal her happiness away from her. Let this drive last forever and a day, she prayed, let it just go on and on and on. It was warm in the car with the rug tucked around her. The rain beat softly on the windows and the windscreen wipers made a soft purring sound as they swept the glass. She felt closeted safely in a cocoon, protected from cold and pain. Nothing bad could touch her here. She basked in his presence beside her, the smell of his tweed coat, of his skin, his breath. She wanted this man beside her always. She wanted the serenity she felt inside, the feeling of having arrived at an emotional destination, never to end.

But at last they pulled up in front of the hotel. It stood on a hill overlooking the sea. Des reached behind him, got an umbrella and sheltered her journey from the car to the hotel so that no rain reached her. He treated her as precious and gave her a feeling of being cosseted, of being – dare she even think it? – of being loved.

It warmed her. It caused a glow deep in her stomach that spread through her body and made her feel weak and pliable. She had a lump in her throat as big as a pigeon's egg and for the first time in her life words escaped her.

He did not seem to mind. He took her hand and led her into a large tea lounge, a Palm Court overlooking the bay. She had never seen such grandeur before, except in movies, and she had to snap her mouth, which had fallen open, shut.

The world out there was tempest-tossed. The rain was beating on the bay windows and the sea was churning greyly under a lowering sky.

'I'm sorry,' he said, settling her at the table in the window that had a 'Reserved' sign on it. The waiter took the sign away. 'I'd planned for the sun to be shining in a placid blue sky on a placid blue sea.'

'I think I'd prefer this,' she said hesitantly. She was so afraid of saying the wrong thing. 'It makes me feel warm and safe. Closer to you.' Blushing at her own audacity. Where did that remark come from? Oh Jasus, what was she saying? She lowered her eyes, afraid to look at him, perhaps find the magic spell broken. But sitting beside her he agreed with her.

'I know. It makes one feel protected. The age-old story of man defeating the elements.'

She nodded, not sure what he meant but certain that if he said it it must be true. Then they were silent, just staring out at the rain.

He ordered tea and it came in a silver pot. There was a tiered cake-stand with éclairs and sandwiches and scones and the china cups were as fine as seashells.

They neither of them ate. They had no appetite. He touched her hand occasionally as if drawn irresistibly to her, and she glanced up at him under her lashes and smiled at him shyly.

It seemed five minutes had passed when it was time to go. He helped her on with her coat, standing behind her, and she could feel him lay his cheek against her hair. She let her body relax against him then turned and looked at him, questioning him with her eyes. The returned look of deep tenderness reassured her and they left the hotel and once more he protected her from the weather.

The evening for her passed in daze. She loved to lose herself in movies, escape from the drabness of life, but that night the film failed to entice her into its world of glamour and romance. Real life was too sweet; the present too precious.

They held hands in the dark, her small one lost in his and her thumb gently massaging his wrist. She leaned her cheek against his tweed sleeve, loving the smell, the nearness of him, the sound deep within him when he laughed.

He drove her home to the flat she now shared with Mavis and she was glad she was free from the anxiety she would have felt if she had still lived in Gardiner Street. Bemused, drowsy with unexpressed feelings but grateful he had given her time to assimilate all she felt on this their first date, she pulled out the sofa, turning it into her bed and, relieved that Mavis had retired and she did not have to give her a blow-by-blow account of the evening or explain how she felt, she undressed and fell into a deep, tranquil sleep.

CHAPTER FORTY-FIVE

After that he drove her home every evening. Sometimes he took her out for a drink, or dinner, or to a film. Sometimes he had a drink with Terry and Mavis in the flat and the girls cooked while the men chatted. They liked each other, Terry and Des, and had a lot in common, both being salesmen.

Mavis taught Breeda how to cook. Breeda hadn't a clue. Mavis introduced her to the mysteries of spaghetti bolognese, garlic, tossed salad, sauces and omelettes. Breeda had never eaten like this before, was dumbfounded at the luxury of plenty. Des introduced her to Indian and French cuisine, foreign films and she, determined to like what he liked, soon acquired a taste for all these good things in life.

She learned quickly. She began to speak differently, dress differently, and was happier than she ever believed it possible. What surprised her most was the abundance of her new life: the constant warm water, the food, the laughter and comfort, all these things were, up to now, foreign to her and had now become more natural than the poverty she had lived in for so long.

The first weekend she did not go home. She went to the General Post Office which was opposite Deary's in O'Connell Street and bought a postal order for thirty shillings and sent it in a registered envelope to her mother. She sent a note with it saying that she would come and see the family at the end of the month.

'Stay away, darlin', once ye leave,' her mother had told her. 'Don't come home for a while till Sean gets the hang of it. For the first few weeks he's bound to argue, give you a hard time. But he'll get used to it an' forget it was ever different.'

She knew her mother was right. Sean was such a fool, forgot so quickly. He'd benefit too from the extra money coming in and he'd be canny enough not to rock the boat in case she kept her word and stopped her contributions. He had always been nervous of her – her contempt disconcerted him and her indifference to his threats unnerved him.

She decided she had to tell Des about Gardiner Street. She wanted everything in their relationship to be above board, no secrets, and now that she had escaped it she was not at all embarrassed by the past and the poverty of the home she had left.

They were in the Metropole having tea after work, something that had become a habit. They had their own private places now that they frequented, laying together pleasant memories, building the file of their relationship, the comfort of familiarity. The Metropole was such a place.

'So you see, Des, I'm from a terrible area, a really terrible place. You'd be shocked if you saw it.'

He shook his head and a brief smile flitted across his face. 'No, sweetheart, I doubt that.'

She looked at him enquiringly and he continued, 'I come from the same sort of place myself.'

She put down her cup on her saucer with a bang and stared at him open-mouthed.

'Yeah! Well there's a tiny lane offa George's Street. My family lived on that tiny street. It was part of a warren of tenements – some of the worst slums in Dublin. A place of bare feet, cold water and hopeless-ness. Like you, I escaped.'

It seemed impossible, yet when she thought about it, why not? No one would guess, to look at her now, her origins, so why not Des? Was that why she had always felt affinity for him? Why she had been drawn to him from the start?

'It's why I liked you right off,' he said, echoing her thoughts, 'I knew where you were coming from. I knew you'd get there. I thought, she's like me.' He smiled at her tenderly, touching her cheek, then cov-ering her hand on the table with his. 'Oh, you don't know how you looked that day,' he said, his voice gruff. 'So brave and buoyant and hopeful. So determined. So vulnerable. And I remembered that was how I had been. See, I *knew* what you felt. I understood you.'

'Is that why you hassled Mrs Lepner?'

'Yes, of course. I thought, *this* one will not be sent away. Not if I'm manager here.'

They laughed together at how unique they were, at the coinci-dence, the strangeness of fate.

The tea lounge was on the balcony of the theatre. There was a duet playing in the corner, old songs – faintly Irish, or rather American–Irish. Waiters rushed here and there and a trickle of customers who did not mind seeing the end of the film first were having their tickets torn as they entered the balcony seats. It was dark where they sat, out of the orbit of the chandelier.

'I had to escape it. That place,' he said. 'It would have destroyed me, turned me to crime. I loathed it.' He shuddered and she was surprised at the vehemence of his feelings. 'There was nothing there, nothing good about it at all. It was horrible, soul-destroying.'

'Yes,' she agreed, her eyes fixed on his face. 'Oh yes.'

'I liked you from the first moment I saw you,' he told her.

The duet – a violinist and the pianist – were playing American numbers now.

> 'I'm a lucky boy,
> You are lucky too . . .
> All our dreams of joy
> Seem to come true,
> Maybe that's because you love me,
> Maybe that's why I love you . . .'

They played rather badly but with great verve and Breeda heard only heavenly music.

'Me too,' she cried eagerly. 'But I never thought . . .'

'Me neither . . . I didn't think you'd give me a second look.'

'I looked all right.' She gave a little sigh of relief. Up to now nothing had actually been said and it was so sweet to put it into words and to find their feelings were mutual. Before there had been the hope, and the doubt. Now they talked of their short past together as if it had been an eternity, their words tumbling over each other, their thoughts like railway tracks running parallel.

He would kiss her tonight, she knew. Where? Outside the flat? In the car? In the doorway? What would it feel like, his lips on hers? She looked at his mouth and ached to press her lips to his. She looked into his eyes and knew he was thinking the same thoughts as her.

He kissed her in the car. He parked on the canal side of the terrace, under the chestnut trees. He turned off the ignition, put the gear in neutral and leaned over and gathered her into his arms. He kissed her gently on her temples and she waited breathless. He kissed her cheeks, the side of her mouth, then she felt his mouth on hers and hers opening in his passionate embrace. He was tasting her as if her mouth was a ripe peach, sweet and moist.

She felt her whole being respond. In that moment she was his. There was no going back. She loved him, she was his woman.

He pulled away from her sharply and took a deep breath as if he'd run a race. Neither of them spoke for a while. She stared out of the window into the lighted street and sighed.

'I better go in,' she said.

'Yeah,' he opened his door. 'Yeah. It's late. I'll see you tomorrow then, after work.'

It was a statement, not a question. And it was not late. In fact it was very early. But she knew how he felt and that his emotions were in the same turmoil as hers. It was no wonder they both needed breathing space.

'Yes. Tomorrow, yes. But on Sunday I'm going to see my mam.'

'Sure,' he said.

There was a constraint between them that was achingly tender. Neither of them trusted speech, neither of them dared to say much in case they shattered the wonder, the magic. He put his arms around her outside the front door and kissed her again and when he let her go and ran back to the car she nearly fell. Her knickers were damp and her body throbbed with a great need she had never felt before.

It was so beautiful, loving a man. His hands, his smile, what he said, his every part, his every utterance was important and now that he had kissed her, every time she looked at him this acute desire swept over her and made her gasp.

She wondered what he would be like without his clothes. Clothes seemed an obstacle when they embraced. His naked body against her naked body would be so very lovely. When she thought of it the blood flooded her face and the parts of her body that yearned for his felt alive and acutely tender and she sucked at her arm as she lay in bed, wanting him, knowing she would eventually be his, knowing that such bliss would be almost beyond bearing.

So she went to see her family in Gardiner Street the last week in November and Sean was nervous of her and her mother was bursting with pride.

'God'n' yer a great girl, Breeda,' she told her eldest, looking over her fine clothes, her new make-up, her smart shoes. 'An' gloves!' she cooed. 'Gloves! Gawney Mac, who'da thought one of our family'd be wearin' gloves, God help us!'

'Jasus, woman! What're ye sayin'? Didn't me mam wear gloves!' Sean protested.

'Yer mam wore gloves once in her life an' they weren't her own.'

'What're ye talkin'?'

'Those gloves belonged to Mrs Flynn up in thirty-six. She borrowed them for yer da's funeral, Sean, an' she sufferin' from arthritis at the time an' the weather cold enough to freeze—'

'The balls offa a dog!' Charlie bellowed gleefully but no one paid any attention to him.

Sean lapsed into silence and glanced up every now and then to scrutinize nervously the strange exotic being that was his stepdaughter.

Outside in the freezing day Lonny wrapped his arms around his body and tried to quell the excitement within. He'd found her!

He'd been on the point of giving up, changing his quarry. He had actually decided not to bother about Breeda Deegan any more and had begun to look at Lizzy. But she was always surrounded by the children and was, in any event, a sharp little urchin, vicious as any boy and lacking the wonderful *joie de vivre* her sister had so abundantly. It was not at all like the other ones – what were their names? He couldn't remember. Well, it was not at all like those ones when he had made a game out of choosing. Oh yes, he remembered, the Masterses. He had had such fun making up his mind which one he would 'do it' to. *His* choice. *His* decision.

Breeda had thwarted him. He had not been able to catch her and that defeat outraged him. Lizzy came a very poor second and he knew he would not find the peace he sought with her. Oh no. That little scrubber was incapable of bringing peace to anyone and he knew without a doubt that if it had to be Lizzy Deegan he would mutilate her. How could he help it?

No. He'd give himself another week to find Breeda. He didn't understand why it was important to him that she be the one. There were a lot of things he didn't understand. He had the feeling that everyone else in the world knew something he didn't. They *understood*. He had only just decided to stick with Breeda Deegan when, on that last Sunday in November, he found her. She walked calmly down Gardiner Street towards the tenement to her home, just like that, out of the blue.

Relief flooded him and he perked up, although to see him, no one would have guessed. He sat, slumped, almost part of the brown bark of the leafless, malformed tree beside the bench. Under his jacket the blood pumped and his heart slammed against his ribs and the saliva flooded his mouth.

She had changed. Boy, had she changed. He tried to hide his excitement inside himself. She was marvellously turned out. She wore high heels, fine dark stockings, a full-skirted crimson coat vaguely military in design, tight-waisted with astrakhan lapels, and the colour with her hair made her look vibrantly alive, a glowing Technicolor figure in a drab monochrome street.

He remained slumped on the bench, his coat pulled around him, his chin sunk under the collar. His knuckles were white around his funeral parlour umbrella. He sat there, adrenalin pumping, and waited. This time he would not lose her.

'Will ye have supper with us, dear?' Nuala asked.

'Not this time, Mam.'

'Too grand for us now,' Lizzy sneered, green with envy, dumbly aware she did not have what it took, what Breeda had, to get her out of this place. It was a common dream, to leave the tenement, but most of the people who inhabited the slum knew they'd never leave. To see Breeda in all her glory was both depressing and a beacon of hope.

'No. I'll see ye next month,' she said.

'What about Christmas?' her mother asked.

Christmas they had chicken. They all sat around and ate bird and potatoes and butter to go with it.

Lizzy had her eye on the handbag Breeda was carrying.

'I'm spending Christmas with my boyfriend,' Breeda announced.

'Oooh! My – my boyfriend!' Charlie snorted with a hoity-toity accent. 'Get her!'

Des had not discussed Christmas with her but she was fairly sure he would not be going home either, that they would spend the day in the flat. Together. Mavis was going to her parents in Wexford, taking Terry with her. And even if her instincts were wrong and Des *did* decide to spend the day without her she would not come home. It would not matter to her that she would be alone in the apartment. She was so happy there. Whatever happened she would not be drawn into a celebration in Gardiner Street. It might seduce her into feeling responsible, make her feel, in spite of her mother, that she was once again part of this terrible place with its peeling walls, its constant smell of piss and stale vegetables.

Nuala understood this and she said quickly, 'Isn't that grand now, Breeda? Aren't things working out just dandy?'

'Oh dandy!' Sean said sarcastically, getting stroppy. Breeda noticed her mother didn't ask her Des's name, almost as if to talk about him here would draw him down.

'That fella's across on the bench again, lookin' up,' Nuala remarked, glancing out of the window, her hand pumping up and down as she squeezed the socks in cold water.

'What fella?' Breeda's attention was elsewhere and the question was casual, not really expecting an answer.

'That undertaker fella. He's been here every day since that funeral. Been here at all times. Sometimes morning. Sometimes afternoon. Sometimes evening or night. Every day he comes. Funny that. Mebbe he knew old Mr Brophy.'

'Brophy?' Sean muttered. 'Who's Brophy?'

'Don't ye remember, Sean. Ould fella lived upstairs. Died.'

Breeda wasn't listening. She threw a large paper bag on the table. 'There,' she said. 'There's something there for alla ye.'

Pandemonium broke out. For Sean she had brought a bottle of Paddy. 'Try not to drink it all at once,' she told him and he smiled at her, his eyes grateful, his thanks sincere. He'd probably be a nice man if he did not have to grift, if he did not live in animal conditions, she thought, looking at him without resentment for the first time ever. Oh, it's easy to be understanding when there's a few bob in your pocket and you have a good job and a wonderful boyfriend!

She had brought a new warm petticoat for Nuala and sweets for the children and an uplift for Lizzy. She brought butter and sausages, fresh bread from Boland's as she had promised. She also gave Lizzy a sweater. It was one that Mavis had given her and the colour did not suit Breeda. Lizzy put it on immediately, bra uneasily underneath. She was nearly speechless with excitement but forgot to thank Breeda, who didn't mind. She left soon after, having pressed an envelope containing the weekly allowance into her mother's hands.

'Are ye sure, darlin', ye can afford it? Seein' as how ye brought all these other things.'

'Sure I can, Mam. It was nuthin'. I get staff discount in Deary's an' the girl I live with – she's got more clothes than a film star, an' she gives me whatever she's finished with. Sometimes she only wears an outfit *once*! Can ye imagine, Mam? An' me boyfriend, well, he has a good job . . . manager . . .'

'Manager! Fancy that now! Janey Mac!' Nuala was impressed.

'Yeah. An' he takes me out all the time an' pays for everything. He buys food for the flat. So does Terry. He's Mavis's fiancé . . .'

'Fi-*an*-céee!' Charlie squealed and Nuala hushed him up.

'So ye see I hardly have to put my hand in my pocket.'

'Lucky for ye!' said Sean. 'An' what's this fine boyo gettin' for all these free gifts . . . Ha? What, me fine young miss, is *yer* contribution? Let me ask ye that!'

'Shut up, Sean. How could ye? Shut up, ye hear.'

Breeda turned slowly and fixed her large eyes upon her stepfather. 'I don't have te pay or contribute a thing, Sean,' she said calmly, not taking the bait. 'Ye see, some of us are worth a lot more than you can imagine. My boyfriend thinks himself lucky if I hold his hand. He respects me, Sean, however difficult you find that to understand. Ye've never respected a woman in yer life so how'd I expect ye to understand? But rest assured, Sean, there's no price to pay at all. He loves me.'

'Yerra don't pay attention te him, Breeda. Sure what would he know. What I canna understand is how someone could have so many clothes that they can give them away.'

'Couple months ago, Mam, I woulda thought the same. I woulda been bewildered. Jasus, it's easy for me to forget! But it is so.'

When she left the house she felt sure there would be a sigh of relief from the family. They could enjoy her gifts without the strain of her company: this new and well-dressed Breeda was awe-inspiring and therefore put a constraint on their spontaneity. The children, like Sean, viewed her now as a rather grand visitor and they were on their best behaviour while she was there.

She shrugged. It did not matter. Her life now had another direction and purpose. She would spend it with Desmond O'Keeffe. They were two of a kind. They both needed success as well as love, and together they would have it. She would always be devoted to her mother, but the others – Sean, Lizzy, Charlie and on down – would travel in a different direction and she was not going to meet them halfway on the ladder down. She could tell how they would turn out. From their lack of interest, their inability to view work as anything but a last choice. No.

They would not fight to get out of the slum but, being Deegans, they'd become adept at surviving in it. And they'd feel hard-done-by. They'd burn with resentment. They'd carry around a heavy load of hate and self-pity all their lives and never see they could do something about it.

She went into the street. The wind was bitterly cold but she was warm. It was the first time that she had felt warm in winter in the street and she smiled to herself and gave a little skip and a jump as she hurried to the bus stop. Des O'Keeffe was in the flat waiting for her with Mavis and Terry. They would be having one of Terry's Martinis, frosted, ice-cold to the taste with that mule-kick to the stomach. They would have one ready for her. She wondered if there was anyone in the whole world as happy as she was.

And Lonny Clebber watched and followed.

CHAPTER FORTY-SIX

Lonny Clebber followed Breeda as she took the bus to Harcourt Terrace. A suffocating feeling of triumph surged through him and he felt as if he might explode. He'd done it! He'd done it! He'd found her. He'd followed her to her lair. He'd won! He was the hunter who after weeks of patience had found his quarry's hide-out and could now afford to wait.

He was not sure how or why she now lived in Harcourt Terrace but there, on a piece of cardboard, neatly cut and printed, was her name in a slot under the second-floor bell: MISS B. DEEGAN.

Eureka!

He stood under the chestnut tree across the road from the house that had her name on the door. He could see the lights on in the second-floor window. The rest of the house both above and below that flat was dark. No one in.

They had not pulled the curtains and there was only fine nylon drapery between them and the street. He could see them moving behind the gauze, their silhouettes. There were four of them as far as he could make out: two men and two girls, one of them Breeda. Even with the light behind her and the gossamer curtains between them he could see the colour of her hair.

The silhouettes mingled, became one as they stood together, split up again, danced a dance backwards and forwards. And they were drinking, he could see that; the outline of glasses in their hands. He could not hear them; the windows were firmly closed against the bitter night, but their pantomime movements seemed full of gaiety and laughter.

He shivered in the freezing wind and looked about him. Better, much better than Gardiner Street. And the canal behind him . . . perfect. The canal would be useful. If only he had been beside the canal when Imelda Manning snuffed it. Ah well.

He had found Breeda but he could do nothing tonight. He didn't want to. He could take his time now. Wait. He'd get her; all uncertainty was gone. He'd found her, tracked her and he would pounce in his own good time. He grinned. She didn't know her days were numbered. Only he knew that.

He looked around and saw there was no one anywhere in the street, no one at all.

CHAPTER FORTY-SEVEN

O'Malley had had to take his boys off the case. Orders had come from above that he was to drop the Imelda Manning enquiry and get on with other things. They implied that he was wasting good men. The smash-and-grabbies were playing games with them, cocking a snook, showing their contempt. The Gardai were expected to do something about this gang so that the merchants and pawnbrokers of Dublin could sleep soundly at night. They had to be made to understand that they couldn't just barge into other people's premises and abscond with whatever stock they could lay their hands on.

'I agree, sir,' O'Malley said. 'But they're cowboys and at worst are only damaging property. Clebber is a murderer and when he strikes next it's a woman he'll injure, perhaps kill. Rape at least.'

'*Only* property? Since when did property become *only*?' Chief Superintendent Davis asked with heavy sarcasm.

'*Only* compared to people, sir.'

'Have you any proof of this Clebber individual's guilt?'

'No, sir. Just the fact he was convicted of rape. Given a suspended sentence.'

'That's *past*, O'Malley.' Davis rose and emerged from behind his desk and paced the small office overlooking Pearce Street. 'You're obsessed with it. With this boyo. Drop it, for God's sake, man, drop it. You're like a bloody terrier. You've had those two men on this for *months* . . .'

'Well, sir . . .'

'Let it *go*. Just let it go. These bastards are laughing so hard at us they're pissing their pants. Jasus, it won't do. I want them locked up. Hear me, O'Malley?'

'Yes, sir.'

'All right then. Get the hell outa here and find me those snotty-nosed little gurriers. And soon, d'ye hear, soon.'

O'Malley let go reluctantly. Very reluctantly. For some reason he could not fathom, Lonny Clebber nagged at him. It was as if someone's prayers were being directed to him. It was an uncanny feeling, and sometimes he thought that Imelda Manning was reaching out to him from the grave.

When McGuigan reported that evening, freezing from the cold, he told O'Malley that Clebber had changed his movements. 'For the first time, sir. In weeks. He's been a permanent fixture in Gardiner Street and the undertaker's in Capel Street. Then he'd go to that grotty little hovel beside the Tolka.'

'And? Well?' O'Malley deplored McGuigan's habit of taking a long time to get to the point.

'And . . . well . . . He went to Harcourt Terrace, sir. Stood about, waiting under a tree. Looking up at a window.'

'Aha! So! The weasel has moved,' the detective sighed. 'But I've been ordered off Clebber. Damn.'

He saw the look of relief cross the young garda's face and suppressed a surge of resentment.

'You're on the smash-and-grab, McGuigan. That ought to please you.' I sound just like Davis, he thought.

When McGuigan had left his office O'Malley's body slumped in his chair and he stretched, then rubbed his eyes tiredly. It had been a long, hard day. He had been in court all morning, which he hated. Jeez, though, it was bloody ridiculous. To compare a few fly boys, buckaneers who robbed premises that were heavily insured, to a foul little pervert who destroyed life, offended decency and pillaged innocent young women, was, to his way of thinking, obscene. Why was it so vital not to look foolish? People were such fools. Why couldn't they, once in a while, slip on banana skin and not believe the end of the world had come? If the police didn't catch the right person or persons, better to admit the error, brazen it out in the certain knowledge that they were pursuing the right and proper course. Catching Lonny Clebber was infinitely more important than how they appeared in the eyes of the public.

He took out a picture of Lonny Clebber. It had appeared in the press at the time of the Shaughnessy rape trial. He stared at it. The eyes in the picture stared back at him. He tried to fathom what those eyes held but could not. The only expression he could decipher in the admittedly bad photograph was one of concealment. Guarded eyes hiding their owner well. He looked at his watch. It was late, but not that late.

He came to a decision. He'd go to Harcourt Terrace and have a look at the rapist himself. He'd play it by ear. He might even get a chance to frighten Lonny Clebber off, throw a scare into him. Although on mature thought Lonny Clebber did not seem to belong to that majority of the public who would be frightened if they felt they were under surveillance.

He'd be doing it in his own time. No one could buck him for that. He rose, suddenly energetic, and reached for his coat.

CHAPTER FORTY-EIGHT

The lights were up for Christmas. Santas in red felt costumes and white beards, smelling strongly of Paddy, rang bells outside all the big stores and inside gave away tacky gifts that broke instantly so that over-excited children with red, fevered faces burst into tears. There had nearly been snow. A fall that had the city looking like a fairy-tale earlier had degenerated into slush and an icy wind blowing from Dublin Bay forced people to hurry indoors.

It had ceased to be comfortable waiting outside the house in Harcourt Terrace. Lonny Clebber had given up doing that, but not on getting Breeda Deegan. Several happenings had changed his plans and made him snigger into his coat.

Firstly the weather. The wind from Siberia via Dun Laoghaire was lethal and even with a knitted cap with ear-flaps (*North by Northwest* and *The 49th Parallel*), gloves and a pair of mountaineer socks it was hell loitering anywhere in Dublin. Then, as the weeks passed, he became aware he was being watched. It gave him a curiously uncomfortable feeling to realize that he, the watcher, was in turn being observed.

First it had been two clowns. Sometimes they were very good and he could not see them at all. But he knew they were there. Other times they were careless and he could see them. Pretending they were part of the scenery, pretending they were innocent. Ha! He had to laugh.

Then he became conscious of a change in the watcher. This time he didn't see the man – no matter how hard he tried he could not catch a glimpse of him. The first time he became conscious of him was one evening beside the canal when Mavis and Breeda came home in the Caddy. Lonny knew the Caddy by now and he knew Desmond's little roadster.

He knew a lot about the inhabitants of the second-floor flat.

This evening, in the middle of December, the lights of the Cadillac swept the pavement just above the canal, caught Lonny in the beam and caught another figure too. A tall broad man, heavily built; a man who, Lonny saw, was watching him.

Why? Lonny was momentarily disconcerted. He shivered. He wanted to run away screaming, shouting at the man to leave him alone. His mother did that, watched him. His fucking mother did that.

Well, not for much longer. This man would have to stop too or Lonny Clebber'd fix him. He did not ask himself how he would get his mother to finally stop or how exactly he'd fix the man but somehow he'd do it. He'd always got his own way before, hadn't he? 'Get offa me', and she had.

Lonny did not look at the car or at the second-floor window. He turned his back and kept his attention on the canal, as if he was engrossed in the murky water flowing past. He grinned mirthlessly; a fisherman without a rod! he thought, then anger swept over him. How dare that man invade his privacy. How dare he!

He could hear voices on the road. The other car had drawn up with a screech of brakes and the voices of the friends laughed greetings at each other. Then he heard the blonde one called Mavis ask Breeda, had she made up her mind about Christmas?

'Sure, I'm staying here. Des will join me in the flat about three in the afternoon.'

'Oh, then you'll have a late lunch?'

'Sure. Jasus, it's cold!'

'We're goin' to leave after work Christmas Eve. We'll go direct to Wexford from the store. Terry is drivin' me, aren't you, Ter?'

Terry, the fellow who drove the Caddy, was locking the car. Lonny turned around and watched them as, laughing and chatting, they went into the house, the four of them together.

Lonny smirked to himself. He had come to a decision. He had made a plan, he had the final blueprint. He was no fool!

That other man was obviously a policeman. Why else was he there? He was much taller than Lonny which made the latter resent him more. He peered up at O'Malley, who had moved closer and closer to the undertaker's assistant, and his eyes went darting like a fish in a pool all over the policeman. He skimmed O'Malley's hair, darted over his lips and back in a nervous dance.

Lonny boldly approached the tall man, and looked up into his face. 'I'm goin' te get you,' he hissed, wet his lips and hissed again, 'I'm gonna get you!' Then with a James Cagney sneer he walked away.

He was pleased with himself. He'd shown the guy. Just like Cagney and Bogart, he'd let him have it.

And he wouldn't be there tomorrow for that stupid motherfucker to gawp at him. Watch him. He wouldn't go to Harcourt Street again.

Until Christmas Day. He'd go on Christmas Day. What she'd said, 'I'm staying here', 'Des will join me at three'. She'd be alone. Waiting. He'd get in. That bit would be simple. And he'd 'do it' to her *in her own flat*. That would be a change. That would show 'em. He'd not be out in the street or in the bushes. He'd be in the fuckin' house! He'd have time. He'd have the canal outside too. He'd be covered.

She'd be alone. Everyone went home for Christmas. Her flatmate was going home. To Wexford. It would be perfect. There would not even be much traffic on Christmas Day. Perfect.

O'Malley went to the front door of the house and checked the plates. He ran his finger down the neat little slots beside the bell. And then he saw it.

Breeda Deegan.

He stabbed his finger against the printed name. 'Eureka!' he whispered, echoing Lonny.

McGuigan had given him a list of the occupants of the tenement in Gardiner Street, and the names of those people were printed on his brain. Deegan was one of them. Why, he wondered, hadn't McGuigan spotted it? They were a large family, he remembered. A long list of names. And a girl about the right age. There it was now. Breeda Deegan. It could *not* be a coincidence.

Lonny Clebber walked along the dark pavement. The lamp's rays left pools of light around them that slipped into shadow and then pitch dark. There were people in the houses in their living-rooms, spot-lit as if on stage. He stared in at their lives; the girl playing a piano by touch in the twilight; the man and the woman decorating a green fir-tree – hanging baubles on it, winding silver tinsel around the massy branches; the old man and woman sitting on either side of the fire which sent shimmering shadows across their faces; the family around the table, the mother serving from a steaming casserole, and he understood none of it. He looked at them as he looked at a movie set in some Technicolor place – *Moon Over Miami*, *Flying down to Rio*, *The Virginian*. The tableaux were as alien to him as those exotic film locations. He was a stranger in a strange land, a stranger to most human experience, and he was fascinated.

O'Malley followed him to the decaying cottage on the Tolka. It was a long, slow journey. The cocky little figure swaggered along, peering into the houses on the way, taking his time. When he watched he became curiously still, almost went into a trance. He was evil, of that O'Malley was sure. Those eyes had looked into his and they were like dark pools in Hades.

'I'm goin' te get you!' The words were immaterial, the expression was terrifying. This was someone who could wait, plan, plot revenge. O'Malley was sure of that. He had no proof of it. Nothing to take into court where a judge had once called him 'diligent and sober'.

Well, perhaps the judge was right. Lonny was diligent and sober, but not in the way the judge meant. O'Malley shivered and felt his stomach turn over as he thought of Lonny Clebber's tenacity as he searched for Breeda Deegan and found her.

He knew now that though Lonny Clebber had never once looked at Breeda that she was the potential victim. She was the only link between the tenement and Harcourt Terrace. She had obviously gone to work in Deary's, then left home a couple of days later, thus confusing the undertaker's assistant. She had gone to live with the other name on that bell, Mavis Harper, in a flat in Harcourt Terrace and Lonny Clebber pitched up at both places. It was too much of a coincidence. And McGuigan's and Rahilly's testimony was that Lonny had kept watch outside the tenement for weeks, patiently waiting, waiting, waiting.

Lonny Clebber had discovered the Harcourt Terrace address. He had waited, been content to wait, in the freezing cold, the driving rain, this inclement winter weather. Then he had followed her. His obsession was unwavering, his concentration to be marvelled at.

O'Malley got on the bus behind him, catching it as it was in motion. It was going north. He lurked at the back, upstairs, and watched Lonny pull on his fag, staring at the darkness outside. O'Malley got off the bus at the stop before the Tolka Bridge, full sure that Lonny was headed home. He walked briskly towards the cottage.

Lonny was leaning on the bridge waiting for him. He was smirking, his eyes glittering in the dark.

He watched O'Malley approach, then stood, straightening his shoulders, made an obscene face, stuck two fingers in the air in an 'up yours' gesture, then turned and sauntered away from the detective down to where the cottage nestled in ivy and fungus and dampness beside the river.

CHAPTER FORTY-NINE

His mother was waiting for him in a sleazy old pink kimono. His father had probably given it to her in the dim and distant past and since then it had kept apace with her decline. It was saggy and faded as she, creased beyond redemption, dirty, stained, long past its usefulness. But she still wore it, behaving as if it were fresh out of Brown Thomas.

She was in a dangerous mood, he saw that at once. She had slavered on some panstick, lipstick and mascara but the make-up hadn't been blended properly and she looked, he thought, like a slag. Yet she simpered as if she was Scarlett O'Hara. Then she spoke and the pit fell out of his stomach.

'How's my big boy?'

It was a long time since she had said anything like that in precisely that way and he wanted to throw up. Instead he looked at her with distaste. 'I'm not your big boy,' he said. She twittered a bit, seemingly unaware of his disgust. She was tight, he decided, and went to his room.

It did not occur to him that she would follow him. It had been so long since she had tried anything like that: 'Get offa me'. He went to his room and threw himself on to the bed and suddenly there she was beside him, plucking at his sleeve, groping him. 'Leave me alone,' he cried coldly, frozen rigid. He was a child again, terrified. But she did not seem to hear him. She was trying to kiss him and grab his balls at the same time. Her breath smelled of stale alcohol and she was panting heavily, the sound harsh in her chest.

He tried to extricate himself from her grasp but she was very heavy and she fell on him like a hungry wild animal and would not be budged by his feeble flailing. Now he felt her push against his leg uttering excited little yelps.

With a sudden superhuman burst of strength he let out a terrifying, blood-curdling scream that echoed on and on and on and his body was galvanized into action, his eyes rolled back in his head. He rolled her over, now on top of her, still howling like a wolf, and caught her hair in one hand, grasping it and yanking her head backwards. He clenched his fist, hearing the mad wailing of a dog, not realizing it was himself, and he began to beat her. All his poisoned hatred spurted from him as he beat her senseless, beat her face to a pulp, grunting screaming as he hit out, chanting foul words, the foul words he used only in such cases as this.

When she was quite unconscious he lay still for a while until the storm inside him blew out, until the tempest passed and he sank back exhausted, his breathing jagged, until the clock's ticking became the only sound in the room as he stared at the ceiling. He became calm at last and a beatific smile lit up his face. He looked gentle now, like the ideal altar-boy. He gazed at his mother for a moment then calmly put his hands around her throat and strangled her. He tightened his grip slowly, with pleasure, smiling all the time. Only now his smile was not angelic. It was triumphant.

When he had finished he stared at her, disgusted. He gathered some saliva in his mouth, then spat full into her bloodied and lifeless face. Then, with a sudden burst of energy, he leaped off the bed.

He wrapped her in the cover they had been lying on just as he was used to doing in the mortuary. It was *his* bed-cover, but he would never use it again. He felt quite pleased when he thought about that. He would buy himself a new one. Then he wondered what he would do with her now. She was much too heavy for him to carry so he pulled her out of his room and into her own room next door. It took some time but he eventually managed it.

He tried to heave her up on to her bed but he was not strong enough. So he left her where she was, on the floor, ass wrapped up in the coverlet.

Then he bent down and felt for her pulse. There was none. He had to search the folds of her flesh but he found nothing. Applying pressure with his thumbs he pressed, pressed, pressed again just in case.

When at last he stopped he knew she was definitely dead. He felt very peaceful. So very peaceful.

He let the feeling flow over him. It was so good, so very good his nerves at rest at last. Everything still.

He looked down at her.

'I told ye to leave me alone,' he said coldly and left the room, closing the door behind him.

CHAPTER FIFTY

He did not go near her room next day. He slept late, feeling calm.

O'Laughlin phoned him to say he would not be needed until the afternoon.

I need *you*, Mr O'Laughlin, darlin', he thought as he pictured the corpse in the next-door bedroom. Only ye knew, I need yer services for me mam, ha-ha-ha! But he said nothing, put down the phone, got all gussied up in his best George Raft outfit and, looking smart as paint, made his way to the public baths.

He went straight to the changing room. The whole place was tiled, the floor as well as the walls and ceiling. When he undressed he folded his clothes carefully and put them in the locker, but shivered as his feet touched the cold, wet floor. He wrapped a towel around his waist and turned to make his way to the showers, his bare feet slapping the tiles. He was whistling – 'I'm looking over a four-leaved clover' – swaggering a bit, feeling at peace with the world when suddenly he saw his pursuer: the man who had followed him the previous night. A wave of panic overwhelmed him and threatened to reduce him to a cringing pulp, but it was gone in an instant as his natural resilience came to the rescue, the fear followed by a surge of cockiness and an acute awareness of his invincibility. He stopped, put his hands on his hips just above the towel and gave the big man a speculative stare.

'Ye follyin' me?' he asked cheekily, smiling a small smile.

But the man did not seem disconcerted. He simply nodded, 'Yes,' he said, 'I'm following you. Until I can nail you dead, Lonny Clebber.'

Lonny shrugged. 'Wish you luck,' he replied tranquilly. He tried to pass the man but he was blocking the way, towering over him, looking down at him with cold eyes. Lonny couldn't meet the man's gaze.

The man bent down. 'You don't have a bloody shirt today, Lonny, by any chance, do you?' he whispered in Lonny's face. 'You not covered in blood today?'

A sudden vision of his mother's body flashed across his brain and he instinctively looked down at his naked torso. He grinned, an insane and foolish look on his face, then he laughed.

'No. Who said I did?' He squinted up at the man.

'The attendant here. Riggs O'Toole. He said you came in one night looking like Jack the Ripper.'

'Musta made a mistake,' Lonny said equably. 'Anyhow you'll have to do better'n that. Riggs O'Toole is half blind.'

'Don't worry, Lonny, I will. I will.'

Lonny looked at the man. 'You polis?' he asked. The man nodded.

'I knew,' Lonny Clebber chuckled. 'Was right.'

'Think you're clever?' the detective queried.

'Oh yeah.' A look of amusement crossed the rapist's face. 'Wish you luck,' he said again and went to the showers. Nothing could touch him now!

When he had finished he got dressed, straightened the handkerchief in his top pocket, pulled a withered petal or two off his carnation buttonhole, rubbed his patents against the backs of his trouser-legs and smoothed down his hair.

He slipped Riggs a tanner on his way out, passed him by, then turned casual-like. 'Oh, Riggs,' he asked the old ex-boxer with his cauliflower-ear and broken nose, who peered at him through filmed eyes.

'Yes, sir?'

'You remember that night I came in covered in red paint . . .?'

'Paint?' the old boxer squinted at him. 'Paint? Me, I thought it was blood.'

Lonny nearly burst himself laughing and after a moment the old boxer joined in.

'Blood? Oh, Riggs, you kill me! It was paint. Jasus, what you bin tellin' people? It was paint. I'd just been decoratin'. God'n' I was covered, wasn't I? But ye know what? That carbolic soap got it all off! Would ye believe? Stripped it. Like turps.'

He slapped the old man's shoulder; mates, old buddies.

'Paint? Just think o' that! Paint. An' me thinkin' it was blood! I'm an eejit, sur, an eejit.'

'No yer not!' Lonny told him stoutly. 'Nonsense. Anyone coulda made the mistake. An' it's dim in here, innit? The lighting is dim.'

Riggs nodded. 'Surely is. I'm always sayin' it. Lightin' here is that dim. Can't see yer hand in front.'

The lighting was bright, naked-bulb bright, but that did not matter. Lonny was satisfied. The old man thought it was dim and was not at all sure now whether it was paint or blood that had covered Lonny's shirt that night.

Lonny left the baths and made his way to Deary's. He needed a new cover for his bed and he decided Deary's was the place to get it.

As soon as he entered the store he saw her. Red hair shining under the artificial lights, standing behind the perfume counter, the blonde one with her. It was nice seeing her like that, it gave him a jolt of pleasure. He felt good. Full of confidence. Strong. The store did not intimidate him any longer.

He walked past Perfumes a couple of times, back and forth, but he made sure he did not linger where Breeda and her friend, the same friend from Harcourt Terrace, could speak to him. He did not want to talk to her.

He bought a bright yellow coverlet for his bed. It had a multi-yellow print as if someone had dipped a large paintbrush into pots of different shades of yellow paint and sploshed it to and fro to make a cheerful and jolly design. He bought some yellow pillow-slips while he was at it, and a bolster cover, and armed with these in a large parcel he left the store, taking one last look at Breeda as he exited.

The policeman was there, waiting outside. Lonny gave him a grin – crooked, like George Raft, who hardly ever smiled but when he did the smile was lopsided and terrifying. He got the number sixteen bus outside the Carlton cinema and so did the garda.

Lonny was not worried. He felt amused and infinitely superior. It would be so simple. His plan was fool-proof. Let this guy follow him. Let him trail behind him everywhere he went. Why should he care? He had the perfect plan.

He would go to the house in Harcourt Terrace on Christmas Day. He'd not go there before. This simpleton would be confused that Lonny did not go there, that was if he suspected, put two and two together as Lonny thought he had. So old flat-foot would follow him around, wasting his time, and Lonny would be doing nothing even vaguely out of order. No more loitering outside Harcourt Terrace, no more hanging about Gardiner Street. He'd wait patiently until Christmas Day when he felt sure the garda would be home in the bosom of his family. Everyone in Dublin would be at home with their families. Breeda Deegan would be waiting for her boyfriend. And Lonny Clebber would pay the girl a surprise visit, and 'do it' to her. Until then, let the fool follow him.

He got out of the bus at the bridge and ran down the slippery slope to the cottage. It looked derelict in the sharp, clear midday light. A cold sun the colour of his new bed-cover wavered in a pearl-grey sky and a rotting smell rose from the river.

He decided he should paint the house. Yellow. Soon. As soon as he'd 'done it' to Breeda Deegan. The prospect excited him. He hadn't made up his mind yet what to do with *her* inside in her bedroom. He really didn't want to think about it now.

He turned. The garda was leaning on the bridge, watching him. The faint mist from the river shrouded him, made him look ghostly. Lonny Clebber grinned and stuck the tip of his thumb on his nose and waved his fingers in a gesture of defiance. The garda didn't budge an inch, just remained there motionless, staring down at him.

CHAPTER FIFTY-ONE

O'Malley was in deep trouble, at home and at work. At work his chief demanded he give up 'this bloody silly obsession', as he put it, but to his dismay O'Malley continued taking time out to follow Lonny Clebber, against whom, he pointed out, there was not a scrap of evidence.

'I *know* that, sir. What in God's name do you think I'm trying to do?'

'I know what you're trying to do, O'Malley. You trying to fit this pathetic little guy up. You've got some bee in your bonnet that he's done the Manning murder and you won't let go. He's done *nothing*, y'hear?'

'Not yet—'

'You've had half the force following him.'

'Two men—'

'And when I told you lay off, that's what I meant. I've been told that you spend more time shadowing this punk than you do at home or on your other cases. Lay off, O'Malley.'

But O'Malley couldn't and between his scheduled work and his overtime on Lonny Clebber he was up to his neck in shit at home.

'You're never here,' Mary told him. 'You'll kill yourself. A man can't do without sleep. It's impossible.' She knew what he was up to and she agreed with his boss. 'The little creep is not your responsibility.'

'Oh, but, Mary, he is!'

'Look, darling.' Her lovely face was creased by frowns of anxiety. 'If you feel you have to personally follow everyone who *may* commit a crime you might as well give up now. It's an impossible task.'

'No. I've never felt I have to do that,' he told her. 'It's just that this is a foul crime. I couldn't bear it if another young woman's life is destroyed. And all because I was not vigilant.'

'You're thinking of Colleen, aren't you?'

He nodded. And Imelda Manning. We're no nearer finding her killer. But I *know* it's him. I know it in my gut. I can't get that poor girl out of my mind . . .'

'It's been months since her murder,' Mary said, sweetly reasonable as usual. 'Since then you've worked yourself to a frazzle.'

'If you saw him, dear. He's laughing at us.'

'Is that why you're so angry?'

'Oh, give me more credit than that!'

'I'm sorry but this *has* become personal and you know that's against the rules.'

'I can't help it. Dear God, can you imagine if—'

'That's the problem. You've been ordered *not* to imagine. And you're on duty twenty-four hours a day. You'll kill yourself. You'll break down, darling, then what'll we do?'

O'Malley sighed. He was unable to disassociate himself from the undertaker's assistant. He was haunted by his weasel face, the smart-ass little gurrier cocking a snook at authority, grinning at him. He was haunted by the dead, defiled body of Imelda Manning and the theatre photographs of her, radiant and vital. He was haunted too by the bright, expectant face of Breeda Deegan.

He was sure now that Breeda was the next intended victim. He was sure too that Lonny Clebber knew that he guessed, but for some reason he didn't care. He obviously had some plan he was convinced would work. But what could he, a lone policeman, do? He could hardly approach her: 'We have reason to believe you are going to be attacked'! No. It would not do. He might terrify her unnecessarily.

He had seen Breeda, caught her bright smile, her vitality and bounce, knew now she was the kind of victim Lonny Clebber chose. 'Put out thy light'. He had asked himself what they had in common – Arlene Shaughnessy, Imelda Manning and Breeda Deegan – and he had come up with that answer: vitality. Light. It had to be that. Arlene Shaughnessy was a big girl, a dyed blonde; Imelda was dark and tall and very slim. Breeda was a luminous redhead, quite small. They were different physical types and they were different classes; they came from different stock and the only thing they had in common was a zest for life. And Lonny liked to put it out. Snuff it. Bastard! O'Malley knew he was incapable of walking away. He tried to let the furious interviews with his chief, the threats, the orders and rather more unpleasant criticisms flow over him but he could not. So he ran away, became unreachable and time passed and nothing happened, nothing at all. Lonny Clebber went about his business undeterred and with a small infuriating smile at the corner of his mouth that irritated O'Malley endlessly.

He was to be seen around the undertaker's in Capel Street, pall-bearing in churches all over Dublin, chauffeuring the hearse or a limousine for the chief mourners, going home in the evening or setting out in the morning from the cottage by the Tolka. He sometimes went into Deary's but he never went near Perfumes. Once O'Malley caught him staring at the truncated top half of a plaster model wearing a Twilfit brassière but the garda knew Lonny was taking the mickey. He was not interested in the plaster forms or the uplift brassière, his aberration was not for the inanimate. He liked live ones, he liked resistance, he liked to master and destroy.

He never appeared to look at Breeda, though, or even register her. O'Malley was beginning to realize the rapist was an actor. He assumed the mannerisms of the actors whose clothes he wore. He shrugged his shoulders like Cagney, became frozen-faced like Raft, smirked and moved his mouth like Bogart and grinned sourly like Garfield. Who was he? O'Malley wondered. What impulses guided him? What hatreds motivated him? What black, foul thoughts live in his head and spurred him on? He could dissimulate; he was good at playing his game. And it was a game O'Malley knew Lonny Clebber was enjoying. He gave every indication he was having fun. He loved the hide-and-seek, the follow-my-leader that he and the detective were involved in. And the more O'Malley tailed the rapist the more he himself got entangled in this game, ensnared by it – unable to extricate himself – and the angrier his boss, his colleagues and his wife became.

CHAPTER FIFTY-TWO

The Masters household was very uneasy. A terrible awkwardness pervaded the atmosphere and the family were uncomfortable when together.

The problem was, Fliss had changed. As her pregnancy progressed she became more and more bovine, seeming to let nature gain the upper hand and take over her completely; and this, as everyone knew, was the sign of a peasant. No lady allowed her pregnancy to show until it was past redemption, obvious to everyone, and even then a truly well-bred girl would do everything in her power to disguise the awkward fact that nature was at work.

It was appalling, in Tessa's opinion, what this terrible pregnancy had done to her eldest daughter. She was quite sure too that if Fliss had married Derry and become *enceinté* in the *normal* way she would never have behaved as she was now doing.

She lay about all day dressed in the most slovenly way, refusing to wear the neat little navy or grey pleated-from-the-yolk dresses with starched white collars and pearls that every respectable pregnant woman wore, but slatterned about in her nightgown, God's sakes! Even coming downstairs in it! Tessa was horrified. Fliss lounged about all day eating dates and Hadji Bey Turkish Delight, or nibbling on celery stalks and chewing bits of cheese and apple. Tessa was quite fed up with her. She behaved like one of those heavily sugges-tive theatrical prints of Sarah Bernhardt playing Cleopatra in what looked like her underwear, or Theda Bara lying sensuously on a tiger-skin toying with feathers or grapes. It was so *sleazy* to Tessa's mind. No well-bred girl, even when encumbered by pregnancy, should behave that way.

Fliss slopped, slouched, lay pecking at snacks in her room, reading about child welfare. Ungirdled, she unselfconsciously did exercises that looked obscene, read magazines and romances and appeared as if she hadn't a care in the world. There was nothing of the tragic victim about her at all.

All in all she left the household bemused, no one too sure how to behave towards her. She refused to be typecast, changed the script and left the rest of them without the plot.

Meriel was deprived of her suffering heroine. Anxious to further her cause, the championship of women, she was let down by Fliss, who refused to speak out or in any way participate in discussions or meetings that were comprised of women fighting for the liberation of their sex. Meriel was very into women's rights, women's freedoms. But Fliss, who should have been head of the list, refused to help in any of her sister's campaigns.

Tessa and Rogan found themselves with a daughter living under their roof who refused to be discreet about her very obvious and shameful state, would not be tactful about the fact that she was not married and was quite outspoken about poor Derry's 'inability to cope with stark reality', as she phrased it. Which made reconciliation with Agnes and Bigger an impossibility and Rogan found the loss of his favourite golfing partner hard to bear. Valentine too was avoiding the Masterses. He found the whole business embarrassing, never having had any children of his own and suffering from a pathological distaste to be near any troubling physical aberrations or discussions. He would prefer if subjects like pregnancy remained rather disgusting mysteries. Fliss's frank handling of the whole matter shocked him and sent him scuttling to the nearest exit or the bar. Nora was covered in confusion and shame at the fact that her mistress's daughter could let the side down so badly. Well-bred people, people that it was no shame to work for, did *not* do things like that, they simply did not have illegitimate babies and she tut-tutted to herself as she went about her work and pursed her lips in disapproval. Only Clemmie remained calm and accepting in the face of Fliss's obduracy.

She was excessively large, bulging out in front like a Rubens model. Sometimes the family could see the baby's movements as Fliss sat, *en déshabille*, on a sofa in their midst.

She was, for the moment, perfectly happy. She had slipped into a broody content and nothing could reach her. She let her hormones take over and if asked she would have had to admit that she really did not care about anybody or anything. She was totally absorbed in the new life within her. She was content to sit back and let her body get on with its momentous task of creating a baby.

CHAPTER FIFTY-THREE

Den Shaughnessy had begun to beat his daughter, Arlene. Resentment built up as the novelty of being in the newspapers wore off and only the stigma remained.

Arlene could have been a nun. She isolated herself in her room, shut herself off from all human contact and refused to budge. This created problems in the household for it meant that Mrs Shaughnessy had to take Arlene up her meals. Just when Den Shaughnessy was holding forth about the latest incident at work, passing on a titbit of gossip or propounding the unfairness of bosses in general and his in particular, his wife would disappear upstairs to cater to his raped daughter's inability to come to terms with what had happened to her, thus spoiling his punch-line, leaving him alone and very frustrated. He was used to his wife as a captive and rapt audience, but since the rape those days were vanished. No longer was there the attentive hush that greeted his every word. He was very touchy and took premature umbrige when Arlene's name was even mentioned. It was all her fault.

Mrs Shaughnessy, whose selfless disposition was one of her great strengths, found even her marvellous patience stretched to the limit. Arlene, confined to her room, was a handful, her depression contagious, her demands (though she herself was unaware of the burden she placed on the family) wearing. Like most depressed people she was monumentally selfish but quite unconscious of it.

Linen had to be changed more often. Chamber-pots emptied. Basins of water carted to and fro. The room tidied and aired. Washing done. Cups of tea or coffee brought to the girl. It was quite a business and put a strain on the whole household.

And for Mrs Shaughnessy there was the worry over her daughter's behaviour and the constant anxiety about her recovery. If she was self-less she was also a worrier, and since the rape Arlene had been the cause of almost perpetual tension. And that made her snappy. And that, in turn, aggravated her husband who blamed it all on Arlene. And the girl had ceased to contribute to the family upkeep and there-fore was a double liability.

So he belted her one. It was a great relief. She didn't scream or weep or beg him to stop. If she had he would have obeyed her for he was shocked by his action. But she didn't. She simply whimpered and cringed and shrank back into a corner and took it. And he felt a surge of unexpected release from the tension that had built and built till he felt he would explode.

So whenever the strain they were all under got too much for him he beat up Arlene.

Arlene felt she deserved it. She was terrified of those beatings, waited in petrified fear for them to happen and afterwards felt the same release as her father. It was as if by beating her he somehow made things better. She did not understand it, it was simply a fact. Fear had become part of her life and her only relief came when she had been punished.

Her friends, those who were once her friends, had romances, got married, started families, but she remained apart, separated from life. Alone. Quite, quite alone. Alone in a world she had entered through the most violent of acts and which she remained trapped in because of repeated violence.

CHAPTER FIFTY-FOUR

Breeda and Des were a couple, an item. Everyone knew they were doing a line. The whole staff at Deary's were breathless with the excitement of it and Breeda felt special and proud when she walked through the store. Even Mr McGillicuddy couldn't dampen her joy and she let his sarcasm and innuendoes wash off her like water off a duck's back.

'This isn't a marriage mart,' he'd grumble. 'Floozies comin' here to catch themselves a fella! Cheek!'

Breeda didn't take the bait. No one was going to spoil it for her. The suffocating turmoil of the first romantic days had settled down to a lovely restrained passion and an obsession for each other's company.

They were in love. It was beautiful and wild and curiously normal. They enjoyed every moment, relishing their happiness, exploring each other's past, sharing memories and trying desperately to keep from 'going too far'. The last thing Des wanted was for Breeda to have to face the consequences of that.

It was difficult. Their bodies were irresistibly drawn to each other. Like magnets they seemed to be pulled together. But Des respected her. It would not be right to take advantage of her and it would be tragic if she got pregnant. So he determined to restrain himself until he could marry her. He had to prove he revered her. After all, he was not an animal.

But it was difficult. Breeda talked it over with Mavis who, after a lot of hedging and beating about the bush, inferences and eye-rolling, imparted the riveting information that there were other ways, alternatives to 'going the whole hog' as it was strangely phrased. One could find satisfaction manually. Or orally. It wasn't as good as intercourse (she said the word primly) but it was better than nothing. This left Breeda a little uncertain, if not shocked, but she adjusted her ideas, opened her mind, and passion did the rest. She adored Des's body, loved his every limb, so there was nothing they did that could seem shocking to her.

She told Des to talk to Terry and soon they had found a few avenues to quite amazing physical excitement through a distinctive style of heavy petting all their own. It took some experimentation but they were so in love that it didn't take long to find ways to please each other.

It became their main activity. They were all over each other every available opportunity. His hands sought hers, his mouth, his body leaped to respond to her touch and she released him and he her in the back of his car (with the hood down) at lunch-time, on the way home, on the sofa in Harcourt Terrace when Mavis and Terry were out, any time at all when they were together – and they were together all the time. She would slip her hand down his trousers, feel him leap like a salmon to her touch, kiss him and massage him until he came and it gave her a feeling of immense power, extraordinary tenderness and a proprietorial and overwhelming warmth towards him. He was hers and she knew secret things about him. She knew how to excite and please him.

And he could excite and please her. She had not known nor dreamed that such pleasure existed. Her whole body felt gloriously alive and all she regretted was they could not plunge into each other, becoming one in full passionate embrace.

They would eventually, they both knew that, and meantime they had to be satisfied with half-measures, congratulating themselves on their restraint in keeping the status quo.

They talked of marriage constantly. Des was all for it, sooner the better. 'Nothing will stop us, love,' he told Breeda. 'We've both come from nothing; the only way is up.'

But Breeda wanted to save a little first. 'We'll do it in the spring,' she decided. 'We'll wait till then. You can move in here when Mavis and Terry leave. It will be our place. We can both save.' She snuggled up beside him on the sofa.

'Oh, it will be wonderful,' he said. 'Just the two of us, together.'

'In bed together,' she whispered. 'Naked. Nothing between us. Together completely.'

'Oh, my darling, I wish we could now. I wish we could . . .'

'No. We haven't much longer to wait . . .' she told him, her hand creeping up his thighs.

He pulled her fiercely to him. 'Jasus, I hope I can. Wait, I mean,' he murmured against her lips.

They moved in a world of sensuous languidity, erotically voluptuous excitement permeating everything they did. It was like moving underwater, slowly, luxuriously, bones weak, senses responsive to the slightest arousal. Yet they were not yet fully awake, and they waited in a state of fervent suspense for that final thrust of passion, that consummation of their desire, that penetration that would turn their semi-dreamlike sensuality into hot, fervid completion.

They heard Mavis laugh in the hall. She always laughed before they entered the room and expected Des and Breeda to warn them in the same fashion. They broke apart.

'We'll plan after Christmas,' Des whispered as their friends burst into the room after a discreet interval, cheeks glowing from the sharp winds off the Liffey.

'We're off tomorrow to Wexford,' Mavis said breathlessly, 'so we thought we'd give you this tonight.' She turned her back, then whirled around holding a gift-wrapped parcel.

'Tar-ah!' she cried. 'Merry Christmas.'

'Oh gosh, Mavis – you shouldn't have,' Breeda laughed excitedly, 'But well . . .' She dived over to one of the armchairs where a curiously shaped parcel was rather badly folded into red paper with green holly and silver tinsel on it. Breeda had had no practice at gift-wrapping.

They exchanged presents with shrieks and squeaks and hugs and excited protests. Breeda's curiously shaped present was a frying pan. 'Ye can hit him wi' it if he doesn't behave,' she giggled and Mavis squealed, 'Oh, it's lovely! I love gettin' stuff for when I'm married. Oh Janey, thanks a ton, Breeda.'

She had given Breeda a bottle of Chanel No 5. She winked at her friend. 'You know an' I know I got it cost . . .' Then she shrieked, 'But it smells the same!'

Terry poured whiskies all round. They toasted each other and talked over plans for their futures. They were in the best of good humours, confident the future held only joy and the fulfilment of their dreams.

It was midnight when Terry and Mavis left. Mavis took a small case with her. When they had gone Desmond held Breeda tightly in his arms. 'I love you, oh I love you,' he cried fiercely.

She smiled. 'I know, darlin'. I know.'

'I'd die if you got fed up with me,' he whispered.

She placed a cautionary finger on his lips. 'Shush, my darling. Don't ever say such a thing. Don't ever think it.'

'What time you want me tomorrow?' he asked, satisfied.

'Three o'clock. We'll eat about five.' She turned a glowing face to him. 'Oh, it will be wonderful.'

'I'll go now. I don't trust myself. I love you so.'

'I love you too, sweetheart.'

'I better let you get some sleep. See you tomorrow.'

O'Malley saw him come out, turn up his coat collar and go to his car. He got in and drove away and O'Malley was left alone beside the canal. He shivered and rubbed his hands together. Lack of sleep made him feel the cold more. He looked around for the umpteenth time but Lonny wasn't there. Lonny hadn't been there all evening. Lonny hadn't been there for days.

Perhaps he was wrong. Perhaps Lonny Clebber was a creep who raped Arlene Shaughnessy, okay, but had not offended again and was innocent of both the rape and murder of Imelda Manning. Perhaps Lonny Clebber simply liked watching. What? Houses? Trees? In Gardiner Street? Christ sakes!

Oh, he was so tired, so very tired. So bone weary he couldn't think straight.

It was past midnight on Christmas Eve and he was here in the cold outside a girl's flat, alone, exhausted, disobeying orders. His wife was in the church at midnight mass with his family. And Lonny Clebber was nowhere to be seen.

O'Malley turned and walked away. He would join Mary and Colleen and his son in the church and sing carols and celebrate the birth of Christ tonight. They would go home and drink spiced wine and open presents, then go to bed. He wondered if he could muster enough energy to make love to Mary. She would enjoy that and perhaps feel a little less neglected.

He lifted his face, glancing up at the stars as he walked away from the house in Harcourt Terrace. He'd take a break tomorrow. He'd obey orders and spend the day with the kids and Mary, eating, drinking, resting. Maybe he'd take Stephen's Day off too. Go back to work the day after. Well rested. Ready for war.

The stars glittered coldly in a black velvet sky and there was silence.

CHAPTER FIFTY-FIVE

Breeda turned over in the warm cocoon of her bed in Harcourt Terrace. She never failed to appreciate awakening in the luxury of fresh, sweet-smelling sheets, in the perfect silence of privacy. She stretched, thinking that soon, in a few months, Desmond would wake up here beside her, and she wriggled contentedly. Mavis and Terry planned an April wedding and then, in May, hopefully, she and Des would tie the knot. It would be wonderful, almost too wonderful to contemplate, and the surge of joy she felt threatened to spill over so she threw off the bedclothes and jumped out of bed. It was warm in the flat even though it was December. Oh, the luxury of it, the opulence of the sumptuous life she led. Fairy-tale stuff.

The windows fitted snugly here, not like Gardiner Street with its broken panes and ill-fitting frames and she had had a fire in the room last night. She had fallen asleep staring into the flames until, at last, her lids had drooped and pulled down the shades over her eyes.

It was Christmas Day. How magical. Christmas presents, friends who had celebrated with her last night, and most of all, Desmond. Desmond would be with her soon. Meantime she had much to do. She had spent every free moment studying recipes. *Woman's Own* had published a detailed schedule giving timings and instructions for a sure-fire successful celebration meal and Breeda had followed it to the letter.

Well almost. She had cheated a little, buying the Christmas pudding and a packet of bread sauce that only required milk and ground nutmeg added to it.

She threw on a chenille dressing-gown and ran into the kitchen. It was all ready. The turkey on the table, a small-sized bird all trimmed and trussed. There was a bowl of breadcrumbs beside it, chestnuts puréed, onions waiting to be chopped. Stems of parsley and thyme in water, salt and pepper, all the ingredients for the stuffing. The pudding waited to be steamed. It looked so exciting, all of it, a feast. She went into the living-room. There were fairy-lights on the tree and she turned them on. Under it was a long, flat parcel, gift-wrapped with a tag that read 'To my darling Desmond from Breeda'.

It was a scarf. A beautiful cashmere scarf, wine-coloured, soft and cosy and luxurious. It would sit snug around his neck. Keep him warm. Caress him. She hugged herself, then collected the torn paper from the presents opened the night before and the four dirty glasses, and returned to the kitchen. She disposed of the crumpled fancy paper, washed the glasses then turned her attention to the stuffing.

She had done most of the work yesterday. She had plucked the turkey, prepared it, peeled the potatoes and she took them from the water now and put them on a fresh dish-cloth, covering them with absorbent kitchen paper to dry them, ready for the oven like the magazine had instructed her. She mixed the ingredients for the stuffing, wiping her eyes as she chopped the onions. She sang to herself as she stuffed the turkey.

The light on the oven switched off and she knew it was hot enough to put the turkey in. She felt a little thrill of excitement as she pushed the baking tin on to the rack, oven centre, thinking of how proud Nuala would be of her daughter if she could see her now.

'I'll tell you every detail, Mam. Describe it all to you,' she whispered to herself, then giggled, thinking of Desmond. 'Well, not *every* detail,' she added.

She looked at the table. The potatoes could stay there drying. She'd put them in later. The Brussels sprouts were in a pot of cold water, salted. She broke the seal on the bread-sauce mix and tipped it into a small saucepan, added the measured milk, then left it to one side ready to cook at the last moment. She put out a sauce-boat to pour it into when it was ready. Later. She wondered if there was anything she'd forgotten.

She went into the living-room. They would eat in front of the fire. She'd put the carols record on the gramophone ready to turn on when the doorbell rang and Desmond arrived.

She began to set the table. Glasses, polished. The crackling fire.

Plates to warm over the stove in the kitchen. Matching cutlery in a land of plenty. Every now and then she gave a little twirl or a skip of pure joy.

The doorbell rang. It shrilled, breaking the silence, slicing the tranquil hush. She jumped. She looked at the clock. Eleven o'clock. Who could it be?

Desmond! It had to be. No one else would call, Christmas morning. Drat! She hadn't bathed. She had planned it all so carefully. Set the table, bathe, dress and make-up, twelve mass, home, last-minute preparations, then, *then* Desmond would ring the bell. That's when he would arrive. Not now. Not yet.

She pulled the chenille dressing-gown around her, tied the tie securely, pushed her hair back and opened the door to the flat, leaving it on the latch, then she ran down the steps and opened the front door.

CHAPTER FIFTY-SIX

The young man standing there was a stranger.

'What is it?' she asked.

'Merry Christmas,' he cried then pushed past her into the hall. She had no time to realize what he was doing as, without hesitation, he ran up the stairs. Taken completely by surprise she lost precious seconds and her chance to run into the street. Escape.

Instead she followed him up the flight of stairs into her flat, angry now at being disturbed, at her schedule being disrupted, at this young whippersnapper charging ahead of her without being asked. It was like bloody Gardiner Street again. She was unaware yet of any danger.

'Hey, now listen!' She rushed into her living-room. 'What do you want. . .?'

He turned to face her, sprang at her suddenly, moving erratically, flinging her to the floor. Furious, she yelled. It was not the terror-filled cry he was used to: it was an angry bellow.

'Shut up!' he hissed, aware the door was open. Jesus, he'd left it open, anyone could pass by.

'You bastard, get offa me,' she yelled.

It threw him. 'Get offa me!' His own words. For a moment he was disconcerted, his concentration slipped, and in that moment she took advantage, drew up her knee and thrust it into his scrotum with sickening force. It made him turn, cry out and curl away from her.

She leaped to her feet, making now for the door and escape, but, spurred on by a surge of demonic anger, he lunged at her, catching hold of the skirt of her dressing-gown.

She was terrified now and she struggled out of the garment, running to the door, trying to reach it, but her struggles delayed her and he read her plan, reached the door first and pushed it over. It closed but bounced back open with the force he used.

'Let me out! Help! Help!' She was shouting at the top of her voice, struggling away from him. He wondered suddenly if there were other people in the house. He had never seen anyone except the landlord and his wife who lived on the ground floor and who he knew were away. He had watched the house carefully. But only when the girls were about. How did he know whether there was someone upstairs or not? But he'd never seen a light. Never seen anyone about.

'Help me!' she screamed. 'Let me go. Bastard!' She was angry, fighting, a wild-cat.

Fear at the noise she was making galvanized him into sudden, vicious action, instilled him with strength, and he hit her face with his open hand, then punched her on the chin with his clenched fist.

She put up a tremendous battle but her violent resistance only served to excite his desire to dominate. He'd show her!

His flies were undone. He was ready, and her screams ceased suddenly when he tore into her, breaking the virginal barrier, forcing his loathsome member into the privacy of her body. The words bubbled out of him, vomited through slack lips, all his hatred, all his loathing squeezed from him like pus as he did his foul work. 'Fuckin' bitch! Whore!'

She blacked out. She withdrew her conscious mind swiftly, like drawing a shutter. She retreated somewhere else and let him get on with it, this act that would destroy her sex-life forever.

He knew she was not unconscious and her mental withdrawal enraged him. He wanted her to suffer. He wanted her to show him her humiliation. He rammed into her again and again, spewing obscenities at her until he, exhausted, came and fell on her, waiting for the flow of peace, the numbness, the death-like calm he craved. But this time it did not come.

It did not come. He lay on her still body waiting, praying, but instead of peace he was filled with a terrible irritability. Instead of blank calm all he felt was a screaming agitation. The red mist before his eyes did not part. There was no surcease of torment.

He would have to kill her. He would perhaps get his peace if she died. Like that actress. Perhaps they had to die to give him quiet. He put his hands around her throat and began to squeeze.

CHAPTER FIFTY-SEVEN

O'Malley smiled across the room at Mary. He *had* found the requisite energy last night and they had made love and it had been beautiful, healing any possible sense of separation they might have had. She returned his smile with a special intimate grin she always gave him the morning after. The look was full of warmth and it made his bones melt.

She was his love. She always had been. She was the sum total of his happiness.

He had been acutely aware of that, kneeling beside her in the church last night. He had stared at her candlelit face and wondered what the hell he was doing, waiting outside the apartment of a red-haired girl whose life he felt was in danger. Fool! It was *his* life that was in danger for if he lost Mary his whole existence would be rendered worthless.

There was a rich smell of cooking in the living-room. Roasting fowl, onions, nutmeg, mincemeat and chestnut – the odours were delectable and appetite-whetting. Mary was humming 'O Come All Ye Faithful' and in the dim winter morning light the Christmas-tree lights twinkled like the stars last night, sharp and bright.

'Come here, Colleen,' O'Malley beckoned his daughter, rosy-cheeked from excitement. She ran to him, arms out, and he felt a warm surge of gratitude for the love of his family, the security that surrounded him.

'Lunch will be ready soon,' Mary said, glancing at the clock. Seamus at the foot of the tree, knee-deep in festive paper, was too absorbed in a new train-set to react as he usually did at the mention of food.

The telephone rang.

Mary jumped up and looked at him with startled eyes. The expression changed to disbelief, then anger. 'Oh no!'

'It might be your mother,' he said without much conviction.

She shook her head. 'She phoned last night.' Her expression was now one of acceptance. Resigned acceptance. 'Go on. You answer it,' she said and rose and went into the kitchen.

He went into the hall, took the receiver off the wall and heard the panic in McGuigan's voice.

'Calm down, calm down. What happened?'

He listened carefully, the room behind him forgotten. He drew the facts from the young policeman who was stuttering and stammering into the other end of the telephone.

'You were right, sur . . . sur . . . ye were right all the time . . . all the time—'

'Shut up, McGuigan. Is she dead?' There was a terrible apprehension in his heart as he waited patiently for the reply.

'I dunno, sur. I dunno that. Sorry.'

Mary heard the door slam. He hadn't even excused himself from the family festivities. He hadn't said goodbye. He'd just upped and left. God only knew when he'd be back. She sighed, putting the Brussels sprouts on the gas ring, opening the oven door to baste the turkey. He was out there being Sir Galahad, saving maidens from danger. He'd never change. She was foolish to let it upset her. She'd known what he was like when she married him. And he loved her. She smiled at the memory of the night before. His passion was ardent. It spilled over into everything, his work as well as his love-making. His work was a cross she'd have to bear but she mustn't take it out on him. He couldn't help it and if she wanted her passionate, loving man then she'd have to accept the other side of him too: the committed, dedicated worker.

Colleen came into the kitchen. 'Where's Dad?' she asked.

Mary glanced over her shoulder at her pretty teenaged daughter. 'Out slaying dragons,' she said, laughing. Then seriously she added, 'Making the streets of Dublin safer for the likes of you.'

CHAPTER FIFTY-EIGHT

Fergus Twomey was sitting in his world of darkness, his fingers running over the raised lettering of the book on his knee when he heard her screams.

Fergus had been almost completely blinded when a drunken driver, a young Trinity student on his way home from an all-night party, had skidded, his car mounting the pavement, and ploughed into the garden where the young Fergus was playing, tossing the ten-year-old boy in the air, very like the way a bull in a bull-ring would flip a tiny matador out of his way. Fergus had been partially-sighted ever since, which meant that he could see vague outlines, shadows, changes of light, but not objects or colours. Except red. And he could tell night from day, sunlight from dark, stormy clouds. The parents of the drunken student had insisted on making Fergus a monthly allowance. The courts had nothing to do with it. The powers that be said, at the inquest and later at the trial (for there *was* a trial), that it was a tragedy and they hoped Fergus would get his sight back. The drunken boy was fined £100 and given a suspended sentence, left on probation in the care of his parents, and that, as far as the courts were concerned, was that. But the boy's parents had felt a terrible guilt and arranged that Fergus would get an index-linked allowance as long as he lived.

He never regained his sight but thanks to the allowance he was able to study, purchase the equipment he needed and afford to have people in to help him. In the end he came to consider himself, if not exactly fortunate, as least not uncomfortable.

His parents had suffocated themselves chain-smoking and both died of emphysema, gasping for breath until there was no more left.

This happened when he was eighteen and he moved then to the top flat in the house in Harcourt Terrace above the one Mavis occupied.

Everyone tried to persuade him to get a ground-floor flat, suggesting it would be easier for him, but he refused and stubbornly maintained that he liked being forced to go up and down stairs. It kept him mobile, he said. And besides, when he opened his window up high he could almost touch the tree-tops. He could hear them whisper, he said, and smell the breezes from the mountains.

He went out every day at midday when everyone else in the house was at work. He made his little sortie to the shops, bought anything he needed, chatted with the shopkeepers, went and had a beer in the pub, conversed with his acquaintances there and, so fortified and having communicated with the world at large, made his way slowly back to his top flat.

He liked the sounds of the girls downstairs. He liked the sweet perfumed scents that rose upwards through the floorboards. He recognized the perfumes they wore. The loss of one of his senses had sharpened the others and his nose was alert as a hound's. He knew the two separate smells of the girls and he was surprised at the Chanel No 5 this morning, not having identified it mingled with the human smells of the newcomer to the flat below. He had not thought of her as a high-flying lady, more a behind-the-counter class of a girl. But he shrugged, thought how wrong he could be and was grateful that there was someone else in the house this Christmas Day. They were company although they did not know it. He loved their tinkling laughter as they left or entered the house. One of them had gone away, he knew that. The new one was in the house and he who was usually alone at the festive time was glad of her presence below. He could hear her singing.

But now she was screaming.

He had prepared himself for church. Adele, his friend and helper, would call for him in the car and take him to midday mass. So he was ready for her, waiting for the bell to ring at eleven forty-five.

Now it was not the bell he heard but the screams. They were terrified. They were agonizing.

He dithered a moment. What was best to do? Phone or hurry down to help? His instinct was to take his white stick and go as quickly as he was able downstairs, but, he reasoned, that was foolish. He was powerless in his blindness to be accurate, to give much assistance. He couldn't rely on his arrival scaring the assailant away.

So he phoned the local police station. He knew the number. Adele had made him learn it along with the numbers of his doctor, the local hospital, ambulance station and others in case of emergency.

'We don't want you panickin' an' blunderin' around,' she told him and she was right. That was just what he would have done, blundered about, if he hadn't known the number off by heart.

He told the garda to hurry. He gave the address clearly. Then he went downstairs.

He was used to negotiating the stairs; nevertheless he had to contain his impulse to rush forward headlong, precipitating a fall. So he went down calmly tapping his way. The door to the girls' flat was not properly shut and he pushed it open with his stick. He stood there, unaware of what exactly he was staring at. But he saw the red. He saw the scarlet splashes on the floor and the shadows there.

At first Lonny did not register this presence, this tall silhouette in the hall, then as he choked the life out of Breeda Deegan, he became aware of an elongated shadowy figure in the open doorway, watching him. The eyes were wide and milky-white; the man was like the figure of death, he had a stick and was tapping it against the wall. The hall-light behind him haloed grey hair around a pink skull and the wide unblinking eyes were fixed on Lonny. This was death, Lonny decided, this was no mortal man. This was the Devil come to get him, the Black Avenger. He froze for a second, terrified, then he dropped the inert body and, pushing past the spectre in the doorway, he ran down the stairs, down the hall and out into the street.

CHAPTER FIFTY-NINE

Nuala had been cooking the turkey Breeda had given them for Christmas. Glowing from the heat of the old range where the bird sizzled nicely in the juices she would make gravy from later, Nuala Deegan couldn't remember being so happy before in her life. Except of course for that time, so far away now, when Sean's brother had courted her. But that was in another life. She had been another person then, and now, in her home, enfolded in the rich scents of a lavish meal, she was content.

Sean lay in the children's room, drunk as a fiddler's bitch, out of it for at least the next twelve hours. She wouldn't be bothered with him until Boxing Day and then he'd not waste time with his family but tumble out of the tenement and take himself off to the *bona fide* in Santry and no doubt remain there until the early hours of the following day. There was no work over the festivities and he'd make the most of the Christmas. So she'd be off the hook, relieved of his dampening the party, and it was thanks to the bottle of twelve-year-old whiskey Breeda had given him for a present. Had she foreseen the benefits to Nuala in so doing? Nuala thought probably, and silently thanked her daughter.

The children were up and washed and dressed since dawn, excited at the prospect of abundant food and pudding, which they had never had before. Even Lizzy was on her best behaviour, unwilling to risk a punishment that would banish her from this warm, inviting atmosphere. Breeda had enabled them to have a wonderful Christmas and Nuala was grateful beyond measure to her daughter.

There had been an unusual gaiety in the room, a joy and excitement so alien to them that they did not recognize it.

And then the Detective Inspector came. He cast a pall over their happiness, terrifying Nuala just by appearing in the doorway. She knew a sudden descent of spirit and with a fateful shrug invited him in. She knew it had been too good to last.

It could only be Breeda. She could hear Sean snoring and God help her she wished it was him and not her lovely girl. Dear God, not Breeda. Not the light of her life. Her hope. Her darling. She stared at the garda, her eyes wide and full of fear and a terrible pleading. Not my darlin' child.

The detective didn't tell her much. Just that her daughter was in hospital and he would take her there.

He had a big shiny car and normally she would have been excited to ride in it: she had never been in an automobile. But now, numb with shock, apprehension clutching her stomach, she was hardly aware of where she was or what she was doing.

'She's all right, though, isn't she?' she kept asking the big man, O'Malley he said his name was, and he kept replying, 'I hope so, Mrs Deegan, indeed I hope so.'

When they reached the hospital they took her to the bed where Breeda lay fighting for her life and Nuala would have fallen if the big detective had not supported her. His strong hand under her elbow kept her upright while the nurse got her a chair and she stared at what someone had done to her lovely girl. Her breath came in little moans of horror and they eased her into the chair. She took the hand that lay on the white sterile counterpane in her own calloused palms, leaned her forehead on those hands, her own and Breeda's, and she wept. Through stiff lips she muttered, talked to the big silent man beside her, lamented over the bruised and battered body of her child.

'I made her,' she moaned to him. 'I made her fair and beautiful, sir. I nurtured her in Gardiner bloody Street, that desert, I tended her there and I did a good job. I hadn't the strength to do the same for the others. Those childer are halfway to lives led in the shadows, they're halfway to petty crime, Mister, and you will get to know them soon. But not Breeda. Breeda was a miracle; a rose in a briar patch. Flourishing in spite of everything. When I thought "There must be more than this", I thought of Breeda. She was all my hopes and dreams. And I knew my daughter would make it, escape the poverty and dirt and exchange the dark streets for brighter lights. An' she did, sir, she did. Now look at her. Is this what they do to ye if ye escape?

They'd never do this to her in Gardiner Street . . . bad though they are they'd never do this . . .' Her voice broke and the monologue petered out into a banshee weeping.

The big detective patted her shoulder. After a time, when her weeping had subsided, he excused himself and went outside and a smaller, slimmer, more boyish policeman took his place. She turned her ravaged, tear-stained face to him, her eyes pleading. 'They'd never do this to her in Gardiner Street,' she repeated and he misunderstood her.

He looked awkward, sympathetic, cleared his throat. 'Well, yes, he would,' he answered. 'He'da got her one way or the other.'

Alert suddenly, her quick wits absorbing his unguarded remark, she chose her words carefully, not wanting to alarm him. 'Would he?'

The young garda nodded, his heart going out to her. 'We watched him there many's the night,' he said, eager to be helpful. 'There an' Harcourt Terrace. We were tryin' to prevent another case like the last one. We did our best, Missus.'

So it had happened before. To another. She controlled herself. Kept her eyes down, away from his guileless innocence, away from the battered and bruised face of her daughter. To look at either would show her hand, break the spell, and his confiding would stop.

'Oh?' She kept the word casual.

He nodded. 'It was Detective Inspector O'Malley, the big man who brought you here. He was afraid this would happen. He said Lonny was follyin' her, yer daughter, but the Chief Super wouldn't listen. They all thought O'Malley was mad. A rape an' a murder couldn't happen again.'

She winced, the pain of what he said piercing her heart like a knife But she forced herself to stay still. Very, very still.

'But O'Malley was sure it was goin' to an' he was right. The Chief Super'll have to eat his words now.' The young garda had a gleam in his eyes.

'Oh?'

'I got the call, see. From this blind fella. Shame he was blind. Mighta stopped him. An' he won't be able to identify him, more's the pity. I knew at once it was Lonny Clebber at it again when I got the call. Phoned the DI at once. Probably saved her life – the blind fella, I mean, not me.'

She cleared her throat. 'Did you – er – watch this Lonny . . . Clebber? Clebber goin' to his home?' she asked softly.

She waited, breath bated for his reply. He nodded, his eager young face glad to impart the information, glad to let her know what had happened, glad to be an expert.

'Yeah! The cottage by the Tolka. At the bridge. Creepy place. We watched it. But the Chief Super took us offa the job. Said DI O'Malley was loosin' his marbles.' That gleam again.

'This Lonny Clebber did it before, you say?'

Suddenly cautious, McGuigan glanced at her. 'Yeah! He got off rape over a year ago. Judge said it was the girl's fault. O'Malley was ragin'. Like a bull, ragin'. Ye shoulda seen him. Then he thought Lonny Clebber was the one killed Imelda Manning. Now we're sure. He did this just as the DI said he would.'

She drew in a sharp breath and the doctor arrived to speak to her, accompanied by O'Malley. The man who had tried to prevent this heinous crime.

They took her away to a small impersonal room that had chairs and old magazines on an occasional table. She did not hear much of what was said. They uttered mainly platitudes and carefully non-committal reassurances. The blood throbbed in her head and she wanted more than anything to run away, out of here. She had a job to do, then she'd come back here and sit by Breeda's body whether it was dead or alive.

That body she had given life to had been defiled. A sacrilege had been committed, and so a sacrifice was demanded. Everyone knew that.

She stood up suddenly. O'Malley's eyes widened. The doctor, more accustomed to the manifestations of grief and shock, looked less startled.

'I need air,' she said, folding her hands together so that they would not see how she trembled.

'Of course. A nurse will accompany you . . .'

'I want to be left alone,' she cried firmly. 'I need a little time on my own. I'll be right back.'

The doctor nodded and she left the small room.

'Is she all right?' O'Malley asked.

'What do you think?' the doctor replied caustically, then seeing O'Malley's expression added, 'It's quite normal to feel claustrophobic. Quite usual. Especially in here.' He glanced around the room, not really seeing it.

'You'll do everything possible for Breeda, Doctor?'

'Naturally!' The doctor sounded miffed.

'When do you think I can speak to her? Ask her some questions?'

The doctor snorted. 'Certainly not yet – if at all. The girl is no way near out of danger.'

O'Malley looked squarely at the doctor. 'The bastard who did this to her is out there,' he said coldly, his lips tight. 'He's done it before. He'll do it again. Breeda Deegan can help us to put the fucking little shit away. Sorry, Doctor.'

'My first priority is to help the girl to live,' the doctor replied crisply.

'And the prognosis?'

The doctor shrugged. 'Will he be convicted?' he asked.

'I don't know,' O'Malley replied. 'I simply don't know.'

The doctor sighed and shook his head and returned to his patient.

O'Malley groaned. Would they, *could* they get Lonny Clebber this time? They had no witnesses. Fergus Twomey was blind. If Breeda died Lonny would walk, free as a bird, to try again, to spoil another young life.

O'Malley's mouth tightened. He'd give the little shit a hard time, come what may. Dublin was not large enough to hide the cocky little creep, the smear on the face of the earth. He wasn't the sort of criminal who ran. He had nowhere to go. O'Malley decided he'd leave McGuigan with Breeda Deegan and he himself would collect Rahilly and a couple of gardai, anyone he could drum up Christmas Day, and go to the cottage on the Tolka, arrest the little git and hope the Deegan girl would recover enough to identify him. It was all he could do.

He shivered, pushing away the awful thought. If Breeda didn't recover then they would probably lose him again. The man who had phoned them was blind, so his testimony wouldn't stand up in court even though he swore he could tell Lonny by his smell. He said his perceptions were extra acute, but no jury would convict on such tenuous evidence.

O'Malley waited a few minutes, marshalling his thoughts, curbing his anger. Then he left the hospital, wondering briefly as he went to his car where Mrs Deegan was, sorry she was not there so he could press her hands and convey a little of the sympathy he felt.

CHAPTER SIXTY

Nuala Deegan stood outside the room for a while gasping for breath. She felt as if someone had punched her in the chest, and she could not seem to recover. The conversation between the doctor and the detective lapped over her, sinking slowly into her brain.

She was an uneducated woman but she was not a stupid one. She understood all that had been said and a lot that had only been implied.

She stared up the hall to where her daughter lay motionless behind drawn curtains, bruised and beaten and defiled, on a sterile white bed. She saw the young policeman who had been speaking to her come out of the cubicle and sit on a chair opposite. The corridor was long and very quiet. People were always quiet around pain and loss of life. Hushed. You heard no laughter. Somewhere someone called a name and it sounded strange in the sober stillness of this house of the sick. The pictures on the wall were all religious: Our Lady, St Anthony, St Francis with the animals. She did not feel like praying just now. She remembered complaining to Breeda once: 'Is that all there is for me? This ceaseless struggle? No prizes? No rewards? Jasus, it's hard!'

'There'll be Heaven, Mammy, when you die.' Breeda had been going through a spiritual phase, deciding whether or not she had a vocation.

'Don't give me Heaven! I'm not sure I believe in Heaven,' Nuala had said. 'All that crap about people on clouds drifting about with harps! What I want is a visit to a hairdresser.'

Breeda had laughed. 'I'll help you, Mam, when I'm older,' she had said, consoling her mother, loving her.

And she had. She had given generously, relieving the strain. She had been so good.

A nurse came down the corridor pushing a trolley. There were phials of pills on the trolley, a roll of bandages, an enormous pair of scissors, a few stainless-steel, kidney-shaped receptacles, blood-splashed lint and some clean lint pads, a sharp knife, a basin full of pink water with clots of blood floating on its surface, a stethoscope and other such medical paraphernalia. A pot on the lower shelf of the trolley was covered with a sheet of paper. The nurse was going in and out of the cubicles, sometimes collecting something, sometimes bringing something in and leaving it there.

Nuala stood running the back of her hand across her nose, watching. She had not realized that she was crying. Her face and nose were damp and slippery. The nurse disappeared into another cubicle, leaving the trolley in the corridor.

Nuala reached out and took a square of clean lint and she wiped her face with it. She put it in her pocket and took another. She heard the nurse moving around in the cubicle. The curtains were partly open and she could see a fat bald man, head bandaged, his face putty-grey. He was propped up on pillows but his eyes were closed. The nurse was filling his carafe of water from a tap in the washbasin. Ministering to him. Looking after his interests. Woman as man's slave, man's victim.

She thought of Sean: 'Where's me tay, woman!' His fist on the table, a loud bang that made the children jump. It upset them until they became used to it and then the boys started imitating him. If Sean needed a glass of water he had to ask her to get it, not sure where the glasses were kept, or the cups for that matter, in the home he had lived in for twenty years! She thought of his friends with their evenings in the pub, how they always raised the money for that and their wives doing without, slaving over the childer, the cold water making their hands swell, making the washing difficult. She thought of the women tending priests, toiling after them, not letting them lift their little fingers and then the clergy telling her what to do. How dare they! Women always mopping up. Bloody fools! All our own fault, she decided.

She thought of the man – what was it – Lonny, yes, Lonny Clebber who lived in that cottage near the Tolka. Everyone knew that cottage. Some said a witch lived there. A story to scare schoolchildren on their way home from school. It was not too far from Gardiner Street, that cottage on the Tolka. She thought of Lonny Clebber, forcing her

Breeda, her child, beating her, despoiling her just because he was bigger, stronger.

That man, the detective had said, might escape justice. A cry burst from her lips.

The nurse hurried out. 'Are you all right? Can I get you . . .?'

'Water. A glass of water, please.'

She didn't want water. She had made up her mind.

The nurse looked to the cubicle behind her where the bandaged man lay. You could see her thinking. Should she? Take his water? The tumbler off his carafe? Nuala could see her come to a decision and turn into the cubicle. After all, the patient was hardly likely to need the glass in the next few minutes.

She filled the tumbler from the carafe and brought it to Nuala. The woman shuddered and drank it gratefully. The nurse put the glass on to the trolley. She was thinking about how she must not forget to put the glass back in the cubicle before the patient awoke, otherwise Sister would kill her.

She didn't notice then that some of the lint was missing. She didn't notice the scissors were gone. She didn't miss the surgical knife. She pushed the trolley towards the end of the corridor and gave a sigh of relief. She would wash the glass, replace it beside the patient's bed and then she would be off duty! Gorgeous. Bliss. Free to go home to her mam and da and join what was left of the Christmas festivities.

CHAPTER SIXTY-ONE

Lonny went to the public baths. They were closed. He cursed and kicked the locked door in a sudden storm of uncontrollable anger, but it was no use; the doors didn't budge.

It was dark in the street. The cobblestones were wet and slimy. Black slippery mud underfoot. It had been dark all day as well as night these last few days. The street-lights gleamed dimly in the foggy air and it seemed as if the world trembled on the brink of darkness. A fog rolled in from the Liffey, slipping across the face of the city.

He mooched out Into the street. Everything was deserted. Shops were boarded up and the pubs were closed. There was no one about.

Bloody Christmas. He slouched along, coat collar up, hands in pockets, morose expression on his tight little ferret face.

It was cold. That accounted for his shaking. That and the fact he'd been interrupted before he got his release.

No. He'd ejaculated. Into the bitch. But he'd had no relief. Jesus, why? Why not? What had gone wrong? His nerves jangled. He felt as if saws were being drawn across his brain, his sinews stretched, his whole system screaming.

He wanted out! He wanted to be somewhere else. Another land. Be someone else. He yearned to find himself suddenly in one of those 'Rooms to Rent' downtown in some American city, the kind of seedy room, no questions asked, that Alan Ladd, Mark Stephens or Richard Widmark were sure to be in after they'd done something bad. He'd like to be there, staring out of the window, a neon sign flashing on and off, and he'd be standing there spinning the barrel of a gun, a cigarette between his lips, his fedora pushed back on his head. That'd be great.

Instead he was in bloody Dublin, everything shut, nowhere to go except the cottage on the Tolka with its now peculiar smell, its dampness, its darkness.

Who was that apparition? The one he'd seen in the hall? Where had it come from? Was it a human being who could identify him? Or was it a ghost, a phantom, an evil wraith come to get him? Was it the Devil?

His mother always promised him the Devil would get him. In the end he thought she was probably right. He had to pay, just as those girls had had to. Everything would be tallied up in the end. Accounted for.

But he was the Avenging Angel. Was the Avenging Angel held to account? Surely not.

He thought of the man, the phantom in the hall, looking at him. It would be the end for Lonny if he could identify him. It would also be the end for him if the apparition *was* Satan. Satan reminding him about the tally. He felt the nerves jumping under his skin like eels, screaming, frightening his heart, making it leap too like a salmon trying to escape.

He remembered his mother and the syrup of figs.

'Drink it up, Lonny. Clear yourself out. Flush it all away. All the dirt – the dirt – the dirt.'

He'd go home. Get the syrup of figs. Purge himself. He hated it but he'd dose himself to clean himself. Get rid of the bad things.

He walked home dragging his feet. He reached the path that was parallel to the bridge but led down to the riverbank, to his cottage.

The ground was damp and squelchy underfoot. The fog lay heavy on the river. It floated in clouds of pearl-grey vapour all about the cow-parsley, the reeds, the nettles, the ferns lying like scarves against the leaves of the willows. He could hear the gurgle of the water as it danced coldly over the stones. He could also hear the plop-plop-splash of the river rats that scuttled about here in their legions.

And something else. He was approaching the cottage and he saw from the thick foliage the river goddess with the kind face rise up out of the mist, like an apparition, rise up and move towards him.

He stared dumbfounded. There she was, her pale face luminous in the mist. She opened her arms, just like in his dream. The face that had floated before him in Gardiner Street, up there in the clouds, that infinitely sympathetic face, that kind, perfect-mother face was here before him when he most needed her, here to help him, here to comfort and tell him what to do.

He was not dreaming. He could see her clearly now as the mist lifted, then descended, lifted again. She rose up as if from the river and opened her arms, her gentle, pale face glowing in the dark, foggy afternoon.

He ran to her. She would save him. She would bring him peace. She was the mother he had always wanted.

As he neared her she raised her right hand. He saw what he had never before noticed in his dreams: there was a knife in her right hand, a knife autopsy-sharp, thin as a reed, a silver sliver of cruel steel. And in her left hand there was a pair of scissors, its blades flashing under the opaque lamp-light from the bridge above them. She was no comforting mother, she was playing *his* role. She was the Avenging Angel.

He could not stop his rush towards her and as he ran to her he opened his mouth.

'Aw-w-maw-maw—' The strangled cry was torn from him as the scissors plunged into his back and he realized that he'd been wrong, wrong, wrong. He was not the Avenging Angel. *She* was. And if he was mistaken about himself that meant . . . that meant . . . The reality was too terrible to contemplate and he was almost glad to feel the steel against his throat. He jerked back his head as the knife sliced him open, clean as a surgeon.

'Get offa me . . .' he gurgled and the blood spurted in a fountain, gushing out and baptising them both in the scarlet torrent.

CHAPTER SIXTY-TWO

They heard the terrible cry and the gurgling sound as they left their cars and hurried down to the cottage.

'Jasus, sir . . . look . . .' Rahilly cried.

O'Malley approached slowly. He knew what had happened. No one needed to explain. He cursed himself for a fool. An imbecile.

The mother had killed the cruddy little git. The stupid fuckin' mother had taken the law into her own hands. Oh shit! He shoulda seen it coming. Now the little bastard wouldn't have to stand trial, was spared the contempt of the whole town, the hatred directed against him by his fellow criminals, the fury of the country. Shit, shit, shit. One of the gardai was vomiting in the reeds. Two others were holding the half-unconscious form of Mrs Deegan. Someone had phoned for an ambulance. It took longer on Christmas Day.

O'Malley looked around. The place, he thought, would make a great setting for the first scenes of *Macbeth*. Or *Dracula*. McGuigan had been right.

Another young garda had reeled out of the cottage, depositing his Christmas dinner outside the front door. There was another body in there, it seemed. A decomposing body. It was a very damp cottage.

They helped Mrs Deegan to the ambulance and as she passed O'Malley she turned glazed eyes upon him and murmured, 'He didn't escape justice after all, did he, Mister?'

O'Malley said nothing. His heart was heavy and he was angry.

She'd not escape, poor Mrs Deegan. She'd get life. They might even hang her, but he hoped not. Her mental state would be taken into consideration. However, it depended on the judge. Judges didn't hold much in Dublin with mental states. Murder, they said, was murder and there was, in O'Malley's opinion, a disproportionate value put on the male of the population. It was presumably historic, but if a man committed murder because his wife was driving him around the bend, there seemed to be a certain amount of sympathy generated in the all-male judiciary. A woman killing – what had the judge in the rape trial called him? O'Malley frowned as he watched the drooping body of Mrs Deegan being led to the ambulance – a 'diligent and sober worker' would not be dealt with so leniently. God forbid Dublin would be deprived of such a man.

All this had begun with that summation. If that judge had called Lonny Clebber what he actually was: a rapist, a menace to society and women in particular, and given him an appropriate sentence, all this might have been avoided.

He stared at Nuala Deegan. Poor lady. Poor, poor woman. She'd be locked up, no account taken that she too was 'a diligent and sober worker'. She'd be, at worst, hanged, at best, imprisoned with the criminally insane. Years of confinement ahead of her, a lifetime of suffering. And all she'd done was rid the world of vermin. But the law was the law.

And Lonny had done it again! Wriggled out of it. It had been clean and swift, his death. It had been quick after all. O'Malley felt a tight band around his chest. He could feel the mud seeping in at the sides of his shoes. His legs were ice-cold. He thought of the fire at home, the sweet smell of the pine-cones.

He'd do as little of the paperwork as was possible. It was all indelibly in his head. It would take him an hour. They didn't have to look for a perpetrator. They knew who did it. All of it.

He'd do that. And then he'd go home. Home to the warmth and sanity. To peace and normal things. To Mary and Seamus and Colleen.

It had been one hell of a Christmas but at least the lovely young girls of Dublin could sleep safe in their beds again now that Lonny Clebber was dead.

EPILOGUE

TWELVE YEARS LATER

CHAPTER SIXTY-THREE

'Can't you stay home tonight, Meriel?' he asked reasonably.

'No! Got to go to the meeting. We're getting ready for the rally Sunday.'

'Where you'll burn your bra again, no doubt!'

'What did you say?' Calling from the kitchen, a little tetchy.

'I'd rather you stayed at home. We could hold hands and have a conversation.'

'Oh, darling, you know I can't.' Her voice calm, implying he should be adult about it.

'I don't *want* you to go!' He sounded petulant and he knew it.

She appeared in the doorway and he thought, as he always did, how attractive she was. Slim as a reed, she had lost all that puppy-fat and resembled her mother now. All smooth lines and elegance. She wore, as she always did, tight-fitting jeans and an open-necked silk shirt. She had on leather boots and held a potato-peeler in one hand, a potato in the other.

'What did you say?' Her voice quiet, boding no good.

He looked up at her from the chair he was sitting in, his little-boy needy look fixed firmly in place. 'I want you *here*, honey. I miss you when you go out. I get lonely.'

'Aw! Poor lamb.' Sarcasm. But she was pleased, he could tell. Or perhaps not displeased was a better way to phrase it.

It would have panned out all right if he had left it at that but then he made a mistake.

'All this women's lib stuff takes you away from me.' Shit! Her eyes had gone cold and dark as pebbles in a pool.

'What was that?'

'Never mind.'

'I heard you. Women's liberty is desperately important to me. You wouldn't understand. Women demand certain rights. If that stupid judge had put Lonny Clebber away that first time, then Fliss wouldn't have been raped. She's never been the same since, and you, Bobby, should know that. You of all people.'

It seemed to him it was always there, somewhere, that day when Fliss Masters had been raped. Poor Meriel had so needed a reason, an answer, and women's lib had given her outrage a channel. And an explanation, however tenuous. Meriel thought there had to be a reason for everything. She had not yet accepted the fact that a lot that happened was without reason. That life was accidental.

'Why did you ask me if you heard?'

'Oh, don't be childish. This is a very exciting time for women, Bobby. You will not succeed in turning me into a copy of my mother. Or your mother.'

'God forbid!'

'Quit the sarcasm. I'm *not* your maid. I'm not your servant . . .'

'Oh, honey, when have I ever . . .'

'Oh, darling, you don't! 'Cept that time you made me get up and cook a late supper – three o'clock, God's sakes, for your card-playing friends . . .'

'One isolated incident—'

'But it *never* occurs to you to cook a meal.'

He looked up surprised, then bewildered.

'Or help me with the housework. You never lend a hand. All you ever do is lift your feet so I can Hoover underneath. Do you know how demeaning that is?'

'But it's your job, sweetie. I give you a generous allowance for the housekeeping. I never stint you or ask you to scrape and scrimp as some husbands do. You can't expect me to help you when I'm out all day earning . . .'

It sounded as though she was unfair when he put it like that. She struggled to be fair, then gave up. She gave an exasperated squeak and threw the potato at him. Then she threw herself at him, kissing him greedily.

'The trouble with you is . . .' she cried when she came up for air, 'trouble is, you always win.'

'But you still go out and leave me,' he complained. 'So I seldom have the last laugh.'

He pulled her to him again, slipped his hand into the silk shirt and began massaging her nipple. She smacked his hand. 'The children will be in any moment,' she said.

'Not for at least ten minutes,' he told her. She sat up on his knee and looked at him squarely. 'Okay,' she said, 'which do you want? Ten minutes now before the kids get back? Twenty minutes after supper when they go to the tennis club at seven-thirty and I go to the meeting at ten to eight? Or an all-night session when I get back?'

'With extras?'

'Every extra in the book. I'm feeling randy as hell this evening, only you knew.'

He kissed her deeply again, aroused by her words, her body, her warmth

'Settle for which?'

'Can't I have them all?'

She giggled. 'Wear me out! Oh, you brute! No, come on, which you want?'

'Night. With extras.'

'Okay,' she said brightly, leaped to her feet and disappeared, then popped her head around the door again. 'And no more about women's lib, okay?'

'Okay,' he agreed and smiled, then settled back to read his newspaper.

CHAPTER SIXTY-FOUR

Arlene Shaughnessy sat in her room. The light was off and she was alone. She sat sucking a Player's Navy Cut not taking any notice of the ash which showered down on to the sheets. There was a plate of sandwiches on the bedside table. They had little boils of blue and grey-green mould all over them. They had been there for a week now and she had not touched them or any other food during that time.

There had been a terrible silence in the house for a long time. She knew her father had been arrested for assault when the next-door neighbours phoned the Gardai. They could hear her screaming, they said, and something was not right at number twelve. That was the house the Shaughnessys lived in.

Her mother was raging. Fit to kill. They came and saw the state Arlene was in, her bruises and unhealed, suppurating wounds, and they took her father away, leaving her mother behind, full of venomous hate for her daughter.

It had been a terrible time. The police had tried to take her out of the room she lived in. Then the ambulance men came and tried to get her to leave and she refused. Then people started pulling at her and she begged them to leave her alone and at last they went.

Almost incoherent with fury her mother had taken over from her father and administered a beating so vicious that Arlene had passed out. Her mother had not spoken to her since, not come to her room or fed her or communicated in any way. Arlene was afraid to leave. She didn't know what to do now so she did nothing. She lay still, propped up by the dirty pillows, and smoked nervously.

Then she ran out of cigarettes and lay there aching for one but still too scared to emerge. So she lay there and bit her lip until it bled.

The hospital people came back to try to take her but she refused to go. She shouted out of the window that she was all right, that she was over twenty-one and could do as she pleased and to please send her father back to her mother. But they didn't and her mother still refused to speak to her.

Arlene hadn't left the room in so long she was afraid to budge. She simply *couldn't* cross the threshold. Her body refused to obey her. Her mother promised the ambulance people she would look after Arlene but when they went she beat her senseless again. Then she brought her the sandwiches and some water. Then she left her alone again.

Arlene could hear her mother below. Her mother talked to herself all the time since her husband had been taken away. The lament seemed angry and bitter and unending and Arlene believed her mother would kill her if she went down there.

Arlene began to cry. It had all got so out of hand. What had started as punishment had become a way of life, had contaminated everyone. She had believed, initially, that she would recover in this room. That if she stayed quietly here the pain, the shame, would go, and people would forget about the rape. But she had found herself trapped. It had got worse and worse until she had driven her father to violence.

Now it had escalated into a nightmare and that other girl, that Arlene Shaughnessy who had stood in the witness box and bravely accused Lonny Clebber of rape, was gone forever, unrecognizable under this bundle of dirty bedclothes. She had done as the Gardai asked. She had taken her courage, every bit of it, and hoped to see justice done, but that sassy young man had got away with it, and the pretty young girl was now a stranger from another world. Time had slipped by her in a dreamlike trance. She felt she had not been present in her own life at all, not *there* while it was happening.

She felt very tired. She'd sleep. In her sleep she was that young girl again, talking about fellas, talking about Lana Turner and dreaming of a Debbie Reynolds house and a husband and children. She rarely looked in the glass. She wasn't sure who the strange woman reflected there was. That woman had grey hair which straggled down over her eyes, she had yellow teeth and she was old.

Dreams would come if she slept. Dreams of a calm and lovely countryside and a little girl, one hand held by her mother and the other by her father, and she, trusting them, loving them as they laughed and supported her when she lifted her legs from under her and let them take her weight. Kindly smiling at her. Loving her.

That was long ago, if ever, and she didn't know the truth of it, but she could dream it.

Couldn't she?

CHAPTER SIXTY-FIVE

Denis Martin stood outside the Gaiety Theatre.

'It's a good photograph, that one,' he said to the PI girl who was fixing the photographs under the glass. She smiled. Actors were so vain.

'You did this play before, Denis? If what they tell me is true,' the PI girl said. He nodded.

'Long time ago,' he murmured, remembering. 'Years!'

'It was your first big success,' she continued. 'I told the *Independent* and the *Evening Herald*. I did get it right, didn't I?'

'Sure,' he replied. 'But I wouldn't call it my first big success. Milo O'Shea was the star. I only played a small part. But I never stopped working on the strength of it.'

'And now you're back in the O'Shea part.'

He laughed. 'If I'm half as good as he was I'll be a wow!'

Suddenly, for no reason, he saw the face of Imelda Manning. Like a photograph. Perhaps it was the way the PI had fixed them. He didn't know what switch in his memory brought her face to mind. He hadn't thought about her in – Lord, it must have been nigh on twelve years, not since that last production.

'There was another beginner in it then,' he said. 'So talented. So lovely. I was very smitten.'

'Oh? Where's she now?'

'She was murdered.'

The PI girl shuddered. 'Jasus! This is a comedy or I'd make use of that bit of info. Pity it's not *Macbeth* we're doing. Murdered, you say?'

'Yes. The night before we opened. She was going to be a big star.'

'Jeez! How gruesome.'

He thought of Imelda and that electric vitality she had. How she shone. He thought of her lost life. All the days of laughter, all the long evenings of love she had been deprived of. All the songs she would have sung and the dances she would have danced. the dazzling performances she would have given.

'Imelda Manning,' he said.

The PI looked over her shoulder at him, puzzled. 'What?'

'Imelda Manning. That was her name.'

The PI girl turned to him, finished with her work. 'Oh,' she said. 'Sorry. Never heard of her.'

CHAPTER SIXTY-SIX

They walked around the yard. They talked in the commonroom. They smoked. Nuala Deegan had never smoked until she went to prison. She had never had the time or the money. Her hands seemed always to be in cold water or performing some household task or holding a babby so she had never had an opportune moment to put a cigarette in her mouth, and her few pennies wouldn't have stretched that far anyway. Now she chain-smoked.

Sean had always had money for a fag. Sean had always managed.

In prison there was little to do. She read what she could but found most of it incomprehensible. People in elevated walks of life with big houses and servant problems debating lofty ideas.

No. There was little to do in prison and time passed slowly.

She worried about the children. Lizzy and Charlie had already been in trouble with the polis. Petty theft. She couldn't find it in her heart to blame them. If society didn't provide work and some little hope of a bare existence then they had only themselves to blame. What could they expect?

Sean never came to see her. He'd brought another woman into the tenement in Gardiner Street and how could she blame him? The poor ould sod hadn't the least idea how to look after himself. He needed a woman.

And he was ashamed of her. He blamed her, obscurely, for everything, and said that no one in his family had ever been to jail. He said it proudly and she couldn't help wondering how he could boast or afford to point the finger when he spent such a deal of his working life semi-comatose, boozed up to the gills. Was what she had done so shameful?

The judge hadn't thought so. He had looked at her with kind eyes. He said he understood the strain she had been under and he took into account all DI O'Malley had said in her favour. But he threw out the psychiatrist's testimony, remarking it was a load of new-fangled twaddle. The judge said anyone might have been seized by a murderous impulse on hearing their daughter had been brutally attacked as Breeda had been, but murder after all was murder and this young man too had been carried away by a murderous impulse. Because of that he had forfeited his life and so should she. She had felt such relief when he said this, his voice ponderous and slow as befitted the seriousness of the crime he had been asked to judge. It would all be over and she could rest.

But the judge instructed the jury that, because they were compassionate people, Christians, because of the extraordinary circumstances, he was not going to recommend the death penalty. He thought that it would be more appropriate to sentence Mrs Nuala Deegan to life imprisonment. And he looked at her as if he expected her to thank him.

They had appealed but nothing had happened and Nuala became accustomed to the deadly monotony of life behind bars. They gave her pills and she got very fat.

Breeda came to see her, brought her fags. Breeda had a new, sharp metallic edge to her. She had been honed by events. Nuala sighed and yearned for her lost, sunny child.

Breeda was beautiful. Elegant. A big success. Married now, not having to work any more, with the horn of plenty spewing forth its goodies into her life, delivering to her the fridges and washing machines, the electric kettles – all the labour-saving devices as they became available on the market. As soon as someone thought of something to save the housewife trouble or strife, Breeda had it installed.

But she also had some of the ancient labour-saving devices, like a maid. A charlady. A cook. A handyman (to mend the modern conveniences). Breeda dressed in Christian Dior and latterly Yves St Laurent, Raymond Kenna and Maurice O'Brien. Breeda had a television set before anyone else in Dublin. She had silver cutlery and linen tablecloths and fluffy towels kept warm on hot pipes. Breeda could bathe in Chanel No 5.

She tried to help her brothers and sisters. Most of them refused her help with that resentful stubbornness Dubliners were famous for.

Nuala Deegan's thoughts of Breeda were a mixture of joy and sadness. The sweetness was triggered by her daughter's success. By the wonderful abundance of worldly goods that proved her victory in the material world. The bitterness came as she realized that her daughter had changed beyond belief. Her spontaneity had disappeared and she had become calculating and reserved. She had lost her innocence and her trust.

It was to be expected, but nevertheless a tragic thing. Nuala knew that the terrible things that happened to one left their mark, no doubt about that. But she missed her daughter's shared joy at her good fortune, she deplored the anxiety and greed with which she *had* to have another reward, another possession. Another manifestation that she was, after all, secure.

Where was that joyous, optimistic girl gone? Death had not eradicated Lonny Clebber's awful influence on her daughter, had not given her back her baby undefiled.

Was there no redress? No healing?

She sighed and lay back on her bunk. She lit another fag. Another day, another night, another fag. She shook her head. It was so meaningless. So utterly meaningless.

The wardress came to give her a pill.

She took it and lay back again, lying as she so often did full length on the bunk. She stared at the walls. There were no cracks to make pictures out of, so, until the drowsiness came, she just lay there and stared at blank nothingness.

CHAPTER SIXTY-SEVEN

Breeda O'Keeffe sat before her dressing-table in the detached house on the Malahide Road. She and her husband, Desmond, had lived here now for ten years. It was a pretty house, set back from the street, green lawns sloping to the gates, roses bordering the driveway and a laburnum near the door. There were roses under the windows and in the summer their scent floated into the house, lifting the heart like a song. The house was full of light. The windows reflected the sunshine and glanced off the cut-glass chandeliers, the candelabra, the glasses on the drinks cabinet.

Breeda polished her nails, buffing them, choosing a nail varnish carefully to match her scarlet dress. Red silk with her red hair always pleased Desmond.

He was so sweet, so kind, so innocent. Sometimes she resented his innocence, his blind belief and trust in her. His faith tormented her.

He had been so good to her after that terrible Christmas Day, the day darkness had engulfed her and she was thrust into a surreal world of nightmare. Hate had contaminated her, forced her to become hard and realistic. To survive. She *had* to survive, and if she wanted to there had to be a shell. Her breeding, her tough upbringing had fashioned her to develop armour against a cruel world. She could not pretend it had not happened, for it had changed irrevocably her approach to sex, to her body, to men. But she had an unyielding determination not to drown in pain and horror, even though the spiritual source of her thoughts and feelings, the centre of her soul, had been poisoned forever.

She thought as little about it as she could, but when Desmond made love to her, so tenderly, so caringly, that presence, albeit fleeting, was always there. Like Banquo's ghost, Lonny Clebber laid a spectral touch on her shoulder. He intruded.

Mostly she dismissed him briskly. But he was there. It was so difficult to forget. Memories have a will of their own. They come in their own time, insinuating themselves between us and the present, tainting it however lightly with their flavour.

When she recovered, when the hospital had done what they could, she left accompanied by Mavis and Desmond. Terry drove them. But she went home to the back room in Gardiner Street, not to Harcourt Terrace, never there again.

Desmond was sensitive enough to realize that all their dreams and plans for Harcourt Terrace had to be scotched.

He spent every available moment he could with her. Mavis and Terry came to see her too. Somehow the fact she lived in a slum didn't seem to matter any more.

Mavis told her that her job was being held open for her, 'They don't know anything,' Mavis hastened to assure her. 'The police never mentioned your name. That was lucky.' Breeda knew it was Detective O'Malley's doing. 'There was a lot about your mam but no one at work made the connection. They think you've got pneumonia and they're keeping the job open.'

That cheered her. She could focus on something outside herself. Quite soon, before January was out, she had returned to Deary's.

But she had lost the old excitement, the enthusiasm. Try as she might she could not rekindle the flame of ambition. She was jumpy and ill-at-ease and the customers did not take to her so easily.

So she acted. She gave consummate performances every day of her life. And she stayed in Gardiner Street.

Desmond was totally loyal to her. He was like a rock, his support constant. But they never talked about it. She never found out how much he knew. Did he know she'd been raped? He never let her speak about exactly what had happened that day and she could never be sure what he felt about it. And she sometimes resented the fact that he couldn't know what she felt, couldn't share her pain. And he hadn't protected her. He, in some frightening way, had failed her. She did not understand why she felt this and she hated herself for even thinking it but nevertheless it lurked there in the back of her mind along with other unwholesome thoughts.

When Breeda broached the subject to Desmond he always said, 'Oh, forget all that, Bree, put it out of your mind. Put it behind you, darling, best thing to do.'

She went to see her mother in the prison and talked to her. But her mother had changed. She seemed indifferent, had become slower, slow and fat. Almost another person, smoking, smoking all the time, chewing the cigarettes, greedily drinking in the smoke.

Later that year she realized she was pregnant. She didn't panic. She simply felt a cold hatred fill her and she knew she could not have the child. It would spoil her whole life. It would push Desmond away and she would lose him. And she would hate that offspring of a rapist, that spawn of evil with her whole heart and soul. The embryo that lived in her body would have to go, so she went to London and got rid of it. The way she would have rid herself of lice, or a tapeworm or a canker.

She had decided, on her return, to blank out London, the experience there, blank it out of her mind, and by and large she had been successful.

She had gone to the big city at the Easter break. Abortion was illegal in England too, but it was possible to procure if one paid enough. She told Desmond that she needed a break away from everyone, that she needed to be alone, and Desmond, trusting her implicitly, allowed her to go without demur. That irritated her. His trust exasperated her and she deplored her contrariness. She told him she was going to see an aunt of Mavis's in Wexford. To be in the country a while.

She went to a back street in Paddington where the prostitutes strutted and there was always someone to fix you up with whatever you wanted, at a price.

She wanted an abortion, she got it.

It was all she saw of London: Paddington. Her train came in there. She left the cold, dirty station and found the bed-and-breakfast place Mavis had discovered for her through another friend whose boyfriend had ditched her and she four months gone. There was a woman in Paddington, Mavis had told her. It would cost £50, Mavis said, and another £50 travel and the B & B. It was a lot of money but Mavis helped.

'Desmond mustn't find out,' Breeda implored. Mavis shook her head and promised. It was a promise she kept.

The B & B was in Sussex Gardens, a clean place, basic in its simplicity, run by a rosy-cheeked, hard-eyed Irishwoman from Cork.

'Yerra ye'll be all right here,' she told Breeda, panting heavily as she climbed the stairs. 'Yer off te Mrs Pendleton, I take it.' Shrewd eyes understanding the predicament. 'God help us, the young girls today – fast lot ye are an' no mistake.' Then seeing the bright red flush on Breeda's cheeks: 'Yerra don't mind me! Sure what's it te me what ye did, what kinda life ye lead, God's sakes.'

Breeda thought of her love for Desmond. She wondered if the priests were right, if sexual experimentation was as grievous a sin as they told you from the pulpit. As if there was no other. Perhaps she had been punished for her love by a raging God. If that was so she simply didn't want to know that God.

She had gone to the tiny house Mrs Pendleton worked out of in the narrow street off Praed Street opposite St Mary's Hospital. The house was boarded up one side and on the other a shop sold medical aids – trusses, false limbs and such like. Breeda shuddered and passed on. The street was sooty, the crowd drably dressed. No one smiled or met her eyes and she tried to suppress the panic that threatened to overcome her.

Mrs Pendleton was a large woman with tired eyes. She seemed kind but Breeda now felt scared to death. Only a fierce determination to put everything about that terrible day behind her kept her from running away.

Mrs Pendleton asked her for the money and she handed it over. She led her into a room, unfurnished except for a bed, a kind of hospital cot. She was told to remove her skirt, then her pants and her stockings. It was freezing in the room even though an electric fire burned. It was a tiny thing, two bars flaming red, like hot pokers. The floor was tiled and cold on the soles of Breeda's feet.

She was told to lie down on the bed. She wished a doctor was there. Or a nurse. The one that had looked after her in the hospital in Dublin. The nurse had got into trouble because her mother had nicked the scissors and the knife. As if she could help it. She was glad her mother had done what she had done, glad at least that Lonny Clebber was dead. But she was sorry her mother had been caught.

Her ankles were put in stirrups and she wanted to curl up and disappear. She had never been so humiliated in her life. Mrs Pendleton didn't speak to her but Breeda could hear her breathing and smell the sickly-sweet smell of sweat from her armpits every time she bent over her.

She was not prepared for the pain. It was excruciating, rending her body assunder. Mrs Pendleton gave her nothing but put a towel over her mouth when she screamed.

'Shut yer trap, you fool. Want te see me in trouble?' she whispered. She remembered the agony ripping her apart and being glad. Feeling the pain was somehow cathartic, removed the filth of Lonny Clebber, exorcised him and the foul deed he had done to her.

She was given aspirin afterwards and hustled into her clothes and out on to the street. She was bleeding profusely. She could feel the sticky mass between her legs, soaking her sanitary pad.

She hurried back to the B & B, where the woman from Cork let her in, shaking her head and tutting.

'Ye can't stay in yer room in the daytime,' she said. 'It's agin the rules. Why ja think it's called bed an' breakfast? God's sake, ye want te get me in trouble?'

So Breeda got her purse and went to Paddington Station, then spent the afternoon there trying not to faint. The station seemed to her like a steel hell, dark and full of smoke. Anonymous grey people hurried about their business, indifferent to her plight. Porters' eyes slid over her with covert contempt, though why, she had no idea. A few toffs and their ladies brushed past her, arrogance in every line of their demeanour, sweeping her out of their path as servants hurried after them obsequiously.

She changed her pads in the ladies', putting the blood-soaked ones down the lavatory even though they said not to. It was there, written up on a yellow notice, but there was no bin and she was too embarrassed to ask. The ladies' lavatory was tiled and smelled strongly of carbolic and Jeyes Fluid. The smell made her feel sicker than she already was. She bought several cups of tea in the cafeteria. It was good strong tea and she drank it gratefully, but she was not hungry.

A couple of men, seedy lookers in raincoats and hats pulled down low over their foreheads, tried to proposition her but she was in too much pain to feel outraged. She just growled, 'Go away or I'll call the police' at them and they sped away like startled rabbits. The fact that she handled herself so well in an unfamiliar situation surprised her. Just like that, bold as brass. On reflection she felt sure that something deep in her was terribly angry but she did not want to dig about in her feelings, so she pushed the thought away and put in the time as best she could.

At seven o'clock she returned to the B & B. The Cork woman

started to protest that she was back too soon but Breeda pushed past her and ran up the stairs.

She had a bath. She had to put a shilling in the meter before she could get any water. When the bath was half-full the water trickled out, but at least it was steaming and Breeda got in and sank back, eyes closed gratefully. It was so good to let everything slip away in the heat of the water, in the steamy room. But when she opened her eyes she was appalled to see that she was surrounded by a sea of bright red and she realized fearfully that she was still bleeding heavily. So she went to bed.

She put a towel beneath her in the bed so that she would not stain the sheets. It felt blissful lying there, warm, the pain subsiding, not thinking, just letting her body recover.

The Cork woman surprised her by bringing her a cup of Bovril and a hot water bottle to her room.

'Can't have ye dyin' on me,' she said brusquely, quite out of breath after the stairs. 'An' we have te look after our own.'

Breeda was grateful for the hot drink and the comfort of the bottle. She fell asleep soon after.

She came home, healing slowly. The body is a wonderfully resourceful machine, self-restorative provided one gives it the right food and rest. She recovered quickly.

Desmond suggested they marry soon. He was worried about her. She needed looking after, he told her tenderly. She alarmed him, she was suddenly so thin and nervy.

In the end they married before Mavis and Terry. They had a simple ceremony, their two friends the only guests. They had a small cele-bratory lunch in the Grand Hotel in Killiney. They got a flat in Ballsbridge.

Desmond climbed the ladder of success very quickly. Usually in big firms progress was slow, but fate, lucky circumstances and his own driving ambition helped him.

First off, Deary's rival store tried to lure him away. They offered him double his salary and so he went to Mr Graham de Vere and gave him his notice. This alarmed Mr Graham de Vere. He did not want to lose his blue-eyed boy and believed that his rivals saw some wondrous potential in O'Keeffe that he, with all his perspicacity, had overlooked. He had always been sure that O'Keeffe was the manager of the future, but now that his belief was confirmed by his competitor, Mr Graham de Vere became determined to keep Desmond at any cost. Desmond O'Keeffe divined this, played a cool hand, and won. Fate helped him because Mr Graham de Vere had been told by his doctor to take things easier, not spend such long hours at the office, as his ticker was not all it should be, in the doctor's words. So Mr Graham de Vere decided to retire early, to his wife's alarm and Desmond O'Keeffe's delight. He handed over the reigns of power to Desmond and looked forward to a life of golf in Lahinch, wintering in Nice, sailing, and summer in the Balearic Islands, so fashionable at that time.

Desmond made Mr McGillicuddy and Mrs Lepner redundant. Mavis was promoted to staff supervisor. Desmond was quite sure that she had the ability to get the right sort of staff so his appointment was not simply partisan.

Mavis was, of course, delighted and she and Terry married and settled into the house of her dreams, all on the never-never and credit in Deary's.

Desmond got rid of all the old pull, push and jangle and installed cash registers. He decided to turn Mr McGillicuddy's office into a soda fountain. The room overlooked the store and its glass front, which had enabled the head cashier to oversee the whole ground floor, would be a perfect place for customers to rest their weary legs and sip a soda. It was fun and modern and was soon making a very healthy profit for the store. Later, when the day of the soda fountain was over, Desmond turned the place into a coffee shop, then a quick-food snack-bar. He installed escalators. He had the joy of his being the first store in Dublin to have them and the satisfaction of seeing all the others follow his example.

Soon they had the house on the Malahide Road. And soon after that they had every luxury any heart could desire. And they loved each other. That was certain.

Yet there was a fever about their relationship that was strange. There was a secrecy too. A lack of spontaneous frankness.

They never had any children. It simply never happened. They led very busy social lives. They gave smart little dinner parties. They went to the theatre. They went to concerts. Everyone envied them. Sometimes malicious people whispered behind their hands. 'Didn't you know – her mother is in jail for murder!' But it did not stop people liking Breeda and respecting her.

She often thought, as she sat buffing her nails, putting on make-up, spraying Chanel No 5 between her breasts: How lucky I am. I've got absolutely everything I want. I've got infinitely more than I ever set out to get. All my dreams have come true. Then she would look at her small pale face in the mirror, framed by bright red hair and she would add, involuntarily, then why am I so sad?

The simple happiness she had had once, long ago, was never there. That happiness she craved seemed to slip coyly out of her grasp whenever she tried to capture it. It was the same when they made love, she and Desmond. Between her and that promise of complete unity the spectre shivered a moment. Always. Everything was interfered with, her love, her fulfilment, her joy. There was a shadow. An intruder. And in a veiled corner of her mind a tiny voice whispered sibilantly: Foul appetite. Foul appetite. Foul appetite.

CHAPTER SIXTY-EIGHT

London

There were people as far as the eye could see and music sweetly flavoured the air. They had, most of them, men and women and children, blossoms in their hair. The women wore long flowered dresses that had lace at the yoke and sleeves, and they wore bracelets on their wrists and ankles and long earrings in their ears that tinkled as they moved. The men had loose cotton or cheese-cloth tops and jeans decorated with flowered patches. They wore chains around their necks and they too had earrings and their hair was soft, new-washed and shoulder-length. The women's hair was long mostly, braided with flowers, and some of the foliage had died. But it didn't seem to matter. They carried babies in their arms and pretty children hung out of their long skirts. Everyone wore Jesus sandals and the air was heavy with the smell of pot.

They moved with graceful slowness and they smiled at each other and at strangers and said 'Peace and Love' a lot. They called each other brother and sister and were sweet-tempered, their mild dispositions induced by the marijuana.

Leaf held Lance's hand. He was twelve and a bit too old to do that, but everyone did, grown-ups as well, and he liked Lance. Lance lived with his mother. He liked his soft blond hair that smelled of jasmine and his smooth skin that was so soft to the touch.

His mother, too, he loved. She was so beautiful, big and soft, her lap copious, her bosom deep and welcoming.

He called her Fliss. Not 'mother'. It was her name and it was the thing to do. Like 'mother' and 'father' were not words they used. Like it was cool to call your mother by her Christian name.

She was not married to Lance. That was cool too. They were children of nature and didn't bother with pieces of paper, officialdom or bureaucracy and the like. They were from the earth. Manmade laws were stupid and stultifying, according to them.

They were often in trouble over his education. It didn't worry them and it didn't worry him, and when the trouble got alarming, with official letters arriving by the bucketful and officials nosing into their affairs, they simply upped sticks and left wherever they were for somewhere else. Fresh fields and pastures new, his mother said, smiling. She had a beautiful smile, like she had captured all the peace in the world in that smile and sent it out to anyone who happened to catch her eye.

They never opened official letters anyway. It was a waste of time. As they had no fixed address it was all right. But Lance and his mother both had money so they were never uncomfortable. Any letters that came, they said were taxes or some nasty official trying to tell them how to run their lives. God had given us the world. It was free, his mother said with a joyous laugh, and played with his hair.

They had been to the States, to France, Italy and now England. England was where all the best music came from, so Lance said, and he should know. Lance was a troubadour, a musician; he played the guitar. Leaf thought he was very good. Fliss and he sang together. The songs all sounded the same to Leaf. They were always about things going: 'Where have all the birds gone to now' and 'Why did Mandy leave me' and 'I'm gonna take my backpack an' leave this State an' find me love aplenty'.

Leaf liked the songs and he liked it when they sat around at night, hanging out beside the campfire, singing.

They lived in a mobile home. They sometimes lived in a commune. Depending on where it was. Leaf liked that. He didn't like it where it was cold and some of the people were poor and had bad trips and screamed and hallucinated. He didn't like it in the rain.

His real name was Charles, but his mother had changed it to Leaf. She said her family paid her to stay away. She said they paid handsomely. They travelled a lot and like-minded people went along too. They called themselves hippies and ordinary people didn't like them.

People who worked nine to five hated them. They had houses and Leaf thought they looked boring.

It was a good life as long as they kept travelling with the sun. They'd made the mistake once of coming to England for the Solstice, and the weather had been freezing. Not comfortable at all. Their mobile home was very comfortable and luxurious and Fliss did not open its doors to any Tom, Dick or Harry. Lance was always teasing her about it but she remained tranquil and refused to feel guilty.

The winter they went to Scotland was another disaster. They'd hardly left the caravan at all.

So they'd gone back to La Jolla in San Diego. It was Lance's favourite place, and they had sublime times there on the beaches in the sun. Leaf adored San Diego.

They had had brushes with the law about marijuana. It was stupid, Lance said. An infringement of civil liberties. They liked the grass smoke and Leaf liked it too. When they smoked of an evening they always allowed him a puff or two. 'Cool, man, cool,' Lance said. 'Far out!' Fliss replied and they lay back on their Indian cushions and smiled blissfully.

Sometimes Leaf wondered who his real father was. Fliss said he was a wild gipsy man but Lance told him he was probably sired by a boring bank clerk, so respectable that he would not do the right thing by Fliss and marry her when she discovered she was pregnant. 'Those respectable folk are the dregs, man!' Lance said. 'They let you down, sure as hell. Bound to.' Leaf hated the thought of that. Imagine how awful it would be to have a boring father who went to work from nine to five and drank pints in the pub with the lads and was respectable.

Leaf loved his laidback life. He was very happy. Fliss told him he could spend a holiday any time he wanted with his grandparents in Dublin provided he was on his best behaviour, but he didn't fancy that in the least and told her so, and she threw back her head and laughed. 'No, I don't imagine you do!' she said. 'Sun, sea and sand are best.'

Fliss taught him to read. She read him poetry and Lance showed him how to play the guitar and he was soon writing his own songs. Whenever the authorities bothered them his mother showed them her Irish passport and said she was on holiday, touring the United States. Lance showed his American passport and said he was visiting from New York, which was true in a way and was the one place they *never* went.

All in all, Leaf, at twelve, was content. His mother was beautiful, her man was good-lookin', they loved each other and him and the life they led was peaceful.

He'd write that into a song. He picked up the guitar, a piece of paper and an apple, threw himself into the hammock and closed his eyes in the sun.

But he knew, deep down, that the day would come, and soon, when he had to find out about his father. He didn't want to. He'd do anything to avoid it. But there it was like a burr in the back of his mind. Irritating him.

He'd have to go to Ireland. To Dublin. He'd have to leave this joyous, sunny place and meet his prudish grandparents, then set about finding out who his real father was, bank clerk or no. They'd tell him. Someone there would know. It was, according to his mother, a small town.

Wild gipsy? Boring bank clerk? He wondered which.

He was sure whoever it was was nice. His mother would not have had any truck with someone who was not kindly. Lance always said he was a lovely child. 'You're a helluva nice fella, Leaf,' he'd say. 'Your pa must've been okay.' And as Leaf grew Lance always reiterated his affirmation: 'Hey, fella – you're okay, y'know. You're ace!'

So some of that must have come from his father.

He'd go to Dublin next spring and find out all about him.

He'd be able to relax then.

Yeah! His father was bound to be a lovely man.

Bound to.